SHE

Ayesha

H. RIDER HAGGARD

SHE

A HISTORY OF ADVENTURE

Introduction by Margaret Atwood

Illustrations by Maurice Greiffenhagen and Charles H. M. Kerr

Notes by James Danly

THE MODERN LIBRARY

NEW YORK

Library of Congress Cataloging-in-Publication Data

Haggard, H. Rider (Henry Rider), 1856–1925.
She: a history of adventure / H. Rider Haggard; introduction by
Margaret Atwood; illustrations by Maurice Greiffenhagen and
Charles H.M. Kerr; notes by James Danly.
p.   cm.
ISBN 0-375-75905-0
1. Ayesha (Fictitious character : Haggard)—Fiction. 2. Women—Africa—Fiction.
3. Reincarnation—Fiction. 4. Immortalism—Fiction. 5. Africa—Fiction. I. Title.

PR4731 .S6 2002
823'.8–dc21
2001044583

Modern Library website address: www.modernlibrary.com

H. RIDER HAGGARD

Henry Rider Haggard, who was to become one of the most popular authors of his era, was born in Bradenham, Norfolk, England, on June 22, 1856. His father, William Meybohm Rider Haggard, the scion of an old Norfolk family—the Haggards claimed descent from a Danish knight—was the third squire of Bradenham, an estate comprising several hundred acres. His mother, Ella Doveton Haggard, had been raised, in part, in Bombay. An amateur writer, she published, in 1857, a poem called "Myra, or the Rose of the East: A Tale of the Afghan War."

Rider, the sixth son and eighth child of ten children, was considered in his childhood, particularly by his father, to be a dull-witted daydreamer. His mother, though, saw something of her own creative nature in him and encouraged his imagination. In a story that Haggard's daughter Lilias told in her biography of her father, and which may or may not be precisely true, young Rider was pacified—or at least controlled—at bedtime by his nurse's leaving him in the charge of "a disreputable doll of particularly hideous aspect, with boot-button eyes, hair of black wool and a sinister leer on its painted face." The doll was called "She-who-must-be-obeyed," a name Rider Haggard eventually found significant literary use for.

Owing to his father's contempt, Rider was denied the proper education his brothers received, and he was haphazardly taught at a London day school and at Ipswich Grammar School. He failed the army entrance examination in 1873, at which point his father sent him to London to a "crammer" to prepare for work in the Foreign Service.

In London, Haggard met Lady Anne Paulet, a Spiritualist whose séances he attended; after one particularly alarming session he swore off Spiritualism for life (though he'd often write about it). He also met and fell in love with Mary Elizabeth Jackson, called "Lilly," the daughter of a rich Yorkshire farmer. Rider's father opposed the romance, and Rider, self-conscious of his lack of money and position, refrained from proposing marriage.

In 1875, he sent by his father to the British colony of Natal, in southern Africa, to be the unpaid secretary to Sir Henry Bulwer, Natal's lieutenant governor (and a nephew of the novelist Edward Bulwer-Lytton). On his visits to the interior, Haggard learned much of the history, language, and customs of the Zulu people, whom he would write about most notably in *King Solomon's Mines* (1885) and in his Zulu trilogy: *Marie* (1912), *Child of Storm* (1913), and *Finished* (1917).

He became the protégé of Sir Theophilus Shepstone, the secretary of native affairs, assisting Shepstone on his mission to annex the Transvaal for the British government, as well as helping to raise the British flag in Pretoria in 1877. Eventually Haggard became the master and registrar of Transvaal's High Court.

By now firmly established in his career, Haggard intended to return to England to propose to Lilly, but his father angrily wrote him, demanding he stay where he was and concentrate on his work. Eventually, Lilly wrote to announce that she was marrying someone else. Haggard was to love her until he died, and harbored some hope that they would be reunited in the afterlife.

Still, he did return to England, where he met and married, in 1880, the heiress Mariana Louisa Margitson, known as "Louie." (This time the opposition came from her side, from an uncle who thought Haggard an undeserving match for his niece.) With his bride, he moved back to southern Africa, to Transvaal, where Haggard owned a share in an ostrich farm, just before the outbreak of the first Anglo-Boer War. As conditions grew dangerous, they returned to England with their newborn son, Arthur John ("Jock"). (The Haggards would have four children: Jock, Agnes Angela, Dorothy, and Lilias.)

Back home, Haggard studied the law, and was admitted to the bar in 1884. He scarcely practiced, though, as he was already fixated on a career as a writer. His first book, a work of nonfiction called *Cetywayo and His White Neighbours; or, Remarks on Recent Events in Zululand,* was published in 1882. He also wrote two not very successful novels, *Dawn* (1882) and *The Witch's Head* (1884).

Haggard's literary and financial fortunes changed, as the story goes, because of a five-shilling bet with one of his brothers that he could pen a more successful novel than Robert Louis Stevenson's *Treasure Island.* Haggard dashed off *King Solomon's Mines*—rapid composition and scant rewriting were to be hallmarks of his oeuvre—in six weeks. After his publisher littered London with handbills promoting "the most amazing story ever written," the African adventure novel, featuring a search for lost diamonds, a treasure map, a noble black king in exile, and a malignant witch, was a furious success (though Stevenson sent Haggard a friendly letter warning of the dangers of writing too quickly). By September 1885, thirty thousand copies of the novel had been sold in England, and in Haggard's lifetime well over a half million copies would be printed.

In 1887, Haggard published the novels *Jess* and *Allan Quatermain,* a sequel to *King Solomon's Mines* in which the hero was killed off ("Well, he died" is how Haggard, in part, phrases it); like Sir Arthur Conan Doyle's Sherlock Holmes, though, Quatermain wouldn't stay dead, and Haggard eventually revived him for a total of sixteen full-length novels and numerous short stories.

More significantly in 1887, Haggard wrote *She: A History of Adventure.* "The fact is," he said, "that it was written at a white heat, almost without rest.... I remember that when I sat down to the task my ideas as to its development were of the vaguest. The only clear notion that I had in my head was that of an immortal woman inspired by an immortal love. All the rest shaped itself round this figure." *She,* telling of a lost African kingdom ruled by a cruel two-thousand-year-old queen, Ayesha, also known as "She-who-must-be-obeyed," was an even greater success than *King Solomon's Mines,* and since its publication has captured the imaginations of countless readers, from Freud, who recommended it to a patient as "a strange book, but full of hidden meaning [about] the eternal feminine, the immortality of our emotions," to C. S. Lewis, Graham Greene, J.R.R. Tolkien, and even Henry Miller. Haggard's biographer Morton N. Cohen found in Ayesha a quintessential femme fatale, "the heartless beauty, the eternally pitiless woman. Ayesha, huge, cold, and beautiful, passes in [the] parade of fictional Victorian superwomen. She is a closer blood relative to Wilde's Salomé ... than to the fainting heroines in Haggard's modern novels or to the characters in the books for boys with whom [*She*] is often shelved." Geoffrey O'Brien, in the *Voice Literary Supplement,* has noted, "Where pulp exotica tends to offer images of buried treasure found or ancient powers restored, generic resolutions for artificial problems, *She* raises real dilemmas and leaves them gapingly unresolved, on a note of unattainable desire and irretrievable loss."

Some of *She's*—and, generally, Haggard's—success may derive from an ability to address a readership on its own terms. The writer John Hallock has commented, "Necrophilia, embalming, and a curious mixture of the modern and the magical illustrate how Haggard meshes the familiar with uncharted realms. The narrator in *She* places a perfectly preserved foot in a Gladstone bag,* and a native goddess is compared with Mary, Queen of Scots. A secret pit leading to a fire of rejuvenation is measured by the dome of Saint Paul's Cathedral; the main thoroughfare of the Temple of Truth is the width of the embankment of the Thames River." However, this mass appeal of Haggard's did not endear him to the critical establishment;

---

*After *She's* serialization in *The Graphic* magazine, Haggard made numerous changes, most of them minor, in the initial hardcover printing and in "New Edition"s published in 1888 and 1891. Most of the changes concerned issues of diction, but notably removed from the text were many of its topical references and contemporary brand names. Though the 1888 edition mentions a Gladstone bag, the reader of the present volume, taken from Haggard's ultimate version, will find references only to a "travelling bag" or "handbag."

though Haggard had his defenders, he was often harshly judged. (A self-delighted essay he published on the art of fiction writing and occasional whiffs of plagiarism in his work may not have helped matters.)

She was immediately dramatized in a production that opened at London's Gaiety Theatre in September 1888, and Ayesha has also been popular with filmmakers: The pioneering Frenchman Georges Méliès adapted the novel as *The Pillar of Fire* in 1899, and the American Edwin S. Porter filmed *She* in 1908; further versions appeared in 1911, 1916, 1917 (with the vamp Valeska Surratt), 1925 (with Betty Blythe), 1935 (from the creators of *King Kong* and featuring Helen Gahagan, better known as Helen Gahagan Douglas, "the Pink Lady," Richard Nixon's later—and besmirched—rival for a congressional seat), and 1965 (with Ursula Andress and horror-movie stalwarts Christopher Lee and Peter Cushing). *King Solomon's Mines* has also been a staple of the cinema, and in the wake of the Indiana Jones movies—which owe a great debt to Haggard—Richard Chamberlain twice played Allan Quatermain (in the company of Sharon Stone).

Haggard would return to Allan Quatermain in, among other works, *Allan's Wife and Other Tales* (1899), *The Ancient Allan* (1920), and *Allan and the Ice-Gods* (published posthumously in 1927), in which—in a plot partly suggested by Haggard's good friend Rudyard Kipling—the hero, in a drug-induced reverie, relives a past life as a caveman at the dawn of the Ice Age. Haggard would also revisit his most memorable female creation: *Ayesha: The Return of She*, depicting She's miraculous reappearance in a Tibetan temple of Isis, was published in 1905; *She and Allan*, a prequel uniting Haggard's two "stars," was published in 1921, and *Wisdom's Daughter*, another prequel, in which Haggard describes more fully Ayesha's origins, came out in 1923.

———

The years 1885–90 were Haggard's most productive and inspired, and his works were continually serialized and widely read. The death of his beloved mother in 1889 and of his young son, Jock, a little more than a year later, were devastating blows, however; though Haggard continued to write compulsively, the quality of his work and his fortunes took a downturn. Still, there are numerous titles to consider: Among Haggard's fifty-odd novels are *Cleopatra* (1889), written after his first trip to Egypt, a land that had fascinated him since he was a boy, in 1887; a Viking novel, *Eric Brighteyes* (1891), composed after an 1888 visit to Iceland; *Montezuma's Daughter* (1894), the result of research done on the trip to Mexico during which Haggard and his wife learned of Jock's death; *Stella Fregelius: A Tale of Three Destinies* (1903), a supernatural love story involving communication with the dead through the use of radio waves; *Pearl-Maiden: A Tale of the Fall of Jerusalem* (1903); *Moon of Israel: A Tale of the Exodus* (1918), which was particularly popular in a Yiddish translation; and *When the World Shook* (1919), involving citizens of Atlantis revived from suspended animation after 250,000 years. In 1911, inspired by an encounter with the ghost of one of his hunting dogs, which convinced him that animals had immortal souls just as people do, Haggard wrote *The Mahatma and the Hare,* and never hunted again.

Haggard was also an expert on agricultural and social conditions in England, and wrote often on gardening, agricultural reform, and rural life. Among his works on these subjects are *A Farmer's Year* (1899), *Rural England* (1902), and *The Poor and the Land* (1905). Though Haggard's 1895 attempt to gain a seat in Parliament was unsuccessful, he served on government commissions on the Salvation Army and on the erosion and deforestation of land, and in this service he toured the world extensively. Haggard was honored as a Knight Bachelor in 1912, and a Knight Commander of the Order of the British Empire in 1919.

In his last years, his popularity dwindled (he made more money from selling the film rights to his books than he did from publishing them) and his eccentricities increased: Formerly an ardent Zionist, he withdrew his support for the idea of establishing a Jewish homeland in Palestine and became notably anti-Semitic. (There are occasional bursts of anti-Semitism in Haggard's fiction, too, along with the unfortunately pervasive sexism and racism that may be attributable to the mind-set of his era but which can be hard for a modern reader to take anyway.)

After a final visit to Egypt in 1924, where, in the aftermath of the King Tut sensation, he was disappointed to find "the ancient land...

degraded with tourists, harlots, and brass bands," he developed a bladder infection and died in a London nursing home on May 14, 1925. He was sixty-eight. His last novel was *Belshazzar,* completed in 1924 and published in 1930. His autobiography, *The Days of My Life,* appeared in 1926.

V. S. Pritchett, commenting bemusedly on Haggard's enduring popularity, said, "Mr. E. M. Forster once spoke of the novelist sending down a bucket into the unconscious; [Haggard] installed a suction pump. He drained the whole reservoir of the people's secret desires."

Contents

ILLUSTRATIONS

Introduction

Margaret Atwood

When I first read Rider Haggard's highly famous novel *She*, I didn't know it was highly famous. I was a teenager, it was the 1950s, and *She* was just one of the many books in the cellar. My father unwittingly shared with Jorge Luis Borges a liking for nineteenth-century yarns with touches of the uncanny coupled with rip-roaring plots; and so, in the cellar, where I was supposed to be doing my homework, I read my way through Rudyard Kipling and Conan Doyle, and *Dracula* and *Frankenstein,* and Robert Louis Stevenson and H. G. Wells, and also Henry Rider Haggard. I read *King Solomon's Mines* first, with its adventures and tunnels and lost treasure, and then *Allan Quatermain,* with its adventures and tunnels and lost civilization. And then I read *She*.

I had no sociocultural context for these books then—the British Empire was the pink part of the map, "imperialism and colonialism" had not yet acquired their special negative charge, and the accusation "sexist" was far in the future. Nor did I make any distinctions between great literature and any other kind. I just liked reading. Any book that began with some mysterious inscriptions on a very old broken pot was fine with me, and that is how *She* begins. There was even a picture at the front of my edition—not a drawing of the pot, but a *photograph* of it, to make the yarn really convincing. (The pot was made to order by Haggard's sister-in-law; he intended it to function like the pirate map at the beginning of *Treasure Island*—a book the popularity of which he hoped to rival—and it did.)

Most outrageous tales state at the very beginning that what follows is so incredible the reader will have trouble believing it, which is both a come-on and a challenge. The messages on the pot stretch credulity, but having deciphered them, the two heroes of *She*—the gorgeous but none too bright Leo Vincey and the ugly but intelligent Horace Holly—are off to Africa to hunt up the beautiful, undying sorceress who is supposed to have killed Leo's distant ancestor. Curiosity is their driving force, vengeance is their goal. Many a hardship later, and after having narrowly escaped death at the hands of the savage and matrilineal tribe of the Amahagger, they find not only the ruins of a vast and once-powerful civilization and the numerous mummified bodies of the same, but also, dwelling among the tombs, the self-same undying sorceress, ten times lovelier, wiser, and more ruthless than they had dared to imagine.

As Queen of the Amahagger, "She-who-must-be-obeyed" wafts around wrapped up like a corpse in order to inspire fear; but once tantalizingly peeled, under those gauzy wrappings is a stunner, and— what's more—a virgin. "She," it turns out, is two thousand years old. Her real name is Ayesha. She claims she was once a priestess of the Egyptian nature-goddess Isis. She's been saving herself for two millenia, waiting for the man she loves: one Kallikrates, a very goodlooking priest of Isis and the ancestor of Leo Vincey. This man broke his vows and ran off with Leo's ancestress, whereupon Ayesha slew him in a fit of jealous rage. For two thousand years she's been waiting for him to be reincarnated; she's even got his preserved corpse enshrined in a side room, where she laments over it every night. A point-by-point comparison reveals—what a surprise!—that Kallikrates and Leo Vincey are identical.

Having brought Leo to his knees with her knockout charms, and having polished off Ustane, a more normal sort of woman with whom Leo has formed a sexual pair-bond, and who just happens to be a reincarnation of Ayesha's ancient Kallikrates-stealing enemy, She now demands that Leo accompany her into the depths of a nearby mountain. There, She says, is where the secret of extremely long and more abundant life is to be found. Not only that, She and Leo can't be One until he is as powerful as She—the union might otherwise kill him (as it does, in the sequel *Ayesha: The Vengeance of She*). So off to the mountain they go, via the ruins of the ancient, once-imperial city of Kôr. To get the renewed life, all one has to do—after the usual Haggard adventures and tunnels—is to traverse some caverns measureless to man, step into a very noisy rolling pillar of fire, and then make one's getaway across a bottomless chasm.

This is how She acquired her powers two thousand years before, and to show a hestitating Leo how easy it is, She does it again. Alas, this time the thing works backward, and in a few instants Ayesha shrivels up into a very elderly bald monkey and then crumbles into dust. Leo and Holly, both hopelessly in love with She and both devastated, totter back to civilization, trusting in Her promise that She will return.

As a good read in the cellar, this was all very satisfactory, despite the overblown way in which She tended to express herself. *She* was an odd book in that it placed a preternaturally powerful woman at the center of things: the only other such woman I'd run into so far had been the Wonder Woman of the comics, with her sparkly lasso and star-spangled panties. Both Ayesha and Wonder Woman went all weak-kneed when it came to the man they loved—Wonder Woman lost her magic powers when kissed by her boyfriend, Steve Trevor; Ayesha couldn't focus on conquering the world unless Leo Vincey would join her in that dubious enterprise—and I was callow enough, at fifteen, to find this part of it not only soppily romantic but pretty hilarious. Then I graduated from high school and discovered good taste, and forgot for a while about *She*.

———

For a while, but not forever. In the early sixties I found myself in graduate school, in Cambridge, Massachusetts. There I was exposed to Widener Library, a much larger and more organized version of the cellar; that is, it contained many sorts of books, not all of which bore the Great Literature Seal of Approval. Once I was let loose in the stacks, my penchant for not doing my homework soon reasserted itself, and it wasn't long before I was snuffling around in Rider Haggard and his ilk once more.

This time, however, I had some excuse. My field of specialization was the nineteenth century, and I was busying myself with Victorian quasi-goddesses; and no one could accuse Haggard of not being Victorian. Like his age, which practically invented archeology, he was an amateur of vanished civilizations; also like his age, he was fascinated by the exploration of unmapped territories and encounters with "undiscovered" native peoples. As an individual, he was such a cookie-cutter county gentleman—albeit with some African traveling in his past—that it was hard to fathom where his overheated imagination had come from, though it may have been this by-the-book-English-establishment quality that allowed him to bypass intellectual analysis completely. He could sink a core-sampling drill straight down into the great English Victorian unconscious, where fears and desires—especially male fears and desires—swarmed in the darkness like blind fish. Or so claimed Henry Miller, among others.

Where did it all come from? In particular, where did the figure of She come from—old-young, powerful-powerless, beautiful-hideous, dweller among tombs, obsessed with an undying love, deeply in touch with the forces of Nature and thus of Life and Death? Haggard and his siblings were said to have been terrorized by an ugly rag doll that lived in a dark cupboard and was named "She-who-must-be-obeyed," but there is more to it than that. *She* was published in 1887, and thus came at the height of the fashion for sinister but seductive women. It looked back also on a long tradition of the same. Ayesha's literary ancestresses include the young-but-old supernatural women in George MacDonald's "Curdie" fantasies, but also various Victorian femmes fatales: Tennyson's Vivien in *The Idylls of the King,* bent on stealing Merlin's magic; the Pre-Raphaelite temptresses created in both poem and picture by Rossetti and William Morris; Swinburne's dominatrixes; Wagner's nasty pieces of female work, including the very old but still toothsome Kundry of *Parsifal;* and, most especially, the Mona Lisa of Walter Pater's famous prose poem, older than the rocks upon which she sits, yet young and lovely, and mysterious, and filled to the brim with experiences of a distinctly suspect nature.

As Sandra Gilbert and Susan Gubar pointed out in their 1989 book, *No Man's Land*, the ascendency in the arts of these potent but dangerous female figures is by no means unconnected with the rise of "Woman" in the nineteenth century, and with the hotly debated issues of her "true nature" and her "rights," and also with the anxieties and fantasies these controversies generated. If women ever came to wield political power—to which they were surely, by their natures, unsuited—what would they do with it? And if they were beautiful and desirable women, capable of attacking on the sexual as well as the political front, wouldn't they drink men's blood, sap their vitality, and reduce them to groveling serfs? As the century opened, Wordsworth's Mother Nature was benign, and "never would betray / The heart that loved her"; but by the end of the century, Nature and the women so firmly linked to her were much more likely to be red in tooth and claw—Darwinian goddesses rather than Wordsworthian ones. When, in *She,* Ayesha appropriates the fiery phallic pillar at the heart of Nature for the second time, it's just as well that it works backward. Otherwise men could kiss their own phallic pillars goodbye.

"You are a whale at parables and allegories and one thing reflecting another," wrote Rudyard Kipling in a letter to Rider Haggard, and there appear to be various hints and verbal signposts scattered over the landscape of *She*. For instance, the Amahagger, the tribe ruled by She, bear a name that not only encapsulates *hag* but also conflates the Latin root for *love* with the name of Abraham's banished wilderness-dwelling concubine, Hagar, and thus brings to mind a story of two women competing for one man. The ancient city of Kôr is named perhaps for *core,* cognate with the French *coeur,* but suggesting also *corps,* for body, and thus *corpse,* for dead body; for She is in part a Nightmare Life-in-Death. Her horrid end is reminiscent of Darwinian evolution played backward—woman into monkey—but also of vampires after the stake-into-the-heart maneuver. (Bram Stoker's *Dracula* appeared after *She,* but Sheridan LeFanu's *Carmilla* predates it, as does many another vampire story.) These associations and more point toward some central significance that Haggard himself could never fully explicate, though he chalked up a sequel and a couple of prequels trying. "*She,*" he said, was "some gigantic allegory of which I could not catch the meaning."

Haggard claimed to have written *She* "at white heat," in six weeks— "It came," he said, "faster than my poor aching hand could set it down," which would suggest hypnotic trance or possession. In the heyday of Freudian and Jungian analysis, *She* was much explored and admired, by Freudians for its womb-and-phallus images, by Jungians for its *anima* figures and thresholds. Northrop Frye, proponent of the theory of archetypes in literature, says this of *She* in his 1975 book, *The Secular Scripture: A Study of the Structure of Romance:*

> In the theme of the apparently dead and buried heroine who comes to life again, one of the themes of Shakespeare's *Cymbeline,* we seem to be getting a more undisplaced glimpse of the earth-mother at the bottom of the world. In later romance there is another glimpse of such a figure in Rider Haggard's *She,* a beautiful and sinister female ruler, buried in the depths of a dark continent, who is much involved with archetypes of death and rebirth.... Embalmed mummies suggest Egypt, which is preeminently the land of death and burial, and, largely because of its Biblical role, of descent to a lower world.

Whatever *She* may have been thought to signify, its impact upon publication was tremendous. *Everyone* read it, especially men; a whole generation was influenced by it, and the generation after that. A dozen or so films have been based on it, and a huge amount of the pulp-magazine fiction churned out in the teens, twenties, and thirties of the twentieth century bears its impress. Every time a young but possibly old and/or dead woman turns up, especially if she's ruling a lost tribe in a wilderness and is a hypnotic seductress, you're looking at a descendant of She.

Literary writers too felt Her foot on their necks. Conrad's *Heart of Darkness* owes a lot to Her, as Gilbert and Gubar have indicated. James

Hilton's Shangri-La, with its ancient, beautiful, and eventually crumbling heroine, is an obvious relative. C. S. Lewis felt Her power, fond as he was of creating sweet-talking, good-looking evil queens; and in Tolkien's *The Lord of the Rings*, She splits into two: Galadriel, powerful but good, who's got exactly the same water-mirror as the one possessed by She; and a very ancient cave-dwelling man-devouring spider-creature named, tellingly, Shelob.

Would it be out of the question to connect the destructive Female Will, so feared by D. H. Lawrence and others, with the malign aspect of She? For Ayesha is a supremely transgressive female who challenges male power; though her shoe size is tiny and her fingernails are pink, she's a rebel at heart. If only she hadn't been hobbled by love, she would have used her formidable energies to overthrow the established civilized order. That the established civilized order was white and male and European goes without saying; thus She's power was not only female—of the heart, of the body—but barbaric, and "dark."

By the time we find John Mortimer's Rumpole of the Bailey referring to his dumpy, kitchen-cleanser-conscious wife as "she who must be obeyed," the once-potent figure has been secularized and de-mythologized, and has dwindled into the combination of joke and rag doll that it may have been in its origins. Nevertheless, we must not forget one of Ayesha's preeminent powers—the ability to reincarnate herself. Like the vampire dust at the end of Christopher Lee movies, blowing away only to reassemble itself at the outset of the next film, She could come back. And back. And back.

No doubt this is because She is in some ways a permanent feature of the human imagination. She's one of the giants of the nursery, a threatening but compelling figure, bigger and better than life. Also worse, of course. And therein lies her attraction.

———

MARGARET ATWOOD is the author of more than twenty-five books, including works of fiction, poetry, and essays. Her most recent works include the bestselling novels *Alias Grace, The Robber Bride,* and *The Blind Assassin* and the collections *Wilderness Tips* and *Good Bones and Simple Murders.* She lives in Toronto.

Sources

Atwood, Margaret. "Superwoman Drawn and Quartered: The Early Forms of *She*." *Alphabet* magazine vol. 10, July 1965.

Frye, Northrop. *The Secular Scripture: A Study of the Structure of Romance.* Cambridge, Mass.: Harvard University Press, 1976.

Gilbert, Sandra M., and Susan Gubar. *No Man's Land: The Place of the Woman Writer in the Twentieth Century, vol. 2: Sexchanges.* New Haven: Yale University Press, 1989.

Karlin, Daniel. Introduction, in Haggard, H. Rider, *She*. Oxford: Oxford University Press, 1991.

I INSCRIBE THIS HISTORY TO

ANDREW LANG

IN TOKEN OF PERSONAL REGARD

AND OF

MY SINCERE ADMIRATION FOR HIS LEARNING AND HIS WORKS

London:
December 1886

In earth and skie and sea
Strange thynges ther be.

SHE

INTRODUCTION

In giving to the world the record of what, considered as an adventure only, is I suppose one of the most wonderful and mysterious experiences ever undergone by mortal men, I feel it incumbent on me to explain my exact connection with it. So I will say at once that I am not the narrator but only the editor of this extraordinary history, and then go on to tell how it found its way into my hands.

Some years ago I, the editor, was stopping with a friend, *"vir doctissimus et amicus meus,"* at a certain University, which for the purposes of this history we will call Cambridge, and one day was impressed with the appearance of two persons whom I saw walking arm-in-arm down the street. One of these gentlemen was, I think without exception, the handsomest young fellow I have ever seen. He was very tall, very broad, and had a look of power and a grace of bearing that seemed as native to him as to a wild stag. In addition his face was almost without flaw—a good face as well as a beautiful one, and when he lifted his hat, which he did just then to a passing lady, I saw that his head was covered with little golden curls growing close to the scalp.

"Do you see that man?" I said to my friend, with whom I was walking; "why, he looks like a statue of Apollo come to life. What a splendid fellow he is!"

"Yes," he answered, "he is the handsomest man in the University, and one of the nicest too. They call him 'the Greek god.' But look at the other one; he is Vincey's (that's the god's name) guardian, and supposed to be full of every kind of information. They call him 'Charon,' either because of his forbidding appearance or because he has ferried his ward across the deep waters of examination—I don't know which."

I looked, and found the older man quite as interesting in his way as the glorified specimen of humanity at his side. He appeared to be about forty years of age, and I think was as ugly as his companion was handsome. To begin with, he was short, rather bow-legged, very deep chested, and with unusually long arms. He had dark hair and small eyes, and the hair grew down on his forehead, and his whiskers grew quite up to his hair, so that there was uncommonly little of his countenance to be seen. Altogether he reminded me forcibly of a gorilla, and yet there was something very pleasing and genial about the man's eye. I remember saying that I should like to know him.

"All right," answered my friend, "nothing easier. I know Vincey; I'll introduce you," and he did, and for some minutes we stood chatting—about the Zulu people, I think, for I had just returned from the Cape at the time. Presently, however, a stout lady, whose name I do not remember, came along the pavement, accompanied by a pretty fair-haired girl, and Mr. Vincey, who clearly knew them well, at once joined these two, walking off in their company. I remember being rather amused by the change in the expression of the elder man, whose name I discovered was Holly, when he saw the ladies advancing. Suddenly he stopped short in his talk, cast a reproachful look at his companion, and, with an abrupt nod to myself, turned and marched off alone across the street. I heard afterwards that he was popularly supposed to be as much afraid of a woman as most people are of a mad dog, which accounted for his precipitate retreat. I cannot say, however, that young Vincey showed much aversion to feminine society on this occasion. Indeed I remember laughing, and remarking to my friend at the time that he was not the sort of man whom it would be desirable to introduce to the lady one was going to marry, since it was exceedingly probable that the acquaintance would end in a transfer of her affections. He was altogether too good-looking, and, what is more, he had none of that self-consciousness and conceit about him which usually afflicts handsome men, and makes them deservedly disliked by their fellows.

That same evening my visit came to an end, and this was the last I saw or heard of "Charon" and "the Greek god" for many a long day. Indeed, I have never seen either of them from that hour to this, and do not think it probable that I shall. But a month ago I received a letter and two packets, one of manuscript, and on opening the former found that it was signed by "Horace Holly," a name which at the moment was not familiar to me. It ran as follows:—

"—— College, Cambridge, May 1, 18—

"MY DEAR SIR,—You will be surprised, considering the very slight nature of our acquaintance, to get a letter from me. Indeed, I think I had better begin by reminding you that we once met, now several years ago, when I and my ward Leo Vincey were introduced to you in the street at Cambridge. To be brief and come to my business. I have recently read with much interest a book of yours describing a Central African adventure. I take it that this book is partly true, and partly an effort of the imagination. However this may be, it has given me an idea. It happens, how you will see in the accompanying manuscript (which together with the Scarab, the 'Royal Son of the Sun,' and the original sherd, I am sending to you by hand), that my ward, or rather my adopted son Leo Vincey, and myself have recently passed through a real African adventure, of a nature so much more marvellous than the one which you describe, that to tell the truth I am almost ashamed to submit it to you lest you should disbelieve my tale. You will see it stated in this manuscript that I, or rather we, had made up our minds not to make this history public during our joint lives. Nor should we alter our determination were it not for a circumstance which has recently arisen. For reasons that, after perusing this manuscript, you may be able to guess, we are going away again, this time to Central Asia, where, if anywhere upon this earth, wisdom is to be found, and we anticipate that our sojourn there will be a long one. Possibly we shall not return. Under these altered conditions it has become a question whether we are justified in withholding from the world an account of a phenomenon which we believe to be of unparalleled interest, merely because our private life is involved, or because we are afraid of ridicule and doubt being cast upon our statements. I hold one view about this matter, and Leo holds another, and finally, after much discussion, we have come to a compromise, namely, to send the history to you, giving you full leave to publish it if you think fit, the only stipulation being that you shall disguise our real names, and as much concerning our personal identity as is consistent with the maintenance of the *bona fides* of the narrative.

"And now what am I to say further? I really do not know, beyond once more repeating that everything is described in the accompanying manuscript exactly as it happened. As regards *She* herself, I have nothing to add. Day by day we have greater occasion to regret that we did not better avail ourselves of our opportunities to obtain more information from that marvellous woman. Who was she? How did she first come to the Caves of Kôr, and what was her real religion? We never ascertained, and now, alas! we never shall, at least not yet. These and many other questions arise in my mind, but what is the good of asking them now?

"Will you undertake the task? We give you complete freedom, and as a reward you will, we believe, have the credit of presenting to the world the most wonderful history, as distinguished from romance, that its records can show. Read the manuscript (which I have copied out fairly for your benefit), and let me know.

"Believe me, very truly yours,
"L. Horace Holly."*

---

*This name is varied here and throughout in accordance with the writer's request.— EDITOR. [This footnote, and all footnotes following, are Haggard's own. Notes for this Modern Library edition may be found beginning on page 315.]

"P.S.—Of course, if any profit results from the sale of the writing, should you care to undertake its publication, you can do what you like with it; but if there is a loss I will leave instructions with my lawyers, Messrs. Geoffrey and Jordan, to meet it. We entrust the sherd, the scarab, and the parchments to your keeping, till such time as we demand them back again.—L. H. H."

This letter, as may be imagined, astonished me considerably; but when I came to look at the MS., which the pressure of other work prevented me from doing for a fortnight, I was still more astonished, as I think the reader will be also, and at once made up my mind to press on with the matter. I wrote to this effect to Mr. Holly, but a week afterwards I received a letter from that gentleman's lawyers, returning my own, with the information that their client and Mr. Leo Vincey had already left this country for Thibet, and they did not at present know their address.

Well, that is all I have to say. Of the history itself the reader must judge. I give it to him, with the exception of a very few alterations, made with the object of concealing the identity of the actors from the general public, exactly as it has come to me. Personally I have made up my mind to refrain from comments. At first I was inclined to believe that this history of a woman, clothed in the majesty of her almost endless years, on whom the shadow of Eternity itself lay like the dark wing of Night, was some gigantic allegory of which I could not catch the meaning. Then I thought that it might be a bold attempt to portray the possible results of practical immortality, informing the substance of a mortal who yet drew her strength from Earth, and in whose human bosom passions yet rose and fell and beat as in the undying world around her the winds and the tides rise and fall and beat unceasingly. But as I read on I abandoned that idea also. To me the story seems to bear the stamp of truth upon its face. Its explanation I must leave to others. With this slight preface, which circumstances make necessary, I introduce the world to Ayesha and the Caves of Kôr.—THE EDITOR.

P.S.—On consideration there is one thing which, after a reperusal of this history, struck me with so much force that I cannot resist calling the attention of the reader to it. He will observe that, so far as we are made acquainted with him, there appears to be nothing in the character of Leo Vincey which in the opinion of most people would have been likely to attract an intellect so powerful as that of Ayesha. He is not even, at any rate to my view, particularly interesting. Indeed, we might imagine that Mr. Holly under ordinary circumstances would have easily outstripped him in the favour of *She*. Can it be that extremes meet, and that the very excess and splendour of her mind led her by means of some strange physical reaction to worship at the shrine of matter? Was the ancient Kallikrates nothing but a splendid animal beloved for his hereditary Greek beauty? Or is the true explanation what I believe it to be—namely, that Ayesha, seeing further than we can see, perceived the germ and smouldering spark of greatness which lay hid within her lover's soul, and well knew that under the influence of her gift of life, watered by her wisdom, and shone upon with the sunshine of her presence, it would bloom like a flower and flash out like a star, filling the world with light and fragrance?

Here also I am unable to answer, but perforce must leave the reader to form his own judgment on the facts before him, as they are detailed by Mr. Holly in the following pages.

I

My Visitor

There are some events of which each circumstance and surrounding detail seem to be graven on the memory in such fashion that we cannot forget them. So it is with the scene that I am about to describe; it rises as clearly before my mind at this moment as though it had happened yesterday.

It was in this very month something over twenty years ago that I, Ludwig Horace Holly, sat one night in my rooms at Cambridge, grinding away at some mathematical work, I forget what. I was to go up for my fellowship within a week, and was expected by my tutor and my college generally to distinguish myself. At last, wearied out, I flung my book down, and, walking to the mantelpiece, took up a pipe and filled it. There was a candle burning on this mantelpiece, and a long, narrow glass at the back of it; and as I was in the act of lighting the pipe I caught sight of my own countenance in the glass, and paused to reflect. The lighted match burnt away till it scorched my fingers, forcing me to drop it; but still I stood and stared at myself in the glass, and reflected.

"Well," I said aloud, at last, "it is to be hoped that I shall be able to do something with the inside of my head, for I shall certainly never do anything by the help of the outside."

This remark will doubtless strike anybody who reads it as being slightly obscure, but in fact I was alluding to my physical deficiencies. Most men of twenty-two are endowed with some share, at any rate, of the comeliness of youth, but to me even this was denied. Short, thick-set, and deep-chested almost to deformity, with long sinewy arms, heavy features, hollow grey eyes, a low brow half overgrown with a mop of thick black hair, like a deserted clearing on which the forest had once more begun to encroach; such was my appearance nearly a quarter of a century ago, and such, with some modification, is it to this day. Like Cain, I was branded—branded by Nature with the stamp of abnormal ugliness, as I was gifted by Nature with iron and abnormal strength and considerable intellectual powers. So ugly was I that the spruce young men of my College, though they were proud enough of my feats of endurance and physical prowess, did not care even to be seen walking with me. Was it wonderful that I was misanthropic and sullen? Was it wonderful that I brooded and worked alone, and had no friends—at least, only one? I was set apart by Nature to live alone, and draw comfort from her breast, and hers only. Women hated the sight of me. Only a week before I had heard one call me a "monster" when she thought I was out of hearing, and say that I had converted her to the monkey theory. Once, indeed, a woman pretended to care for me, and I lavished all the pent-up affection of my nature upon her. Then money that was to have come to me went elsewhere, and she discarded me. I pleaded with her as I have never pleaded with any living creature before or since, for I was caught by her sweet face, and loved her; and in the end by way of answer she took me to the glass, and stood side by side with me, and looked into it.

"Now," she said, "if I am Beauty, who are you?"

That was when I was only twenty.

And so I stood and stared, and felt a sort of grim satisfaction in the sense of my own loneliness—for I had neither father, nor mother, nor brother; and as I stared there came a knock at my door.

I listened before I went to answer it, for it was nearly twelve o'clock at night, and I was in no mood to admit any stranger. I had but one friend in the College, or, indeed, in the world—perhaps it was he.

Just then the person outside the door coughed, and I hastened to open it, for I knew the cough.

A tall man of about thirty, with the remains of singular personal beauty, hurried in, staggering beneath the weight of a massive iron box, which he carried by a handle with his right hand. He placed the box upon the table, and then fell into an awful fit of coughing. He coughed and coughed till his face became quite purple, and at last he sank into a chair and began to spit up blood. I poured out some whisky into a tumbler, and gave it to him. He drank it, and seemed better; although his better was very bad indeed.

"Why did you keep me standing there in the cold?" he asked pettishly. "You know the draughts are death to me."

"I did not know who it was," I answered. "You are a late visitor."

"Yes; and verily I believe it is my last visit," he answered, with a ghastly attempt at a smile. "I am done for, Holly. I am done for. I do not believe that I shall see to-morrow!"

"Nonsense!" I said. "Let me go for a doctor."

He waved me back imperiously with his hand. "It is sober sense; but I want no doctors. I have studied medicine and I know all about it. No doctors can help me. My last hour has come! For a year past I have only lived by a miracle. Now listen to me as you never listened to anybody before; for you will not have the opportunity of getting me to repeat my words. We have been friends for two years; tell me how much do you know about me?"

"I know that you are rich, and have had the fancy to come to College long after the age when most men leave it. I know that you have been married, and that your wife died; and that you have been the best, indeed almost the only, friend I ever made."

"Did you know that I have a son?"

"No."

"I have. He is five years old. He cost me his mother's life, and I have never been able to bear to look upon his face in consequence. Holly, if you will accept the trust, I am going to leave you as that boy's sole guardian."

I sprang almost out of my chair. *"Me!"* I said.

"Yes, you. I have not studied you for two years for nothing. I have known for some time that I could not last, and since I faced the fact I have been searching for someone to whom I could confide the boy and this," and he tapped the iron box. "You are the man, Holly; for, like a rugged tree, you are hard and sound at core.

"Listen; this boy will be the only representative of one of the most ancient families in the world, that is, so far as families can be traced. You will laugh at me when I say it, but one day it will be proved to you beyond a doubt that my sixty-fifth or sixty-sixth lineal ancestor was an Egyptian priest of Isis, though he was himself of Grecian extraction, and was called Kallikrates.* His father was one of the Greek mercenaries raised by Hak-Hor, a Mendesian Pharaoh of the twenty-ninth dynasty, and his grandfather or great-grandfather, I believe, was that very Kallikrates mentioned by Herodotus.† In or about the year 339 before Christ, just at the time of the final fall of the Pharaohs, this Kallikrates (the priest) broke his vows of celibacy and fled from Egypt with a Princess of royal blood who had fallen in love with him. His ship was wrecked upon the coast of Africa, somewhere, as I believe, in the neighbourhood of where Delagoa Bay now is, or rather to the north of it, he and his wife being saved, and all the remainder of their company destroyed in one way or another. Here they endured great hardships, but were at last entertained by the powerful Queen of a

*The Strong and Beautiful, or, more accurately, the Beautiful in strength.

†The Kallikrates here referred to by my friend was a Spartan, spoken of by Herodotus (Herod. ix. 72) as being remarkable for his beauty. He fell at the glorious battle of Platæa (September 22, B.C. 479), when the Lacedæmonians and Athenians under Pausanias routed the Persians, putting nearly 300,000 of them to the sword. The following is a translation of the passage: "For Kallikrates died out of the battle, he came to the army the most beautiful man of the Greeks of that day—not only of the Lacedæmonians themselves, but of the other Greeks also. He, when Pausanias was sacrificing, was wounded in the side by an arrow; and then they fought, but on being carried off he regretted his death, and said to Arimnestus, a Platæan, that he did not grieve at dying for Greece, but at not having struck a blow, or, although he desired so to do, performed any deed worthy of himself." This Kallikrates, who appears to have been as brave as he was beautiful, is subsequently mentioned by Herodotus as having been buried among the ιρένες (young commanders), apart from the other Spartans and the Helots.—L. H. H.

savage people, a white woman, of peculiar loveliness, who, under circumstances which I cannot enter into, but which you will one day learn, if you live, from the contents of the box, finally murdered my ancestor Kallikrates. His wife, however, escaped, how, I know not, to Athens, bearing a child with her, whom she named Tisisthenes, or the Mighty Avenger.

"Five hundred years or more afterwards the family migrated to Rome under circumstances of which no trace remains, and here, probably with the idea of preserving the idea of vengeance which we find set out in the name of Tisisthenes, they appear with some regularity to have assumed the cognomen of Vindex, or Avenger. Here, too, they remained for another five centuries or more, till about 770 A.D., when Charlemagne invaded Lombardy, where they were then settled, whereon the head of the family seems to have attached himself to the great Emperor, to have returned with him across the Alps, and finally to have settled in Brittany. Eight generations later his lineal representative crossed to England in the reign of Edward the Confessor, and in the time of William the Conqueror was advanced to great honour and power. From that time to the present day I can trace my descent without a break. Not that the Vinceys—for that was the final corruption of the name after its bearers took root in English soil—have been particularly distinguished—they never came much to the fore. Sometimes they were soldiers, sometimes merchants, but on the whole they have preserved a dead level of respectability, and a still deader level of mediocrity. From the time of Charles II till the beginning of the present century they were merchants. About 1790 my grandfather made a considerable fortune out of brewing, and retired. In 1821 he died, and my father succeeded him, and dissipated most of the money. Ten years ago he died also, leaving me a net income of about two thousand a year. Then it was that I undertook an expedition in connection with *that*," and he pointed to the iron chest, "which ended disastrously enough. On my way back I travelled in the South of Europe, and finally reached Athens. There I met my beloved wife, who might well also have been called the 'Beautiful,' like my old Greek ancestor. There I married her, and there, a year afterwards, when my boy was born, she died."

He paused a while, his head sunk upon his hand, and then continued:

"My marriage had diverted me from a project which I cannot enter into now. I have no time, Holly—I have no time! One day, if you accept my trust, you will learn all about it. After my wife's death I turned my mind to it again. But first it was necessary, or, at least, I conceived that it was necessary, that I should attain to a perfect knowledge of Eastern dialects, especially Arabic. It was to facilitate my studies that I came here. Very soon, however, my disease developed itself, and now there is an end of me." And as though to emphasise his words he burst into another terrible fit of coughing.

I gave him some more whisky, and after resting he went on:

"I have never seen my boy, Leo, since he was a tiny baby. I could never bear to see him, but they tell me that he is a quick and handsome child. In this envelope," and he produced a letter from his pocket addressed to myself, "I have jotted down the course I wish followed in the boy's education. It is a somewhat peculiar one. At any rate, I could not entrust it to a stranger. Once more, will you undertake it?"

"I must first know what I am to undertake," I answered.

"You are to undertake to have the boy, Leo, to live with you till he is twenty-five years of age—not to send him to school, remember. On his twenty-fifth birthday your guardianship will end, and you will then, with the keys that I give you now" (and he placed them on the table), "open the iron box, and let him see and read the contents, and say whether or no he is willing to undertake the quest. There is no obligation on him to do so. Now, as regards terms. My present income is two thousand two hundred a year. Half of that income I have secured to you by will for life, contingently on your undertaking the guardianship—that is, one thousand a year remuneration to yourself, for you will have to give up your life to it, and one hundred a year to pay for the board of the boy. The rest is to accumulate till Leo is twenty-five, so that there may be a sum in hand should he wish to undertake the quest of which I spoke."

"And suppose I were to die?" I asked.

"Then the boy must become a ward of Chancery and take his chance. Only, be careful that the iron chest is passed on to him by your will. Listen, Holly; don't refuse me. Believe me, this is to your advantage. You are not fit to mix with the world—it would only embitter you. In a few weeks you will become a Fellow of your College, and the income which you will derive from it combined with what I have left you will enable you to live a life of learned leisure, alternated with the sport of which you are so fond, such as will exactly suit you."

He paused and looked at me anxiously, but I still hesitated. The charge seemed so very strange.

"For my sake, Holly. We have been good friends, and I have no time to make other arrangements."

"Very well," I said, "I will do it, provided there is nothing in this paper to make me change my mind," and I touched the envelope he had put upon the table by the keys.

"Thank you, Holly, thank you. There is nothing at all. Swear to me by God that you will be a father to the boy, and follow my directions to the letter."

"I swear it," I answered solemnly.

"Very well; remember that perhaps one day I shall ask for the account of your oath, for though I am dead and forgotten, yet shall I live. There is no such thing as death, Holly, only a change, and, as you may perhaps learn in time to come, I believe that even here that change could under certain circumstances be indefinitely postponed," and again he broke into one of his dreadful fits of coughing.

"There," he said, "I must go; you have the chest, and my will can be found among my papers, under the authority of which the child will be handed over to you. You will be well paid, Holly, and I know that you are honest; but if you betray my trust, by Heaven, I will haunt you."

I said nothing, being, indeed, too bewildered to speak.

He held up the candle, and looked at his own face in the glass. It had been a beautiful face, but disease had wrecked it. "Food for the worms," he said. "Curious to think that in a few hours I shall be stiff and cold—the journey done, the little game played out. Ah me, Holly! life is not worth the trouble of life, except when one is in love—at least, mine has not been; but the boy Leo's may be if he has the courage and the faith. Good-bye, my friend!" and with a sudden access of tenderness he flung his arm about me and kissed me on the forehead, and then turned to go.

"Look here, Vincey," I said; "if you are as ill as you think, you had better let me fetch a doctor."

"No, no," he said earnestly. "Promise me that you won't. I am going to die, and, like a poisoned rat, I wish to die alone."

"I don't believe that you are going to do anything of the sort," I answered. He smiled, and, with the word "Remember" on his lips, was gone. As for myself, I sat down and rubbed my eyes, wondering if I had been asleep. As this idea would not bear investigation I gave it up, and began to think that Vincey must have been drinking. I knew that he was, and had been, very ill, but still it seemed impossible that he could be in such a pass as to be able to know for certain that he would not outlive the night. Had he been so near dissolution surely he would scarcely have been able to walk, and to carry a heavy iron box with him. The story, on reflection, seemed to me utterly incredible, for I was not then old enough to be aware how many things happen in this world that the common sense of the average man would set down as so improbable as to be absolutely impossible. This is a fact that I have only recently mastered. Was it likely that a man would have a son five years of age whom he had never seen since he was a tiny infant? No. Was it likely that he could foretell his own death so accurately? No. Was it likely that he could trace his pedigree for more than three centuries before Christ, or that he would suddenly confide the absolute guardianship of his child, and leave half his fortune, to a college friend? Most certainly not. Clearly Vincey was either drunk or mad. That being so, what did it mean? And what was in the sealed iron chest?

The position baffled and puzzled me to such an extent that at last I could bear the thought of it no longer, and determined to sleep over it. So having put away the keys and the letter that Vincey had left into my despatch-box, and hidden the iron chest in a large portmanteau, I went to bed, and was soon fast asleep.

As it seemed to me, I had only been asleep for a few minutes when I was awakened by somebody calling me. I sat up and rubbed my eyes; it was broad daylight—eight o'clock, in fact.

"Why, what is the matter with you, John?" I asked of the gyp who waited on Vincey and myself. "You look as though you had seen a ghost!"

"Yes, sir, and so I have," he answered, "leastways I've seen a corpse, which is worse. I've been in to call Mr. Vincey, as usual, and there he lies stark and dead!"

Mr. Vincey — 5 yr old son; trip to Africa; descendent of Egyptian priest Isis;

Holly — college friend of Mr. Vincey

II

The Years Roll By

As might be expected, poor Vincey's sudden death created a great stir in the College; but, as he was known to be very ill, and a satisfactory doctor's certificate was forthcoming, no inquest was held. They were not so particular about inquests in those days as we are now; indeed, they were generally disliked, because of the attendant scandal. Under these circumstances, being asked no questions, I did not feel it necessary to volunteer information about our interview on the night of Vincey's decease, beyond saying that, as was not unusual with him, he had come into my rooms. On the day of the funeral a lawyer came down from London and followed my poor friend's remains to the grave, and then returned with his papers and effects, except, of course, the iron chest which had been left in my keeping. For a week after this I heard no more of the matter; and, indeed, my attention was amply occupied in other ways, for I was up for my Fellowship, a fact that had prevented me from attending the funeral or seeing the lawyer. At last, however, the examination was over, and I came back to my rooms and sank into an easy chair with a happy consciousness that I had got through it very fairly.

Soon, however, my thoughts, relieved of the pressure that had crushed them into a single groove during the last few days, turned to the events of the night of poor Vincey's death, and again I asked myself what it all meant, and wondered if I should hear anything more of the matter, and if I did not, what it would be my duty to do with the curious iron chest. I sat there and thought and thought till I began to grow seriously disturbed over the occurrence: the mysterious midnight visit, the prophecy of death so shortly to be fulfilled, the solemn oath that I had taken, and which Vincey had called on me to answer to in another world than this. Had the man committed suicide? It looked like it. And what was the quest of which he spoke? The circumstances were uncanny, so much so that, though I am by no means nervous, or apt to be alarmed at anything which may seem to cross the bounds of the natural, I grew afraid, and began to wish I had nothing to do with them. How much more do I wish it now, over twenty years afterwards!

As I sat and thought, there came a knock at the door, and a letter, in a big blue envelope, was brought to me. I saw at once that it must be a lawyer's letter, and an instinct told me that it was connected with my trust. The letter, which I still have, runs thus:—

"SIR,—Our client, the late M. L. Vincey, Esq., who died on the 9th instant in —— College Cambridge, has left behind him a Will, of which we are the executors, whereof you will please find copy enclosed. Under this Will you will perceive that you take a life-interest in about half of the late Mr. Vincey's property, now invested in Consols, subject to your acceptance of the guardianship of his only son, Leo Vincey, an infant, aged five. Had we not ourselves drawn up the document in question in obedience to Mr. Vincey's clear and precise instructions, both personal and written, and had he not then assured us that he had very good reasons for what he was doing, we ought to tell you that its provisions seem to us of so unusual a nature, that we should have felt bound to call the attention of the Court of Chancery to them, in order that such steps might be taken as seemed desirable to it, either by contesting the capacity of the testator or otherwise, to safeguard the interests of the infant. As it is, knowing that Mr. Vincey was a gentleman of the

highest intelligence and acumen, and that he has absolutely no relations living to whom he could have confided the guardianship of the
child, we do not feel justified in taking this course.

"Awaiting such instructions as you may please to send us as regards the delivery of the infant and the payment of the proportion
of the dividends due to you,

"We remain, Sir, faithfully yours,
"GEOFFREY AND JORDAN.

"Horace L. Holly, Esq."

I put down the letter, and ran my eye through the Will, which appeared, from its utter unintelligibility, to have been drawn on the
strictest legal principles. So far as I could discover, however, it exactly
bore out what my friend Vincey had told me on the night of his death.
Then it was true after all. I must take the boy. Suddenly I remembered
the letter which Vincey had left with the box. I fetched and opened it.
It contained only such directions as he had already given to me as to
opening the chest on Leo's twenty-fifth birthday, and laid down the
outlines of the boy's education, which was to include Greek, the
higher Mathematics, and *Arabic.* At the end there was a postscript to
the effect that if the child died under the age of twenty-five, which,
however, the writer did not believe would occur, I was to open the
chest, and act on the information therein contained if I saw fit. If I did
not see fit, I was to destroy all the contents. On no account was I to pass
them on to a stranger.

As this letter added nothing material to my knowledge, and certainly raised no further objection in my mind to entering on the task I
had promised my dead friend to undertake, there was only one course
open to me—namely, to write to Messrs. Geoffrey and Jordan, and express my acceptance of the trust, stating that I should be willing to
commence my guardianship of Leo in ten days' time. This done I
went to the authorities of my college, and having told them as much of
the story as I considered desirable, which was not very much, after
some difficulty I succeeded in persuading them to stretch a point, and,
in the event of my having obtained a fellowship, which I was almost

certain was the case, to allow me to take the child to live with me. Their consent, however, was only granted on the condition that I vacated my rooms in college and took lodgings. This I did, and after an active search I obtained very good apartments quite close to the college gates. The next thing was to find a nurse. Now on this point I came to a decision. I would have no woman to lord it over me about the child, and steal his affections from me. The boy was old enough to do without female assistance, so I set to work to find a suitable male attendant. After some difficulty I was fortunate in hiring a most respectable round-faced young man, who had been a helper in a hunting-stable, but who said that he was one of a family of seventeen and well-accustomed to the ways of children, and professed himself quite willing to undertake the charge of Master Leo when he arrived. Then, having carried the iron box to town, and with my own hands deposited it at my banker's, I bought some books upon the health and management of infants, and read them, first to myself, then aloud to Job—that was the young man's name—and waited.

At length the child arrived in the charge of an elderly person, who wept bitterly at parting with him; and a beautiful boy he was. Indeed, I do not think that I ever saw such a perfect child before or since. His eyes were grey, his forehead was broad, and his face, even at that early age, clean cut as a cameo, without being pinched or thin. But perhaps his most attractive point was his hair, which was pure gold in colour and tightly curled over his shapely head. He cried a little when at last his nurse tore herself away and left him with us. Never shall I forget the scene. There he stood, with the sunlight from the window playing upon his golden curls, his fist screwed over one eye, while he took us in with the other. I was seated in a chair, and stretched out my hand to him to induce him to come to me, while Job, in the corner, made a sort of clucking noise, which, arguing from his previous experience, or from the analogy of the hen, he judged would have a soothing effect, and inspire confidence in the youthful mind, and ran a wooden horse of peculiar hideousness backwards and forwards in a way that was little short of inane. This went on for some minutes, and then all of a sudden the lad stretched out both his little arms and ran to me.

"I like you," he said: "you is ugly, but you is good."

Ten minutes afterwards he was eating large slices of bread-and-butter, with every sign of satisfaction; Job wanted to put jam on to them, but I sternly reminded him of the excellent works that we had read, and forbade it.

In a very little while (for, as I expected, I gained my fellowship) the boy became the favourite of the whole College—where, orders and regulations to the contrary notwithstanding, he was continually in and out—a sort of infant libertine, in whose favour all rules were relaxed. The offerings made at his shrine were without number, and thereon I had a serious difference of opinion with one old resident Fellow, now long dead, who was supposed to be the crustiest man in the University, and to abhor the sight of a child. And yet I discovered, when a frequently recurring fit of sickness had forced Job to keep a strict lookout, that this unprincipled old man was in the habit of enticing the boy to his rooms and there feeding him upon unlimited quantities of "brandy-balls," and of making him promise to say nothing about it. Job told him that he ought to be ashamed of himself, "at his age, too, when he might have been a grandfather if he had done what was right," by which Job understood had married. Thence arose the quarrel.

But I have no space to dwell upon those delightful years, around which happy memories still linger. One by one they went by, and as they passed we two grew dearer and yet more dear to each other. Few sons have been loved as I love Leo, and few fathers know the deep and continuous affection that Leo bears to me.

The child grew into the boy, and the boy into the young man, while one by one the remorseless years flew by, and as he grew and increased so did his beauty and the beauty of his mind grow with him. When he was about fifteen they christened him Beauty about the College, and me they nicknamed the Beast. Beauty and the Beast was what they called us when we went out walking together, as we were wont to do every day. Once Leo attacked a strapping butcher's man, twice his size, because he sang it out after us, and thrashed him, too—thrashed him fairly. I walked on and pretended not to see, till the combat grew too exciting, when I turned round and cheered him on to victory. It was the chaff of the College at the time, but I could not help it. Then, when he was a little older the undergraduates found fresh names for us. They styled me Charon, and Leo the Greek god! I will pass over my own appellation with the humble remark that I was never handsome, and did not grow more so as I aged. As for his title, there was no doubt about its fitness. Leo at twenty-one might have stood for a statue of the youthful Apollo. I never saw anybody to equal him in looks, nor anybody so absolutely unconscious of them. As for his mind, he was brilliant and keen-witted, but no scholar. He had not the dulness necessary to that result. We followed out his father's instructions as to his education strictly enough, and on the whole the results, especially with regard to Greek and Arabic, were satisfactory. I learnt the latter language in order to help to teach it to him, but after five years of it he knew it as well as I did—almost as well as the professor who instructed us both. I was always a great sportsman—it is my one passion—and every autumn we went away shooting or fishing, sometimes to Scotland, sometimes to Norway, once indeed to Russia. I am a good shot, but even in this he learnt to excel me.

When Leo was eighteen I moved back into my rooms, and entered him at my own College, and at twenty-one he took his degree—a respectable degree, but not a very high one. Then it was that, for the first time, I told him something of his own story, and of the mystery which loomed ahead. Naturally he was very curious about it, and of course I explained to him that his curiosity could not be gratified at present. After this, to pass the time away, I suggested that he should read for the Bar; and this he did, studying at Cambridge, and going to London to eat his dinners.

I had only one trouble about Leo, and it was that every young woman whom he met, or, if not every one, most of them, insisted on falling in love with him. Hence arose difficulties into which I need not enter here, though they were troublesome enough at the time. On the whole he behaved fairly well; I cannot say more than that.

And so the years went by till at last Leo reached his twenty-fifth birthday, at which date this strange and, in some ways, awful history really begins.

III

The Sherd of Amenartas

On the day preceding Leo's twenty-fifth birthday we both journeyed to London, and extracted the mysterious chest from the bank where I had deposited it twenty years before. It was, I recollect, brought up by the same clerk who had taken it down. He perfectly remembered having hidden away the box. Had he not done so, he said, he should have had difficulty in finding it, it was so covered up with cobwebs.

In the evening we returned with our precious burden to Cambridge, and I think that we might both of us have given away all the sleep we won that night and not have been much the poorer. At daybreak Leo arrived in my room in a dressing-gown, and suggested that we should at once proceed to business, an idea which I scouted as showing an unworthy curiosity. The chest had waited twenty years, I said, so it could very well continue to wait until after breakfast. Accordingly at nine—an unusually sharp nine—we breakfasted; and so occupied was I with my own thoughts that I regret to state that I put a piece of bacon into Leo's tea in mistake for a lump of sugar. Job, too, to whom the contagion of excitement had, of course, spread, managed to

break the handle off my Sèvres china teacup, the identical one, I believe, that Marat had used just before he was stabbed in his bath.

At last, however, breakfast was cleared away, and Job, at my request,
fetched the chest, and placed it upon the table in a somewhat gingerly
fashion, as though he mistrusted it. Then he prepared to leave the
room.

"Stop a moment, Job," I said. "If Mr. Leo has no objection, I should
prefer to have an independent witness to this business, who can be re-
lied upon to hold his tongue unless he is asked to speak."

"Certainly, Uncle Horace," answered Leo; for I had brought him up
to call me uncle—though he varied the appellation somewhat disre-
spectfully by styling me "old fellow," or even "my avuncular relative."

Job touched his head, not having a hat on.

"Lock the door, Job," I said, "and bring me my despatch-box."

He obeyed, and from the box I took the keys that poor Vincey, Leo's
father, had given me on the night of his death. There were three of
them: the largest a comparatively modern key, the second an exceedingly ancient one, and the third entirely unlike anything of the sort
that we had ever seen before, being fashioned apparently from a strip
of solid silver, with a bar placed across it to serve as a handle, and having some nicks cut in the edge of the bar. It was more like a clumsy
railway key than anything I can think of.

"Now are you both ready?" I said, as people do when they are about
to fire a mine. There was no answer, so I took the big key, rubbed some
salad oil into the wards, and after one or two mistakes, for my hands
were shaking, managed to fit it, and shoot the lock. Leo bent over and
caught the massive lid in both his hands, and with an effort, for the
hinges had rusted, he forced it back, revealing another case covered
with dust. This we extracted from the iron chest without any difficulty,
and removed the accumulated filth of years from it with a clothes-
brush.

It was, or appeared to be, of ebony, or some such close-grained
black wood, and was bound in every direction with flat bands of iron.
Its antiquity must have been extreme, for in parts the dense heavy
wood was commencing to crumble from age.

The Casket

"Now for it," I said, inserting the second key.

Job and Leo bent forward in breathless expectancy. The key turned, I flung back the lid and uttered an exclamation; and no wonder, for inside the ebony case was a magnificent silver casket, about twelve inches square by eight high. It was doubtless of Egyptian workmanship, for the four legs were formed of Sphinxes, and the dome-shaped cover was also surmounted by a Sphinx. The casket was of course much tarnished and dinted with age, but otherwise in very sound condition.

I drew it out and set it on the table, and then, in the midst of the most perfect silence, I inserted the strange-looking silver key, and pressed this way and that until at last the lock yielded, and the casket stood open before us. It was filled to the brim with some brown shredded material, more like vegetable fibre than paper, the nature of which I have never been able to discover. This I carefully removed to the depth of some three inches, when I came to a letter enclosed in an ordinary modern-looking envelope, and addressed, in the handwriting of my dead friend Vincey:

"To my son Leo, should he live to open this casket."

I handed the letter to Leo, who glanced at the envelope, and then put it down upon the table, making a motion to me to continue the investigation of the casket.

The next thing that I found was a parchment carefully rolled up. I unrolled it, and seeing that it was also in Vincey's handwriting, and headed, "Translation of the Uncial Greek Writing on the Potsherd," I put it down by the letter. Then followed another ancient roll of parchment, that had become yellow and crinkled with the passage of years. This I also unrolled. It was likewise a translation of the same Greek original, but into black-letter Latin, which at the first glance from the style and character appeared to me to date from about the beginning of the sixteenth century.

Immediately beneath this roll was something hard and heavy, wrapped up in yellow linen, and reposing upon another layer of the fibrous material. Slowly and carefully we unrolled the linen, exposing to view a very large but undoubtedly ancient potsherd of a dirty yellow colour! This potsherd, in my judgment, had once been a part of an ordinary amphora of medium size. For the rest, it measured ten and a half inches in length by seven in width, was about a quarter of an inch thick, and densely covered on the convex side that lay towards the bottom of the box with writing in the later uncial Greek character, faded here and there, but for the most part perfectly legible, the inscription having evidently been executed with the greatest care, and by means of a reed pen, such as the ancients often used. I must not forget to mention that in some remote age this wonderful fragment had been broken in two, and rejoined with cement and eight long rivets. Also there were numerous inscriptions on the inner side, but these were of the most erratic character, and clearly had been made by different hands and in many different ages. Of them, together with the writings on the parchments, I shall have to speak presently.

"Is there anything more?" asked Leo, in an excited whisper.

I groped about, and produced something hard, done up in a little linen bag. Out of the bag we took first a very beautiful miniature painted upon ivory, and, secondly, a small chocolate-coloured composition *scarabæus*, marked thus:—

symbols which, we have since ascertained, mean "Suten se Rā," that is, being translated, the "Royal Son of Rā or the Sun." The miniature was a picture of Leo's Greek mother—a lovely, dark-eyed creature. On the back of it was written, in poor Vincey's handwriting, "My beloved wife."

"That is all," I said.

"Very well," answered Leo, putting down the miniature, at which he had been gazing affectionately; "and now let us read the letter," and without further ado he broke the seal, and read aloud as follows:—

"MY SON LEO,—When you open this, if you ever live to do so, you will have attained to manhood, and I shall have been long enough dead to be absolutely forgotten by nearly all who knew me. Yet in reading remember that I have been, and for anything you know may still be, and that herein, through this link of pen and paper, I stretch out my hand to you across the gulf of death, and my voice speaks to you from the silence of the grave. Though I am dead, and no memory of me remains in your mind, yet am I with you in this hour as you read. Since your birth to this day I have scarcely seen your face. Forgive me this. Your life supplanted the life of one whom I loved better than women are often loved, and the bitterness of it endureth yet. Had I lived I should in time have conquered this foolish feeling, but I am not destined to live. My sufferings, physical and mental, are more than I can bear, and when such small arrangements as I have to make for your future well-being are completed it is my intention to put a period to them. May God forgive me if I do wrong. At the best I could not live more than another year."

"So he killed himself," I exclaimed. "I thought so."
"And now," Leo went on, without replying,

"enough of myself. What has to be said belongs to you who live, not to me, who am dead, and almost as much forgotten as though I had never been. Holly, my friend (to whom, if he will accept the trust, it is my intention to confide you), will have told you something of the extraordinary antiquity of your race. In the contents of this casket you will find sufficient to prove it. The strange legend that you will see inscribed by your remote ancestress upon the potsherd was communicated to me by my father on his deathbed, and took strong hold in my imagination. When I was only nineteen years of age I determined, as, to his misfortune, did one of our ancestors about the time of Elizabeth, to investigate its truth. Into all that befell me I cannot enter now. But this I saw with my own eyes. On the coast of Africa, in a hitherto unexplored region, some distance to the north of where the Zambesi falls into the sea, there is a headland, at the extremity of which a peak towers up, shaped like the head of a negro, similar to that whereof the writing speaks. I landed there, and learnt from a wandering native, who had been cast out by his people because of some crime which he had committed, that far inland are great mountains shaped like cups, and caves surrounded by measureless swamps. I learnt also that the people there speak a dialect of Arabic, and are ruled over by a *beautiful white woman* who is seldom seen by them, but who is reported to have power over all things living and dead. Two days after I had ascertained this the man died of fever contracted in crossing the swamps, and I was forced by want of provisions and by symptoms of an illness which afterwards prostrated me to take to my dhow again.

"Of the adventures that befell me after this I need not now speak. I was wrecked upon the coast of Madagascar, and rescued some months afterwards by an English ship that brought me to Aden, whence I started for England, intending to prosecute my search as soon as I had made sufficient preparations. On my way I stopped in Greece, and there, for *Omnia vincit amor,* I met your beloved mother, and married her, and there you were born and she died. Then it was that my last illness seized me, and I returned hither to die. But still I hoped against hope, and set myself to work to learn Arabic, with the intention, should I ever get better, of returning to the coast of Africa, and solving the mystery of which the tradition has lived so many centuries in our family. But I have not got better, and, so far as I am concerned, the story is at an end.

"For you, however, my son, it is not at an end, and to you I hand on these the results of my labour, together with the hereditary proofs of its origin. It is my purpose to provide that they shall not be put into your hands until you have reached an age when you will be able to judge for yourself whether or no you will choose to investigate what, if it is true, must be the greatest mystery in the world, or to put it by as an idle fable, originating in the first place in a woman's disordered brain.

"I do not believe that it is a fable; I believe that if it can only be re-discovered, there is a spot where the vital forces of the world visibly exist. Life exists; why therefore should not the means of preserving it indefinitely exist also? But I have no wish to prejudice your mind about the matter. Read and judge for yourself. If you are inclined to undertake the search, I have so provided that you will not lack for means. If, on the other hand, you are satisfied that the legend is a chimera, then, I adjure you, destroy the potsherd and the writings, and let a cause of troubling be removed from our race for ever. Perhaps that will be wisest. The unknown is generally taken to be terrible, not, as the proverb would infer, from the inherent superstition of man, but because it so often *is* terrible. He who would tamper with the vast and secret forces that animate the world may well fall a victim to them. And if the end were attained, if at last you emerged from the trial ever beautiful and ever young, defying time and evil, and lifted above the natural decay of flesh and intellect, who shall say that the awesome change would bring you happiness? Choose, my son, and may the Power who rules all things, and who says 'thus far shalt thou go, and thus much shalt thou learn,' direct the choice to your own welfare and the welfare of the world, which, in the event of your success, you would one day certainly rule by the pure force of accumulated experience.—Farewell!"

Thus the letter, which was unsigned and undated, abruptly ended.

"What do you make of that, Uncle Holly?" said Leo, with a gasp, as he replaced the paper on the table. "We have been looking for a mystery, and certainly we seem to have found one."

"What do I make of it? Why, that your poor dear father was off his head, of course," I answered, testily. "I guessed as much that night, twenty years ago, when he came into my room. You see he evidently hurried his own end, poor man. It is absolute balderdash."

"That's it, sir!" said Job, solemnly. Job was a most matter-of-fact specimen of a matter-of-fact class.

"Well, let's see what the potsherd has to say, at any rate," said Leo, taking up the translation in his father's writing, and commencing to read:—

"I, *Amenartas*, of the Royal House of the Pharaohs of Egypt, wife of *Kallikrates* (the Beautiful in Strength), *a Priest of Isis whom the gods*

I.

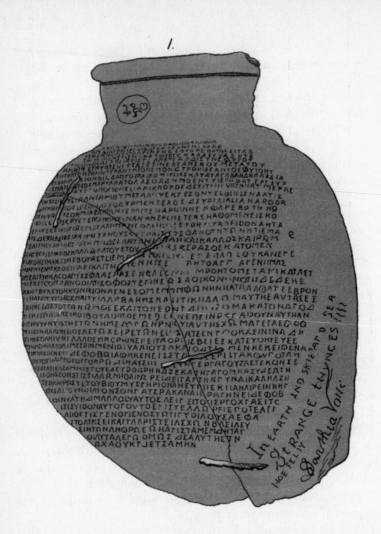

FACSIMILE OF THE SHERD OF AMENARTAS.

ONE ½ SIZE.

Greatest length of the original ... 10½ inches.

Greatest breadth 7   "

Weight ... ... 1 lb 5½ oz.

2

DYA ANLI   YIN   VEYOLEISY
MICDENIIN KA ΛΛΙΚΡΑΤΕΠΤΙΙD
ΛΙΔΙ
Lionel Vincey
Ætate sua 7   ΚΡΛΕΙΙΡΖΗ

KIA   III ΔIHC   W
ΤΙΣΚΘΕΝΗ   ΤΙΣΚ ΠΕΛΚΙ
ΚΟΛΝΚΡΥ ΖLΙΤΝ ΔISS
ΠLOL ΘΕΝΕΝLΙC ΓOLSI
ΚΑΛΛΙΚΡΒΓΥS
ΤΙGΙΘ ΘΕΝHS
C.FVFIDIVS.C F VINDEK   ROMAEAIU   CVI.
C. CAECIL VINDEX   AOVSIVS VIND
M.AIMILIVS VIN DEX   VALERIVS GOMINVS
SEX MARIVS MARVLIVS   VINDEX
OSOSIVSPRISCVS SENECIO VINDEX
LABERIA POMPEIANA CCNIVX MACRINI VINDKIS
A.V.   ICINIVS FAVSTVS
1800 SEX OTACIL IV SMIF
MANILIA LVCILLA CHIVX MARVW VINDIEIS

one that dydtost my fatherhis
a most strawgeitisione   uponthe eaftr goast of
lyfe for m setkynge for the ylaee
Africa his own   nce was fund by a Yorbuayuese
galleonols fore an masquez am hy hvmfetfper shed
1564
John Vincey
Yherewnd mow thmigs m neawen and
earth than aus Iw aml of m yom

J.PITCHER & CO., LT₀ LITH.

FACSIMILE OF THE REVERSE OF THE SHERD OF AMENARTAS.
ONE ½ SIZE.

cherish and the demons obey, being about to die, to my little son Tisisthenes (the Mighty Avenger). *I fled with thy father from Egypt in the days of Nectanebes,* causing him through love to break the vows that he had vowed. We fled southward, across the waters, and we wandered for twice twelve moons on the coast of Libya (Africa) that looks towards the rising sun, where by a river is a great rock carven like the head of an Ethiopian. Four days on the water from the mouth of a mighty river were we cast away, and some were drowned and some died of sickness. But us wild men took through wastes and marshes, where the sea fowl hid the sky, bearing us ten days' journey till we came to a hollow mountain, where a great city had been and fallen, and where there are caves of which no man hath seen the end; and they brought us to the Queen of the people who place pots upon the heads of strangers, who is a magician having a knowledge of all things, and life and loveliness that does not die. And she cast eyes of love upon thy father, Kallikrates, and would have slain me, and taken him to husband, but he loved me and feared her, and would not. Then did she take us, and lead us by terrible ways, by means of dark magic, to where the great pit is, in the mouth of which the old philosopher lay dead, and showed to us the rolling Pillar of Life that dies not, whereof the voice is as the voice of thunder; and she did stand in the flames, and come forth unharmed, and yet more beautiful. Then did she swear to make thy father undying even as she is, if he would but slay me, and give himself to her, for me she could not slay because of the magic of my own people that I have, and that prevailed thus far against her. And he held his hand before his eyes to hide her beauty, and would not. Then in her rage did she smite him by her magic, and he died; but she wept over him, and bore him thence with lamentations; and being afraid, me she sent to the mouth of the great river where the ships come, and I was carried far away on the ships where I gave thee birth, and hither to Athens I came at last after many wanderings. Now I say to thee, my son, Tisisthenes, seek out the woman, and learn the secret of Life, and if thou mayest find a way slay her, because of thy father Kallikrates; and if thou dost fear or fail, this I say to all of thy seed who come after thee, till at last a brave man be found among them who shall bathe in the fire and sit in the place*

---

*Nekht-nebf, or Nectanebo II, the last native Pharaoh of Egypt, fled from Ochus to Ethiopia, B.C. 339.—EDITOR.

of the Pharaohs. I speak of those things, that though they be past belief, yet I have known, and I lie not."

"May the Lord forgive her for that," groaned Job, who had been listening to this marvellous composition with his mouth open.

As for myself, I said nothing: my first idea being that my poor friend, when demented, had composed the whole tale, though it scarcely seemed likely that such a story could have been invented by anybody. It was too original. To solve my doubts I took up the potsherd and began to read the close uncial Greek writing on it; and very good Greek of the period it is, considering that it came from the pen of an Egyptian born. Here is an exact transcript of it:—

```
ΑΜΕΝΑΡΤΑΣΤΟΥΒΑΣΙΛΙΚΟΥΓΕΝΟΥΣΤΟΥΑ
ΙΓΥΠΤΙΟΥΗΤΟΥΚΑΛΛΙΚΡΑΤΟΥΣΙΣΙΔΟΣΙΕΡ
ΕΩΣΗΝΟΙΜΕΝΘΕΟΙΤΡΕΦΟΥΣΙΤΑΔΕΔΑΙΜΟ
ΝΙΑΥΓΟΤΑΣΣΕΤΑΙΗΔΗΤΕΛΕΥΤΩΣΑΤΙΣΙΣ
ΘΕΝΕΙΤΩΠΑΙΔΙΕΠΙΣΤΕΛΛΕΙΤΑΔΕΣΥΝΕΦΥΓΟ
ΝΓΑΡΠΟΤΕΕΚΤΗΣΑΙΓΥΠΤΙΑΣΕΠΙΝΕΚΤΑΝΕΒ
ΟΥΜΕΤΑΤΟΥΣΟΥΓΑΤΡΟΣΔΙΑΤΟΝΕΡΩΤΑΤΟ
ΝΕΜΟΝ ΕΠΙΟΡΚΗΣΑΝΤΟΣΦΥΓΟΝΤΕΣ ΔΕΠΡΟ
ΣΝΟΤΟΝΔΙΑΓΟΝΤΙΟΙΚΑΙΚΔΜΗΝΑΣΚΑΤΑΤΑ
ΓΑΡΑΘΑΛΑΣΣΙΑΤΗΣΛΙΒΥΗΣΤΑΠΡΟΣΗΛΙΟΥ
ΑΝΑΤΟΛΑΣΠΛΑΝΗΘΕΝΤΕΣΕΝΘΑΓΕΡΠΕΤΡΑ
ΤΙΣΜΕΓΑΛΗΓΛΥΠΤΟΝΟΜΟΙΩΜΑΑΙΘΙΟΠΟΣ
ΚΕΦΑΛΗΣΕΙΤΑΗΜΕΡΑΣΔΑΠΟΣΤΟΜΑΤΟΣΓΟ
ΤΑΜΟΥΜΕΓΑΛΟΥΕΚΓΕΣΟΝΤΕΣΟΙΜΕΝΚΑΤΕ
ΓΟΝΤΙΣΘΗΜΕΝΟΙΔΕΝΟΣΩΙΑΠΕΘΑΝΟΜΕΝΤ
ΕΛΟΣΔΕΥΠΑΓΡΙΩΝΑΝΘΡΩΓΩΝΕΦΕΡΟΜΕΘΑ
ΔΙΑΕΛΕΩΝΤΕΚΑΙΤΕΝΑΓΕΩΝΕΝΘΑΓΕΡΠΤΗΝ
ΩΝΠΛΗΘΟΣΑΓΟΚΡΥΠΤΕΙΤΟΝΟΥΡΑΝΟΝΗΜ
ΕΡΑΣΙΕΩΣΗΛΘΟΜΕΝΕΙΣΚΟΙΛΟΝΤΙΟΡΟΣΕΝ
ΘΑΓΟΤΕΜΕΓΑΛΗΜΕΝΠΟΛΙΣΗΝΑΝΤΡΑΔΕΑΓ
ΕΙΡΟΝΑΗΓΑΓΟΝΔΕΩΣΒΑΣΙΛΕΙΑΝΤΗΝΤΩΝΞ
ΕΝΟΥΣΧΥΤΡΑΙΣΣΤΕΦΑΝΟΥΝΤΩΝΗΤΙΣΜΑΓΕ
ΙΑΜΕΝΕΧΡΗΤΟΕΠΙΣΤΗΜΗΔΕΓΑΝΤΩΝΚΑΙΔ
ΗΚΑΙΚΑΛΛΟΣΚΑΙΡΩΜΗΝΑΓΗΡΩΣΗΝΗΔΕΚΑ
ΛΛΙΚΡΑΤΟΥΣΤΟΥΣΟΥΓΑΤΡΟΣΕΡΑΣΘΕΙΣΑΤ
ΟΜΕΝΠΡΩΤΟΝΣΥΝΟΙΚΕΙΝΕΒΟΥΛΕΤΟΕΜΕΔ
ΕΑΝΕΛΕΙΝΕΓΕΙΤΑΩΣΟΚΑΝΕΓΕΙΘΕΝΕΜΕΓΑ
ΡΥΓΕΡΕΦΙΛΕΙΚΑΙΤΗΝΞΕΝΗΝΝΕΦΟΒΕΙΤΟΑΓΗ
ΓΑΓΕΝΗΜΑΣΥΓΟΜΑΓΕΙΑΣΚΑΘΟΔΟΥΣΣΦΑΛ
```

ΕΡΑΣΕΝΘΑΤΟΒΑΡΑΘΡΟΝΤΟΜΕΓΑΟΥΚΑΤΑΣ
ΤΟΜΑΕΚΕΙΤΟΟΓΕΡΩΝΟΦΙΛΟΣΟΦΟΣΤΕΘΝΕ
ΩΣΑΦΙΚΟΜΕΝΟΙΣΔΕΔΕΙΞΕΦΩΣΤΟΥΒΙΟΥΕΥ
ΘΥΟΙΟΝΚΙΟΝΑΕΛΙΣΣΟΜΕΝΟΝΦΩΝΗΝΙΕΝΤ
ΑΚΑΘΑΓΕΡΒΡΟΝΤΗΣΕΙΤΑΔΙΑΓΥΡΟΣΒΕΒΗΚ
ΥΙΑΑΒΛΑΒΗΣΚΑΙΕΤΙΚΑΛΛΙΩΝΑΥΤΗΕΑΥΤΗΣ
ΕΞΕΦΑΝΗΕΚΔΕΤΟΥΤΩΝΩΜΟΣΕΚΑΙΤΟΝΣΟ
ΝΓΑΤΕΡΑΑΘΑΝΑΤΟΝΑΓΟΔΕΙΞΕΙΝΕΙΣΥΝΟΙΚ
ΕΙΝΟΙΒΟΥΛΟΙΤΟΕΜΕΔΕΑΝΕΛΕΙΝΟΥΓΑΡΟΥ
ΝΑΥΤΗΑΝΕΛΕΙΝΙΣΧΥΕΝΥΓΟΤΩΝΗΜΕΔΑΓΩ
ΝΗΝΚΑΙΑΥΤΗΕΧΩΜΑΓΕΙΑΣΟΔΟΥΔΕΝΤΙΜΑ
ΛΛΟΝΗΘΕΛΕΤΩΧΕΙΡΕΤΩΝΟΜΜΑΤΩΝΓΡΟΙ
ΣΧΩΝΙΝΑΔΗΤΟΤΗΣΓΥΝΑΙΚΟΣΚΑΛΛΟΣΜΗ
ΟΡΩΗΓΕΙΤΑΟΡΓΙΣΘΕΙΣΑΚΑΤΕΓΟΗΤΕΥΣΕΜ
ΕΝΑΥΤΟΝΑΓΟΛΟΜΕΝΟΝΜΕΝΤΟΙΚΛΑΟΥΣΑ
ΚΑΙΟΔΥΡΟΜΕΝΗΕΚΕΙΘΕΝΑΓΗΝΕΓΚΕΝΕΜΕΔ
ΕΦΟΒΩΙΑΦΗΚΕΝΕΙΣΣΤΟΜΑΤΟΥΜΕΓΑΛΟΥΓ
ΟΤΑΜΟΥΤΟΥΝΑΥΣΙΓΟΡΟΥΓΟΡΡΩΔΕΝΑΥΣΙ
ΝΕΦΩΝΓΕΡΓΛΕΟΥΣΑΕΤΕΚΟΝΣΕΑΓΟΓΛΕΥΣ
ΑΣΑΜΟΛΙΣΓΟΤΕΔΕΥΡΟΑΘΗΝΑΖΕΚΑΤΗΓΑΓ
ΟΜΗΝΣΥΔΕΩΤΙΣΙΣΘΕΝΕΣΩΝΕΓΙΣΤΕΛΛΩΜ
ΗΟΛΙΓΩΡΕΙΔΕΙΓΑΡΤΗΝΓΥΝΑΙΚΑΑΝΑΖΗΤΕΙ
ΝΗΝΓΩΣΤΟΤΟΥΒΙΟΥΜΥΣΤΗΡΙΟΝΑΝΕΥΡΗ
ΣΚΑΙΑΝΑΙΡΕΙΝΗΝΓΟΥΓΑΡΑΣΧΗΔΙΑΤΟΝΣΟ
ΝΓΑΤΕΡΑΚΑΛΛΙΚΡΑΤΗΝΕΙΔΕΦΟΒΟΥΜΕΝΟ
ΣΗΔΙΑΑΛΛΟΤΙΑΥΤΟΣΛΕΙΓΕΙΤΟΥΕΡΓΟΥΓΑ
ΣΙΤΟΙΣΥΣΤΕΡΟΝΑΥΤΟΤΟΥΤΟΕΓΙΣΤΕΛΛΩΕ
ΩΣΓΟΤΕΑΓΑΘΟΣΤΙΣΓΕΝΟΜΕΝΟΣΤΩΓΥΡΙΛ
ΟΥΣΑΣΘΑΙΤΟΛΜΗΣΕΙΚΑΙΤΑΑΡΙΣΤΕΙΑΕΧΩΝ
ΒΑΣΙΛΕΥΣΑΙΤΩΝΑΝΘΡΩΓΩΝΑΓΙΣΤΑΜΕΝΔ
ΗΤΑΤΟΙΑΥΤΑΛΕΓΩΟΜΩΣΔΕΑΑΥΤΗΕΓΝΩΚ
ΑΟΥΚΕΨΕΥΣΑΜΗΝ

For general convenience in reading, I have here accurately transcribed this inscription into the cursive character.

Ἀμενάρτας, τοῦ βασιλικοῦ γένους τοῦ Αἰγυπτίου, ἡ τοῦ Καλλικράτους Ἴσιδος ἱερέως, ἣν οἱ μὲν θεοὶ τρέφουσι τὰ δὲ δαιμόνια ὑποτάσσεται, ἤδη τελευτῶσα Τισισθένει τῷ παιδὶ ἐπιστέλλει τάδε· συνέφυγον γάρ ποτε ἐκ τῆς Αἰγυπτίας ἐπὶ Νεκτανέβου μετὰ τοῦ σοῦ πατρός, διὰ τὸν ἔρωτα τὸν ἐμὸν ἐπιορκήσαντος. φυγόντες δὲ πρὸς νότον διαπόντιοι καὶ κδʹ μῆνας κατὰ τὰ παραθαλάσσια τῆς Λιβύης τὰ πρὸς ἥλιου ἀνατολὰς πλανηθέντες, ἔνθαπερ πέτρα τις μεγάλη, γλυπτὸν ὁμοίωμα Αἰθίοπος κεφαλῆς,

εἶτα ἡμέρας δ᾽ ἀπὸ στόματος ποταμοῦ μεγάλου ἐκπεσόντες,
οἱ μέν κατεποντίσθημεν, οἱ δὲ νόσῳ ἀπεθάνομεν· τέλος
δὲ ὑπ᾽ ἀγρίων ἀνθρώπων ἐφερόμεθα διὰ ἑλέων τε καὶ τενα-
γέων ἔνθαπερ πτηνῶν πλῆθος ἀποκρύπτει τὸν οὐρανόν,
ἡμέρας ἱ, ἕως ἤλθομεν εἰς κοῖλόν τι ὄρος, ἔνθα ποτὲ μεγάλη
μὲν πόλις ἦν, ἄντρα δὲ ἀπείρονα· ἤγαγον δὲ ὡς βασίλειαν
τὴν τῶν ξένους χύτραις στεφανούντων, ἥτις μαγείᾳ μὲν
ἐχρῆτο ἐπιστήμῃ δὲ πάντων καὶ δὴ καὶ κάλλος καὶ ῥώμην
ἀγήρως ἦν· ἡ δὲ Καλλικράτους τοῦ σοῦ πατρὸς ἐρασθεῖσα
τὸ μὲν πρῶτον συνοικεῖν ἐβούλετο ἐμὲ δὲ ἀνελεῖν· ἔπειτα,
ὡς οὐκ ἀνέπειθεν, ἐμὲ γὰρ ὑπερεφίλει καὶ τὴν ξένην ἐφο-
βεῖτο, ἀπήγαγεν ἡμᾶς ὑπὸ μαγείας καθ᾽ ὁδοὺς σφαλεράς
ἔνθα τὸ βάραθρον τὸ μέγα, οὗ κατὰ στόμα ἔκειτο ὁ γέρων
ὁ φιλόσοφος τεθνεώς, ἀφικομένοις δ᾽ ἔδειξε φῶς τοῦ βίου
εὐθύ, οἷον κίονα ἑλισσόμενον φωνὴν ἱέντα καθάπερ βροντῆς,
εἶτα διὰ πυρὸς βεβηκυῖα ἀβλαβὴς καὶ ἔτι καλλίων αὐτὴ
ἑαυτῆς ἐξεφάνη. ἐκ δὲ τούτων ὤμοσε καὶ τὸν σὸν πατέρα
ἀθάνατον ἀποδείξειν, εἰ συνοικεῖν οἱ βούλοιτο ἐμὲ δε ἀνελεῖν, οὐ γὰρ οὖν αὐτὴ ἀνελεῖν ἴσχυεν ὑπὸ τῶν ἡμεδαπῶν
ἣν καὶ αὐτὴ ἔχω μαγείας. ὁ δ᾽ οὐδέν τι μᾶλλον ἤθελε,
τὼ χεῖρε τῶν ὀμμάτων προΐσχων ἵνα δὴ τὸ τῆς γυναικὸς
κάλλος μὴ ὁρῴη· ἔπειτα ὀργισθεῖσα κατεγοήτευσε μὲν
αὐτόν, ἀπολόμενον μέντοι κλάουσα καὶ ὀδυρομένη ἐκεῖθεν
ἀπήνεγκεν, ἐμὲ δὲ φόβῳ ἀφῆκεν εἰς στόμα τοῦ μεγάλου
ποταμοῦ τοῦ ναυσιπόρου, πόρρω δὲ ναυσίν, ἐφ᾽ ὧνπερ
πλέουσα ἔτεκόν σε, ἀποπλεύσασα μόλις ποτὲ δεῦρο Ἀθη-
νάζε κατηγαγόμην. σὺ δέ, ὦ Τισίσθενες, ὧν ἐπιστέλλω
μὴ ὀλιγώρει· δεῖ γὰρ τὴν γυναῖκα ἀναζητεῖν ἥν πως τὸ τοῦ
βίου μυστήριον ἀνεύρῃς, καὶ ἀναιρεῖν, ἤν που παρασχῇ,
διὰ τὸν σὸν πατέρα Καλλικράτην. εἰ δὲ φοβούμενος ἢ διὰ
ἄλλο τι αὐτὸς λείπει τοῦ ἔργου, πᾶσι τοῖς ὕστερον αὐτὸ
τοῦτο ἐπιστέλλω, ἕως ποτὲ ἀγαθός τις γενόμενος τῷ πυρὶ
λούσασθαι τολμήσει καὶ τὰ ἀριστεῖα ἔχων βασιλεῦσαι
τῶν ἀνθρώπων· ἄπιστα μὲν δὴ τὰ τοιαῦτα λέγω, ὅμως
δὲ ἃ αὐτὴ ἔγνωκα οὐκ ἐψευσάμην.

The English translation is, as I discovered on further investigation, and as the reader may easily see for himself by comparison, both accurate and elegant.

Besides the uncial writing on the convex side of the sherd, at the top, painted in dull red on what had once been the lip of the amphora, was the cartouche already mentioned as appearing on the *scarabæus,* which we had found in the casket. The hieroglyphics or symbols, however, were reversed, just as though they had been pressed on wax. Whether this was the cartouche of the original Kallikrates,* or of some Prince or Pharaoh from whom his wife Amenartas was descended, I am not sure, nor can I tell if it was drawn upon the sherd at the same time that the uncial Greek was inscribed, or copied more recently from the Scarab by some other member of the family. Nor was this all. At the foot of the writing, painted in the same dull red, appeared the outline of a somewhat rude drawing of the head and shoulders of a Sphinx wearing two feathers, symbols of majesty, which, though common enough upon the effigies of sacred bulls and gods, I have never before met with on a Sphinx.

Also on the right-hand side of this surface of the sherd, written obliquely in red on the space not covered by the uncial characters, and signed in blue paint, was the following quaint inscription:—

IN EARTH AND SKIE AND SEA
STRANGE THYNGES THER BE.
HOC FECIT
DOROTHEA VINCEY.

Perfectly bewildered, I turned the relic over. It was covered from top to bottom with notes and signatures in Greek, Latin, and English. The first in uncial Greek was by Tisisthenes, the son to whom the writing was addressed. It was, "I could not go. Tisisthenes to his son, Kallikrates." Here it is in fac-simile with its cursive equivalent:—

ΟΥΚΑΝΔΥΝΑΙΜΗΝΓΟΡΕΥΕϹΘΑΙΤΙϹΙϹΘΕΝΗ
ϹΚΑΛΛΙΚΡΑΤΕΙΤΩΙΓΑΙΔΙ

οὐκ ἂν δυναίμην πορεύεσθαι.
Τισισθένης Καλλικράτει τῷ παιδί.

*The cartouche, if it be a true cartouche, cannot have been that of Kallikrates, as Mr. Holly suggests. Kallikrates was a priest and not entitled to a cartouche, which was the prerogative of Egyptian royalty, though he might have inscribed his name or title upon an *oval.*—EDITOR.

This Kallikrates (probably, in the Greek fashion, so named after his grandfather) evidently made some attempt to start on the quest, for his entry written in very faint and almost illegible uncial is, "I ceased from my going, the gods being against me. Kallikrates to his son." Here it is also:—

ΤΩΝΘΕΩΝΑΝΤΙΣΤΑΝΤΩΝΕΓΑΥΣΑΜΗΝΤΗΣ
ΓΟΡΕΙΑΣΚΑΛΛΙΚΡΑΤΗΣΤΩΙΓΑΙΔΙ

τῶν θεῶν ἀντιστάντων ἐπαυσάμην τῆς πορείας.
Καλλικράτης τῷ παιδί.

Between these two ancient writings, the second of which was inscribed upside down, and was so faint and worn that had it not been for the transcript of it executed by Vincey I should scarcely have been able to read it, since, owing to its having been written on that portion of the tile which, in the course of ages, had undergone the most handling, it was nearly rubbed out, was the bold, modern-looking signature of one Lionel Vincey, "Ætate sua 17," inscribed thereon, as I think, by Leo's grandfather. To the right of this were the initials "J. B. V.," and below came a variety of Greek signatures, in uncial and cursive character, and what appeared to be some carelessly executed repetitions of the sentence "τῷ παιδί" (to my son), showing that the relic was passed on religiously from generation to generation.

The next thing legible after the Greek signatures was the word "ROMAE, A.U.C.," indicating that the family had now migrated to Rome. Unfortunately, however, with the exception of its termination (cvi) the date of their settlement there is for ever lost, for just where it had been placed a piece of the potsherd is broken away.

Then followed twelve Latin signatures, jotted about here and there, wherever there was a space upon the tile suitable to their inscription. These signatures, with three exceptions only, ended with the name "Vindex" or "the Avenger," which seems to have been adopted by the family after its migration to Rome as a kind of equivalent to the Grecian "Tisisthenes," which also means an avenger. Ultimately, as might be expected, this Latin cognomen of Vindex was transformed first into De Vincey, and then into the plain, modern Vincey. It is curious to observe how this hereditary duty of revenge, bequeathed by an Egyptian who lived before the time of Christ, is thus, as it were, embalmed in an English family name.

A few of the Roman names inscribed upon the sherd I have since found mentioned in history and other records. They are, if I remember right,

MVSSIVS. VINDEX

SEX. VARIVS. MARVLLVS

C. FVFIDIVS. C. F. VINDEX

and

LABERIA POMPEIANA. CONIVX. MACRINI. VINDICIS

the last being, of course, the name of a Roman lady.

The following list, however, comprises all the Latin names upon the sherd:—

C. CAECILIVS VINDEX

M. AIMILIVS VINDEX

SEX. VARIVS. MARVLLVS

Q. SOSIVS PRISCVS SENECIO VINDEX

L. VALERIVS COMINIVS VINDEX

SEX. OTACILIVS. M. F.

L. ATTIVS. VINDEX

MVSSIVS VINDEX

C. FVFIDIVS. C. F. VINDEX

LICINIVS FAVSTVS

LABERIA POMPEIANA CONIVX MACRINI VINDICIS

MANILIA LVCILLA CONIVX MARVLLI VINDICIS

After the series of Roman names there is a gap of very many centuries. Nobody will ever know now what was the history of the relic during those dark ages, or how it came to be preserved in the family. My poor friend Vincey, it will be remembered, had told me that his

Roman ancestors finally settled in Lombardy, and when Charlemagne invaded it, returned with him across the Alps, and made their home in Brittany, whence they crossed to England in the reign of Edward the Confessor. How he knew this I am not aware, for there is no reference to Lombardy or Charlemagne upon the tile, though, as will be seen presently, there is a reference to Brittany. To continue: the next entries on the sherd, if I may except a long splash either of blood or red colouring matter of some sort, consist of two crosses drawn in red pigment, probably representing Crusaders' swords, and a rather neat monogram ("D. V.") in scarlet and blue, perhaps executed by that same Dorothea Vincey who wrote, or rather painted, the doggerel couplet. To the left of this, inscribed in faint blue, are the initials A. V., and after them a date, 1800.

Then came what was perhaps as curious an item as anything upon this extraordinary relic of the past. It is executed in black letter, written over the crosses or Crusaders' swords, and dated fourteen hundred and forty-five. As the best plan will be to allow it to speak for itself, I here give the black-letter fac-simile, together with the original Latin without the contractions, from which it will be seen that the writer was a fair mediæval Latinist. Further we discovered what is still more curious, an English version of the black-letter Latin. This, also written in black letter, we found inscribed on a second parchment that was in the coffer, apparently somewhat older in date than that on which was written the mediæval Latin translation of the uncial Greek of which I shall speak presently. This I also give in full.

FACSIMILE OF BLACK-LETTER INSCRIPTION ON
THE SHERD OF AMENARTAS.

𝔍ſta reliᵭia eſt balde miſticū et myrificū oꝑs
ᵭd maiores mei ex Armorica ſſ Brittania
mīore secū cōbeᵭebāt et ᵭdm ſᵭ cleriᵭ ſeper ꝓi
meo in manb ferebat ᵭd pᵉitus illbd deſtrueret

affirmãs ꝗᵭ eſſet ab ipſo ſathana cõſſatᵬ preſtigi⸗
oſa et ꝺyabolica arte ꝗre ꝑter meᵭs cõfregit illᵬᵭ
ĩ ꝺᵬas ꝑteꝫ ꝗs ꝗᵭm ego Ꝗohꝫ de Ꝯiceto ſalᵬas
ſerᵬabi et aꝺaptabi ſicᵬt aꝑparet die lũe ꝓ̄ poſt
ſeſt beate Ꝟrie birᵹ̃ anni gᵗ̄e mccccxlᵬ.

Expanded Version of the above Black-Letter Inscription.

"Ista reliquia est valde misticum et myrificum opus, quod ma-
jores mei ex Armorica, scilicet Britannia Minore, secum convehe-
bant; et quidam sanctus clericus semper patri meo in manu ferebat
quod penitus illud destrueret, affirmans quod esset ab ipso Sathana
conflatum prestigiosa et dyabolica arte, quare pater meus confregit
illud in duas partes, quas quidem ego Johannes de Vinceto salvas
servavi et adaptavi sicut apparet die lune proximo post festum beate
Marie Virginis anni gratie MCCCCXLV."

Facsimile of the Old English Black-Letter Translation of the above Latin Inscription from the Sherd of Amenartas found inscribed upon a parchment.

Ꞇhyꝫ rellike yꝫ a ryghte miſtycall worke &
    a marbeylous yᵉ whyche myne abnceteres
afore tyme ꝺyꝺ conbeighe hider wᵗ yᵐ ffrom
Armoryke whᵉ yꝫ to ſeien Ꞵritapne yᵉ leſſe & a
certapne holpe clerke ſhoulde allwepes beare mp
ffaꝺir on honde yᵗ he owghte bttirlp ffor to
ffruſſhe yᵉ ſame affirmynge yᵗ pt was ffourmpꝺ &
confflatpꝺ off ſathanas hym ſelffe bp arte magike
& ꝺybellpſſhe wherefore mp ffaꝺir ꝺyꝺ take yᵉ
ſame & to braſt pt yn twepne but Ꝗ Ꝗohn ꝺe

𝔙incey dyd save whool yͤ tweye p̄tes therof & topeecyd pͫ togydder agayne soe as yee se on yˢ depe mondaye next ffolowynge after yͤ ffeeste of seynte 𝔐arye yͤ blessed vyrgyne yn yͤ yeere of salvacioun ffowertene hundreth & ffyve & ffowrti.

MODERNISED VERSION OF THE ABOVE BLACK-LETTER TRANSLATION.

"THYS rellike ys a ryghte mistycall worke and a marvaylous, ye whyche myne aunceteres aforetyme dyd conveigh hider with them from Armoryke which ys to seien Britaine ye Lesse and a certayne holye clerke should allweyes beare my fadir on honde that he owghte uttirly for to frusshe ye same, affyrmynge that yt was fourmed and conflatyd of Sathanas hym selfe by arte magike and dyvellysshe wherefore my fadir dyd take ye same and tobrast yt yn tweyne, but I, John de Vincey, dyd save whool ye tweye partes therof and topeecyd them togydder agayne soe as yee se, on this daye mondaye next fol-lowynge after ye feeste of Seynte Marye ye Blessed Vyrgyne yn ye yeere of Salvacioun fowertene hundreth and fyve and fowerti."

The next and, save one, last entry was Elizabethan, and dated 1564: "A most strange historie, and one that did cost my father his life; for in seekynge for the place upon the east coast of Africa, his pinnance was sunk by a Portuguese galleon off Lorenzo Marquez, and he himself perished.—JOHN VINCEY."

Then came the last entry, which, to judge by the style of writing, had been made by some representative of the family in the middle of the eighteenth century. It was a misquotation of the well-known lines in "Hamlet," and ran thus: "There are more things in Heaven and earth than are dreamt of in your philosophy, Horatio."*

*Another thing that makes me fix the date of this entry at the middle of the eighteenth

And now there remained but one more document to be examined—namely, the ancient black-letter translation into mediæval Latin of the uncial inscription on the sherd. As will be seen, this translation was executed and subscribed in the year 1495, by a certain "learned man," Edmundus de Prato (Edmund Pratt) by name, licentiate in Canon Law, of Exeter College, Oxford, who had actually been a pupil of Grocyn, the first scholar who taught Greek in England.[†] No doubt, on the fame of this new learning reaching his ears, the Vincey of the day, perhaps that same John de Vincey who years before had saved the relic from destruction and made the black-letter entry on the sherd in 1445, hurried to Oxford to discover if perchance it might avail to solve the secret of the mysterious inscription. Nor was he disappointed, for the learned Edmundus was equal to the task. Indeed his rendering is so excellent an example of mediæval scholarship and Latinity that, even at the risk of sating the learned reader with too many antiquities, I have made up my mind to give it in fac-simile, together with an expanded version for the benefit of those who find the contractions troublesome. The translation has several peculiarities, whereon this is not the place to dwell, but I would in passing call the attention of scholars to the passage "duxerunt autem nos ad reginam *advenaslasaniscoronantium*," which strikes me as a delightful rendering of the original, "ἤγαγον δὲ ὡσ βασίλειαν τὴν τῶν ξένουσ χύτραισ στεφούντων."

---

century is that, curiously enough, I have an acting copy of "Hamlet," written about 1740, in which these two lines are misquoted almost exactly in the same way, and I have little doubt but that the Vincey who wrote them on the potsherd heard them so misquoted at that date. Of course, the true reading of the lines is:—

> There are more things in heaven and earth, Horatio,
> Than are dreamt of in your philosophy.—L. H. H.

[†]Grocyn, the instructor of Erasmus, studied Greek under Chalcondylas the Byzantine at Florence, and first lectured in the Hall of Exeter College, Oxrford, in 1491.—EDITOR.

Mediæval Black-Letter Latin Translation of the Uncial Inscription on the Sherd of Amenartas, executed by Edmundus de Prato in 1495.

Amenartas e gen. reg. Egyptii vxor Callicratis sacerdos Isidis quã dei fovēt demonia at= tedūt filiol' svo Tisistheni iã moribūda ita mãdat: Effugi quodã ex Egypto regnãte Nectanebo cū patre tvo, ppter mei amorē pejerato. Fvgiētes autē v'sus Notū trans mare et xxiiij mēses p'r litora Libye v'sus Oriētē errans vbi est petra quedã mgna scvlpta instar Ethiop capis, deinde dies iiij ab ost stuñ mgni eiecti p'tim submersi sumus p'tim morbo mortui suñ : in sine autē a ser hoībs portabamur pr palvd̄ et vada. vbi aviū m'titvdo celū obūbrat dies x. donec advenim̃ ad cavū quedã montē, ubi olim mgna vrbs erat, cauerne quoñ imēse : dvrerūt autē nos ad reginā Aduenaslasaniscoronãtiū que magic̃ vtebasr et peritia omniū rer et saltē pvlcrii et vigore īsēesci= bil' erat. Hec mgno patr tui amore pevlsa p'mū q'dē ei coñubiū michi mortē parabat. postea v'ro recvsãte Callicrate amore mei et timore regine affecto nos pr magicã abduxit p'r vias horribil' vbi est puteus ille psūdus, cuius iurta aditū iacebat senior philosophi cadauer, et advēiētib mōstravit siamā Uite erectã, īstar columne volu= tãtis, voces emittētē ñsi tonitrvs : tūc pr ignē īpetu nociuo expers trāsiit et iã ipsa sese formosior visa est.

Quib saci iuravit se patrē tuū quoñ imortalē ostēsurã esse, si me prius occisa regine cōtvberniū

mallet; neq enī ipsa me occidere valuit, ꝓpter nos̄
tratū m̄gicā cuius egomet ꝑtem habeo. Ille vero
nichil huius̄ gen̄ maluit, manib ante ocuł passis̄
ne mulier̄ formositatē adspiceret: postea eū m̄gica
ꝑcussit arte, at mortuū esserebat īde cū ssetib et
vagitib, me ꝑr timorē expulit ad ostiū m̄gni
ssumin̄ veliuoli porro in nave in qua te peperi,
uir post dies̄ hvc Athenas̄ invecta sū. At tu,
O Tisisthen̄, ne q'd quorū mādo nauci fac: necesse
enī est mulierē exqvirere si qva Uite mpsteriū
īpetres̄ et vīdicare, quātū in te est, patrē tuū
Callicraī in regine morte. Sin timore seu aliq̄
cavsa rē reliquis̄ īfectā, hoc ipsū oīb poster̄ mādo
dū bonvs̄ q̄s inveniatur qvi ignis̄ lauacrū nō
ꝓrhorrescet et ꝑtentia dign̄ dōīabir̄ hōīū.

Talia dico incredibilia q̄dē at mn̄e n̄cta de reb
michi cognitis̄.

Hec Grece scripta Latine reddidit vir doctus̄
Edm̄ds̄ de Prato, in Decretis̄ Licenciatus̄ e Coll.
Exon: Oxon: doctissimi Grocyni quondam e
pupillis̄, Id. Apr. A°. Dn̄i. MCCCCLXXXV°.

EXPANDED VERSION OF THE ABOVE MEDIÆVAL LATIN
TRANSLATION.

AMENARTAS, e genere regio Egyptii, uxor Callicratis, sacerdotis
Isidis, quam dei fovent demonia attendunt, filiolo suo Tisistheni jam
moribunda ita mandat: Effugi quondam ex Egypto, regnante
Nectanebo, cum patre tuo, propter mei amorem pejerato. Fugientes
autem versus Notum trans mare, et viginti quatuor menses per
litora Libye versus Orientem errantes, ubi est petra quedam magna
sculpta instar Ethiopis capitis, deinde dies quatuor ab ostio fluminis

magni ejecti partim submersi sumus partim morbo mortui sumus: in fine autem a feris hominibus portabamur per paludes et vada, ubi avium multitudo celum obumbrat, dies decem, donec advenimus ad cavum quendam montem, ubi olim magna urbs erat, caverne quoque immense; duxerunt autem nos ad reginam Advenaslasaniscoronantium, que magicâ utebatur et peritiâ omnium rerum, et saltem pulcritudine et vigore insenescibilis erat. Hec magno patris tui amore perculsa, primum quidem ei connubium michi mortem parabat; postea vero, recusante Callicrate, amore mei et timore regine affecto, nos per magicam abduxit per vias horribiles ubi est puteus ille profundus, cujus juxta aditum jacebat senioris philosophi cadaver, et advenientibus monstravit flammam Vite erectam, instar columne volutantis, voces emittentem quasi tonitrus: tunc per ignem impetu nocivo expers transiit et jam ipsa sese formosior visa est.

Quibus factis juravit se patrem tuum quoque immortalem ostensuram esse, si me prius occisa regine contubernium mallet; neque enim ipsa me occidere valuit, propter nostratum magicam cujus egomet partem habeo. Ille vero nichil hujus generis malebat, manibus ante oculos passis, ne mulieris formositatem adspiceret: postea illum magica percussit arte, at mortuum efferebat inde cum fletibus et vagitibus, et me per timorem expulit ad ostium magni fluminis, velivoli, porro in nave, in qua te peperi, vix post dies huc Athenas vecta sum. At tu, O Tisisthenes, ne quid quorum mando nauci fac: necesse enim est mulierem exquirere si qua Vite mysterium impetres et vindicare, quantum in te est, patrem tuum Callicratem in regine morte. Sin timore seu aliqua causa rem relinquis infectam, hoc ipsum omnibus posteris mando, dum bonus quis inveniatur qui ignis lavacrum non perhorrescet, et potentia dignus dominabitur hominum.

Talia dico incredibilia quidem at minime ficta de rebus michi cognitis.

Hec Grece scripta Latine reddidit vir doctus Edmundus de Prato, in Decretis Licenciatus, e Collegio Exoniensi Oxoniensi doctissimi Grocyni quondam e pupillis, Idibus Aprilis Anno Domini MCCCCLXXXXV°.

———

"Well," I said, when at length I had read out and carefully examined these writings and paragraphs, at least those of them that were still easily legible, "that is the conclusion of the whole matter, Leo, and now you can form your own opinion on it. I have already formed mine."

"And what is it?" he asked, in his quick way.

"It is this. I believe the potsherd to be perfectly genuine, and that, wonderful as it may seem, it has come down in your family from since the fourth century before Christ. The entries absolutely prove it, therefore, however improbable it may seem, the fact must be accepted. But there I stop. That your remote ancestress, the Egyptian princess, or some scribe under her direction, wrote that which we see on the sherd I have no doubt, nor have I the slightest doubt but that her sufferings and the loss of her husband had turned her head, and that she was not of sound mind when she did write it."

"How do you account for what my father saw and heard there?" asked Leo.

"Coincidence. No doubt there are bluffs on the coast of Africa that look something like a man's head, and plenty of people who speak bastard Arabic. Also, I believe that there are lots of swamps. Another thing is, Leo, though I am sorry to say it, I do not think that your poor father was quite sane when he wrote that letter. He had met with a great trouble, also he had allowed this story to prey on his imagination, and he was a very imaginative man. Anyway, I believe that the legend as it reaches us is rubbish. I know that there are curious forces in nature which we rarely meet with, and that, when we do meet them, we cannot understand. But until I see it with my own eyes, which I am not likely to do, I never will believe that there exist means of avoiding death, even for a time, or that there is or was a white sorceress living in the heart of an African swamp. It is bosh, my boy, all bosh!—What do you say, Job?"

"I say, sir, that it is a lie, and, if it is true, I hope Mr. Leo won't meddle with no such things, for no good can't come of it."

"Perhaps you are both right," said Leo, very quietly. "I express no opinion. But I say this. I intend to set the matter at rest once and for all, and if you won't come with me I will go by myself."

I looked at the young man, and saw that he meant what he said.

When Leo means what he says one may always know it by a curious expression about the mouth, which has been a trick of his from a child. Now, as a matter of fact, I had no intention of allowing Leo to go anywhere by himself, for my own sake, if not for his. I was far too much attached to him for that. I am not a man of many ties or affections. Circumstances have been against me in this respect, and men and women shrink from me, or at least I fancy that they do, which comes to the same thing, thinking, perhaps, that my somewhat forbidding exterior is a key to my character. Rather than be thus shunned I have, to a great extent, retired from society, and cut myself off from those opportunities which with most men result in the formation of ties more or less intimate. Therefore Leo was all the world to me—brother, child, and friend—and until he wearied of me, where he went there I should go too. But, of course, it would not do to let him see how great a hold he had over me; so I cast about for some means whereby I might surrender with a good grace.

"Yes, I shall go, Uncle," he repeated; "and if I don't find the 'rolling Pillar of Life,' at any rate I shall get some first-class shooting."

Here was my opportunity, and I took it.

"Shooting?" I said. "Ah! yes; I never thought of that. It must be a very wild stretch of country, and full of big game. I have always wanted to kill a buffalo before I die. Do you know, my boy, I don't believe in the quest, but I do believe in big game, and really on the whole, if, after thinking it over, you make up your mind to start, I will take a holiday, and come with you."

"Ah," said Leo, "I thought that you would not lose such a chance. But how about money? We shall want a good lot."

"You need not trouble about that," I answered. "There is all your income which has been accumulating for years, and besides that I have saved two-thirds of what your father left to me, as I consider, in trust for you. There is plenty of cash."

"Very well, then, we may as well stow these things away and go up to town to see about our guns. By the way, Job, are you coming too? It's time you began to see the world."

"Well, sir," answered Job, stolidly, "I don't hold much with foreign parts, but if both you gentlemen are going you will want somebody to look after you, and I am not the man to stop behind after serving you for twenty years."

"That's right, Job," said I. "You won't find out anything wonderful, but you will get some good shooting. And now look here, both of you. I won't have a word said to a living soul about this nonsense," and I pointed to the potsherd. "If it were known, and anything happened to me, my next of kin would dispute my will on the ground of insanity, and I should become the laughing-stock of Cambridge."

—

That day three months we were on the ocean, bound for Zanzibar.

IV

The Squall

How different is the scene whereof I have now to tell from that which has just been told! Gone are the quiet college rooms, gone the wind-swayed English elms, the cawing rooks, and the familiar volumes on the shelves, and in their place there rises a vision of the great calm ocean gleaming in shaded silver lights beneath the beams of a full African moon. A gentle breeze fills the huge sail of our dhow, and draws us through the water that ripples musically against her sides. Most of the men are sleeping forward, for it is near midnight, but a stout swarthy Arab, Mahomed by name, stands at the tiller, lazily steering by the stars. Three miles or more to our starboard is a low dim line. It is the Eastern shore of Central Africa. We are running to the southward, before the north-east monsoon, between the mainland and the reef that for hundreds of miles fringes this perilous coast. The night is quiet, so quiet that a whisper can be heard fore and aft the dhow; so quiet that a faint booming sound rolls across the water to us from the distant land.

The Arab at the tiller holds up his hand, and says one word:— "*Simba* (lion)!"

We all sit up and listen. Then it comes again, a slow, majestic sound that thrills us to the marrow.

"To-morrow by ten o'clock," I say, "we ought, if the captain is not out in his reckoning, which I think very probable, to make this mysterious rock with a man's head, and begin our shooting."

"And begin our search for the ruined city and the Fire of Life," corrected Leo, taking his pipe from his mouth, and laughing a little.

"Nonsense!" I answered. "You were airing your Arabic with that man at the tiller this afternoon. What did he tell you? He has been trading (slave trading probably) up and down these latitudes for half of his iniquitous life, and once landed on this very 'man' rock. Did he ever hear anything of the ruined city or the caves?"

"No," answered Leo. "He says that the country is all swamp behind, and full of snakes, especially pythons, and game, and that no man lives there. But then there is a belt of swamp all along the East African coast, so that does not go for much."

"Yes," I said, "it does—it goes for malaria. You see what sort of an opinion these gentry have of the country. Not one of them will come with us. They think that we are mad, and upon my word I believe that they are right. If ever we see old England again I shall be astonished. However, it does not greatly matter to me at my age, but I am anxious for you, Leo, and for Job. It's a Tom Fool's business, my boy."

"All right, Uncle Horace. So far as I am concerned, I am willing to take my chance. Look! What is that cloud?" and he pointed to a dark blotch upon the starry sky some miles astern of us.

"Go and ask the man at the tiller," I said.

He rose, stretched his arms, and went. Presently he returned.

"He says it is a squall, but that it will pass far on one side of us."

Just then Job came up, looking very stout and English in his shooting-suit of brown flannel, and with a sort of perplexed appearance upon his honest round face that had been very common with him since he sailed into these strange waters.

"Please, sir," he said, touching his sun hat, which was stuck on to the back of his head in a somewhat ludicrous fashion, "as we have got all those guns and things in the whale-boat astern, to say nothing of the provisions in the lockers, I think it would be best if I slipped down and slept in her. I don't like the looks" (here he dropped his voice to a portentous whisper) "of these black gentry; they have such a wonderful thievish way about them. Supposing now that some of them were to sneak into the boat at night and cut the cable, and make off with her? That would be a pretty go, that would."

The whale-boat, I may explain, was one specially built for us at Dundee, in Scotland. We had brought it with us as we knew that this coast is a network of creeks, and that we might require something in which to navigate them. She was a beautiful boat, thirty feet in length, with a centre-board for sailing, copper-bottomed to keep the worm out of her, and full of water-tight compartments. The captain of the dhow had told us that when we reached the rock, which he knew, and that appeared to be identical with the one described upon the sherd and by Leo's father, he would probably not be able to run up to it on account of the shallows and breakers. Therefore we had employed three hours that very morning, whilst we were totally becalmed, the wind having dropped at sunrise, in transferring most of our goods and chattels to the whale-boat, and placing the guns, ammunition, and preserved provisions in the water-tight lockers specially prepared for them, so that when we did sight the fabled rock we should have nothing to do but get into the boat, and run her ashore. Another reason that induced us to take this precautionary step was that Arab captains are apt to run past the point which they are making, either from carelessness or owing to a mistake in its identity. Now, as sailors know, it is quite impossible for a dhow that is only rigged to run before the monsoon to beat back against it. Therefore we made our boat ready to row for the rock at any moment.

"Yes, Job," I said, "perhaps it would be as well. There are plenty of blankets there, only be careful to keep out of the moon, as it may turn your head or blind you."

"Lord, sir! I don't think it would much matter if it did, it is that turned already with the sight of these blackamoors and their filthy, thieving ways. They are only fit for muck, they are; and they smell bad enough for it already."

Job, it will be perceived, was no admirer of the manners and customs of our dark-skinned brothers.

Accordingly we hauled up the boat by the tow-rope till it was right under the stern of the dhow, and Job bundled into her with all the grace of a falling sack of potatoes. Then we returned and sat down on the deck again, and smoked and talked in little gusts and jerks. The night was so lovely, and our brains were so full of suppressed excitement of one sort and another, that we did not feel inclined to turn in. For nearly an hour we sat thus, and then, I think, we both dozed off. At least I have a faint recollection of Leo sleepily explaining that the head was not a bad place to hit a buffalo, if you could catch him exactly between the horns, or send your bullet down his throat, or some nonsense of the sort.

I remember no more; till quite suddenly—a frightful roar of wind, a shriek of terror from the awakening crew, and a whip-like sting of water in our faces. Some of the men ran to let go the halyards and lower the sail, but the parrel jammed and the yard would not come down. I sprang to my feet and hung on to a rope. The sky aft was dark as pitch, but the moon still shone brightly ahead of us and lit up the blackness. Beneath its sheen a huge white-topped breaker, twenty feet high or more, was rushing on to us. It was on the break—the moon shone on its crest and tipped its foam with light. On it rushed beneath the inky sky, driven by the awful squall behind it. Suddenly, in the twinkling of an eye, I saw the black shape of the whale-boat cast high into the air on the crown of the breaking wave. Then—a shock of water, a wild rush of boiling foam, and I was clinging for my life to the shroud, ay, swept straight out from it like a flag in a gale.

We were pooped.

The wave passed. It seemed to me that I was under water for minutes—really it was seconds. I looked forward. The blast had torn out the great sail, and high in the air it was fluttering away to leeward like a huge wounded bird. Now for a moment there was comparative calm, and in it I heard Job's voice yelling wildly, "Come here to the boat!"

Bewildered and half drowned as I was, I had the sense to rush aft. I felt the dhow sinking beneath me—she was full of water. Under her counter the whale-boat was tossing furiously, and I saw the Arab Mahomed, who had been steering, leap into her. I gave one desperate pull at the taut tow-rope to bring her alongside. Wildly I sprang also, Job caught me by one arm, and I rolled into the bottom of the boat. Down went the dhow bodily, and as she sank Mahomed drew his curved knife and severed the fibre rope by which we were fast to her, and in another second we were driving before the storm over the place where the dhow had been.

"Great Heaven!" I shrieked, "where is Leo? *Leo! Leo!*"

"He's gone, sir, God help him!" roared Job into my ear; and such was the fury of the squall that his voice sounded like a whisper.

I wrung my hands in agony. Leo was drowned, and I was left alive to mourn him.

"Look out," yelled Job; "here comes another."

I turned; a second huge wave was overtaking us, which I half hoped would drown me. With a curious fascination I watched its awful advent. The moon was nearly hidden now by the wreaths of the rushing storm, but a little light still caught the crest of the devouring breaker. There was something dark on it—a piece of wreckage. It was on us now, and the boat was nearly full of water. But she was built in air-tight compartments—Heaven bless the man who invented them!—and lifted up through it like a swan. Amidst the foam and turmoil I saw the black thing on the wave hurrying right at me. I put out my right arm to ward it from me, and my hand closed on another arm, the wrist of which my fingers gripped like a vice. I am a very strong man, and had something to hold to, but my shoulder was nearly torn from its socket by the strain and weight of the floating body. Had the rush lasted another two seconds I must either have let go or gone with it. But it passed, leaving us up to our knees in water.

"Bail out! bail out!" shouted Job, suiting the action to the word.

But I could not bail just then, for as the moon went out and left us in total darkness, one faint, flying ray of light lit upon the face of the man I had gripped, who was now half lying, half floating in the bottom of the boat.

It was *Leo*. Leo brought back by the wave—back, dead or alive, from the very jaws of Death.

"Bail out! bail out!" yelled Job, "or we shall founder."

I seized a large tin bowl with a handle to it, which was fixed under one of the seats, and the three of us bailed away for dear life. The furious tempest drove over and round us, flinging the boat this way and that, the wind and the storm wreaths and the sheets of stinging spray blinded and bewildered us, but through it all we worked like demons with the wild exhilaration of despair, for even despair can exhilarate. One minute! three minutes! six minutes! The boat began to lighten, and no fresh wave swamped us. Five minutes more, and she was almost clear. Then, suddenly, above the awful shriekings of the hurricane came a duller, deeper roar. Great Heavens! It was the voice of breakers!

At that instant the moon began to shine forth again—this time behind the path of the squall. Out far across the torn bosom of the ocean shot the ragged arrows of her light, and there, half a mile ahead of us, ran a white line of foam, then a little space of open-mouthed blackness, and beyond another streak of white. It was the breakers, and their roar sounded clearer and yet more clear as we sped down upon them like a swallow. There they were, boiling up in snowy spouts of spray, smiting and gnashing their crests together like the gleaming teeth of hell.

"Take the tiller, Mahomed!" I roared in Arabic. "We must try and shoot them." At the same moment I seized an oar, and got it out, motioning to Job to do likewise.

Mahomed clambered aft, and took hold of the tiller, and with some difficulty Job, who had at times pulled a tub upon the homely Cam, shipped his oar. In another minute the boat's head was straight on to the ever-nearing foam, towards which she plunged and tore with the speed of a racehorse. Just in front of us the first line of breakers seemed a little thinner than to the right or left, for here was a gap of rather deeper water. I turned and pointed to it.

"Steer for your life, Mahomed!" I yelled. He was a skilful steersman, and well acquainted with the dangers of this most perilous coast, and I saw him grip the tiller, bend his heavy frame forward, and stare at the foaming terror till his big round eyes looked as though they would start out of his head. The send of the sea was driving the boat's head round to starboard. If we struck the line of breakers fifty yards to starboard of the gap we must sink, for there was a great field of twisting, spouting waves. Mahomed planted his foot against the seat before him, and, glancing at him, I saw his brown toes spread out like a hand beneath the weight he put upon them as he took the strain of the tiller. She came round a bit, but not enough. I roared to Job to back water, whilst I dragged and laboured at my oar. She answered now, and not too soon.

"Steer for your life, Mahomed!"

Heavens, we were in them! And then followed a couple of minutes of heart-breaking excitement such as I cannot hope to describe. All that I remember is a shrieking sea of foam, out of which the billows rose here, there, and everywhere like avenging ghosts from their ocean grave. Once we were whirled right round, but either by chance, or through Mahomed's skilful steering, the boat's head came straight again before a breaker filled us. One more—a monster. We were through it or over it—more through than over—and then, with a wild yell of exultation from the Arab, we shot out between the teeth-like lines of gnashing waves into the comparatively smooth water of the mouth of sea.

But we were nearly full of water again, and not more than half a mile ahead raved the second line of breakers. Again we set to and bailed furiously. Fortunately the storm had now quite gone by, and the moon shone brightly, revealing a rocky headland running half a mile or more out into the sea, of which point these breakers appeared to be a continuation. At any rate, they boiled around its foot. Probably the ridge that formed the headland pushed out into the ocean, only at a lower level, and made the reef also. This bluff terminated in a curious peak that seemed to be not more than a mile away from us. Just as we bailed the boat clear for the second time, Leo, to my immense relief, opened his eyes, remarking that the clothes had tumbled off his bed, and that he supposed it was time to get up for chapel. I told him to shut his eyes and keep quiet, which he did without in the slightest degree realising the position. As for myself, his reference to chapel made me reflect, with a sort of sick longing, on my comfortable rooms at Cambridge. Why had I been such a fool as to leave them? This is a reflection that has often recurred to me since that night, and with an ever-increasing force.

But now again we were drifting down on the breakers, though with lessened speed, for the wind had fallen, and only the current or the tide (it afterwards proved to be the tide) was driving us.

Another minute, and with a dismal howl to Allah from the Arab, a pious ejaculation from myself, and something that was not pious from Job, we were in them. Thereon the performance, down to our final escape, repeated itself, only not quite so violently. Mahomed's skilful steering and the airtight compartments saved our lives. In five minutes we were through, and drifting—for we were too exhausted to do anything to help ourselves except keep the boat's head straight—with the most startling rapidity round the headland which I have described.

Round we went with the tide, until we got well under the lee of the point, when suddenly the speed slackened, we ceased to make way, and finally appeared to be in dead water. The storm had passed, leaving a calm, clean-washed sky behind it; the headland intercepted the heavy sea that was occasioned by the squall, and the tide, which had been running so fiercely up the river (for we were now in the mouth of a river), was sluggish as it turned, so we floated at peace, and before the moon went down managed to bail out the boat thoroughly and get her a little ship-shape. Leo was sleeping profoundly, and on the whole I judged it wise not to wake him. It was true he was lying in wet clothes, but the night was now so warm that I thought (and so did Job) that this was not likely to injure a man of his unusually vigorous constitution. Besides, we had no dry change at hand.

Presently the moon went down, and we were left floating on the waters, now only heaving like some troubled woman's breast, with leisure to reflect upon all that we had gone through and all that we had escaped. Job stationed himself at the bow, Mahomed kept his post at the tiller, and I sat on a seat in the middle of the boat close to where Leo was lying.

The moon went slowly down in loveliness; she departed into the depth of the horizon, and long veil-like shadows crept up the sky through which the stars appeared. Soon, however, they too began to pale before a splendour in the east, and the advent of the dawn declared itself in the new-born blue of heaven. Quieter and yet more quiet grew the sea, quiet as the soft mist that brooded on her bosom, and covered up her troubling, as in our tempestuous life the transitory wreaths of sleep brood upon a pain-racked soul, causing it to forget its sorrow. From the east to the west sped those angels of the Dawn, from sea to sea, from mountain-top to mountain-top, scattering light from breast and wing. On they sped out of the darkness, perfect, glorious; on, over the quiet sea, over the low coast-line, and the swamps beyond, and the mountains above them; over those who slept in peace and those who woke in sorrow; over the evil and the good; over the living and the dead; over the wide world and all that breathes or has breathed thereon.

It was a beautiful sight, and yet a sad one, perhaps because of its excess of beauty. The arising sun; the setting sun! There we have the symbol and the type of humanity, and of all things with which humanity has to do. On that morning this came home to me with a peculiar force. The sun that rose to-day for us had set last night for eighteen of our fellow-voyagers!—had set everlastingly for eighteen whom we knew!

The dhow had gone down with them; they were tossing among the rocks and seaweed, so much human drift on the great ocean of Death! And we four were saved!

V

THE HEAD OF THE ETHIOPIAN

At length the heralds and forerunners of the royal sun had done their work, and, searching out the shadows, caused them to flee away. Then up he came in glory from his ocean bed, and flooded the earth with warmth and light. I sat there in the boat listening to the gentle lapping of the water and watched him rise, till presently the slight drift of the boat brought the odd-shaped rock, or peak, at the end of the promontory which we had weathered with so much peril, between me and the majestic sight, blotting it from my view. I still continued, however, to stare at the rock, absently enough, till presently it became edged with the fire of the growing light behind it. Then I started, as well I might, for I perceived that the top of the peak, which was about eighty feet high by one hundred and fifty thick at its base, was shaped like a negro's head and face, whereon was stamped a most fiendish and terrifying expression. There was no doubt about it; before me were the thick lips, fat cheeks, and squat nose standing out with startling clearness against that flaming background. There, too, was the round skull, washed into shape perhaps by thousands of years of wind and weather, and, to complete the resemblance, there was a scrubby growth of weeds or lichen upon it, which against the sun looked for all the world like the wool on a colossal negro's head. Certainly it was very odd; so odd that now I believe this is not a mere freak of nature but a gigantic monument fashioned, like the well-known Egyptian Sphinx, by a forgotten people out of a pile of rock that lent itself to their design, perhaps as an emblem of warning and defiance to any enemies who approached the harbour. Unfortunately, we were never able to ascertain whether or not this was the case, inasmuch as the rock is difficult of access both from the land and the waterside, and we had other things to attend to. To-day, considering the matter in the light of what we saw afterwards, I believe that it was fashioned by man; but however this may be, there the effigy stands, and stares from age to age across the changing ocean—there it stood two thousand years and more ago, when Amenartas, the Egyptian princess, and the wife of Leo's remote ancestor Kallikrates, gazed upon its devilish face—and there I have no doubt it will still stand when as many centuries as are numbered between her day and our own are added to the year which bore us to oblivion.

"What do you think of that, Job?" I asked of our retainer, who was seated on the edge of the boat, trying to absorb as much sunshine as possible, and generally looking very wretched, and I pointed to the fiery and demoniacal head.

"Oh Lord, sir!" answered Job, who now perceived the object for the first time, "I think that the Old Gentleman must have been sitting for his portrait on them rocks."

I laughed, and the laugh woke up Leo.

"Hullo!" he said, "what's the matter with me? I am all stiff. Where is the dhow? Give me some brandy, please."

"You may be thankful that you are not stiffer, my boy," I answered. "The dhow is sunk, everybody on board of her is drowned with the exception of us four, and your own life was only saved by a miracle." Then whilst Job, now that it was light enough, searched about in a locker for the brandy for which Leo asked, I told him the history of our night's adventure.

"Great Heavens!" he said faintly; "and to think that we should have been chosen to live through it!"

By this time the brandy was forthcoming, and we all took a good pull, and thankful enough we were for it. Also the sun was beginning to gain strength, and warm our chilled bones, for we had been wet through for five hours or more.

"Why," said Leo, with a gasp, as he put down the brandy bottle, "there is the head the writing talks of, the 'rock carven like the head of an Ethiopian.' "

"Yes," I said, "there it is."

"Well, then," he answered, "the whole thing is true."

"I don't at all see that it follows," I answered. "We knew this head was here: your father saw it. Very likely it is not the same head of which the writing tells; or if it is, it proves nothing."

Leo smiled at me in a superior way. "You are an unbelieving Jew, Uncle Horace," he said. "Those who live will see."

"Exactly so," I answered; "and now perhaps you will observe that we are drifting across a sandbank into the mouth of the river. Get hold of your oar, Job, and we will row in and see if we can find a place to land."

The river mouth which we were entering did not appear to be a very wide one, though as yet the long banks of steaming mist that clung about its shores had not lifted sufficiently to enable us to see its exact measure. As is the case with nearly every East African river, there was a considerable bar at the mouth, which, when the wind was on shore and the tide running out, no doubt was absolutely impassable even for a boat drawing only a few inches. But as things were it proved manageable enough, and we did not ship a cupful of water. In twenty minutes we were well across, with but slight assistance from ourselves, and being carried by a strong though somewhat variable breeze straight up the harbour. By this time the mist had vanished beneath the sun, which was growing uncomfortably hot, and we saw that the mouth of the little estuary was here about half a mile across, and that the banks were very marshy, and crowded with crocodiles lying on the mud like logs. A mile or so ahead of us, however, lay what appeared to be a strip of firm land, and for this we steered. In another quarter of an hour we were there, and making the boat fast to a beautiful tree with broad shining leaves, and flowers of the magnolia species, only they were rose-coloured and not white,* which hung over the water, we dis-embarked. This done we undressed, washed ourselves, and spread our clothes in the sun to dry, together with the contents of the boat, which they did very quickly. Then, taking shelter from the heat under some trees, we made a hearty breakfast off an excellent potted tongue, of which we had brought a quantity with us, congratulating ourselves the while on our good fortune in having loaded and provisioned the boat on the previous day before the hurricane destroyed the dhow. By the time that we had finished our meal our clothes were quite dry, and we hastened to put them on, feeling not a little refreshed. Indeed, with the exception of weariness and a few bruises, none of us was the worse for the terrifying adventure which had been fatal to all our companions. Leo, it is true, had been half drowned, but that is no great matter to a vigorous young athlete of five-and-twenty.

After breakfast we started to look round us. We were on a strip of dry land about two hundred yards broad by five hundred long, bor-dered on one side by the river, and on the other three by endless deso-late swamps, that stretched far as the eye could reach. This strip of land was raised about twenty-five feet above the plain of the sur-rounding morasses and the river level: indeed it had every appearance of having been made by the hand of man.

"This place has been a wharf," said Leo, dogmatically.

"Nonsense," I answered. "Who would be stupid enough to build a wharf in the middle of these dreadful marshes in a country inhabited by savages—that is, if it is inhabited at all?"

"Perhaps it was not always marsh, and perhaps the people were not always savage," he said drily, looking down the steep bank, for we were standing by the river. "See there," he went on, pointing to a spot where the hurricane of the previous night had torn up by its roots one of the magnolia trees which had grown on the extreme edge of the bank just where it sloped down to the water, and lifted a large cake of earth with them. "Is not that stonework? If not, it is very like it."

"Nonsense," I said again; but we clambered down to the spot, and stood between the upturned roots and the bank.

*There is a known species of magnolia with pink flowers. It is indigenous in Sikkim, and known as *Magnolia Campbellii.*—EDITOR.

"Well?" he said.

But this time I did not answer. I only whistled. For there, bared by the removal of the earth, was an undoubted facing of solid stone laid in large blocks, bound together with brown cement so hard that I could make no impression on it with the file in my shooting-knife. Nor was this all; seeing something projecting through the soil at the bottom of the bared patch of walling, I removed the loose earth with my hands, and revealed a huge stone ring, a foot or more in diameter, and about three inches thick. This discovery absolutely silenced me.

"Looks rather like a wharf where good-sized vessels have been moored, does it not, Uncle Horace?" said Leo, with an excited grin.

I tried to say "Nonsense" again, but the word stuck in my throat— the worn ring spoke for itself. In some past age vessels *had* been moored there, and this stone wall was undoubtedly the remnant of a solidly constructed wharf. Probably the city to which it had belonged lay buried beneath the swamp behind it.

"Begins to look as though there were something in the story after all, Uncle Horace," said the exultant Leo: and reflecting on the mysterious negro's head and the equally mysterious stonework, I made no direct reply.

"A country like Africa," I said, "is sure to be full of the relics of long dead and forgotten civilisations. Nobody knows the age of the Egyptian civilisation, and very likely it had offshoots. Then there were the Babylonians and the Phœnicians, and the Persians, and other peoples, all of them more or less civilised, to say nothing of the Jews whom everybody 'wants' nowadays. It is possible that they, or any one of them, may have had colonies or trading stations about here. Remember those buried Persian cities that the Consul showed us at Kilwa."*

"Quite so," said Leo, "but that is not what you said before."

*Near Kilwa, on the East Coast of Africa, about 400 miles south of Zanzibar, is a cliff which has been recently washed by the waves. On the top of this cliff are Persian tombs known to be at least seven centuries old by the dates still legible upon them. Beneath these tombs is a layer of *débris* representing a city. Farther down the cliff is a second layer representing an older city, and farther down still a third layer, the remains of yet another city of vast and unknown antiquity. Beneath the bottom city were recently found some specimens of glazed earthenware, such as are occasionally to be met with on that coast to this day. I believe that they are now in the possession of Sir John Kirk.—EDITOR.

"Well, what is to be done now?" I asked, turning the conversation.

As no answer was forthcoming we walked to the edge of the swamp, and looked over it. Apparently it was boundless, and vast flocks of every sort of waterfowl flew from its recesses, till it was sometimes difficult to see the sky. Also, now that the sun was heightening it drew sickly looking clouds of poisonous vapour from the surface of the marsh and from the scummy pools of stagnant water.

"Two things are clear to me," I said, addressing my three companions, who stared at this spectacle in dismay: "first, that we can't go across there" (I pointed to the swamp), "and, secondly, that if we stop here we shall certainly die of fever."

"That's as plain as a haystack, sir," said Job.

"Very well, then; there are two alternatives before us. One is to 'bout ship, and try to run for some port in the whale-boat, which would be a sufficiently risky proceeding, and the other to sail or row on up the river, and see where we come to."

"I don't know what you are going to do," said Leo, setting his mouth, "but I am going up that river."

Job turned up the whites of his eyes and groaned, and the Arab murmured "Allah," and groaned also. For my part, I remarked sweetly that as we seemed to be between the devil and the deep sea, it did not much matter where we went. But in reality I was as anxious to proceed as Leo. The colossal negro's head and the stone wharf had excited my curiosity to an extent of which I was secretly ashamed, and I was prepared to gratify it at any cost. Accordingly, having carefully fitted the mast, restowed the boat, and got out our rifles, we embarked. Fortunately the wind was blowing on shore from the ocean, so we were able to hoist the sail. Indeed, we afterwards discovered that as a general rule the wind set on shore from daybreak for some hours, and off shore again at sunset. The explanation that I offer of this fact is, that when the earth is cooled by the dew and the night the hot air rises, and the draught rushes in from the sea till the sun has once more heated it through. At least that appears to be the rule in this latitude.

Taking advantage of this favouring wind, we sailed merrily up the river for three or four hours. Once we came across a school of hippopotami, which rose, and bellowed dreadfully at us within ten or a dozen fathoms of the boat, much to Job's alarm, and, I will confess, to my own. These were the first hippopotami that we had ever seen, and, to judge by their insatiable curiosity, I should say that we were the first white men whom they had ever seen. Upon my word, I thought once or twice that they were coming into the boat to gratify it. Leo wanted to fire at them, but I dissuaded him, fearing the consequences. Also, we saw hundreds of crocodiles basking on the muddy banks, and thousands upon thousands of waterfowl. Some of these birds we shot, among them a wild goose, which, in addition to the sharp-curved spurs on its wings, had a third spur, three-quarters of an inch long, growing from its skull just between the eyes. We never shot another like it, so I do not know if it was a "sport" or a distinct species. In the latter case this incident may interest naturalists. Job named it the Unicorn Goose.

About midday the sun grew intensely hot, and the stench drawn up by it from the marshes which the river drains was something too awful, and caused us instantly to swallow precautionary doses of quinine. Shortly afterwards the breeze died away altogether, and as rowing our heavy boat against stream in the heat was out of the question, we were thankful to clamber under the shade of a group of trees—a species of willow—that grew by the edge of the river, and lie there and gasp till at length the approach of sunset put a period to our miseries. Seeing what appeared to be an open space of water straight ahead of us, we determined to row thither before settling what to do for the night. Just as we were about to loosen the boat, however, a beautiful waterbuck, with great horns curving forward, and a white stripe across the rump, came down to the river to drink, without perceiving us hidden away within fifty yards under the willows. Leo was the first to catch sight of it, and, being an ardent sportsman, thirsting for the blood of big game, about which he had been dreaming for months, instantly he stiffened all over, and pointed like a setter dog. Seeing what was the matter, I handed him his Express rifle, at the same time taking my own.

"Now then," I said, "mind you don't miss."

"Miss!" he whispered contemptuously; "I could not miss it if I tried."

He lifted the rifle, and the roan-coloured buck, having drunk his fill, raised his head and looked across the river. He was standing out against the sunset sky on a little eminence, or ridge of ground, which ran through the swamp, evidently a favourite path for game, and there was something very beautiful about him. Indeed, I do not think if I live to a hundred that I shall ever forget this desolate and yet most fascinating scene; it is stamped upon my memory. To the right and left were wide stretches of lonely death-breeding swamp, unbroken and unrelieved so far as the eye could reach except here and there by ponds of black and peaty water that, mirror-like, flashed up the red rays of the setting sun. Behind and before us stretched a vista of the sluggish river, ending in glimpses of a reed-fringed lagoon, on whose surface the long lights of the evening played as the faint breeze stirred the shadows. To the west loomed the huge red ball of the sinking sun, now vanishing into the vapoury horizon, and filling the great heaven, high across whose arch the cranes and wildfowl streamed in line, square, and triangle, with flashes of flying gold and the lurid stain of blood. And then ourselves—three modern Englishmen in a modern English boat—seeming to jar upon and be out of tone with that measureless desolation; and in front of us the noble buck limned upon a background of ruddy sky.

Bang! Away he goes with a mighty bound. Leo has missed him. *Bang!* right under him again. Now for a shot. I must have one, though he is flying like an arrow, and a hundred yards away and more. By Jove! over and over and over! "Well, I think I've wiped your eye there, Master Leo," I say, struggling against the ungenerous exultation that in such a supreme moment of existence will rise in the best-mannered sportsman's breast.

"Confound you! yes," growled Leo; and added, with the quick smile that is one of his charms lighting up his handsome face like a ray of light, "I beg your pardon, old fellow. I congratulate you; it was a lovely shot, and mine were vile."

We leapt from the boat and ran to the buck, which was shot through the spine and stone-dead. It took us a quarter of an hour or more to clean it and cut off as much of the best meat as we could carry, so that, having packed this away, we had barely enough light to row to the lagoon-like space, into which, there being a hollow in the swamp, the river here expanded. Just as the darkness fell we cast anchor about thirty fathoms from the edge of this lake. We did not dare to go ashore, not knowing if we should find dry ground to camp on, and greatly fearing the poisonous exhalations from the marsh, of which we thought we should be freer on the water. So we lighted a lantern, and made our evening meal off another potted tongue in the best fashion that we could, and then prepared to go to sleep, only, however, to find that sleep was impossible. For, whether they were attracted by the lantern, or by the unaccustomed smell of a white man that they had awaited for the last thousand years or so, I know not; but certainly we were attacked presently by tens of thousands of the most bloodthirsty, pertinacious, and huge mosquitoes that I ever read of or saw. In clouds they came, and pinged and buzzed and bit till we were nearly mad. Tobacco-smoke only seemed to stir them into a merrier and more active life, till at length we were driven to covering ourselves with blankets, heads and all, and sitting to stew slowly and scratch and swear continually beneath them. And as we sat, suddenly rolling out like thunder through the silence rose the deep roar of a lion, and then of a second lion, moving among the reeds within sixty yards of us.

"I say," said Leo, poking out his head from under the blanket, "lucky we ain't on the bank, eh, Avuncular?" (Leo sometimes addressed me in this disrespectful way.) "Curse it! a mosquito has bitten me on the nose," and the head vanished again.

Shortly after this the moon came up, and notwithstanding every variety of roar that echoed over the water to us from the lions on the banks, thinking ourselves perfectly secure, we began to doze.

I do not quite know what it was that caused me to lift my head from the friendly shelter of the blanket, perhaps because I found that the mosquitoes were biting through it. Anyhow, as I did so I heard Job whisper, in a frightened voice—

"Oh, my stars, look there!"

Instantly we all of us looked, and this was what we saw in the moonlight. Near the shore were two wide and ever-widening circles of concentric rings rippling away across the surface of the water, and in the heart and centre of these circles appeared two dark and moving objects.

"What is it?" asked I.

"It is those damned lions, sir," answered Job, in a tone which suggested an odd mixture of a sense of personal injury, habitual respect, and acknowledged fear, "and they are swimming here to *h*eat us," he added nervously, picking up an "h" in his agitation.

I looked again: there was no doubt about it; I could catch the glare of their ferocious eyes. Attracted either by the smell of the newly killed waterbuck meat or of ourselves, the hungry beasts were storming our position.

Leo already had a rifle in his hand. I called to him to wait till they were nearer, and meanwhile found my own. Some fifteen feet from us the water shallowed on a bank to the depth of about fifteen inches, and presently the first of them—it was the lioness—waded to it, shook herself, and roared. At that moment Leo fired; the bullet travelled down her open mouth and out at the back of her neck, and down she dropped, with a splash, dead. The other lion—a full-grown male—was some two paces behind her. At this second he set his forepaws on the bank, when something happened. There was a rush and disturbance of the water, such as one sees in a pond in England when a pike takes a little fish, only a thousand times fiercer and larger, then suddenly the lion uttered a terrific snarling roar and sprang forward on to the bank, dragging something black with him.

"Allah!" shouted Mahomed, "a crocodile has got him by the leg!" and sure enough he had. We could see the long snout with its gleaming lines of teeth and the reptile body behind it.

Then followed a most extraordinary scene. The lion managed to struggle on to the bank, the crocodile half standing and half swimming, still nipping his hind leg. He roared till the air quivered with the sound; then, with a savage, shrieking snarl, he turned and clawed hold of the crocodile's head. The reptile shifted his grip, having, as we discovered afterwards, had one of his eyes torn out, and advanced slightly; whereon the lion took him by the throat and held it, and over and over they rolled upon the bank, struggling hideously. It was impossible to follow their movements, but when next we had a clear view the tables were turned, for the crocodile, whose head seemed to be a mass of gore, held the lion's body in his iron jaws just above the hips, and was squeezing him, shaking him to and fro. For his part, the tortured brute, roaring in agony, clawed and bit madly at his enemy's scaly head, and fixing his great hind claws in the softer skin of the crocodile's throat, ripped it open as one would rip a glove.

Then, of a sudden, the end came. The lion's head fell forward on the reptile's back, and with an awful groan he died, and the crocodile, after standing for a minute motionless, slowly rolled over on to his side, his jaws still fixed across the carcase of the lion, which, as we found, he had bitten almost in halves.

This duel to the death was a wonderful and a shocking sight, and one that I suppose few men have seen. And thus it ended.

When it was all over, leaving Mahomed to keep a look out, we spent the rest of the night in such comparative peace as the mosquitoes would allow.

VI

An Early Christian Ceremony

Next morning, at the earliest light of dawn, we rose, performed such ablutions as circumstances would allow, and made ourselves ready to start. I am bound to say that when there was sufficient light to enable us to see each other's faces I, for one, was moved to laughter, for Job's fat and comfortable countenance had swollen to nearly twice its natural size from mosquito bites, and Leo's condition was not much better. Indeed, of the three I had come off the best, probably owing to the toughness of my dark skin, and to the fact that a good deal of it was covered by hair, for since we sailed from England I had allowed my naturally luxuriant beard to grow at its own will. But the other two were comparatively clean shaved, which of course afforded the enemy a larger extent of open country to explore, although in Mahomed's case the mosquitoes, recognising the taste of a true believer, would not touch him at any price. How often, I wonder, during the next week or so did we wish that we were flavoured like an Arab!

By the time that we had done laughing as heartily as our swollen lips would allow it was daylight, and the morning breeze, drawing up from the sea, cut lanes through the dense marsh mists, here and there rolling them before it in great balls of fleecy vapour. So we set our sail, and having carefully examined the two dead lions and the alligator, which we were of course unable to skin, being destitute of means of curing the pelts, we started, and, sailing through the lagoon, followed the course of the river on its further side. At midday, when the breeze dropped, we were fortunate enough to find a convenient spot of dry land on which to camp and light a fire, and here we cooked two wild-ducks and some of the waterbuck's flesh—not in a very appetising way, it is true, but still sufficiently. The rest of the buck's flesh we cut into strips and hung in the sun to dry into "biltong," as, I believe, the South African Dutch call flesh thus prepared. On this welcome patch of dry land we stayed till the following dawn, as before, spending the night in warfare with the mosquitoes, but without other troubles. The next day or two passed in similar fashion, and without noticeable adventures, except that we shot a specimen of a peculiarly graceful hornless buck, and saw many varieties of water-lilies in full bloom, some of them blue and of exquisite beauty, though few of the flowers were perfect, owing to the presence of a white water-maggot with a green head that fed upon them.

It was on the fifth day of our journey, when we had travelled, so far as we could reckon, about one hundred and thirty-five to a hundred and forty miles westwards from the coast, that the first event of any real importance occurred. On that morning the usual wind failed us about eleven o'clock, and after pulling a little way we were forced to halt, more or less exhausted, at what appeared to be the junction of our stream with another of a uniform width of about fifty feet. Some trees grew near at hand—the only trees in all this country were along the banks of the river—and under these we rested; then, the land being fairly dry just here, we walked a little way along the edge of the river to prospect, and shoot a few waterfowl for food. Before we had gone fifty yards we perceived that all hopes of pushing further up the stream in the whale-boat were at an end, for not two hundred yards above where we had landed we found a succession of shallows and mud-banks, with not six inches of water over them. It was a watery *cul de sac*.

Turning back, we walked some way along the banks of the other river, and soon came to the conclusion, from various indications, that it was not a river at all, but an ancient canal, like the one which is to be seen above Mombasa, on the Zanzibar coast, connecting the Tana River with the Ozy, in such a way as to enable the shipping coming down the Tana to cross to the Ozy, and reach the sea by it, and thus avoid the very dangerous bar that blocks the mouth of the Tana. The canal before us evidently had been dug out by man at some remote period of the world's history, and the results of his digging still remained in the shape of the raised banks that had no doubt once formed towing-paths. Except here and there, where they had been hollowed out by the water or fallen in, these banks of stiff binding clay were at a uniform distance from each other, and the depth of the stream also appeared to be uniform. Current there was little or none, and, as a consequence, the surface of the canal was choked with vegetable growth, intersected by little paths of clear water, made, I suppose, by the constant passage of waterfowl, iguanas, and other vermin. Now, as it was evident that we could not proceed up the river, it became equally evident that we must either try the canal or else return to the sea. We could not stop where we were, to be baked by the sun and eaten up by the mosquitoes, till we died of fever in that dreary marsh.

"Well, I suppose that we must try it," I said; and the others assented in their various ways—Leo, as though it were the best joke in the world; Job, in respectful disgust; and Mahomed, with an invocation to the Prophet, and a comprehensive curse upon all unbelievers and their ways of thought and travel.

Accordingly, so soon as the sun sank low, having little or nothing more to hope for from our friendly wind, we started. For the first hour or so we managed to row the boat, though with great labour; but after that the weeds became too thick to allow of it, and we were obliged to resort to the primitive and most exhausting resource of towing her. For two hours we laboured, Mahomed, Job, and I, who was supposed to be strong enough to pull against the two of them, on the bank, while Leo sat in the bow of the boat, and brushed away the weeds which collected round the cutwater with Mahomed's sword. At dark we halted for some hours to rest and enjoy the mosquitoes, but about midnight we went on again, taking advantage of the comparative cool of the night. At dawn we rested for three hours, then started once more, and laboured on till about ten o'clock, when a thunderstorm, accompanied by a deluge of rain, overtook us, and we spent the next six hours practically under water.

I do not know that there is any necessity for me to describe the next four days of our voyage in detail, further than to say that they were, on the whole, the most miserable that I ever spent in my life, forming one monotonous record of heavy labour, heat, misery, and mosquitoes. All that dreary way we passed through a region of almost endless swamp, and I can only attribute our escape from fever and death to the constant doses of quinine and purgatives that we swallowed, and the unceasing toil which we were forced to undergo. On the third day of our journey up the canal we had sighted a round hill that loomed dimly through the vapours of the marsh, and on the evening of the fourth night, when we camped, this hill seemed to be within five-and-twenty or thirty miles of us.

By now we were utterly exhausted, and felt as though our blistered hands could not pull the boat a yard farther, and that the best thing which we could do would be to lie down to die in that dreadful wilderness of swamp. It was an awful position, and one in which I trust no other white men will often be placed; and as I threw myself down in the boat to sleep the sleep of utter exhaustion, bitterly I cursed my folly in having become a party to such a mad undertaking, which could, I saw, only end in our deaths in this ghastly land. I thought, I remember, as I slowly sank into a doze, of what the appearance of the boat and her unhappy crew would be in two or three months' time from that night. There she would lie, with gaping seams and half filled with fœtid water, which, when the mist-laden wind stirred her, would wash backwards and forwards through our mouldering bones, and that must be the end of her, and of those in her who would follow after myths and seek out the secrets of Nature.

Already I seemed to hear the water rippling against the desiccated bones, and rattling them together, rolling my skull against Mahomed's, and his against mine, till at last the Arab's stood straight upon its vertebræ, and, glaring at me through its empty eyeholes, cursed me with its grinning jaws because I, a dog of a Christian, disturbed the last sleep of a true believer. I opened my eyes, shuddering at the horrid dream, then shuddered again at something that was not a dream, for two great eyes were gazing at me through the misty darkness. I struggled to my feet, and in my terror and confusion shrieked, and shrieked again, so that the others sprang up too, reeling, and drunken with sleep and fear. Then all of a sudden there was a flash of cold steel, and a broad spear was held against my throat, and behind it other spears gleamed cruelly.

"Peace," said a voice, speaking in Arabic, or rather in some dialect into which Arabic entered very largely; "who are you that come hither swimming on the water? Speak, or ye die," and the steel pressed sharply against my throat, sending a cold chill through me.

"We are travellers, and have come hither by chance," I answered in my best Arabic, which appeared to be understood, for the man turned his head, and, addressing a tall form that was visible in the background, said, "Father, shall we slay?"

"What is the colour of the men?" asked a deep voice in answer.

"White is their colour."

"Slay not," was the reply. "Four suns since was the word brought to me from 'She-who-must-be-obeyed,' 'White men come; if white men come, kill them not.' Let them be brought to the house of 'She-who-must-be-obeyed.' Bring forth the men, and let that which they have with them be brought forth also."

"Come!" said the man, half leading and half dragging me from the boat, and as he did so I perceived others doing the same kind office to my companions.

On the bank were gathered a company of some fifty men. In that light all I could discover was that they were armed with huge spears, were very tall, and strongly built, comparatively light in colour, and naked, save for a leopard skin tied round the middle.

Presently Leo and Job were thrust forward and placed beside me.

"What on earth is the matter?" asked Leo, rubbing his eyes.

"Oh, Lord! sir, here's a rum go," ejaculated Job; and just at that moment a disturbance ensued, and Mahomed tumbled between us, followed by a shadowy form with an uplifted spear.

"Allah! Allah!" howled Mahomed, feeling that he had little to hope from man, "protect me! protect me!"

"Father, it is a black one," said a voice. "What was the word of '*She-who-must-be-obeyed*' about the black one?"

"She said no word of him; but slay him not. Come hither, my son."

The man advanced, and the tall shadowy form bent forward and whispered something.

"Yes, yes," answered the other, and chuckled in a rather blood-curdling tone.

"Are the three white men there?" asked the form.

"Yes, they are there."

"Then bring up that which is made ready for them, and take with you all that can be brought from the thing which floats."

Hardly had he spoken when men advanced, carrying on their shoulders several covered palanquins, each borne by four bearers and two spare men, into which it was indicated that we were expected to mount.

"Well!" said Leo, "it is a blessing to find anybody to carry us after having to carry ourselves so long."

Leo always takes a cheerful view of things.

As there was no help for it, after seeing the others into theirs I climbed into my own litter, and very comfortable I found it. It appeared to be manufactured of cloth woven from grass-fibre, which stretched and yielded to every motion of the body, and, being bound top and bottom to the bearing-pole, gave a grateful support to the head and neck.

Scarcely had I settled myself when, accompanying their steps with a monotonous song, the bearers started at a swinging trot. For half an hour or so I lay still, reflecting on the very remarkable experiences that we were going through, and wondering whether any of my eminently respectable fossil friends at Cambridge would believe me if I were miraculously to be set at the familiar dinner-table for the purpose of relating them. I do not wish to convey any imputation or slight when I call those good and learned men fossils, but my experience is that people are apt to petrify, even at a University, if they follow the same paths too persistently. I was becoming fossilised myself, but of late my stock of ideas has been very much enlarged. Well, I lay and reflected, and wondered what on earth would be the end of it all, till at last I ceased to wonder, and went to sleep.

I suppose I must have slept for seven or eight hours, taking the first real rest that I had won since the night before the loss of the dhow, for when I woke the sun was high in the heavens. We were still journeying on at a pace of about four miles an hour. Peeping out through the thin curtains of the litter, which were fixed ingeniously to the bearing-pole, I perceived, to my infinite relief, that we had passed out of the region of eternal swamp, and were now travelling over swelling grassy plains towards a cup-shaped hill. Whether or not it was the same hill that we had seen from the canal I do not know, and have never since been able to discover, for, as we learned afterwards, these people will give little information upon such points. Next I glanced at the men who were bearing me. They were of a magnificent build, few of them being under six feet in height, and yellowish in colour. Generally their appearance had a good deal in common with that of the East African Somali, only their hair was not frizzed up, but hung in thick black locks upon their shoulders. Their features were aquiline, and in many cases exceedingly handsome, the teeth being especially regular and beautiful. But notwithstanding their beauty, it struck me that, on the whole, I had never seen more evil faces. There was an aspect of cold and sullen cruelty stamped upon them that revolted me, which, indeed, in some cases was almost uncanny in its intensity.

Another thing which I noticed about them was that they never seemed to smile. Sometimes they sang the monotonous song whereof I have spoken, but when they were not singing they remained almost perfectly silent, and the light of a laugh never came to brighten their sombre and wicked countenances. Of what race could these people be? Their language was a bastard Arabic, and yet they were not Arabs; I was quite sure of that. For one thing they were too dark, or rather yellow. I could not say why, but I know that their appearance filled me with a sick fear of which I felt ashamed. While I was still wondering another litter ranged alongside of mine. In it—for the curtains were drawn—sat an old man, clothed in a whitish robe, made, apparently, from coarse linen, that hung loosely about him, who, as I at once concluded, was the shadowy figure that had stood on the bank and been addressed as "Father." He was a wonderful-looking old man, with a snowy beard, so long that the ends of it hung over the sides of the litter, and he had a hooked nose, above which flashed a pair of eyes as keen as a snake's, while his whole countenance was instinct with a look of wise and sardonic humour impossible to describe on paper.

"Art thou awake, stranger?" he said in a deep and low voice.

"Surely, my father," I answered courteously, feeling certain that I should do well to conciliate this ancient Mammon of Unrighteousness.

He stroked his beautiful white beard, and smiled faintly.

"From whatever country thou wanderest," he said, "and by the way it must be from one where somewhat of our language is known, they teach their children courtesy there, my stranger son. And now, wherefore comest thou unto this land, which scarce an alien foot has pressed from the time that man knoweth? Art thou and are those with thee weary of life?"

"We came to find new things," I answered boldly. "We are tired of the old things; we have risen up out of the sea to know that which is unknown. We are of a brave race who fear not death, my very much respected father—that is, if we can win a little fresh information before we die."

"Humph!" said the old gentleman, "that may be true; it is rash to contradict, otherwise I should declare that thou wast lying, my son. However, I dare to say that *'She-who-must-be-obeyed'* will meet thy wishes in the matter."

"Who is *'She-who-must-be-obeyed'*?" I asked, curiously.

The old man glanced at the bearers, and then answered, with a little smile that somehow sent my blood to my heart—

"Surely, my stranger son, thou wilt learn soon enough, if it be her pleasure to see thee at all in the flesh."

"In the flesh?" I answered. "What may my father wish to convey?"

But the old man only laughed a dreadful laugh, and made no reply.

"What is the name of my father's people?" I asked.

"The name of my people is Amahagger, the People of the Rocks."

"And if a son might ask, what is the name of my father?"

"My name is Billali."

"And whither go we, my father?"

"That shalt thou see," and at a sign from him his bearers started forward at a run till they reached the litter in which Job was reposing (with one leg hanging over the side). Apparently, however, he could not make much out of Job, for presently I saw his bearers trot forward to Leo's litter.

After this, as nothing fresh occurred, I yielded to the pleasant swaying motion of the litter, and went to sleep again. I was dreadfully tired. When I woke I found that we were passing through a rocky defile of a lava formation with precipitous sides, in which grew many beautiful trees and flowering shrubs.

Presently this defile took a turn, and a lovely sight unfolded itself to my eyes. Before us was a vast cup of earth from four to six miles in extent, and moulded to the shape of a Roman amphitheatre. The sides of this great cup were rocky, and clothed with bush, but its centre was of the richest meadow land, studded with single trees of magnificent growth, and watered by meandering brooks. On this rich plain grazed herds of goats and cattle, but I saw no sheep. At first I could not imagine what this strange spot might be, but presently it flashed upon me that it must represent the crater of some long-extinct volcano which afterwards had been a lake, and ultimately was drained in some unexplained fashion. And here I may state that from my subsequent experience of this and a much larger, but otherwise similar, place, which I shall have occasion to describe by-and-by, I have every reason to believe that this conclusion was correct. What puzzled me, however, was, that although there were people moving about herding the goats and cattle, I saw no signs of any human habitation. Where did they all live? I wondered. My curiosity was soon destined to be gratified. Turning to the left the string of litters followed the cliffy sides of the crater for a distance of about half a mile, or perhaps a little less, and then halted. Seeing my adopted "father," Billali, emerge from his litter, I followed his example, and so did Leo and Job. The first thing I noticed was our wretched Arab companion, Mahomed, lying exhausted on the ground.

It appeared that he was not provided with a litter, but had been forced to run the entire distance, and, as he was already quite worn out when we started, his condition now seemed one of great prostration.

On looking round us we saw that the place where we had halted was a platform in front of the mouth of a great cave, and that piled upon this platform were the contents of the whale-boat, even to the oars and sail. Round the cave stood groups of the men who had escorted us, and other men like to them. They were all tall and all handsome, though they varied in their degree of darkness of skin, some being as black as Mahomed, and some as yellow as a Chinese. They were naked, except for the leopard skin round the waist, and each of them carried a huge spear.

There were also some women among them, who, instead of the leopard skin, wore a tanned hide of a small red buck, something like that of the oribé, only rather darker in colour. These women were, as a class, exceedingly good-looking, with large, dark eyes, well-cut features, and a thick bush of curling hair—not crisped like a negro's—ranging from black to chestnut in hue, with all shades of intermediate colour. Some, but very few of them, wore a yellowish linen garment, such as I have described as worn by Billali; but this, as we afterwards discovered, was a mark of rank, rather than an attempt at clothing. For the rest, their appearance was not quite so terrifying as that of the men, and they smiled sometimes, though rarely. As soon as we had alighted they gathered round us and examined us with curiosity, but without excitement. Leo's tall, athletic form and clear-cut Grecian face, however, evidently excited their attention, and when he politely lifted his hat to them, and showed his curling yellow hair, there was a slight murmur of admiration. Nor did it stop there; for, after regarding him critically from head to foot, the handsomest of the young women—one wearing a robe, and with hair of a shade between brown and chestnut—deliberately advanced to him, and, in a way that would have been winning had it not been so determined, quietly put her arm round his neck, bent forward, and kissed him on the lips.

I gasped aloud, expecting to see Leo instantly speared; and Job ejaculated, "The hussy!—well, I never!" As for Leo, he looked slightly astonished; and then, remarking that clearly we had reached a country where they followed the customs of the early Christians, he deliberately returned the embrace.

Again I gasped, thinking that something would happen; but, to my surprise, though some of the young women showed traces of vexation, the older ones and the men only smiled faintly. When we came to understand the customs of this extraordinary people the mystery was explained. It then appeared that, in direct opposition to the habits of almost every other savage race in the world, women among the Amahagger live upon conditions of perfect equality with the men, and are not held to them by any binding ties. Descent is traced only through the line of the mother, and while individuals are as proud of a long and superior female ancestry as we are of our families in Europe, they never pay attention to, or even acknowledge, any man as their father, even when their male parentage is perfectly well known. There is but one titular male parent of each tribe, or, as they call it, "Household," and he is its elected and immediate ruler, with the title of "Father." For instance, the man Billali was the father of this "household," which consisted of about seven thousand individuals all told, and no other man was ever called by that name. When a woman chanced to favour a man she signified her preference by advancing and embracing him publicly, in the same way that this handsome and exceedingly prompt young lady, who was called Ustane, had embraced Leo. If he kissed her back it was a token that he accepted her, and the arrangement continued till one of them wearied of it. I am bound, however, to add that the change of husbands was not nearly so frequent as might have been expected. Nor did quarrels arise out of it, at least among the men, who, when their wives deserted them in favour of a rival, accepted the matter much as we accept the income tax or our marriage laws, as something not to be disputed, and as tending to the good of the community, however disagreeable they may prove to the individual in particular instances.

It is very curious to observe how the customs of mankind on this question vary in different countries, making morality an affair of latitude and religion, and what is right in one place wrong and improper in another. It must, however, be understood that, since all civilised nations appear to accept it as an axiom that ceremony is the touchstone of morals, there is, even according to our canons, nothing immoral about this Amahagger custom, since the public interchange of an embrace answers to our ceremony of marriage, which, as we know, justifies most things.

VII

USTANE SINGS

When the kissing *coram populo* was done—by the way, none of the young ladies offered to pet me in this fashion, though I saw one hovering round Job, to that respectable individual's evident alarm—the old man Billali advanced, and graciously waved us into the cave, whither we went, followed by Ustane, who did not seem inclined to take the hints I gave her that we liked privacy.

Before we had gone five paces it struck me that the cave which we were entering was none of Nature's handiwork, but, on the contrary, had been hollowed by the labour of man. So far as we could judge it appeared to be about one hundred feet in length by fifty wide, and very lofty, resembling a cathedral aisle more than anything else. From this main aisle opened passages at a distance of every twelve or fifteen feet, leading, I supposed, to smaller chambers. About fifty feet from the entrance of the cave, just where the light began to fade, a fire was burning, which threw huge shadows upon the gloomy walls around. Here Billali halted, and asked us to be seated, saying that the people would bring us food, and accordingly we sat ourselves down upon the rugs of skins which were spread for us, and waited. Presently the food, consisting of goat's flesh boiled, fresh milk in an earthenware pot, and roasted cobs of Indian corn, was brought by young girls. We were almost starving, and I do not think that in my life I ever before ate with such satisfaction. Indeed, before we finished we had devoured everything that was set before us.

When we had eaten, our somewhat saturnine host, Billali, who was watching us in absolute silence, rose and addressed us. He said that it was a wonderful thing which had happened. No man had ever known or heard of white strangers arriving in the country of the People of the Rocks. Sometimes, though rarely, black men had come here, and from them they had heard of the existence of men much whiter than themselves, who sailed on the sea in ships, but for the arrival of such there was no precedent. We had, however, been seen dragging the boat up the canal, and he told us frankly that he at once gave orders for our destruction, since it was unlawful for any stranger to enter here, when a message arrived from *"She-who-must-be-obeyed,"* saying that our lives must be spared, and that we were to be brought hither.

"Pardon me, my father," I interrupted at this point; "but if, as I understand, *'She-who-must-be-obeyed'* lives yet farther off, how could she have known of our approach?"

Billali turned, and seeing that we were alone—for the young lady, Ustane, had withdrawn when he began to speak—said, with a curious little laugh—

"Are there none in your land who can see without eyes and hear without ears? Ask no questions; *She* knew."

I shrugged my shoulders at this, and he went on to say that no further instructions had been received on the subject of our disposal, and this being so he was about to start to interview *"She-who-must-be-obeyed,"* generally spoken of, for the sake of brevity, as "Hiya" or *She* simply, who, he gave us to understand, was the Queen of the Amahagger, and learn her wishes.

I asked him how long he proposed to be absent, and he said that by travelling hard he might be back on the fifth day, but there were many miles of marsh to cross before he came to where *She* was. He then said that every arrangement would be made for our comfort during his absence, and that, as personally he had taken a fancy to us, he trusted sincerely that the answer he should bring from *She* would be one favourable to the continuation of our existence. At the same time he did not wish to conceal from us that he thought this doubtful, as every stranger who had ever come into the country during his grandmother's life, his mother's life, and his own life, had been put to death without mercy, and in a way which he would not harrow our feelings by describing. This had been done by the order of *She* herself, at least he supposed that it was by her order. At any rate, she never interfered to save them.

"Why," I said, "but how can that be? You are an old man, and the time you talk of must reach back three men's lives. How, therefore, could *She* have ordered the death of anybody at the beginning of the life of your grandmother, seeing that herself she would not have been born?"

Again Billali smiled—that same peculiar smile—and with a deep bow departed, without making any answer; nor did we see him again for five days.

When he had gone we discussed the situation, which filled me with alarm. I did not at all like the accounts of this mysterious Queen, *"She-who-must-be-obeyed,"* or more shortly *She,* who apparently ordered the execution of any unfortunate stranger in a fashion so unmerciful. Leo, too, was depressed about it, but consoled himself by triumphantly pointing out that this *She* was undoubtedly the person referred to in the writing on the potsherd and in his father's letter, in proof of which he advanced Billali's allusions to her age and power. I was by this time so overwhelmed with the course of events that I had not the heart left even to dispute a proposition so absurd, therefore I suggested that we should try to go out to take a bath, of which all of us stood sadly in need.

Accordingly, indicating our wish to a middle-aged individual of an unusually saturnine cast of countenance, even among this saturnine people, who appeared to be deputed to look after us now that the Father of the hamlet had departed, we started in a body—having first lit our pipes. Outside the cave we found quite a crowd of people evidently watching for our appearance, but when they saw us emerge smoking they vanished this way and that, calling out that we were mighty magicians. Indeed, nothing about us created so great a sensation as our tobacco-smoke—not even our firearms.* After this we succeeded in reaching a stream that had its source in a strong ground spring, and taking our bath in peace, though some of the women, not excepting Ustane, showed a decided inclination to follow us even there.

By the time that we had finished this most refreshing bathe the sun was setting; indeed, when we came back to the big cavern it had already set. The cave itself was full of people gathered round fires—for several had now been lighted—who were eating their evening meal by the lurid glare, and by the light of lamps which were set about or hung upon the walls. These lamps were of a rude manufacture of baked earthenware, and of all shapes, some of them graceful enough. The larger ones were formed of big red earthenware pots, filled with clarified melted fat, and having a reed wick let through a wooden disk which fitted the top of the pot. This sort of lamp required the most constant care to prevent its extinction whenever the wick burnt down, as there was no means of turning it up. The smaller hand lamps, however, which were also made of baked clay, were furnished with wicks manufactured from the pith of a palm-tree, or sometimes from the stem of a very handsome variety of fern. This kind of wick was passed through a round hole at the end of the lamp, to which a sharp piece of hard wood was attached wherewith to pierce and draw it up whenever it showed signs of burning low.

For a while we sat down and watched this grim people eating their evening meal in a silence grim as themselves, till at length, growing tired of contemplating them and the dark moving shadows on the rocky walls, I suggested to our new keeper that we should like to go to bed.

Without a word he rose, and, taking me politely by the hand, advanced with a lamp to one of the small passages that I had noticed opening out of the central cave. This we followed for about five paces, when suddenly it widened into a small chamber, about eight feet

*We found tobacco growing in this country as it does in every other part of Africa, and, although they are so absolutely ignorant of its other blessed qualities, the Amahagger use it habitually in the form of snuff, and also for medicinal purposes.—L. H. H.

square, and hewn from the living rock. On one side of this chamber was a stone slab, raised three feet above the ground, and running its entire length like a bunk in a cabin, whereon my guide intimated that I was to sleep. There was no window or air-hole to the chamber, and no furniture; and, on looking at it more closely, I came to the disturbing conclusion—in which, as I afterwards discovered, I was quite right—that it had served originally as a sepulchre for the dead rather than a sleeping-place for the living, the slab being designed to receive the corpse of the departed. This thought made me shudder in spite of myself; but, seeing that I must sleep somewhere, I stifled my feelings as best I might, and returned to the cavern to fetch my blanket, which had been brought from the boat with the other things. There I met Job, who, having been inducted to a similar apartment, had declined flatly to stop in it, saying that the look of the place "gave him the horrors," and that he might as well be dead and buried in his grandfather's brick grave at once. Now he expressed his determination of sleeping with me if I would allow him. This, of course, I was only too glad to do.

The night passed very comfortably on the whole. I say on the whole, for personally I experienced a horrible nightmare, wherein I was buried alive, induced, no doubt, by the sepulchral nature of my surroundings. At dawn we were aroused by a loud trumpeting sound, produced, as we discovered afterwards, by a young Amahagger blowing through a hole bored in its side into a hollowed elephant tusk, which was kept for the purpose.

Taking the hint, we rose and went down to the stream to wash, after which the morning meal was served. At breakfast one of the women, no longer quite young, advanced and publicly kissed Job. Putting its impropriety aside for a moment, I think it was in its way the most delightful thing that I ever saw. Never shall I forget the respectable Job's abject terror and disgust. Job, like myself, is something of a misogynist—owing I fancy to the fact of his having been born one of a family of seventeen—and the feelings expressed upon his countenance when he realised that he was not only being embraced publicly, and without authorisation on his own part, but also in the presence of his masters, were too mixed and painful to admit of accurate description. He sprang to his feet, and pushed the woman, a buxom person of about thirty, from him.

"Well, I never!" he gasped, whereupon probably thinking that he was only coy, she embraced him again.

"Be off with you! Get away, you minx!" he shouted, waving the wooden spoon, with which he was eating his breakfast, up and down before the lady's face. "Beg your pardon, gentlemen, I am sure I haven't encouraged her. Oh, Lord! she's coming for me again. Hold her, Mr. Holly! please hold her! I can't stand it; I can't, indeed. This has never happened to me before, gentlemen, never. There's nothing against my character." Here he broke off, and ran as hard as he could down the cave, and for once I saw the Amahagger laugh. As for the woman, however, she did not laugh. On the contrary, she seemed to bristle with fury, which the mockery of the other women about her only served to intensify. She stood there literally snarling and shaking with indignation, and, seeing her, I wished Job's scruples had been at Jericho, for I could guess that his admirable behaviour had endangered our throats. Nor, as the sequel shows, was I wrong.

The lady having retreated, Job returned in a state of great nervousness, and looking with an anxious eye upon every woman who came near him. I took an opportunity to explain to our hosts that Job was a married man, who had met with unhappy experiences in his domestic relations, which accounted for his presence here and his terror at the sight of women. My remarks, however, were received in silence, it being evident that our retainer's behaviour was considered as a slight to the "household" at large, although the women, after the manner of some of their more civilised sisters, made merry at the rebuff of their companion.

After breakfast we took a walk and inspected the Amahagger herds, also their cultivated lands. They have two breeds of cattle, one large and angular, with no horns, but yielding beautiful milk; and the other, a red strain, very small and fat, excellent for meat, but of no value for milking purposes. This last breed closely resembles the Norfolk red-poll stock, only it has horns which generally curve forward over the head, sometimes to such an extent that they must be sawn to prevent them from growing into the bones of the skull. The goats are long-haired, and are used for eating only, at least I never saw them milked. As for the Amahagger cultivation, it is primitive in the extreme, their only implement being a spade made of iron, for these people smelt and work iron. This spade is shaped more like a big spear-head than anything else, and has no shoulder to it on which the foot can be set. As a consequence, the labour of digging is very great. It is, however, all done by the men, the women, contrary to the habits of most savage races, being entirely exempt from manual toil. But then, as I think I have said elsewhere, among the Amahagger the weaker sex has established its rights.

At first we were much puzzled as to the origin and laws of this most extraordinary race, points upon which they were singularly uncommunicative. As time went on, however—for the next four days passed without any striking event—we learnt something from Leo's lady friend, Ustane, who, by the way, clung to that young gentleman like his own shadow. As to origin, they had none, at least so far as she was aware. There were, however, she informed us, mounds of masonry and many pillars, called Kôr, near to the place where *She* lived, which the wise said had once been houses wherein men dwelt, and it was suggested that the Amahagger were descended from these men. No one, however, dared to go near these great ruins, because they were haunted: they only looked on them from a distance. Other similar ruins were to be seen, she had heard, in various parts of the country, that is, wherever one of the mountains rose above the level of the swamp. Also the caves in which they abode had been hollowed out of the rocks by men, perhaps the same who built the cities. They themselves had no written laws, only custom, which was, however, quite as binding as law. If any man offended against the custom, he was put to death by order of the Father of the "Household." I asked how he was put to death, but she only smiled in answer, and said that I might see one day soon.

They had a Queen, however. *She* was their Queen, but she appeared very rarely, perhaps once in two or three years, when she came forth to pass sentence on some offenders, and when seen she was muffled up in a big cloak, so that nobody could look upon her face. Those who waited upon her were deaf and dumb, and therefore could tell no tales, but it was reported that she was lovely as no other woman was lovely, or ever had been. It was rumoured also that she was immortal, and had power over all things, but she, Ustane, knew nothing about this. What she believed was that the Queen chose a husband from time to time, and so soon as a female child was born, this husband, who was never seen again, was put to death. Then the female child grew up and took the place of the Queen when its mother died, and had been buried in the great caves. But of these matters none could speak with certainty. Only *She* was obeyed throughout the length and breadth of the land, and to question her command was instant death. She kept a guard, but had no regular army, and to disobey her was to die.

I asked what size the land was, and how many people lived in it. She answered that there were ten "Households" like this that she knew of, including the big "Household," where the Queen was; that all the "Households" lived in caves, in places resembling this stretch of raised country, dotted about in a vast extent of swamp, which could only be threaded by secret paths. Often the "Households" made war on each other until *She* sent word that it was to stop, when they instantly obeyed her. Wars and the fever which they caught in crossing the swamps prevented their numbers from increasing too much. They had no connection with any other race, indeed none lived near them; also the swamps could not be crossed by foes. Once an army from the direction of the great river (presumably the Zambesi) had attempted to attack them, but lost themselves in the marshes, and at night, seeing the great balls of fire that move about there, tried to come to them, thinking that they marked the enemy's camp, and half of them were drowned. As for the rest, they soon died of fever and starvation, not a blow being struck at them. The marshes, she repeated, were absolutely impassable except to those who knew the paths, adding, what I could well believe, that we should never have reached this place where we now were had we not been brought thither.

These and many other things we learned from Ustane during the four days' pause before our real adventures began, and, as may be imagined, they gave us considerable cause for thought. The whole story was exceedingly remarkable, almost incredibly so, indeed, and the oddest part of it was that so far it did more or less correspond to the ancient writing on the sherd. And now it appeared that there was a mysterious Queen clothed by rumour with dread and wonderful attributes, and commonly known by the impersonal, but, to my mind, rather awesome title of *She*. Altogether, I could not understand it, nor could Leo, though of course he was triumphant exceedingly over me because I had persistently mocked at the legend. As for Job, he had long since abandoned any attempt to call his reason his own, and left it to drift upon the sea of circumstance. Mahomed, the Arab, who, by the way, was treated civilly indeed, but with chilling contempt, by the Amahagger, was, I discovered, in a great fright, though I could not quite make out what it was that frightened him. He would sit crouched in a corner of the cave all day long, calling upon Allah and the Prophet for protection. When I pressed him about it, he said that he was afraid because these people were not men and women at all, but devils, and that this was an enchanted land; and, upon my word, once or twice since then I have been inclined to agree with him. And so the time went on, till the night of the fourth day after Billali had left, when something happened.

We three and Ustane were sitting round a fire in the cave just before bedtime, when suddenly the woman, who had been brooding in silence, rose, and laid her hand upon Leo's golden curls, and addressed him. Even now, when I shut my eyes, I can see her proud, shapely form, clothed alternately in dense shadow and the red flickering light of the fire, as she stood, the wild centre of as wild a scene as I ever witnessed, and delivered herself of the burden of her thoughts and forebodings in a rhythmical speech that ran something as follows:—

Thou art my chosen—I have waited for thee from the beginning!
Thou art very beautiful. Who hath hair like unto thee, or skin so white?
Who hath so strong an arm, who is so much a man?
Thine eyes are the sky, and the light in them is the stars.
Thou art perfect and of a happy face, and my heart turned itself towards thee.

Ay, when mine eyes fell upon thee I did desire thee,—
Then did I take thee to me—O thou Beloved,
And hold thee fast, lest harm should come unto thee.
Ay, I did cover thine head with mine hair, lest the sun should strike it;
And altogether was I thine, and thou wast altogether mine.
And so it went for a little space, till Time was in labour with an evil Day;
And then, what befell on that day? Alas! my Beloved, I know not!
But I, I saw thee no more—I, I was lost in the blackness.
And she who is stronger did take thee; ay, she who is fairer than Ustane.

"Thou art my chosen."

Yet didst thou turn and call upon me, and let thine eyes search in the darkness.
But, nevertheless, she prevailed by Beauty, and led thee down horrible places,
And then, ah! then my Beloved——

Here this extraordinary woman broke off her speech, or chant, which was so much musical gibberish to us who could not understand of what she was talking, and seemed to fix her flashing eyes upon the deep shadow before her. Then in a moment they acquired a vacant, terrified stare, as though they were striving to picture some half-seen horror. She lifted her hand from Leo's head, and pointed into the darkness. We all looked, and could see nothing; but she saw something, or thought she did, and something evidently that affected even her iron nerves, for, without another sound, down she fell senseless between us.

Leo, who had grown really attached to this remarkable young person, became greatly alarmed and distressed, and, to be perfectly candid, my own condition was not far removed from that of superstitious fear. The scene and circumstances were so very uncanny.

Presently, however, she recovered, and sat up with a convulsive shudder.

"What didst thou mean, Ustane?" asked Leo, who, thanks to years of tuition, spoke Arabic very prettily.

"Nay, my chosen," she answered, with a little forced laugh, "I did but sing unto thee after the fashion of my people. Surely, I meant nothing. How could I speak of that which is not yet?"

"And what didst thou see, Ustane?" I asked, looking her sharply in the face.

"Nay," she answered again, "I saw naught. Ask me not what I saw. Why should I affright you?" Then, turning to Leo with a look of the most utter tenderness that I ever saw upon the face of a woman, civilised or savage, she took his head between her hands, and kissed him on the forehead as a mother might.

"When I am gone from thee, my chosen," she said; "when at night thou stretchest out thine hand and canst not find me, then shouldst thou think at times of me, for of a truth I love thee well, though I be not fit to wash thy feet. And now let us love and take that which is given us, and be happy; for in the grave there is no love and no warmth, nor any touching of the lips. Nothing perchance, or perchance but bitter memories of what might have been. To-night the hours are our own; how know we to whom they shall belong to-morrow?"

VIII

The Feast, and After!

On the day following this remarkable scene—a scene calculated to make a deep impression upon anybody who beheld it, more because of what it suggested and seemed to foreshadow than of what it revealed—it was announced to us that a feast would be held that evening in our honour. I did my best to decline it, saying that we were modest people, who cared little for feasts, but as my remarks were received with the silence of displeasure, I thought it wisest to make no further objections.

Accordingly, just before sundown, I was informed that everything was ready, and, accompanied by Job, went into the cave, where I met Leo, who as usual was followed by Ustane. These two had been out walking somewhere, and knew nothing of the projected festivity till that moment. When Ustane heard of it I saw an expression of horror start upon her handsome features. Turning, she caught a man who was passing up the cave by the arm, and asked him something in an imperious tone. His answer seemed to reassure her a little, for she looked relieved, though far from satisfied. Next she appeared to attempt some remonstrance with the man, who was a person in authority, but he spoke angrily to her, and shook her off. Then, changing his mind, he took her by the arm, and sat her down between himself and another man in the circle round the fire, and I perceived that for some reason of her own she thought it best to submit.

The fire in the cave was unusually large that night, and in a wide circle round it were gathered about thirty-five men and two women— Ustane and the woman to avoid whom Job had played the *rôle* of another Scriptural character. The men were sitting in perfect silence, as was their custom, each with his great spear set upright behind him, in a socket cut in the rock for that purpose. Only one or two wore the yellowish linen garment of which I have spoken, the rest had nothing on except the leopard skin about the middle.

"What's up now, sir?" said Job, doubtfully. "Bless us and save us, there's that woman again. Now, surely, she can't be after me, seeing that I have given her no encouragement. They give me the creeps, the whole lot of them, and that's a fact. Why, look, they have asked Mahomed to dine, too. There, that lady of mine is talking to him in as nice and civil a way as possible. Well, I'm glad it isn't me, that's all!"

We looked, and surely enough the woman in question had risen, and was escorting the wretched Mahomed from his corner, where, overcome by some acute prescience of horror, he had been seated, shivering, and calling on Allah. He appeared unwilling enough to comply, if for no other reason perhaps because it was an unaccustomed honour, for hitherto his food had been given to him apart. Anyway, I could see that he was in a state of great terror, for his tottering legs would scarcely support his stout, bulky form, and I think it was rather owing to the resources of barbarism behind him, in the shape of a huge Amahagger with a proportionately huge spear, than to the seductions of the lady who led him by the hand, that he consented to come at all.

"Well," I said to the others, "I don't at all like the look of things, but I suppose we must face it out. Have you fellows got your revolvers on? because, if so, you had better see that they are loaded."

"I have, sir," said Job, tapping his Colt, "but Mr. Leo has only got his hunting-knife, though that is big enough, surely."

Feeling that it would not do to wait while the missing weapon was fetched, we advanced boldly, and seated ourselves in a line, with our backs against the side of the cave.

So soon as we were seated an earthenware jar was passed round containing a fermented fluid of by no means unpleasant taste, though apt to turn upon the stomach, made from crushed grain—not Indian corn, but a small brown grain that grows upon its stem in clusters, not unlike that which in the southern part of Africa is known by the name of Kafir corn. The vase which contained this liquor was very curious, and as it more or less resembled many hundreds of others in use among the Amahagger I may as well describe it. These vases are of a very ancient manufacture, and of all sizes. None such can have been made in the country for hundreds, or rather thousands, of years. They are found in the rock tombs, of which I shall give a description in their proper place, and my own belief is that they were used to receive the viscera of the dead, after the fashion of the Egyptians, with whom the former inhabitants of this country may have had some connection. Leo, however, is of opinion that, as in the case of Etruscan amphoræ, they were placed there for the spiritual use of the deceased. They are mostly two-handled, and of all sizes, some measuring nearly three feet, and running from that height down to as many inches. In shape they vary, but are all exceedingly beautiful and graceful, being made of a very fine black ware, not lustrous, but slightly rough. On this groundwork are inlaid figures much more graceful and lifelike than any others that I have seen on antique vases. Some of these inlaid pictures represent love-scenes with a child-like simplicity and freedom of manner which would not commend itself to the taste of the present day. Others again give pictures of maidens dancing, and yet others of hunting-scenes. For instance, the very vase from which we were then drinking had on one side a most spirited drawing of men, apparently white in colour, attacking a bull-elephant with spears, while on the reverse was a picture, not quite so well done, of a hunter shooting an arrow at a running antelope, I should say from the look of it either an eland or a koodoo.

This is a digression at a critical moment, but it is not too long for the occasion, for the occasion itself was very long. With the exception of the periodical passing of the vase, and the movement necessary to throw fuel on to the fire, nothing happened for the best part of a whole hour. Nobody spoke a word. There we all sat in perfect silence, staring at the glare and glow of the large fire, and at the shadows thrown by the flickering earthenware lamps—which, by the way, were not ancient. On the open space between us and the fire lay a large wooden tray, with four short handles to it, exactly like a butcher's tray, only not hollowed out. By the side of the tray was a great pair of long-handled iron pincers, and on the other side of the fire was a similar pair. Somehow I did not at all like the appearance of this tray and of the accompanying pincers. There I sat contemplating them and the silent circle of the fierce moody faces of the men, reflecting that it was all very awful, and that we were absolutely in the power of this fearsome people, who, to me at any rate, were all the more formidable because their true character was still very much of a mystery to us. They might be better than I thought them, or they might be worse. I feared that they were worse, and I was not wrong. It was a curious sort of a feast, I reflected, in appearance indeed an entertainment of the Barmecide stamp, for there was absolutely nothing to eat.

At last, just as I had begun to feel as though I were being mesmerised, a move was made. Without the slightest warning, a man from the other side of the circle called out in a loud voice—

"Where is the flesh that we shall eat?"

Thereon everybody in the circle answered in a deep measured tone, and stretching out the right arm towards the fire as he spoke—

"The flesh will come."

"Is it a goat?" said the same man.

"It is a goat without horns, and more than a goat, and we shall slay it," they answered with one voice, and turning half round one and all they grasped the handles of their spears with the right hand, and then simultaneously released them.

"Is it an ox?" said the man again.

"It is an ox without horns, and more than an ox, and we shall slay it," was the answer, and again the spears were grasped, and again released.

And turning half round one and all they grasped the handles of their spears.

Then came a pause, and I noticed, with horror and a rising of the hair, that the woman next to Mahomed began to fondle him, patting his cheeks, and calling him by names of endearment while her fierce eyes played up and down his trembling form. I do not know why the sight frightened me, but it did frighten us all dreadfully, especially Leo. The caressing was so snake-like, and so evidently a part of some ghastly formula that had to be gone through.* I saw Mahomed turn white under his brown skin, sickly white with fear.

"Is the meat ready to be cooked?" asked the voice, more rapidly.

"It is ready; it is ready."

"Is the pot hot to cook it?" it continued, in a sort of scream that echoed painfully down the great recesses of the cave.

"It is hot; it is hot."

*We afterwards learnt that its motive was to pretend to the victim that he was the object of love and admiration, and so to soothe his injured feelings, and cause him to expire in a happy and contented frame of mind.—L. H. H.

"Great heavens!" shouted Leo, "remember the writing, *'The people who place pots upon the heads of strangers.'*"

As he said the words, before we could stir, or even take the matter in, two great ruffians sprang up, and, grasping the long pincers, plunged them into the heart of the fire, while the woman who had been caressing Mahomed suddenly produced a fibre noose from under her girdle or moocha, and, slipping it over his shoulders, ran it tight, the men next him seizing him by the legs. These two men with the pincers heaved simultaneously, and, scattering the fire this way and that upon the rocky floor, lifted from it a large earthenware pot, heated to a white glow. In an instant, almost with a single movement, they had reached the spot where Mahomed was struggling. He fought like a fiend, shrieking in the abandonment of his despair, and notwithstanding the noose round him, and the efforts of the men who held his legs, the advancing wretches were for the moment unable to accomplish their purpose, which, horrid and incredible as it seems, was *to put the red-hot pot upon his head.*

I sprang to my feet with a yell of horror, and drawing my revolver I fired it by instinct straight at the diabolical woman who had been caressing Mahomed, and who was now gripping him in her arms. The bullet struck her in the back and killed her, and to this day I am glad of it, for, as it transpired afterwards, she had availed herself of the anthropophagous customs of the Amahagger to organise this sacrifice in revenge of the slight put upon her by Job. She sank down dead, and as she dropped, to my terror and dismay, Mahomed, by a superhuman effort, burst from his tormentors, and, springing high into the air, fell dying upon her corpse. The heavy bullet from my pistol had driven through the bodies of both, at once striking down the murderess and saving her victim from a death a hundred times more dreadful. It was an awful and yet a most merciful accident.

For a moment there was a silence of astonishment. The Amahagger had never heard the report of a firearm before, and its effects dismayed them. The next instant a man close to us recovered himself, and seized his spear preparatory to making a lunge with it at Leo, who was the nearest to him.

"Run for it!" I shouted, setting the example by starting up the cave as hard as my legs would carry me. I would have headed for the open if it had been possible, but there were men in the way, besides I had caught sight of the forms of a crowd of people standing out clearly against the skyline beyond the entrance to the cave. Up the cave I went, and after me came the others, and after them thundered the whole crowd of cannibals, mad with fury at the death of the woman. With a bound I cleared the prostrate form of Mahomed. As I flew over him I felt the heat from the red-hot pot, which was lying close by, strike upon my legs, and by its glow saw his hands—for he was not quite dead—still feebly moving. At the top of the cave was a little platform of rock three feet or so high by about eight deep, on which two large lamps were placed at night. Whether this platform had been left as a seat, or as a raised point afterwards to be cut away when it had served its purpose as a standing-place from which to carry on the excavations, I do not know—at least, I did not then. At least we reached it, all three of us, and, jumping on to it, prepared to sell our lives as dearly as we could. For a few seconds the crowd that was pressing on our heels hung back when they saw us face round upon them. Job was on one side of the rock to the left, Leo in the centre, and I to the right. Behind us were the lamps. Leo bent forward, and looked down the long lane of shadows, terminating in the fire and lighted lamps, through which the quiet forms of our would-be murderers flitted to and fro with the faint light glinting on their spears, for even their fury was silent as a bulldog's. The only other thing visible was the red-hot pot still glowing angrily in the gloom. There was a curious gleam in Leo's eyes, and his handsome face was set like a stone. In his right hand was his heavy hunting-knife. He shifted its thong a little up his wrist, then he put his arm round me and embraced me.

"Good-bye, old fellow," he said, "my dear friend—my more than father. We have no chance against those scoundrels; they will finish us in a few minutes, and eat us afterwards, I suppose. Good-bye. I led you into this. I hope you will forgive me. Good-bye, Job."

"God's will be done," I said, setting my teeth, as I prepared for the end. At that moment, with an exclamation, Job lifted his revolver, fired, and hit a man—not the man he had aimed at, by the way: anything that Job shot *at* was perfectly safe.

On they came with a rush, and I fired too as fast as I could, and checked them—between us, Job and I, besides the woman, killed or mortally wounded five men with our pistols before they were emptied. But we had no time to reload, and still they came on in a way which was almost splendid in its recklessness, since they did not know but that we could continue shooting for ever.

A great fellow bounded upon the platform, and Leo struck him dead with one blow of his powerful arm, sending the knife right through him. I did the same by another, but Job missed his stroke, and I saw a brawny Amahagger grip him by the middle and whirl him off the rock. The knife not being secured by a thong fell from Job's hand at that moment, and, by a most happy accident for him, lit upon its handle on the rock, just as the body of the Amahagger, who was undermost, struck upon its point and was transfixed thereon. What happened to Job after that I am sure I do not know, but my own impression is that he lay still upon the corpse of his deceased assailant, "playing 'possum," as the Americans say. As for myself, soon I was involved in a desperate encounter with two ruffians, who, luckily for me, had left their spears behind them; and for the first time in my life the great physical power with which Nature has endowed me stood me in good stead. I had hacked at the head of one man with my hunting-knife, which was almost as big and heavy as a short sword, with such vigour that the sharp steel split his skull down to the eyes, and was held so fast by it that as he suddenly fell from me sideways the knife was twisted out of my hand.

Then it was that the two others sprang upon me. I saw them coming, and wound an arm round the waist of each, and down we all fell upon the floor of the cave together, rolling over and over. They were strong men, but I was mad with rage, and that awful lust of battle which will creep into the hearts of the most civilised of us when blows are flying, and life and death tremble on the turn. My arms were about the two swarthy demons, and I hugged them till I heard their ribs crack and crunch up beneath my gripe. They twisted and writhed like snakes, and clawed and battered at me with their fists, but I held on. Lying on my back there, so that their bodies might protect me from spear thrusts from above, I slowly crushed the life out of them, and as

I did so, strange as it may seem, I thought of what the amiable Head of my College at Cambridge (who is a member of the Peace Society) and my brother Fellows would say if by clairvoyance they could see me, of all men, playing such a bloody game. Soon my assailants grew faint, and almost ceased to struggle; their breath had failed them, and they were dying, but still I dared not leave them, for they died very slowly. I knew that if I relaxed my grip they would revive. The other savages probably thought—for the three of us were lying in the shadow of the ledge—that we were all dead together, at any rate they did not interfere with our little tragedy.

I turned my head, and as I lay gasping in the throes of that awful struggle I could see that Leo was off the rock now, for the lamplight fell full upon him. He was still on his feet, but in the centre of a surging mass of struggling men, who were striving to pull him down as wolves pull down a stag. Up above them towered his beautiful pale face crowned with its bright curls as he swayed to and fro, and I saw that he was fighting with a desperate abandonment and an energy that was at once splendid and hideous to behold. He drove his knife through one man—they were so close to and mixed up with him that they could not come at him to kill him with their big spears, and they had no knives or sticks. The man fell, and then somehow the knife was wrenched from Leo's hand, leaving him defenceless, and I thought that the end had come. But no; with a desperate effort he broke loose from them, seized the body of the man he had just slain, and lifting it high in the air hurled it right at the mob of his assailants, so that the shock and weight of it swept some five or six of them to the earth. But in a minute they were up again, all except one, whose skull was smashed, and had once more fastened upon him. And now slowly, and with infinite labour and struggling, the wolves bore the lion down. Once even then he recovered himself, and felled an Amahagger with his fist, but it was more than man could do to hold his own for long against so many, and at last he came crashing down upon the rock floor, falling as an oak falls, and bearing with him to the earth all those who clung about him. They gripped him by his arms and legs, and then cleared off his body.

Up above them towered his beautiful pale face.

"A spear," cried a voice—"a spear to cut his throat, and a vessel to catch his blood."

I shut my eyes, for I saw a man run up with the spear, and myself, I could not stir to Leo's help, for I was growing weak: the two men on me were not yet dead, and a deadly sickness overcame me.

Then suddenly there was a disturbance, and involuntarily I opened my eyes again, and looked towards the scene of murder. The girl Ustane had thrown herself on Leo's prostrate form, covering his body with her body, and fastening her arms about his neck. They tried to drag her from him, but she twisted her legs round his, and hung on like a bulldog, or rather like a creeper to a tree, and they could not. Then they tried to stab him in the side without hurting her, but somehow she shielded him, and he was only wounded.

At last they lost patience.

"Drive the spear through the man and the woman together," said a voice, the same voice which had asked the questions at that ghastly feast, "so of a verity shall they be wed."

Then I saw the man with the weapon straighten himself for the effort. I saw the cold steel gleam on high, and once more I shut my eyes.

Even as I did so I heard the voice of a man thunder out, in tones that rang and echoed down the rocky ways—

"*Cease!*"

Then I fainted, and as I sank away it flashed through my darkening mind that I was passing down into the last oblivion of death.

IX

A LITTLE FOOT

When I opened my eyes again I found myself lying on a skin mat not far from the fire round which we had been gathered for that dreadful feast. Near to me lay Leo, still lost in a swoon, and over him bent the tall form of the girl Ustane, who was washing a deep spear wound in his side with cold water before binding it up with linen. Leaning against the wall of the cave behind her stood Job, apparently uninjured, but bruised and trembling. On the other side of the fire, tossed about this way and that, as though they had thrown themselves down to sleep in some moment of absolute exhaustion, were the bodies of those whom we had killed in our frightful struggle for life. I counted them: there were twelve besides the woman, and the corpse of poor Mahomed, who had died by my hand, which, the fire-stained pot at its side, was placed at the end of the irregular line. To the left a number of men were engaged in binding behind them the arms of the survivors of the cannibals, and in fastening them two and two. These villains were submitting to their fate with an air of sulky indifference which accorded ill with the baffled fury that gleamed in their sombre eyes. In front of the prisoners, directing the operations, stood no other than our friend Billali, looking rather tired, but particularly patriarchal with his flowing beard, and as cool and unconcerned as though he were superintending the cutting up of an ox.

Presently he turned, and perceiving that I was sitting up advanced to me, and with the utmost courtesy said that he trusted that I felt better. I answered that at present I scarcely knew how I felt, except that I ached all over.

Then he bent down and examined Leo's wound.

"It is an evil cut," he said, "but the spear has not pierced the entrails. He will recover."

"Thanks to thy arrival, my father," I answered. "In another minute we should all have been beyond the reach of recovery, for those devils of thine sought to slay us as they would have slain our servant," and I pointed towards Mahomed.

The old man ground his teeth, and I saw an extraordinary expression of malignity flare in his eyes.

"Fear not, my son," he answered. "Vengeance shall be taken on them such as would make the flesh twist upon the bones merely to hear of it. To *She* shall they go, and her revenge shall be worthy of her greatness. That man," pointing to Mahomed, "I tell thee that man would have died a merciful death to the death these hyæna-men shall die. Tell me, I pray of thee, how it came about."

In a few words I sketched what had happened.

"Ah, so!" he answered. "Thou seest, my son, here there is a custom that if a stranger comes into this country he may be slain by 'the pot,' and eaten."

"That is hospitality turned upside down," I answered feebly. "In our country we entertain a stranger, and give him food to eat. Here you eat him, and are entertained."

"It is a custom," he answered, with a shrug. "Myself, I think it an evil one; but then," he added by an afterthought, "I do not like the taste of strangers, especially after they have wandered through the swamps and lived on wildfowl. When *She-who-must-be-obeyed* sent orders that you were to be saved alive she said naught of the black man, therefore, being hyænas, these men lusted after his flesh, and it was the woman, whom thou didst rightly slay, who put it into their evil hearts to 'hotpot' him. Well, they will have their reward. Better for them would it be if they had never seen the light than that they should stand before *She* in her terrible anger. Happy are those of them who died by your hands.

"Ah," he went on, "it was a gallant fight that you fought. Knowest thou, long-armed old baboon that thou art, that thou hast crushed in the ribs of those two who are laid out there as though they were but the shell on an egg? And the young one, the lion, it was a beautiful stand that he made—one against so many; three did he slay outright, and that one there"—and he pointed to a body which was still moving a little—"will die anon, for his head is cracked across, and others of those who are bound are hurt. It was a gallant fight, and thou and he have made a friend of me by it, for I love to see a well-fought fray. But tell me, my son, the Baboon—and now I think of it thy face, too, is hairy, and altogether like a baboon's—how was it that you slew those with a hole in them?—You made a noise, they say, and slew them—they fell down on their faces at the noise?"

I explained to him as well as I could, but very shortly—for I felt terribly wearied, and was only persuaded to talk through fear of offending one so powerful if I refused to do so—what were the properties of gunpowder, whereupon he suggested that I should illustrate my words by operating on the person of one of the prisoners. One, he said, never would be counted, and the experiment would not only interest him, but would give me an immediate opportunity of revenge. He was greatly astounded when I told him that it was not our custom to wreak our wrongs in cold blood, and that we left vengeance to the law and a higher Power, of which he knew nothing. I added, however, that when I recovered I would take him out shooting with us, and that he should kill an animal for himself. With this prospect he was as pleased as is a child at the promise of a new toy.

Just then Leo opened his eyes beneath the stimulus of some brandy, of which we still had a little, that Job had poured down his throat, and our conversation came to an end.

After this we managed to carry Leo, who was in a very poor way indeed, and only half conscious, safely to bed, supported by Job and that brave girl Ustane, whom, had I not been afraid that she might resent it, I would certainly have kissed in acknowledgment of her courage in saving my boy's life at the risk of her own. But Ustane was a young person with whom I felt that it would be unadvisable to take liberties unless certain that they might not be misunderstood, so I repressed my inclinations. Then, bruised and battered, but with a sense of safety in my breast to which I had for some days been a stranger, I crept off to my own little sepulchre, not forgetting before I laid down in it to thank Providence from the bottom of my heart that it was not a sepulchre indeed, as, save for a merciful combination of events that I can only attribute to its protection, it would certainly have been for me this night. Few men have been nearer their end and yet escaped it than we were on that dreadful day.

I am a bad sleeper at the best of times, and my dreams that night when at last I sank to rest were not of the pleasantest. The awful sight of poor Mahomed struggling to escape the red-hot pot would haunt them. Then in the background of the vision a draped form hovered continually, which, from time to time, seemed to draw the coverings from its body, revealing now the perfect shape of a lovely blooming woman, and again the white bones of a grinning skeleton, which, as it veiled and unveiled, uttered the mysterious and apparently meaningless sentence:—

"That which is alive hath known death, and that which is dead yet can never die, for in the Circle of the Spirit life is naught and death is naught. Yea, all things live for ever, though at times they sleep and are forgotten."

The morning dawned at last, but when it came I found that I was too stiff and sore to rise. About seven Job arrived, limping terribly, his round face the colour of a rotten apple, and told me that Leo had slept fairly, but was very weak. Two hours afterwards Billali (Job called him "Billy-goat," to which animal his white beard gave him some resemblance, or more familiarly "Billy") came too, bearing a lamp in his hand, his towering form reaching nearly to the roof of the little chamber. I pretended to be asleep, and through the cracks of my eyelids I watched his sardonic but handsome old face. He fixed his hawk-like eyes upon me, and stroked his glorious white beard, which, by the way, would have been worth a hundred a year to any London barber as an advertisement.

"Ah!" I heard him mutter (Billali had a habit of muttering to himself), "he is ugly—ugly as the other is beautiful—a very Baboon; it was a good name. But I like the man. Strange now, at my age, that I should like a man. What says the proverb—'Mistrust all men, and slay him whom thou mistrustest overmuch; and as for women, flee from them, for they are evil, and in the end will destroy thee.' It is a good proverb, especially the last part of it: I think that it must have come down from the ancients. Nevertheless I like this Baboon, and I wonder where they taught him his tricks, and I trust that *She* will not bewitch him. Poor Baboon! he must be wearied after that fight. I will go lest I should awake him."

I waited till he had turned and was nearly through the entrance, walking softly on tiptoe, then I called after him.

"My father," I said, "is it thou?"

"Yes, my son, it is I; but let me not disturb thee. I did but come to see how thou didst fare, and to tell thee that those who would have slain thee, my Baboon, are by now far on their road to *She*. *She* said that you also were to come at once, but I fear you cannot yet."

"Nay," I said, "not till we have recovered a little; but have me borne out into the daylight, I pray thee, my father. I love not this place."

"Ah, no," he answered, "it hath a sad air. I remember when I was a boy I found the body of a fair woman lying where thou liest now—yes, on that very bench. She was so beautiful that I was wont to creep in hither with a lamp and gaze upon her. Had it not been for her cold hands, almost could I think that she slept and would one day awake, so fair and peaceful was she in her robes of white. White was she, too, and her hair was yellow, and fell down her almost to the feet. There are many such still in the tombs at the place where *She* is, for those who set them there had a way I know naught of whereby to save their beloved from the crumbling hand of Decay, even when Death had slain them. Ay, day by day I came hither, and gazed on her, till at last—laugh not at me, stranger, for I was but a silly lad—I learned to love that dead form, the shell which once had held a life that no more is. I would creep up to her and kiss her cold face, and wonder how many men had lived and died since she was, and who had loved her and embraced her in the days that long have passed away. And, my Baboon, I think I learned wisdom from that dead one, for of a truth it taught me of the littleness of Life, and the length of Death, and how all things that are under the sun go down one path, and are for ever forgotten. And so I mused, and it seemed to me that knowledge flowed into me from the dead, till one day my mother, a watchful woman, but hasty-minded, seeing I was changed, followed me, and saw the beautiful white one, and feared that I was bewitched, as, indeed, I was. So, half in dread and half in anger, she took the lamp, and standing the dead woman up against the wall yonder, set fire to her hair, and she burnt fiercely, even down to the feet, for those who are thus kept burn excellently well.

"See, my son, the smoke of her burning still hangs upon the roof."

I looked up doubtfully, and there, sure enough, on the rock of the sepulchre, was spread an unctuous and sooty mark, three feet or more across. Doubtless in the course of years it had been rubbed off the sides of the little cave, but on the roof it remained, and there was no mistaking its appearance.

"She burned," he went on in a meditative voice, "even to the feet, but the feet I came back and saved, cutting the charred bone from them, and I hid them under the stone bench yonder, wrapped in a piece of linen. Surely, I remember it as though it were but yesterday. Perchance they are there, if none have found them, even to this hour. Of a truth I have not entered the chamber from that time to this very day. Stay, I will look," and, kneeling down, Billali groped with his long arm in the recess under the stone bench. Presently his face brightened, and with an exclamation he drew something forth which was caked in dust that he shook on to the floor. It was covered with the remains of a rotting rag, which he undid, and revealed to my astonished gaze a beautifully shaped and almost white woman's foot, looking as fresh and firm as though it had been placed there yesterday.

"Thou seest, my son, the Baboon," he said, in a sad voice, "I spake

Holly and Billali

the truth to thee, for here is yet one foot remaining. Take it, my son, and gaze upon it."

I took this cold fragment of mortality in my hand, and looked at it in the light of the lamp with feelings which I cannot describe, so compounded were they of astonishment, fear, and fascination. It was light, much lighter I should say than it had been in the living state, and the flesh to all appearance was still flesh, though about it there clung a faintly aromatic odour. For the rest it was not shrunk or shrivelled, or even black and unsightly, like the flesh of Egyptian mummies, but plump and fair, and, except where it had been slightly scorched, perfect as on the day of death—a very triumph of embalming.

Poor little foot! I set it down upon the stone bench where it had lain for so many thousand years, and wondered whose was the beauty that it had upborne through the pomp and pageantry of a forgotten civilisation—first as a merry child's, then as a blushing maid's, and lastly as that of a perfect woman. Through what halls of Life had its step echoed, and in the end, with what courage had it trodden down the dusty ways of Death! To whose side had it stolen in the hush of night when the black slave slept upon the marble floor, and who had listened for its coming? Shapely little foot! Well might it have been set upon the proud neck of a conqueror bent at last to woman's beauty, and well might the lips of nobles and of kings have been pressed upon its jewelled whiteness.

I wrapped this relic of the past in the remnants of the old linen rag which, I believe, had been a portion of its owner's grave-clothes, for it was partially burnt, and hid it away in my travelling bag—a strange resting-place, I thought. Then with Billali's help I staggered out to see Leo. I found him dreadfully bruised, worse even than myself, perhaps owing to the excessive whiteness of his skin, and faint and weak with the loss of blood from the flesh wound in his side, but for all that very cheerful, and asking for some breakfast. Job and Ustane lifted him on to the bottom, or rather the sacking, of a litter, which was taken from its pole for that purpose, and with the aid of old Billali carried him out into the shade at the mouth of the cave, from which, by the way, every trace of the slaughter of the previous night had now been removed. There we all breakfasted, and indeed spent that day, and most of the two which followed.

On the third morning Job and myself were practically recovered. Leo also was so much better that I yielded to Billali's often expressed entreaty, and agreed to set out at once upon our journey to Kôr, which we were told was the name of the place where the mysterious *She* lived, though I still feared for its effect upon Leo, and especially lest the motion should cause his wound, which was scarcely skinned over, to break open again. Indeed, had it not been for Billali's evident anxiety to start, which led us to suspect that some difficulty or danger might threaten us if we did not comply with it, I would not have consented to go so soon.

X

SPECULATIONS

Within an hour of our final decision to start five litters were brought up to the door of the cave, each accompanied by four bearers and two spare hands, and with them a band of fifty armed Amahagger, who were to form the escort and carry the baggage. Three of these litters, of course, were for us, and one for Billali, who, I was immensely relieved to hear, proposed to accompany us, while the fifth I presumed was for the use of Ustane.

"Does the lady go with us, my father?" I asked of Billali, as he stood superintending things in general.

He shrugged his shoulders as he answered—

"If she wills. In this country the women do what they please. We worship them, and give them their way, because without them the world could not go on; they are the source of life."

"Ah!" I said, the matter never having struck me quite in that light before.

"We worship them," he continued, "up to a point, till at last they grow unbearable, which," he added, "happens about every second generation."

"And then what do you do?" I asked, with curiosity.

"Then," he answered, with a faint smile, "we rise, and kill the old ones as an example to the young ones, and to show them that we are the strongest. My poor wife was killed in that way three years ago. It was very sad, but to tell thee the truth, my son, life has been happier since, for my age protects me from the maidens."

"In short," I replied, quoting the saying of a politician whose wisdom has not yet lightened the darkness of the Amahagger, "thou hast found thy position one of greater freedom and less responsibility."

This phrase puzzled him a little at first from its vagueness, though I think my translation hit off the sense very well, but at last he understood, and appreciated it.

"Yes, yes, my Baboon," he said, "I see it now, but all the 'responsibilities' are killed, at least some of them are, and that is why there are so few old women about just now. Well, they brought it on themselves. As for this girl," he went on, in a graver tone, "I know not what to say. She is a brave girl, and she loves the Lion; thou sawest how she clung to him, and saved his life. Also, according to our custom, she is wed to him, and has a right to go where he goes, unless," he added significantly, "*She* would say her no, for her word overrides all rights."

"And if *She* bade her leave him, and the girl refused? What then?"

"If," he said, with a shrug, "the hurricane bids the tree to bend, and it will not, what happens?"

Then, without waiting for an answer, he turned and walked to his litter, and in ten minutes from that time we were all well under way.

It took us an hour and more to cross the cup of the volcanic plain, and another half-hour or so to climb the edge on the farther side. Once there, however, the view was a very fine one. Before us lay a long steep slope of grassy plain, broken here and there by clumps of trees, mostly of the thorn tribe. At the bottom of this gentle slope, some nine or ten miles away, we could discern a dim sea of marsh, over which the foul vapours hung like smoke about a city. It was easy work for the bearers down the slopes, and by midday we had reached the borders of the dismal swamp. Here we halted to eat our midday meal, then, following a winding and devious track, we plunged into the morass. Presently the path, at any rate to our unaccustomed eyes, grew so faint as to be almost indistinguishable from those made by the aquatic beasts and birds, and it is to this day a mystery to me how our bearers found their way across the marshes. Ahead of the cavalcade marched two men with long poles, which they now and again plunged into the ground before them, the reason of this being that the nature of the soil frequently changed from causes with which I am not acquainted, so that places which might be safe enough to cross one month would certainly swallow the wayfarer the next. Never did I see a more dreary and depressing scene. Miles on miles of quagmire, varied only by bright green strips of comparatively solid ground, and by deep and sullen pools fringed with tall rushes, in which the bitterns boomed and the frogs croaked incessantly: miles upon miles of it without a break, unless the fever fog can be called a break. The only life in this great morass was that of the aquatic birds, and the animals that fed on them, of both of which there were vast numbers. Geese, cranes, ducks, teal, coot, snipe, and plover swarmed all around us, many being of varieties which were quite new to me, and all so tame that one could almost have knocked them over with a stick. Among these birds I noticed especially a very beautiful variety of painted snipe, almost the size of a woodcock, and with a flight more resembling that bird's than an English snipe's. In the pools, too, lived a species of small alligator or enormous iguana, I do not know which, that fed, Billali told me, upon the waterfowl, also large quantities of a hideous black water-snake, of which the bite is dangerous, though not, I gathered, so deadly as that of a cobra or a puff adder. The bullfrogs were also very large, with voices proportionate to their size; and as for the mosquitoes—the "musqueteers," as Job called them—they were, if possible, even worse than they had been on the river, and tormented us greatly. Undoubtedly, however, the worst feature of the swamp was the awful smell of rotting vegetation that hung about it, which at times was positively overpowering, and the malarious exhalations that accompanied it, which we were of course obliged to breathe.

On we went through it all, till at last the sun sank in sullen splendour just as we reached a spot of rising ground about two acres in extent—an oasis of dry land in the midst of the miry wilderness—where Billali announced that we were to camp. The camping, however, turned out to be a very simple process, and consisted, in fact, in sitting down on the ground round a scanty fire built of sere reeds and some wood that had been brought with us. However, we made the best we could of it, and smoked and ate with such appetite as the smell of damp, stifling heat would allow, for it was very hot on this low land, and yet, oddly enough, chilly at times. But, however hot it was, we were glad enough to keep near the fire, because we found that the mosquitoes did not like the smoke. Presently we rolled ourselves up in our blankets and tried to go to sleep, but so far as I was concerned the bullfrogs, and the extraordinary roaring and alarming sound produced by hundreds of snipe hovering high in the air, made sleep an impossibility, to say nothing of our other discomforts. I turned and looked at Leo, who was next me; he was dozing, but his face had a flushed appearance that I did not like, and by the flickering firelight I saw Ustane, who was lying on the other side of him, raise herself from time to time upon her elbow, and glance at him anxiously enough.

However, I could do nothing to help him, for we had already taken a good dose of quinine, the only preventive we possessed; so I lay and watched the stars come out by thousands, till all the immense arch of heaven was strewn with glittering points, and every point a world! Here was a glorious sight by which man might well measure his own insignificance! Soon I gave up thinking about it, for the mind wearies easily when it strives to grapple with the Infinite, and to trace the footsteps of the Almighty as He strides from sphere to sphere, or deduce His purpose from His works. Such things are not for us to know. Knowledge is to the strong, and we are weak. Too much wisdom perchance would blind our imperfect sight, and too much strength would make us drunk, and over-weight our feeble reason till it fell and we were drowned in the depths of our own vanity. For what is the first result of man's increased knowledge interpreted from Nature's book by the persistent effort of his purblind observation? Is it not but too often to make him question the existence of his Maker, or, indeed, of any intelligent purpose beyond his own? Truth is veiled, because we could no more look upon her glory than we can upon the sun. It would destroy us. Full knowledge is not for man as man is here, for his capacities, which he is apt to think so great, are indeed but small. The vessel is soon filled, and were one-thousandth part of the unutterable and silent Wisdom that directs the rolling of those shining spheres, and the Force which makes them roll, pressed into it, it would be shattered into fragments. Perhaps in some other place and time it may be otherwise. Who can tell? Here the lot of man born of the flesh is but to endure midst toil and tribulation; to catch at the bubbles blown by Fate, which he calls pleasures, thankful if before they burst they rest a moment in his hand, and when the tragedy is played out, and his hour comes to perish, to pass humbly whither he knows not.

Above me as I lay shone the eternal stars, and there at my feet the impish marsh-born balls of fire rolled this way and that, vapour-tossed and earth-desiring, and I thought that in the two I saw a type and image of what man is, and of what man may perchance become, if the living Power who ordained him and them should so ordain this also.

Many such speculations passed through my mind that night. They come to torment us all at times. I say to torment, for, alas! thinking can only serve to measure out the helplessness of thought. What is the purpose of our feeble crying in the silences of space? Can our dim intelligence read the secrets of that star-strewn sky? Does any answer come out of it? Never any at all—nothing but echoes and fantastic visions! And yet we believe that beyond the horizon of the grave there is an answer, and that Faith supplies it. Without Faith we should suffer moral death, and by the help of Faith we yet may climb to Heaven.

Wearied, but still sleepless, I fell to considering our undertaking, and how wild it was. Yet how strangely the story seemed to fit in with what had been written centuries ago upon the sherd! Who was this extraordinary woman, Queen over a people apparently as extraordinary as herself, and reigning amidst the vestiges of a lost civilisation? And what was the meaning of this story of the Fire which gave unending life? Could it be possible that any fluid or essence should exist which might so fortify these fleshy walls that they could from age to age resist the mines and batterings of decay? It was possible, though not probable. The indefinite continuation of life would not, as poor Vincey said, be so marvellous a thing as the production of life and its temporary endurance. And if it were true, what then? The person who found it might no doubt rule the world. He could accumulate all the wealth in the world, and all the power, and all the wisdom that is power. He might give a lifetime to the study of each art or science. Well, if that were so, and if this *She* were practically immortal, which I did not for one moment believe, how was it that, with all these things at her feet, she preferred to remain in a cave amongst a society of cannibals? Surely this settled the question. The story was monstrous, and only worthy of the superstitious days in which it was written. At any rate, I was very certain that *I* would not attempt to attain unending life. I had known far too many worries and disappointments and secret bitternesses during my forty odd years of existence to wish that this state of affairs should be continued indefinitely. And yet I suppose that, comparatively speaking, my life has been a happy one.

And then, reflecting that at the present moment there was far more likelihood of our earthly careers being cut exceedingly short than of their being unduly prolonged, at last I managed to fall asleep, a fact for which anybody who reads this narrative, if anybody ever does, may very probably be thankful.

When I woke again it was just dawning, and the guards and bearers were moving about like ghosts through the dense morning mists, making ready for our start. The fire had died quite down, and I rose and stretched myself, shivering in every limb with the damp cold of the dawn. Then I looked at Leo. He was sitting up, holding his hands to his head, and I saw that his face was flushed and his eyes bright, and yet yellow round the pupils.

"Well, Leo," I said, "how do you feel?"

"I feel as though I were going to die," he answered hoarsely. "My head is splitting, my body is trembling, and I am deathly sick."

I whistled, or if I did not whistle I felt inclined to, for Leo had a sharp attack of fever. I went to Job, and asked him for the quinine, of which, fortunately, we had still a good supply, only to find that Job himself was not much better. He complained of pains across the back, and dizziness, and was almost incapable of helping himself. Then I did the only thing it was possible to do under the circumstances—gave them both about ten grains of quinine, and took a slightly smaller dose myself as a matter of precaution. After that I found Billali, and explained to him how matters stood, asking at the same time what he thought had best be done. He came with me, and looked at Leo and Job, whom, by the way, he had named the Pig on account of his fatness, round face, and small eyes.

"Ah!" he said, when we were out of earshot, "the fever! I thought so. The Lion has it badly, but he is young, and he may live. As for the Pig, his attack is not so bad; it is the 'little fever' which he has; that always begins with pains across the back; it will spend itself upon his fat."

"Can they go on, my father?" I asked.

"Nay, my son, they must go on. If they stop here they will certainly die; also, they will be better in the litters than on the ground. By to-night, if all goes well, we shall be across the marsh and in good air. Come, let us lift them into the litters and start, for it is very bad to stand still in this morning fog. We can eat our meal as we go."

This we did accordingly, and with a heavy heart I set out once more upon our strange journey. For the first three hours all went as well as could be expected, and then an accident happened that nearly lost us the pleasure of the company of our venerable friend Billali, whose litter was leading the procession. We were wading through a particularly dangerous stretch of quagmire, in which the bearers sometimes sank up to their knees. Indeed it was a mystery to me how they contrived to carry the heavy litters at all over such ground as that which we were traversing, though the two spare men, as well as the four bearers, had of course to put their shoulders to the pole.

Presently, as we blundered and floundered along, there was a sharp cry, then a storm of exclamations, and, last of all, a most tremendous splash, and the whole caravan halted.

I jumped out of my litter and ran forward. About twenty yards ahead was the lip of one of those sullen peaty pools of which I have spoken, the path we were following running along the top of its bank, that, as it happened, was a steep one. Looking towards this pool, to my horror I saw that Billali's litter was floating on it, while as for Billali himself, he was nowhere to be seen. To make matters clear I may as well explain at once what had happened. One of Billali's bearers had unfortunately trodden on a basking snake, which bit him in the ankle, whereon not unnaturally he had let go of the pole, and then, finding that he was tumbling down the bank, grasped at the litter to save himself. The result was exactly what might have been expected. The litter was pulled over the edge of the bank, the bearers let go, and together with Billali and the man who had been bitten, rolled into the slimy pool. When I reached the edge of the water neither of them was to be seen; indeed, the unfortunate bearer never was seen again. Either he struck his head against something, or was wedged in the mud, or possibly the snake-bite paralysed him. At any rate he vanished. But though Billali had disappeared, his whereabouts was clear enough from the agitation of the floating litter, in the bearing cloth and curtains of which he lay entangled.

"He is there! Our father is there!" said one of the men, but he did not stir a finger to help him, nor did any of the others. They simply stood and stared at the water.

"Out of the way, you brutes!" I shouted in English, and, throwing off my hat, I took a run and sprang well out into the horrid slimy-looking pool. A couple of strokes took me to where Billali was struggling beneath the cloth.

Somehow, I do not quite know how, I managed to push it free of him, and his venerable head all covered with green slime, like that of a yellowish Bacchus with ivy leaves, emerged upon the surface of the water. The rest was easy, for Billali was an eminently practical individual, and had the common sense not to grasp hold of me as drowning people often do. So I caught him by the arm, and towed him to the bank, through the mud of which we were dragged with difficulty. Such a filthy spectacle as we presented I have never seen before or since, and it will perhaps give some idea of the almost superhuman dignity of Billali's appearance when I say that, coughing, half drowned, and covered with mud and green slime as he was, with his beautiful beard drawn to a dripping point, like a Chinaman's freshly oiled pigtail, he still looked venerable and imposing.

"You dogs!" he said, addressing the bearers, so soon as he had recovered sufficiently to speak, "you left me, your father, to drown. Had it not been for this stranger, my son the Baboon, assuredly I should have drowned. Well, I will remember it," and he fixed them with his gleaming though slightly watery eye, in a way I saw that they did not like, although they tried to appear sulkily indifferent.

"As for thee, my son," the old man went on, turning towards me and grasping my hand, "rest assured that I am thy friend through good and evil. Thou hast saved my life: perchance a day may come when I shall save thine."

After that we cleaned ourselves as best we could, rescued the litter, and went on, *minus* the man who had been drowned. I do not know if it was because he chanced to be unpopular, or from native indifference and selfishness of temperament, but I am bound to say that nobody seemed to grieve much over his sudden and final disappearance, except the men who had to do his share of the work.

XI

The Plain of Kôr

About an hour before sundown, at last, to my unbounded gratitude, we emerged from the great belt of marsh on to land that swelled upwards in a succession of rolling waves. Just on the hither side of the crest of the first wave we halted for the night. My first care was to examine Leo's condition. It was, if anything, worse than in the morning, and a new and very distressing feature, vomiting, set in, and continued till dawn. Not one hour of sleep did I get that night, for I passed it in assisting Ustane, who was one of the most gentle and indefatigable nurses I ever saw, to wait upon Leo and Job. However, the air here was warm and genial without being too hot, and there were not many mosquitoes. Also we were above the level of the marsh mist, which lay stretched beneath us like the dim smoke-pall over a city, lit up here and there by the wandering globes of fen fire. Thus it will be seen that we were, speaking comparatively, very well off.

By dawn on the following morning Leo was quite light-headed, and fancied that he was divided into halves. I was dreadfully distressed, and began to wonder with a sort of sick fear what the end of his attack would be. Alas! I had heard but too much of how these fevers generally terminate. As I was wondering Billali came up and said that we must be moving on, more especially as, in his opinion, if Leo did not reach some spot where he could be quiet, and have proper nursing, within the next twelve hours, his death would only be a matter of a day or two. I could not but agree with him, so we placed Leo in the litter, and started, Ustane walking by his side to keep the flies off him, and watch that he did not throw himself out on to the ground.

Within half an hour of sunrise we had reached the top of the rise of which I have spoken, and a most beautiful view broke upon our gaze. Beneath us was a rich stretch of country, verdant with grass and lovely with foliage and flowers. In the background, at a distance, so far as I could judge, of some eighteen miles from where we then stood, a huge and extraordinary mountain rose abruptly from the plain. The base of the great mountain appeared to consist of a grassy slope, but rising upon this, I should say, from subsequent observation, at an altitude of about five hundred feet above the level of the plain, was a tremendous and absolutely precipitous wall of bare rock, quite twelve or fifteen hundred feet in height. The shape of the mountain, which was undoubtedly of volcanic origin, seemed to be round, but, as only a segment of its circle was visible, it proved difficult to estimate its exact size, which was enormous. Afterwards I discovered that it could not cover less than fifty square miles of ground. Anything more grand and imposing than the sight presented by this great natural castle, starting in solitary grandeur from the level of the plain, I never saw, and I suppose I never shall. Its very solitude added to its majesty, and its towering cliffs seemed to kiss the sky. Indeed for the most part they were clothed in clouds that lay in fleecy masses upon their broad and even battlements.

I sat up in my hammock and gazed across the plain at this thrilling and majestic prospect, and I suppose that Billali noticed me, for he brought his litter alongside.

"Behold the House of '*She-who-must-be-obeyed*'!" he said. "Had ever a queen such a throne before?"

"It is wonderful, my father," I answered. "But how do we enter? Those cliffs look hard to climb."

"Thou shalt see, my Baboon. Look now at the path below us. What thinkest thou that it is? Thou art a wise man. Come, tell me."

I looked, and saw what appeared to be the line of roadway running straight towards the base of the mountain, though it was covered with turf. There were high banks on each side of it, broken here and there, but fairly continuous on the whole, the meaning of which I did not understand. It seemed so very odd that anybody should embank a roadway.

"Well, my father," I answered, "I suppose that it is a road, otherwise I should have been inclined to say that it was the bed of a river, or rather," I added, observing the extraordinary directness of the cutting, "of a canal."

Billali—who, by the way, was none the worse for his immersion of the day before—nodded his head sagely as he replied—

"Thou art right, my son. It is a channel cut out by those who were before us in this place to carry away water. Of this I am sure: within the rocky circle of the mountain whither we journey was once a great lake till those who lived before us, by wonderful arts of which I know nothing, hewed a path for the water through the solid rock of the mountain, piercing even to the bed of the lake. But first they cut the channel that thou seest across the plain. Then, when at last the water burst out, it rushed down the channel that had been made to receive it, and crossed this plain till it reached the low land behind the rise, and there, perchance, it made the swamp through which we have come. Then, when the lake was drained dry, the people of whom I speak built a mighty city on its bed, whereof naught but ruins and the name of Kôr yet remaineth, and from age to age hewed out the caves and passages that thou wilt see."

"It may be," I answered; "but if so, how is it that the lake does not fill up again with the rains and the water of the springs?"

"Nay, my son, the people were a wise people, and they left a drain to keep it clear. Seest thou that river to the right?" and he pointed to a fair-sized stream which wound away across the plain, some four miles from us. "That is the drain, and it comes out through the mountain wall where this cutting goes in. At first, perhaps, the water ran down this canal, but afterwards the people turned it, and used the cutting for a road."

"And is there, then, no other place where one may enter into the great mountain," I asked, "except through the drain?"

"There is a place," he answered, "where cattle and men on foot may cross with much labour, but it is secret. A month mightest thou search and never find it. It is only used once a year, when the herds of cattle that have been fatting on the slopes of the mountain, and on this plain, are driven into the space within."

"And does *She* live there always?" I asked, "or does she come at times without the mountain?"

"Nay, my son, where she is, there she is."

By now we were well on to the great plain, and I was examining with delight the varied beauty of its semi-tropical flowers and trees, the latter of which grew singly, or at most in clumps of three or four, much of the timber being of large size, and belonging apparently to a variety of evergreen oak. There were also many palms, some of them more than one hundred feet high, and the largest and most beautiful tree ferns that I ever saw, about which hung clouds of jewelled honey-suckers and great-winged butterflies. Wandering there among the trees or crouching in the long and feathered grass were all varieties of game, from rhinoceroses to hares. I saw a rhinoceros, buffalo in large herds, eland, quagga, and sable antelope, the most beautiful of all the bucks, not to mention many smaller varieties of game, and three os-triches, which scudded away at our approach like white drift before a gale. So plentiful was the game that at last I could refrain no longer. With me in the litter I had a single-barrel sporting Martini, the "Ex-press" being too cumbersome, and espying a beautiful fat eland rub-bing himself under one of the oak-like trees, I jumped out, and proceeded to creep as near to him as I could. He allowed me to come within some eighty yards, then turned his head and stared at me, preparatory to running away. I lifted the rifle, and taking him about midway down the shoulder, for he was side on to me, fired. I never made a cleaner shot or a better kill in all my small experience, for the great buck sprang right up into the air and fell dead. The bearers, who had halted to see what happened, gave a murmur of surprise, an unwonted compliment from these sullen people, who never appear to be surprised at anything, and a party of the guard at once ran off to cut up the animal. As for myself, though I was longing to inspect him, I sauntered back to my litter as though I had been in the habit of killing eland all my life, feeling that I had risen several degrees in the estimation of the Amahagger, who looked on the performance as a very high-class manifestation of witchcraft. As a matter of fact, however, I had never seen an eland in a wild state before. Billali received me with enthusiasm.

"It is wonderful, my son the Baboon," he cried; "wonderful! Thou art a very great man, though so ugly. Had I not seen, surely I would never have believed. And thou sayest that thou wilt teach me to slay in this fashion?"

"Certainly, my father," I said airily; "it is nothing."

But all the same I firmly made up my mind that when "my father" Billali began to fire I would without fail lie down or take refuge behind a tree.

After this little incident nothing happened of any note till about an hour and a half before sundown, when we arrived beneath the shadow of the towering volcanic mass whereof I have already written. It is quite impossible for me to describe its grim grandeur as it appeared to me while my patient bearers toiled along the bed of the ancient watercourse towards the spot where the rich brown-hued cliff shot up from precipice to precipice till its crown lost itself in cloud. All I can say is that it almost awed me by the intensity of its lonesome and most solemn greatness. On we went up the bright and sunny slope, till at last the creeping shadows from above swallowed its brightness, and presently we began to pass through a cutting hewn in the living rock. Deeper and deeper grew this marvellous work, which must, I should say, have employed thousands of men for many years. Indeed, how it was ever executed at all without the aid of blasting-powder or dynamite I cannot to this day imagine. That is and must remain one of the mysteries of this wild land. I can only suppose that these cuttings and the vast caves that have been hollowed out of the rocks they pierced were the State undertakings of the people of Kôr, who lived here in the dim lost ages of the world, and that, as in the case of the Egyptian monuments, they were executed by the labour of tens of thousands of captives, carried on through an indefinite number of centuries. But who were the people?

At last we reached the face of the precipice itself, and found ourselves looking into the mouth of a dark tunnel that reminded me forcibly of those undertaken by our nineteenth-century engineers in the construction of railway lines. Out of this tunnel flowed a considerable stream of water. Indeed, though I do not think that I have mentioned it, from the spot where the cutting in the solid rock commenced we had followed this stream, which ultimately developed into the river I have already described as winding away to the right. Half of this cutting formed a channel for the stream, and half, which was placed on a slightly higher level—eight feet, perhaps—was devoted to the purposes of a roadway. At the termination of the cutting, however, the stream turned off across the plain and followed a bed of its own. At the mouth of the cave the cavalcade was halted, and, while the men employed themselves in lighting some earthenware lamps which they had brought with them, Billali, descending from his litter, informed me politely but firmly that the orders of *She* were that we must now be blindfolded, so that we should not learn the secret of the paths through the bowels of the mountains. To this of course I assented cheerfully enough, but Job, who was now very much better, notwithstanding the journey, did not like it at all, believing, I think, that it was but a preliminary step to being hot-potted. He was, however, a little consoled when I pointed out to him that there were no hot pots at hand, and, so far as I knew, no fire to heat them in. As for poor Leo, after turning restlessly for hours, to my deep thankfulness, at last he had dropped off into a sleep or stupor, I do not know which, so that there was no need to blindfold him. This blindfolding was performed by binding tightly round the eyes a piece of the yellowish linen whereof those of the Amahagger made their dresses who condescended to wear anything in particular. This linen I discovered afterwards was taken from the tombs, and was not, as I had at first supposed, of native manufacture.

The bandage was then fastened at the back of the head, and the ends knotted under the chin to prevent slipping.

Ustane, by the way, was also blindfolded, I do not know why, unless it was from fear lest she should impart the secrets of the route to us.

This operation performed we started on once more, and soon, by the echoing sound of the footsteps of the bearers and the increased noise of the water caused by reverberation in a confined space, I knew that we were entering into the bowels of the great mountain. It was an eerie sensation, that of being borne into the dead heart of the rock we knew not whither, but I was growing accustomed to such experiences by this time, and not to be surprised at anything. So I lay still, and listened to the *tramp, tramp* of the bearers and the rushing of the water, and tried to believe that I was enjoying myself. Presently the men set up the melancholy little chant that I had heard on the evening when we were captured in the whaleboat, and the effect produced by their voices was very curious; indeed quite indescribable. After a while the stagnant air became exceedingly thick and heavy, so much so, indeed, that I felt as though I were about to choke, till at length the litter turned a corner, then another and another, and the sound of the running water ceased. After this the air grew fresher again, but the turns were continuous, and to me, blindfolded as I was, most bewildering. I tried to keep a map of them in my mind in case it might ever be necessary for us to try to escape by this route, but, needless to say, I failed utterly. Another half-hour or so went by, when suddenly I became aware that we had passed into the open air. I could see the light through my bandage and feel its freshness on my face. A few more minutes and the litters halted, and I heard Billali order Ustane to remove her bandage and undo ours. Without waiting for her attentions I loosed the knot of mine, and looked out.

As I anticipated, we had journeyed through the precipice, and were now on the farther side, and immediately beneath its beetling face. The first thing I noticed was that the cliff is not nearly so high here, not so high I should say by five hundred feet, which proved that the bed of the lake, or rather of the vast ancient crater in which we stood, was much above the level of the surrounding plain. For the rest, we found ourselves in a huge rock-surrounded cup, not unlike that of the first place where we had sojourned, only ten times its size. Indeed, I could but just discern the frowning line of the opposite cliffs. A great portion of the plain thus enclosed by Nature was cultivated, and fenced in with walls of stone, placed there to prevent the cattle and goats, of which there were large herds, from breaking into the gardens.

Dotted about this plain rose grass mounds, and some miles away towards its centre I thought that I could see the outline of colossal ruins. I had no time to observe anything more at the moment, for we were instantly surrounded by crowds of Amahagger, similar in every particular to those with whom we were already familiar, who, though they spoke little, pressed round us so closely as to obscure the view to a person lying in a hammock. Then of a sudden a number of armed men arranged in companies appeared, running swiftly towards us, marshalled by officers who held ivory wands in their hands, having, so far as I could discover, emerged from the face of the precipice like ants from their burrows. These men as well as their officers were all robed in addition to the usual leopard skin, and, as I gathered, they formed the bodyguard of *She* herself.

Their leader advanced to Billali, saluted him by placing his ivory wand transversely across his forehead, and then asked some question which I could not catch. Billali having answered him briefly, the regiment turned and marched along the side of the cliff, our cavalcade of litters following in their track. After journeying thus for half a mile we halted once more in front of the mouth of a tremendous cave, measuring about sixty feet in height by eighty wide. Here Billali descended from his litter, requesting Job and myself to follow him, Leo, of course, being too ill to do anything of the sort. I obeyed, and we entered the great cave, into which the beams of the setting sun penetrated for some distance, while beyond the reach of the daylight it was faintly illuminated with lamps which seemed to me to stretch away for an almost immeasurable distance, like the gaslights of an empty London street.

The first thing I noticed was that the walls were covered with sculptures in bas-relief, for the most part of a sort similar to those upon the vases that I have described:—love-scenes principally, then hunting pieces, pictures of executions, and of the torture of criminals by the placing of a pot upon the head, presumably red-hot, thus showing whence our hosts had derived this pleasant practice. There were very few battle-scenes, though many of duels, and of men running and wrestling, and from this fact I am led to believe that this people were not much subject to attack by exterior foes, either on account of the isolation of their position or because of their great strength. Between the pictures were columns of stone characters of a nature absolutely new to me; at any rate they were neither Greek, nor Egyptian, nor Hebrew, nor Assyrian—this I am sure of. They looked more like Chinese writings than any other that I am acquainted with. Near to the entrance of the cave both pictures and writings were worn away, but further on in many cases they were absolutely fresh and perfect as the day on which the sculptor had ceased to work upon them.

The regiment of guards did not come further than the entrance to the cave, where they formed up to let us pass through. On entering the place itself, however, we were met by a man robed in white, who bowed humbly, but said nothing, which was not very wonderful, as afterwards it appeared that he was a deaf mute.

Running at right angles to the great cave, at a distance of some twenty feet from its entrance, lay a smaller cave or wide gallery, that was pierced into the rock both to the right and to the left of the main cavern. In front of the gallery to our left stood two guards, from which circumstance I argued that it might be the entrance to the apartments of *She* herself. The mouth of the right-hand gallery was unguarded, and the mute indicated that we were to pass along it. Walking a few yards down this passage, which was lighted with lamps, we came to the entrance of a chamber having a curtain made of some grass material hung over the doorway, not unlike a Zanzibar mat in appearance. This the mute drew back with another profound obeisance, and led the way into a good-sized apartment, hewn, as usual, out of the solid rock, but to my great relief lighted by means of a shaft pierced in the face of the precipice. In this room were a stone bedstead, pots full of water for washing, and leopard skins beautifully tanned to serve as blankets.

Here we left Leo, who was still sleeping heavily, and Ustane stayed with him. I noticed that the mute gave her a very sharp look, as much as to say, "Who are you, and by whose orders do you come here?" Next he conducted us to a very similar room, which Job took possession of, and then to two more that were occupied respectively by Billali and myself.

XII

"She"

The first care of Job and myself, after attending to Leo, was to wash ourselves and put on clean clothing, for what we were wearing had not been changed since the loss of the dhow. Fortunately, as I think that I have said, by far the greater part of our personal baggage had been packed into the whaleboat, and therefore was saved, and brought hither by the bearers, although the stores laid in by us for barter and presents to the natives were lost. Nearly all our clothing was made of a well-shrunk and very strong grey flannel, and excellent I found it for travelling in these places. Though a Norfolk jacket, shirt, and pair of trousers of this material only weighed about four pounds, a consideration in tropical countries, where every extra ounce tells on the wearer, it was warm, and offered a good resistance to the rays of the sun, and best of all to chills, which are so apt to result from sudden changes of temperature.

Never shall I forget the comfort of that "wash and brush-up," and of those clean flannels. The only thing that was wanting to complete my joy was a cake of soap, of which we had none.

Afterwards I discovered that the Amahagger, who do not reckon dirt among their many disagreeable qualities, use a kind of burnt earth for washing purposes, which, though unpleasant to the touch till one is accustomed to it, forms a very fair substitute for soap.

By the time that I was dressed, and had combed and trimmed my black beard, the previous condition of which was certainly sufficiently unkempt to give weight to Billali's appellation for me of "Baboon," I began to feel most uncommonly hungry. Therefore I was by no means sorry when, without the slightest preparatory sound or warning, the curtain over the entrance to my cave was flung aside, and another mute, a young girl this time, announced to me by signs that I could not misunderstand—namely, by opening her mouth and pointing down it—that there was something ready to eat. Accordingly I followed her into the next chamber, which we had not yet entered, where I found Job, who, to his great embarrassment, had also been conducted thither by a fair mute. Job never forgot the advances the "hot-pot" lady had made towards him, and suspected every girl who came near to him of similar designs.

"These young parties have a way of looking at one, sir," he would say apologetically, "which I don't call respectable."

This chamber was twice the size of the sleeping caves, and I saw at once that originally it had served as a refectory, and also, probably, as an embalming-room for the Priests of the Dead; for I may as well explain here that these hollowed-out caves were nothing more nor less than vast catacombs, in which for tens of ages the mortal remains of the great extinct race whose monuments surrounded us had been first preserved, with an art and a completeness that have never since been equalled, and then hidden away for all time. On each side of this particular rock-chamber ran a long and solid stone table, about three feet wide by three feet six in height, hewn out of the living rock, of which it had formed part, and was still attached to at the base. These tables were slightly hollowed out or curved inward, to give room for the knees of any one sitting on the stone ledge that had been cut as a bench along the side of the cave at a distance of about two feet from them. Each of them, also, was so arranged that it ended just under a shaft pierced in the rock for the admission of light and air. On examining them carefully, however, I saw that there was a difference between them which had escaped my attention at first; namely, that one of the tables, that to the left as we entered the cave, had evidently been used, not to eat upon, but for the purposes of embalming. That this was beyond all question the case was clear from five shallow depressions in the stone of the table, all shaped like a human form, with a separate place for the head to lie in, and a little bridge to support the neck, each depression being of a different size, to accommodate bodies varying in stature from a full-grown man's to that of a child, and having holes bored in it at intervals to carry off fluid. Indeed, if any further confirmation were required, we had but to look at the wall of the cave above to find it. For there, sculptured round the apartment, looking nearly as fresh as on the day of completion, was the pictorial representation of the death, embalming, and burial of an old man with a long beard, probably an ancient king or grandee of this country.

The first picture represented his death. He was lying upon a couch supported by four curved corner-posts fashioned to a knob at the end, and in appearance resembling written notes of music. Evidently he was in the very act of expiring, for gathered round the couch were women and children weeping, the former with their hair hanging down their backs. The next scene represented the embalmment of the body, which lay stark upon a table with depressions in it, similar to the one before us; probably, indeed, it was a picture of the same table. Three men were employed at the work—one superintending; one supporting a funnel shaped exactly like a port-wine strainer, of which the narrow end was fixed in an incision in the breast, no doubt in the great pectoral artery; while the third, who was depicted as standing straddle-legged over the corpse, held a very large jug high in his hand, and poured from it some steaming fluid which fell accurately into the funnel. The most curious part of this sculpture is that both the man with the funnel and the man who pours the fluid are depicted as holding their noses, either I suppose because of the stench arising from the body, or more probably to keep out the aromatic fumes of the hot fluid which was being forced into the dead man's veins. Another curious thing which I am unable to explain is that all three men are represented with a band of linen tied round the face having holes in it for the eyes.

The third sculpture was a picture of the burial of the deceased. There he lay, stiff and cold, clothed in a linen robe, and reposing on a stone slab such as I had slept upon at our first sojourning-place. At his head and feet burnt lamps, and by his side were placed several of the beautiful painted vases that I have described, which were perhaps supposed to be full of provisions. The little chamber was crowded with mourners, and with musicians playing on instruments resembling a lyre, while near the foot of the corpse stood a man holding a sheet, with which he was about to cover it from view.

These sculptures, looked at merely as works of art, were so remarkable that I make no apology for describing them rather fully. I consider them also of surpassing interest as representing, probably with studious accuracy, the rites of the dead as practised among an utterly lost people, and even then I thought how envious some antiquarian friends of my own at Cambridge would be if ever I found an opportunity of describing these wonderful remains to them. Probably they would say that I was exaggerating, notwithstanding that every page of this history must bear so much internal evidence of its truth that obviously it would have been quite impossible for me to have invented it.

To return. So soon as I had hastily examined these sculptures, which I think I omitted to mention are executed in relief, we sat down to a very excellent meal of boiled goat's-flesh, fresh milk, and cakes made of meal, the whole being served upon clean wooden platters.

When we had eaten we returned to see how poor Leo went on, Billali saying that he must now wait upon *She*, and hear her commands. On reaching Leo's room we found him exceedingly ill. He had awakened from his torpor altogether off his head, and was inclined to be violent, babbling incessantly about some boat-race on the Cam. Indeed, when we entered the room Ustane was holding him down. I spoke to him, and my voice seemed to soothe him; at any rate he grew much quieter, and was persuaded to swallow a dose of quinine.

I had been sitting with him for an hour, perhaps—at least I remember it was becoming so dark that I could only just see his head lying like a gleam of gold upon the pillow which we had extemporised out of a bag covered with a blanket—when suddenly Billali arrived with an air of great importance, and informed me that *She* herself had deigned to express a wish to see me—an honour, he added, accorded to but very few. I think that he was a little horrified at my cool way of taking the honour, but the truth is that I did not feel overwhelmed with gratitude at the prospect of meeting some savage, dusky queen, however absolute and mysterious she might be, more especially as my mind was full of dear Leo, for whose life I began to have great fears. However, I rose to follow him, and as I went I caught sight of something bright lying on the floor, which I picked up. Perhaps the reader will remember that with the potsherd in the casket was a "composition" scarabæus marked with a round O, a goose, and another curious hieroglyphic, the meaning of which signs is "Suten se Rā," or "Royal Son of the Sun." This scarab, which is a very small one, Leo had insisted upon having set in a massive gold ring, such as is generally used for signets, and it was this very ring that I now found. He had pulled it off in the paroxysm of his fever, at least I suppose so, and flung it down upon the rock-floor. Thinking that if I left it about it might be lost, I slipped it on to my own little finger, and then followed Billali, leaving Job and Ustane with Leo.

We passed down the passage, crossed the great aisle-like cave, and came to the corresponding passage on the other side, at the mouth of which the guards stood like two statues. As we came they bowed their heads in salutation, and then, lifting their long spears, placed them transversely across their foreheads, as the leader of the soldiers that met us had done with his ivory wand. We stepped between them, and found ourselves in a gallery exactly similar to that which led to our own apartments, only this passage, by comparison, was brilliantly lighted. A few paces down it we were met by four mutes—two men and two women—who bowed low and then disposed themselves, the women in front and the men behind of us, and in this order we continued our procession past several doorways hung with curtains resembling those in our own quarters, which I afterwards discovered opened into chambers occupied by the mutes who attended on *She*. A few paces more and we came to another doorway facing us, and not to our left like the others, which seemed to mark the termination of the passage. Here two more white-, or rather yellow-robed guards were standing, who also bowed, saluted, and let us pass through heavy curtains into a great antechamber, quite forty feet long by as many wide, in which some eight or ten yellow-haired women, most of them young and handsome, sat on cushions, working with ivory needles at what had the appearance of being embroidery-frames. These women were also deaf and dumb. At the farther end of this great lamp-lit apartment was a second opening, closed in with heavy Oriental-looking tapestries, quite unlike those that hung before the doors of our own rooms, where stood two particularly handsome girl mutes, their heads bowed upon their bosoms and their hands crossed in an attitude of the humblest submission. As we advanced they each stretched out an arm and drew back the curtains. Thereupon Billali did a curious thing. Down he went, that venerable-looking old gentleman—for Billali is a gentleman at the bottom—down on to his hands and knees, and in this undignified position, with his long white beard trailing on the ground, he began to creep into the apartment beyond. I followed him, standing on my feet in the usual fashion. Looking over his shoulder he perceived it.

"Down, my son; down, my Baboon; down on to thy hands and knees. We enter the presence of *She*, and, if thou art not humble, of a surety she will blast thee where thou standest."

I halted, and felt frightened. Indeed, my knees began to give way of their own mere motion; but reflection came to my aid. I am an Englishman, and why, I asked myself, should I creep into the presence of some savage woman as though I were a monkey in fact as well as in name? I would not and could not do it, that is, unless I was absolutely sure that my life or comfort depended thereon. If once I began to creep upon my knees I should always have to creep, which would be a patent acknowledgment of inferiority. So, fortified by an insular prejudice against "kootooing" that, like most of our so-called prejudices, has a good deal of common sense to recommend it, I marched in boldly. Presently I found myself in another apartment, considerably smaller than the anteroom, of which the walls were hung about with rich-looking curtains of the same make as those over the door, the work, I discovered subsequently, of the mutes who sat in the antechamber and wove them in strips, that were afterwards sewn together. Also, here and there about the room stood settees of a beautiful black wood of the ebony species, inlaid with ivory, and spread upon the floor were other tapestries, or rather rugs. At the top end of this apartment was what appeared to be a recess, also draped with curtains, through which shone rays of light. For the rest the place was empty and untenanted.

Painfully and slowly old Billali crept up the length of the cave, and with the most dignified stride which I could command I followed after him. But I felt that it was more or less of a failure. To begin with, it is not possible to appear dignified when you are following in the wake of an old man writhing along on his stomach like a snake. Thus, in order to walk sufficiently slowly, either I had to wave my leg for some seconds in the air at every step, or else to advance with a full stop between each stride, like Mary, Queen of Scots, going to execution in a play. Billali was not expert at crawling—I suppose his years stood in the way—and our progress up that apartment was a very long affair. I was immediately behind him, and on several occasions was sorely tempted to help him forward with a kick. It seemed absurd to advance into the presence of savage royalty after the fashion of an Irishman driving a pig to market. That is what we looked like, and the idea nearly made me laugh aloud. Indeed, I was obliged to work off the tendency to unseemly merriment by blowing my nose, a proceeding which filled old Billali with horror, for he looked over his shoulder and, making a ghastly face at me, murmured, "Oh, my poor Baboon!"

At last we reached the curtains, where Billali collapsed flat on to his breast, with his hands stretched out before him as though he were dead, and I, not knowing what to do, began to stare about the chamber. Presently I became aware that somebody was looking at me from behind the curtains. I could not see the person, but I could distinctly feel his or her gaze, and, what is more, it produced a very odd effect upon my nerves. I was frightened, I do not know why. The place was a strange one, it is true, and looked lonely, notwithstanding its rich hangings and the soft glow of the lamps—indeed, these accessories added to, rather than detracted from, its loneliness, just as an empty lighted street at night has always a more solitary appearance than one that is dark. It was so silent, and there lay Billali like a corpse before the heavy curtains, through which the odour of perfumes seemed to float up towards the gloom of the arched roof above. Minute grew into minute, and still there was no sign of life, nor did the hangings move; but I felt the gaze of a watching being sink through and through me, filling me with a nameless terror, till the perspiration stood in beads upon my brow.

At length the curtain began to stir. Who could be behind it?—some naked savage queen, a languishing Oriental beauty, or a nineteenth-century young lady, drinking afternoon tea? I had not the slightest idea, and should not have been astonished at seeing any of the three. Indeed, I was beyond astonishment. Presently the hanging agitated itself, then from between its folds there appeared a most beautiful white hand, white as snow, and with long tapering fingers, ending in the pinkest nails. This hand grasped the curtain, drawing it aside, and a voice spoke, I think the softest and yet most silvery voice that I ever heard. It reminded me of the murmur of a brook.

"Stranger," said the voice in Arabic, but much purer and more classical Arabic than the Amahagger talk—"stranger, wherefore art thou so much afraid?"

Now I flattered myself that, in spite of my inward terrors, I had kept a complete command of my countenance, and was therefore a little astonished at this question. Before I had made up my mind how to answer it, however, the curtain was drawn, and a tall figure stood before us. I say a figure, for not only the body, but also the face, was wrapped with a soft white and gauzy material in such a way as at first sight to remind me most forcibly of a corpse in its grave-clothes. And yet I do not know why it should have given me this idea, seeing that the wrappings were so thin that I could distinctly see the gleam of the pink flesh beneath them. I suppose it was owing to the way in which they were arranged, either accidentally, or more probably by design. Anyhow, I felt more frightened than ever at this ghost-like apparition, and the hair began to rise upon my head as a certainty crept over me that I was in the presence of something that was not canny. I could clearly distinguish, however, that the swathed mummy-like form before me was that of a tall and lovely woman, instinct with beauty in every part, and also with a certain snake-like grace which heretofore I had never seen anything to equal. When she moved a hand or foot her entire frame seemed to undulate, and the neck did not bend, it curved.

"Why art thou so frightened, stranger?" asked the sweet voice again—a voice which, like the strains of softest music, seemed to draw the heart out of me. "Is there that about me which should affright a man? Then surely are men changed from what they used to be!" And with a little coquettish movement she turned herself, holding up one arm, so as to reveal all its loveliness and the rich hair of raven blackness that streamed in soft ripples down the snowy robes, almost to her sandalled feet.

"It is thy beauty that makes me fear, O Queen," I answered humbly, scarcely knowing what to say, and I thought that as I spoke I heard old Billali, who was still lying prostrate on the floor, mutter, "Good, my Baboon, good!"

"I see that men still know how to beguile us women with false words," she answered, with a laugh which sounded like distant silver bells. "Ah, stranger, thou wast afraid because mine eyes were searching out thine heart; therefore wast thou afraid. Yet, being but a woman, I will forgive thee the lie, for it was courteously said. And now tell me how came ye hither to this land of the dwellers among caves—a land of swamps and evil things and dead old shadows of the dead? What came ye for to see? How is it that ye hold your lives so cheap as to place them in the hollow of the hand of *Hiya*, into the hand of '*She-who-must-be-obeyed*'? Tell me also how comest thou to know the tongue I talk. It is an ancient tongue, that sweet child of the old Syriac. Liveth it yet in the world? Thou seest that I dwell among caves and the dead, and naught know I of the affairs of men, nor have I cared to know. I have lived, O stranger, with my memories, and my memories are in a grave which mine hands hollowed, for it hath been truly said that the child of man maketh his own path evil;" and her beautiful voice quivered, and broke in a note as soft as any wood-bird's. Suddenly her eye fell upon the sprawling frame of Billali, and she seemed to recollect herself.

"Ah! thou art there, old man. Tell me how it is that things have gone wrong in thine household. Forsooth, it seems that these my guests were set upon. Ay, and one was nigh to being slain by the 'hot-pot,' to be eaten of those brutes, thy children, and had not the others fought gallantly they too had been slain, and not even I could have called back the life which once was loosed from the body. What means it, old man? What hast thou to say that I should not give thee over to those who execute my vengeance?"

The woman's voice had risen in her anger till it rang clear and cold against the rocky walls and I thought that I could see her eyes flash through the gauze which hid them. Poor Billali, whom I had believed to be a very fearless person, positively quivered with terror at her words.

"O 'Hiya!' O *She!*" he said, without lifting his white head from the floor. "O *She,* as thou art great, be merciful, for I am now as ever thy servant to obey. It was no plan or fault of mine, O *She;* it was those wicked ones who are called my children. Led on by a woman whom thy guest the Pig had scorned, they would have followed the ancient custom of the land, and eaten the fat black stranger who came hither with these thy guests the Baboon and the Lion who is sick, thinking that no word had come from thee about the Black One. But when the Baboon and the Lion saw what they would do, they slew the woman, and slew also their servant to save him from the horror of the pot. Then those evil ones, ay, those children of the Wicked One who lives in the Pit, they went mad with the lust of blood, and flew at the throats of the Lion and the Baboon and the Pig. But gallantly they fought. O *Hiya!* they fought like very men, and killed many, and held their own, and then I came and saved them, and the evildoers have I sent on hither to Kôr to be judged of thy greatness, O *She!* and here they are."

"Ay, old man, I know it, and to-morrow I will sit in the great hall and do justice upon them, fear not. And for thee, I forgive thee, though hardly. See that thou dost keep thine household better. Go!"

Billali rose upon his knees with astonishing alacrity, bowed his head thrice, and, his white beard sweeping the ground, crawled down the apartment as he had crawled up it, till finally he vanished through the curtains, leaving me, not a little to my alarm, alone with this terrible but most fascinating woman.

XIII

AYESHA UNVEILS

"There," said *She*, "he has gone, the white-bearded old fool! Ah! how little knowledge does a man acquire in his life. He gathers it up like water, but like water it runs between his fingers, and yet, if his hands be but as though with dew, behold a generation of fools call out, 'See, he is a wise man!' Is it not so? But how call they thee? 'Baboon,' he says," and she laughed; "but that is the way of these savages, who lack imagination, and fly to the beasts they are kin to for a name. How do they call thee in thine own country, stranger?"

"They call me Holly, O Queen," I answered.

"Holly," she said, speaking the word with difficulty, and yet with a most charming accent; "and what is 'Holly'?"

"'Holly' is a prickly tree," I replied.

"So. Well, thou hast a prickly and yet a tree-like look. Strong art thou, and ugly, but, if my wisdom be not at fault, honest at the core, and a staff to lean on; also one who thinks. But stay, thou Holly, stand not there; enter with me and be seated by me. I would not see thee crawl before me like those slaves. I am aweary of their worship and their terror; sometimes when they vex me I could blast them for very sport, and to see the rest turn white, even to the heart." And she held the curtain aside with her ivory hand that I might pass in.

I entered, shuddering. This woman was very terrible. Within the curtains was a recess measuring about twelve feet by ten, and in it a couch, and a table on which were fruit and sparkling water. By it, at its end, stood a vessel like a font cut in carved stone, also full of pure water. The place was softly lit with lamps formed out of the beautiful vessels of which I have spoken, and the air and curtains were laden with a subtle perfume. Perfume too seemed to emanate from the glorious hair and white clinging vestments of *She* herself. I entered the little room, and stood there uncertain.

"Sit," said *She*, pointing to the couch. "As yet thou hast no cause to fear me. If thou hast cause, thou shalt not fear for long, for I shall slay thee. Therefore let thy heart be light."

I sat down on the foot of the couch near to the font-like basin of water, and *She* sank down slowly on to its other end.

"Now, Holly," she said, "how comest thou to speak Arabic? It is my own dear tongue, for Arabian am I by my birth, even 'al Arab al Ariba,' an Arab of the Arabs, and of the race of our father Yárab, the son of Kâhtan, for in that fair and ancient city Ozal I was born, in the province of Yaman the Happy. Yet thou dost not speak it as we used to speak. Thy talk lacks the music of the sweet tongue of the tribes of Hamyar which I was wont to hear. Some of the words, too, seemed changed, even as among these Amahagger, who have debased and defiled its purity, so that I must speak with them in what is to me another tongue."*

"I have studied it," I answered, "for many years. Also the language is spoken in Egypt and elsewhere."

"So it is still spoken, and there is yet an Egypt? And what Pharaoh sits upon the throne? Still one of the spawn of the Persian Ochus, or are the Achæmenians gone, for it is far to the days of Ochus?"

---

*Yárab, the son of Kâhtan, who lived some centuries before the time of Abraham, was the father of the ancient Arabs, and gave its name Araba to the country. In speaking of herself as "al Arab al Ariba," *She* no doubt meant to convey that she was of the true Arab blood as distinguished from the naturalised Arabs, the descendants of Ismael, the son of Abraham and Hagar, who were known as "al Arab al mostáreba." The dialect of the Koreish was usually called the clear or "perspicuous" Arabic, but the Hamaritic dialect approached nearer to the purity of the mother Syriac.—L. H. H.

"The Persians have been gone from Egypt for nigh two thousand years, and since then the Ptolemies, the Romans, and many others have flourished and held sway upon the Nile, to fall when their time was ripe," I said, aghast. "What canst thou know of the Persian Artaxerxes?"

She laughed, making no answer, and again a cold chill went through me. "And Greece," she said; "is there still a Greece? Ah, I loved the Greeks. They were beautiful as the day, and clever, but fierce at heart and fickle, notwithstanding."

"Yes," I said, "there is a Greece; and, just now, it is once more a people. Yet the Greeks of to-day are not what the Greeks of the old time were, and Greece herself is but a mockery of the Greece that was."

"So! The Hebrews, are they yet at Jerusalem? And does the Temple stand that the Wise King built, and if so, what God do they worship there? Is that Messiah come, of whom they preached so much and prophesied so loudly, and doth He rule the earth?"

"The Jews are broken and gone; the fragments of their people strew the world, and Jerusalem is no more. As for the temple that Herod built——"

"Herod!" she said. "I know not Herod. But tell on."

"The Romans burnt it, and the Roman eagles flew across its ruins, and now Judæa is a desert."

"So, so! They were a great people, those Romans, and went straight to their end—ay, they sped to it like Fate, or like their own eagles on the prey!—and left peace behind them."

"Solitudinem faciunt, pacem appellant," I suggested.

"Ah, thou canst speak the Latin tongue, too!" she said, in surprise. "It has a strange ring in my ears after all these days, and I doubt me that thy accent does not fall as the Romans put it. Who was it wrote that? I know not the saying, but it is a true one of this great people. It seems that I have found a learned man—one whose hands have held the water of the world's knowledge. Knowest thou Greek also?"

"Yes, O Queen, and something of Hebrew, but not to speak them well. They are all dead languages now."

She clapped her hands in childish glee. "Of a truth, ugly tree that thou art, thou growest the fruits of wisdom, O Holly," she said; "but of those Jews whom I hated, for they called me 'Gentile' and 'heathen' when I would have taught them my philosophy—did their Messiah come, and doth He rule the world?"

"Their Messiah came," I answered with reverence; "but He came poor and lowly, and they would have none of Him. They scourged Him, and crucified Him upon a tree, but yet His words and His works live on, for He was the Son of God, and now of a truth He doth rule half the world, but not with an empire of the world."

"Ah, the fierce-hearted wolves," she said, "the followers of Sense and many gods—greedy of gain and faction-torn. I can see their dark faces yet. So they crucified their Messiah? Well can I believe it. That He was a Son of the Living Spirit would be naught to them, if indeed He was so, and of that we will talk afterwards. They would care little for any God if He came not with pomp and power. They, a chosen people, a vessel of Him they call Jehovah, ay, and a vessel of Baal, and a vessel of Astoreth, and a vessel of the gods of the Egyptians—a high-stomached people, eager of aught that brought them wealth and power. So they crucified their Messiah because He came in lowly guise—and now they are scattered about the earth? Why, if I remember, so said one of their prophets that it should be. Well, let them go— they broke my heart, those Jews, and made me look with evil eyes across the world, ay, and drove me to this wilderness, this place of a nation that was before them. When I would have taught them wisdom in Jerusalem they stoned me, yes, at the Gate of the Temple those white-bearded hypocrites and Rabbis hounded the people on to stone me! See, here is the mark of it to this day!" and with a sudden movement she rolled back the gauzy wrapping on her rounded arm, and pointed to a little scar that showed red against its milky beauty.

I shrank back horrified.

"Pardon me, O Queen," I said, "but I am bewildered. Nigh upon two thousand years have rolled across the earth since the Jewish Messiah hung upon His cross at Golgotha. How, then, canst thou have taught thy philosophy to the Jews before He was? Thou art a woman, and no spirit. How can a woman live two thousand years? Why dost thou befool me, O Queen?"

She leaned back on the couch, and once more I felt her hidden eyes playing upon me and searching out my heart.

"O man!" she said at last, speaking very slowly and deliberately, "it seems that there remain secrets upon the earth of which thou knowest little. Dost thou still believe that all creations die, even as those very Jews believed? I tell thee that naught dies. There is no such thing as Death, although there be a thing called Change. See," and she pointed to some sculptures on the rocky wall. "Three times two thousand years have passed since the last of the great race that hewed those pictures fell before the breath of the pestilence which destroyed them, yet they are not dead. Even now they live; perchance their spirits are drawn toward us at this very hour," and she glanced round. "Of a surety it sometimes seems to me that my eyes can see them."

"Yes, but to this world they are dead."

"Ay, for a time; but even to the world they are born again and yet again. I, yes I, Ayesha*—for that, stranger, is my name—I say to thee that I wait now for one I loved to be born anew, and I tarry here till he finds me, knowing of a surety that hither he will come, and that here, and here only, he shall greet me. Why dost thou believe that I, who am all-powerful, I, whose loveliness is more than the loveliness of that Grecian Helen of whom poets used to sing, and whose wisdom is wider, ay, far more wide and deep than the wisdom of Solomon the Wise,—I, who know the secrets of the earth and its riches, and can turn all things to my uses,—I, who have even for a while overcome Change, that ye call Death,—why, I say, O stranger, dost thou think that I herd here with barbarians lower than beasts?"

"I cannot tell," I said humbly.

"Because I wait for him I love. My life has perchance been evil—I know not, for who can say what is evil and what good? Therefore I fear to die to go to find him where he is, even if I could die, which I may not until mine hour comes; for between us there might rise a wall I could not climb; at the least, I dread it. Surely it would be easy also to lose the way in seeking him through those great spaces wherein the planets wander on for ever. But the day must come, it may

*Pronounced Assha.—L. H. H.

be when five thousand more years have passed, and are lost and melted into the vault of Time, even as the little clouds melt into the gloom of night, or it may be to-morrow, when he, my love, shall be born again, and then, following a law that is stronger than any human plan, he shall find me *here*, where once we kissed, and of a surety his heart will soften towards me, although I sinned against him. Ay, even if he knew me not again, yet must he love me, if only for my beauty's sake!"

For a moment I was dumbfounded, and could not answer. The matter was too overpowering for my intellect to grasp.

"But even thus, O Queen," I said at last, "even if we men be born again and again, that is not so with thee, if thou speakest truly." Here she looked up sharply, and once more I caught the flash of those hidden eyes; "thou," I went on hurriedly, "who hast never died?"

"That is so," she said; "and it is so because, half by chance and half by learning, I have solved one of the great secrets of the world. Tell me, stranger: life is—why, therefore, should not life be lengthened for a while? What are ten or twenty or fifty thousand years in the history of life? Why, in ten thousand years scarce will the rain and storms lessen a mountain top by a span in thickness. In two thousand years these caves have not changed, nothing has changed but the beasts, and man, who is as the beasts. There is naught that is wonderful about the matter, couldst thou but understand. Life is wonderful, ay, but that it should be a little lengthened is not wonderful. Nature hath her animating spirit as well as man, who is Nature's child, and he who can find that spirit, and let it breathe upon him, shall live with her life. He shall not live eternally, for Nature is not eternal, and she herself must die, even as the nature of the moon hath died. She herself must die, I say, or rather change, and sleep till it be time for her to live again. But when shall she die? Not yet, I ween, and while she lives, so shall he who hath all her secret live with her. All I have not, yet I have some, more perchance than any who were before me. Now, to thee I doubt not that this thing is a great mystery, therefore I will not overcome thee with it now. Another time I will tell thee more if the mood be on me, though perchance I shall never speak thereof again. Dost thou wonder how I knew that ye were coming to this land, and so saved your heads from the burning?"

"Ay, O Queen," I answered feebly.

"Then gaze upon that water," and, pointing to the font-like vessel, she bent forward and held her hand over it.

I rose and gazed, and instantly the water darkened. Then it cleared, and I saw as distinctly as I ever saw anything in my life—I saw, I say, our boat upon that horrible canal. There was Leo lying at the bottom asleep in it, with a coat thrown over him to keep off the mosquitoes, in such a fashion as to hide his face, and there were myself, Job, and Mahomed towing on the bank.

I started back aghast, and cried out that it was magic, for I recognised every detail of the pictured scene—it was one which had actually occurred.

"Nay, nay; O Holly," she answered, "it is no magic—that is a dream of ignorance. There is no such thing as magic, though there is such a thing as knowledge of the hidden ways of Nature. This water is my glass; in it I see what passes when at times it is my will to summon it before me. Therein I can show thee what thou wilt of the past, if it be anything that has to do with this country and with what I have known, or anything that thou, the gazer, hast known. Think of a face if thou wilt, and it shall be reflected from thy mind upon the water. I know not all the secret yet—I can read nothing in the future. But it is an old secret; I did not find it. In Arabia and in Egypt the sorcerers found it centuries ago. Thus one day I chanced to bethink me of that old canal—some twenty ages since I sailed upon it, and I was minded to look thereon again. So I looked, and there I saw the boat, and three men walking, and one, whose face I could not see, but a youth of noble form, sleeping in the boat, and so I sent and saved you. And now farewell. But stay, tell me of this youth—the Lion, as the old man calls him. I would look upon him, but he is sick, thou sayest—sick with the fever, and also wounded in the fray."

"He is very sick," I answered sadly; "canst thou do nothing for him, O Queen! who knowest so much?"

"Of a surety I can; I can cure him. But why speakest thou so sadly? Dost thou love the youth? Is he perchance thy son?"

"He is my adopted son, O Queen! Shall he be brought in before thee?"

"Nay. How long hath the fever taken him?"

"This is the third day."

"Good; let him lie another day. Then he will perchance throw it off by his own strength, and that is better than that I should cure him, for my medicine is of a sort to shake the life in its very citadel. If, however, by to-morrow night, at that hour when the fever first took him, he doth not begin to mend, then I will come to him and cure him. Stay; who nurses him?"

"Our white servant, he whom Billali names the Pig; also," and here I spoke with some little hesitation, "a woman called Ustane, a very handsome woman of this country, who came and embraced him when first she saw him, and hath stayed by him ever since, as I understand is the fashion of thy people, O Queen."

"My people! Speak not to me of my people," she answered hastily; "these slaves are no people of mine, they are but dogs to do my bidding till the day of my deliverance comes; and as for their customs, I have naught to do with them. Also, call me not Queen—I am weary of flattery and titles—call me Ayesha; the name hath a sweet sound in mine ears, it is an echo from the past. As for this Ustane, I know not. I wonder if it be she against whom I was warned, and whom I in turn did warn? Hath she—stay, I will see;" and, bending forward, she passed her hand over the font of water and gazed intently into it. "See," she said quietly, "is that the woman?"

I looked into the water, and there, mirrored upon its placid surface, was the silhouette of Ustane's stately face. She was bending forward, a look of infinite tenderness upon her features, watching something beneath her, and with her chestnut locks falling on to her right shoulder.

"It is she," I said, in a low voice, for once more I felt much disturbed at this most uncommon sight. "She watches Leo asleep."

"Leo!" said Ayesha, in an absent voice; "why, that is 'lion' in the Latin tongue. The old man has named happily for once. It is strange," she went on, speaking to herself, "most strange. So like—but it is not possible!" With an impatient gesture she passed her hand over the water once more. It darkened, and the image vanished silently and mysteriously as it had risen, and once more the lamplight, and the lamplight only, shone on the placid surface of that limpid, living mirror.

"Hast thou aught to ask me before thou goest, O Holly?" she said, after a few moments of reflection. "It is but a rude life that thou must live here, for these people are savages, and know not the ways of cultivated man. Not that I am troubled thereby, for behold my food," and she pointed to the fruit upon the little table. "Naught but fruit doth ever pass my lips—fruit and cakes of flour, and a little water. I have bidden my girls to wait upon thee. They are mutes, thou knowest, deaf are they and dumb, and therefore the safest of servants, save to those who can read their faces and their signs. I bred them so—the task has needed many centuries and much trouble; but at the last I triumphed. Once I succeeded before, but the breed was too ugly, so I let it die away; but now, as thou seest, they are otherwise. Once, too, I reared a race of giants, but after a while Nature sickened of it, and it withered away. Hast thou aught to ask of me?"

"Ay, one thing, O Ayesha," I said boldly, but feeling by no means so bold as I trust I looked. "I would gaze upon thy face."

She laughed out in her bell-like notes. "Bethink thee, Holly," she answered; "bethink thee. It seems that thou knowest the old myths of the gods of Greece. Was there not one Actæon who perished miserably because he looked on too much beauty? If I show thee my face, perchance thou wouldst perish miserably also; perchance thou wouldst eat out thy life in impotent desire; for know I am not for thee—I am for no man, save one, who hath been, but is not yet."

"As thou wilt, Ayesha," I said. "I fear not thy beauty. I have turned my heart away from such vanity as woman's loveliness, that passes like a flower."

"Nay, thou errest," she said; "that does *not* pass. My loveliness endures even as I endure; still, if thou wilt, O rash man, have thy will; but blame not me if passions mount thy reason, as the Egyptian breakers used to mount a colt, and guide it whither thou wilt not. Never may the man to whom my beauty is once unveiled put it from his mind, and therefore even among these savages I go hidden, lest they vex me, and I should slay them. Say, wilt thou see?"

"I will," I answered, my curiosity overpowering me.

Ayesha Unveils

She lifted her white and rounded arms—never had I seen such arms before—and slowly, very slowly, she withdrew some fastening beneath her hair. Then of a sudden the long, corpse-like wrappings fell from her to the ground, and my eyes travelled up her form, now robed only in a garb of clinging white that did but serve to show its rich and imperial shape, instinct with a life that was more than life, and with a certain serpent-like grace which was more than human. On her little feet were sandals, fastened with studs of gold. Then came ankles more perfect than ever sculptor dreamed of. About the waist her white kirtle was fastened by a double-headed snake of solid gold, above which her gracious form swelled up in lines as pure as they were lovely, till the kirtle ended at the snowy argent of her breast, whereon her arms were folded. I gazed above them at her face, and—I do not romance—shrank back blinded and amazed. I have heard of the beauty of celestial beings, now I saw it; only this beauty, with all its awful loveliness and purity, was *evil*—or rather, at the time, it impressed me as evil. How am I to describe it? I cannot—simply I cannot! The man does not live whose pen could convey a sense of what I saw. I might talk of the great changing eyes of deepest, softest black, of the tinted face, of the broad and noble brow, on which the hair grew low, and delicate, straight features. But, beautiful, surpassingly beautiful as were all these, her loveliness did not lie in them. It lay rather, if it can be said to have had any abiding home, in a visible majesty, in an imperial grace, in a godlike stamp of softened power, which shone upon that radiant countenance like a living halo. Never before had I guessed what beauty made sublime could be—and yet, the sublimity was a dark one—the glory was not all of heaven—but none the less was it glorious. Though the face before me was that of a young woman of certainly not more than thirty years, in perfect health and the first flush of ripened beauty, yet it bore stamped upon it a seal of unutterable experience, and of deep acquaintance with grief and passion. Not even the slow smile that crept about the dimples of her mouth could hide this shadow of sin and sorrow. It shone even in the light of those glorious eyes, it was present in the air of majesty, and it seemed to say: "Behold me, lovely as no woman was or is, undying and half-divine; memory haunts me from age to age, and passion leads me by the hand—evil have I done, and with sorrow have I made acquaintance from age to age, and from age to age evil I shall do, and sorrow shall I know till my redemption comes."

Drawn by some magnetic force which I could not resist, I let my eyes rest upon her shining orbs, and felt a current pass from them to me that bewildered and half blinded me.

She laughed—ah, how musically!—and nodded her little head at me with an air of sublime coquetry that would have been worthy of the Venus Victrix.

"Rash man!" she said; "like Actæon, thou hast had thy will; be careful lest, like Actæon, thou too dost perish miserably, torn to pieces by the ban-hounds of thine own passions. I too, O Holly, am a virgin goddess, not to be moved of any man, save one, and it is not thou. Say, hast thou seen enough?"

"I have looked on beauty, and I am blinded," I said hoarsely, lifting my hand to cover up my eyes.

"So! what did I tell thee? Beauty is like the lightning: it is lovely, but it destroys—especially trees, O Holly!" and again she nodded and laughed.

Ayesha paused, and through my fingers I saw an awful change come upon her countenance. The great eyes suddenly fixed themselves into an expression in which horror seemed to struggle with some tremendous hope arising through the depths of her dark soul. The lovely face grew rigid, and the gracious willowy form seemed to erect itself.

"Man!" she half whispered, half hissed, throwing back her head like a snake about to strike—"Man! whence hadst thou that scarab on thy hand? Speak, or by the Spirit of Life I will blast thee where thou standest!" and she took one light step towards me, while from her eyes there shone such an awful light—to me it seemed almost like a flame—that I fell, then and there, to the ground before her, babbling confusedly in my terror.

"Peace!" she said, with a sudden change of manner, and speaking in her former soft voice, "I did affright thee. Forgive me! But at times, O Holly, the almost infinite mind grows impatient of the slowness of the very finite, and I am tempted to use my power out of vexation. Very nearly wast thou dead, but I remembered———. But the scarab—about the scarabæus?"

"I found it," I stammered feebly, as I gained my feet once more, and it is a solemn fact that my mind was so disturbed that at the moment I could remember nothing else about the ring except the finding of it in Leo's cave.

"It is very strange," she said with a sudden access of woman-like trembling and agitation which seemed out of place in this awful woman—"but once I knew a scarab fashioned thus. It—hung round the neck—of one I loved," and she gave a little sob, and I saw that after all she was only a woman, although she might be a very old one.

"So," she went on, "it must be one like to it, and yet never did I see its fellow, for thereto hung a history, and he who wore it prized it much.* But the scarab that I knew was not set thus in the bezel of a ring. Go now, Holly, go, and, if thou canst, try to forget that of thy folly thou hast looked on Ayesha's beauty," and, turning from me, she threw herself upon her couch, and buried her face in the cushions.

As for me, I stumbled from her presence, and how I reached my own cave I do not remember.

---

*I am informed by a renowned and most learned Egyptologist, to whom I have submitted this very interesting and beautifully finished scarab, "Suten se Rā," that he has never seen one resembling it. Although it bears a title frequently given to Egyptian royalty, he is of opinion that it is not necessarily the cartouche of a Pharaoh, on which either the throne or personal name of the monarch is generally inscribed. What the history of this particular scarab may have been we can now, unfortunately, never know, though I have little doubt but that it played some part in the tragic story of the Princess Amenartas and her lover Kallikrates, the forsworn priest of Isis.—EDITOR.

XIV

A Soul in Hell

It was nearly ten o'clock at night when I cast myself down upon my bed, and began to gather my scattered wits, and to reflect upon what I had seen and heard. But the more I reflected the less I could understand it. Was I mad, or drunk, or dreaming, or was I merely the victim of a gigantic and most elaborate hoax? How was it credible that I, a rational man, not unacquainted with the leading scientific facts of our history, and hitherto an absolute and utter disbeliever in all the hocus-pocus which in Europe goes by the name of the supernatural, could believe that within the last few minutes I had been engaged in conversation with a woman two thousand and odd years old? The thing was quite adverse to the experience of humanity, and absolutely and utterly impossible. It must be a hoax, and yet, if it were a hoax, what was I to make of it? What, too, could be said of the figures in the water, of the woman's extraordinary acquaintance with the remote past, and her ignorance, or apparent ignorance, of any subsequent history? What, too, of her wonderful and awful loveliness? This, at any rate, was a patent fact, and beyond the experience of the world. No merely mortal woman could shine with such a supernatural radiance. As to that, at least, she had been in the right—it was not safe for any man to look upon such beauty. I was a hardened vessel in such matters, with the exception of one painful experience of my green and tender youth, having thrust the softer sex (I sometimes think that this is a misnomer) almost entirely out of my thoughts. But now, to my intense horror, I *knew* that I could never put away the vision of those glorious eyes; and alas! the very *diablerie* of the woman, whilst it horrified and repelled, attracted in an even greater degree. A person with the experience of two thousand years behind her, with the command of such tremendous powers, and the knowledge of a mystery that could hold off death, was certainly worth falling in love with, if ever woman was. But, alas! it was not a question of whether or no she were worth it, for so far as I could judge, not being versed in such matters, I, a Fellow of my college, noted for what my acquaintances are pleased to call my misogyny, and a respectable man now well on in middle life, had succumbed absolutely and hopelessly before this white sorceress. Nonsense; it must be nonsense! She had warned me fairly, and I had refused to take the warning. Curses on the fatal curiosity that is ever prompting man to draw the veil from woman, and curses on the natural impulse which begets it! It is the cause of half—ay, and more than half—of our misfortunes. Why cannot man rest content to live alone and be happy, and let the women live alone and be happy also? But perhaps they would not be happy, and I am not sure that we should either. Here was a nice state of affairs—I, at my age, to fall a victim to this modern Circe! But then she was not modern, at least she said not. She was almost as ancient as the original Circe.

I tore my hair, and jumped up from my couch, feeling that if I did not do something I should go quite mad. What did she mean about the scarabæus, too? It was Leo's scarabæus, and had come out of the old coffer that Vincey had left in my rooms nearly one-and-twenty years before. Could it be, after all, that the story was true, and that the writing on the sherd was *not* a forgery, or the invention of some crack-brained, long-forgotten individual? And if so, could it be that *Leo* was the man whom *She* awaited—the dead man who was to be born again!

Impossible! The supposition was insane! Who ever heard of a man being reborn?

But if it were possible that a woman could exist for two thousand years, this might be possible also—anything might be possible. For aught I knew I myself might be a reincarnation of some other forgotten self, or perhaps the last of a long line of ancestral selves. Well, *vive la guerre!* why not? Only, unfortunately, I had no recollection of these previous conditions. The idea was so absurd to me that I burst out laughing, and, addressing the sculptured picture of a grim-looking warrior on the cave wall, called out to him aloud, "Who knows, old fellow?—perhaps I was your contemporary. By Jove! perhaps I was you and you are I," and then I laughed again at my own folly, and the sound of my laughter rang dismally along the vaulted roof, as though the ghost of the warrior had echoed the ghost of a laugh.

Next I bethought me that I had not been to see how Leo fared, so, taking one of the lamps which were burning at my bedside, I slipped off my shoes and crept down the passage to the entrance of his sleeping-cave. The draught of the night air was lifting his curtain to and fro gently, as though spirit hands were drawing and redrawing it. I slid into the vault-like apartment, and looked round. There was a light by which I could see that Leo was lying on the couch, tossing restlessly in his fever, but asleep. At his side, half prostrate on the floor, half leaning against the stone couch, was Ustane. She held his hand in one of hers, but she too dozed, and the two made a pretty, or rather a pathetic, picture. Poor Leo! his cheek was burning red, there were dark shadows beneath his eyes, and his breath came heavily. He was very, very ill; and again the horrible fear seized me that he might die, and I be left alone in the world. And yet if he lived he would perhaps be my rival with Ayesha; even if he were not the man, what chance should I, middle-aged and hideous, have against his bright youth and beauty? Well, thank Heaven! my sense of right was not dead. *She* had not killed that yet; and, as I stood there, I prayed to Heaven in my heart that my boy, my more than son, might live—ay, even if he proved to be the man.

Then I went back as softly as I had come, but still I could not sleep; the sight and thought of Leo lying so ill yonder had but added fuel to the fire of my unrest. My wearied body and overstrained mind awakened all my imagination into preternatural activity. Ideas, visions, almost inspirations, floated before it with startling vividness. Most of them were grotesque enough, some were ghastly, some recalled thoughts and sensations that for years had been buried in the *débris* of my past life. But behind and above them all hovered the shape of that awful woman, and through them gleamed the memory of her entrancing loveliness. Up and down the cave I strode—up and down.

Suddenly I observed, what I had not noticed before, that there was a narrow aperture in the rocky wall. I took up the lamp and examined it; the aperture led to a passage. Now I was still sufficiently sensible to remember that it is not pleasant, in such a situation as was ours, to find passages running into your bedchamber from no one knows where. If there are passages, people can come along them; they can come when one is asleep. Partly to see where it went to, and partly from a restless desire to be doing something, I followed this passage. It led to a stone stair, which I descended; the stair ended in another passage, or rather tunnel, also hewn out of the bed-rock, and running, so far as I could judge, exactly beneath the gallery that led to the entrance of our rooms, and across the great central cave. I went down it: it was silent as the grave, but still, drawn by some sensation or attraction that I cannot define, I followed on, my stockinged feet falling without noise on the smooth and rocky floor. When I had traversed some fifty yards of space, I came to a third passage running at right angles, and here an awful thing happened to me: the sharp draught caught my lamp and extinguished it, leaving me in utter darkness in the bowels of that mysterious place. I took a couple of strides forward so as to clear the bisecting tunnel, being terribly afraid lest I should turn up it in the dark if once I grew confused as to the direction. Then I paused to think. What was I to do? I had no match; it seemed awful to attempt that long journey back through the utter gloom, and yet I could not stand there all night, and, if I did, probably it could not help me much, for in the bowels of the rock it would be as dark at midday as at midnight. I looked back over my shoulder—not a sight or a sound. I peered forward down the darkness: surely, far away, I saw something like the faint glow of fire. Perhaps it was a cave where I could find a light—at any rate, it was worth investigating. Slowly and painfully I crept along the tunnel, keeping my hand against its wall, and feeling at every step with my foot before I set it down, fearing lest I should fall into some pit. Thirty paces—there was a light, a broad light that came and went, shining through curtains! Fifty paces—it was at hand! Sixty—oh, great heaven!

I was at the curtains, and they did not hang close, so I could see clearly into the little cavern beyond them. This had the appearance of a tomb, and was lit up by a fire that burnt in its centre with a whitish flame and without smoke. Indeed, there, to the left, was a stone shelf with a little ledge to it three inches or so high, and on the shelf lay what I imagined to be a corpse; at any rate, it looked like one, with something white thrown over it. To the right was a similar shelf, on which broidered coverings were strewn. Over the fire bent the figure of a woman who seemed to be staring at the flickering flame; she knelt sideways to me, facing the corpse, and was wrapped in a dark mantle that hid her like a nun's cloak. Suddenly, as I was trying to make up my mind what to do, with a convulsive movement that suggested an impulse of despairing energy, the woman rose to her feet and cast the dark cloak from her.

It was *She* herself!

She was clothed, as I had seen her when she unveiled, in the kirtle of clinging white, cut low upon her bosom, and bound in at the waist with the barbaric double-headed snake, and her rippling black hair fell in heavy masses almost to her feet. But it was her face that caught my eye, and held me as in a vice, not this time by the force of its beauty, but with the power of fascinated terror. The beauty was still there, indeed, but the agony, the blind passion, and the awful vindictiveness displayed upon those quivering features, and in the tortured look of the upturned eyes, were such as surpass my powers of description.

For a moment she stood still, her hands raised high above her head, and as she stood the white robe slipped from her down to her golden girdle, baring the blinding loveliness of her form. She stood there, her fingers clenched, while the awful look of malevolence gathered and deepened on her face.

Suddenly I thought of what would happen if she discovered me, and the reflection turned me sick and faint. But, even if I had known that I must die if I stayed, I do not believe that I could have moved, for I was absolutely fascinated. Still I knew my danger. Supposing that she should hear me, or see me through the curtain, supposing I even sneezed, or that her magic told her that she was being watched—swift indeed would be my doom.

Down came the clenched hands to her sides, then up they rose above her head, and, as I am a living and honourable man, the white flame of the fire leapt after them, almost to the roof, throwing a fierce and ghastly glare upon *She* herself, upon the white figure beneath the covering, and every scroll and detail of the rockwork.

Down came the ivory arms again, and as they fell she spoke, or rather hissed, in Arabic, in a note that curdled my blood, and for a second stopped my heart.

"Curse her, may she be everlastingly accursed."

The arms sank and the flame sank. Up they went again, and the broad tongue of fire shot after them; and then again they fell.

"Curse her memory—accursed be the memory of the Egyptian."

Up again, and again down.

"Curse her, the daughter of the Nile, because of her beauty.

"Curse her, because her magic hath prevailed against me.

"Curse her, because she held my beloved from me."

And again the flame dwindled and shrank.

She placed her hands before her eyes, and, abandoning the hissing tone, she cried aloud:—

"Where is the use of cursing?—she prevailed, and she is gone."

Then she recommenced with an even more frightful energy:—

"Curse her where she is. Let my curses reach her where she is and disturb her rest.

"Curse her through the starry spaces. Let her shadow be accursed.

"Let my power find her even there.

"Let her hear me even there. Let her hide herself in the black-ness.

"Let her go down into the pit of despair, because I shall one day find her."

Again the flame fell, and again she covered her eyes with her hands.

"Curse her, may she be everlastingly accursed."

"It is folly," she wailed; "who can reach those who sleep beneath the wings of Power? Not even I can reach them."

Then once more she began her unholy rites.

"Curse her when she shall be born again. Let her be born accursed.

"Let her be utterly accursed from the hour of her new birth until sleep finds her.

"Yea then, let her be accursed; for then shall I overtake her with my vengeance, and utterly destroy her."

———

And so on. The flame rose and fell, reflecting itself in Ayesha's agonised eyes; the hissing sound of her terrible maledictions, and no words of mine can convey how terrible they were, ran round the walls and died away in little echoes, and the fierce light and deep gloom alternated themselves on the white and dreadful form stretched upon that bier of stone.

But at length she seemed to wear herself out and ceased. She sat herself down upon the rocky floor, shaking the dense cloud of beautiful hair over her face and breast, and began to sob terribly in the torture of a heartrending despair.

"Two thousand years," she moaned—"two thousand years have I waited and endured; but though century doth still creep on to century, and time give place to time, the sting of memory hath not lessened, the light of hope doth not shine more bright. Oh, to have lived two thousand years, with all my passion eating at my heart, and with my sin ever before me! Oh, that for me life cannot bring forgetfulness! Oh, for the weary ages that have been and are yet to come, and evermore to come, endless and without end!

"My love! my love! my love! Why did that stranger bring thee back to me after this sort? For five long centuries I have not suffered thus. Oh, if I sinned against thee, have I not wiped away the sin? When wilt thou come back to me who have all, and yet without thee have naught? What is there that I can do? What? What? What? And perchance she— perchance that Egyptian doth abide with thee where thou art, and mock my memory. Oh, why could I not die with thee, I who slew thee? Alas, that I cannot die! Alas! Alas!" and she flung herself prone upon the ground, and sobbed and wept till I thought that her heart must burst.

Suddenly she ceased, raised herself to her feet, rearranged her robe, and, tossing back her long locks impatiently, swept across to where the body lay upon the bench.

"O Kallikrates!" she cried, and I trembled at the name, "I must look upon thy face again, though it be agony. It is a generation since I looked upon thee whom I slew—slew with mine own hand," and with trembling fingers she seized the corner of the sheet-like wrapping that covered the form upon the stone bier, and paused. When she spoke again, it was in an awed whisper, as though her thought were terrible even to herself.

"Shall I raise thee," she said, apparently addressing the corpse, "so that thou standest there before me, as of old? I *can* raise thee," and she held out her hands over the sheeted dead, while her frame became rigid and terrible to see, and her eyes grew fixed and dull. I shrank in horror behind the curtain, my hair stood up upon my head, and, whether it was my imagination or a fact I am unable to say, but I thought that the quiet form beneath the covering began to quiver, and the winding sheet to lift as though it lay on the breast of one who slept. Suddenly Ayesha withdrew her hands, and the motion of the corpse seemed to me to cease.

"To what purpose?" she said heavily. "Of what service is it to recall the semblance of life when I cannot recall the spirit? Even if thou stoodest before me thou wouldst not know me, and couldst do but what I bid thee. The life in thee would be *my* life, and not *thy* life, Kallikrates."

For a moment she remained thus, brooding; then she cast herself down on her knees beside the form, and began to press her lips against the sheet, and to weep. There was something so horrible about the sight of this awe-inspiring woman letting loose her passion on the dead—so much more horrible even than anything which had gone before—that I could no longer bear to look at it, and, turning, began to creep, shaking as I was in every limb, slowly along the pitch-dark passage, feeling in my trembling heart that I had seen a vision of a Soul in Hell.

On I stumbled, I scarcely know how. Twice I fell, once I turned up the bisecting passage, but fortunately found out my mistake in time. For twenty minutes or more I crept along, till at last it occurred to me that I must have passed the little stair by which I had descended. So, utterly exhausted, and nearly frightened to death, I lay down there on the stone flooring, and sank into oblivion.

When I came to myself I noticed a ray of light in the passage behind me. I crept to it, and found that the weak dawn was stealing down to the little stair. Passing up it, I gained my chamber in safety, and, flinging myself on the couch, was soon lost in sleep, or rather in stupor.

XV

Ayesha Gives Judgment

The next thing that I remember was opening my eyes and perceiving the form of Job, who had now almost recovered from his attack of fever. He was standing in a beam of light that pierced into the cave from the outer air, shaking out my clothes as a makeshift for brushing them, which he could not do because there was no brush, then folding them up neatly and laying them on the foot of the stone couch. This done, he took my leather dressing-case out of the travelling bag, and opened it ready for my use. First he stood it on the foot of the couch also, then, being afraid, I suppose, that I should kick it off, he placed it upon a leopard skin on the floor, and stepped back a pace or two to observe the effect. It was not satisfactory, so he shut up the bag, turned it on end, and, having stood it against the end of the couch, rested the dressing-case on it. Next he looked at the pots full of water, which constituted our washing apparatus. "Ah!" I heard him murmur, "no hot water in this beastly place. I suppose these poor creatures only use it to boil each other in," and he sighed deeply.

"What is the matter, Job?" I said.

"Beg pardon, sir," he said, touching his hair. "I thought you were asleep, sir: and I am sure you seem as though you want it. One might think from the look of you that you had been having a night of it."

I only groaned by way of answer. I had, indeed, been "having a night of it," such as I hope never to have again.

"How is Mr. Leo, Job?"

"Much the same, sir. If he don't soon mend, he'll end, sir; and that's all about it; though I must say that that there savage, Ustane, do do her best for him, almost like a baptised Christian. She is always hanging round and looking after him, and if I ventures to interfere it's awful to see her; her hair seems to stand on end, and she curses and swears away in her heathen talk—at least I fancy she must be cursing, from the look of her."

"And what do you do then?"

"I make her a perlite bow, and I say, 'Young woman, your position is one that I don't quite understand, and can't recognise. Let me tell you that I has a duty to perform to my master as is incapacitated by illness, and that I am going to perform it until I am incapacitated too,' but she don't take no heed, not she—only curses and swears away worse than ever. Last night she put her hand under that sort of nightshirt she wears, and whips out a knife with a kind of a curl in the blade; so I whips out my revolver, and we walks round and round each other till at last she bursts out laughing. It isn't nice treatment for a Christian man to have to put up with from a savage, however handsome she may be, but it is what people must expect as is *fools* enough" (Job laid great emphasis on the "fools") "to come to such a place to look for things no man is meant to find. It's a judgment on us, sir—that's my view; and I, for one, is of opinion that the judgment isn't half done yet, and when it is done we shall be done too, and just stop in these beastly caves with the ghosts and the corpseses for once and all. And now, sir, I must be seeing about Mr. Leo's broth, if that wild cat will let me; and perhaps you would like to get up, sir, because it's past nine o'clock."

Job's remarks were not exactly of a cheering order to a man who had just passed through such a night; and, what is more, they had the weight of truth. Taking one thing with another, it appeared to me to be an utter impossibility that we should escape from this place where we were. Supposing that Leo recovered, and supposing that *She* would let us go, which was exceedingly doubtful, and that she did not "blast" us in some moment of vexation, and that we were not "hot-potted" by the Amahagger, it would be quite impracticable for us to find our way across the network of marshes which, stretching for scores and scores of miles, formed a stronger and more impassable fortification round the various Amahagger "households" than any that could be built or designed by man. No, there was but one thing to do—face it out; and, speaking for my own part, I was so intensely interested in the whole weird story that, notwithstanding the shattered state of my nerves, I asked nothing better, even if my life paid forfeit to my curiosity. What man for whom physiology has charms could forbear to study such a character as that of this wonderful Ayesha when the opportunity presented itself? The very terror of the pursuit added to its fascination; moreover, as I was forced to own to myself even now in the sober light of day, the woman had attractions that I could not forget. Not even the dreadful sight which I had witnessed during the night could drive that folly from my mind; and, alas that I should have to admit it! it has not been driven thence to this hour.

After I had dressed myself I passed into the eating, or rather embalming chamber, and took some food, which as before was brought to me by the girl mutes. When I had finished I went to see poor Leo, who was quite light-headed, and did not even know me. I asked Ustane how she thought he did; but she only shook her head and began to cry a little. Evidently her hopes were small; and then and there I made up my mind that, if it were possible, I would persuade *She* to come to see him. Surely she would cure him if she had the power—at any rate she said so. While I was in the room, Billali entered, and also shook his head.

"He will die at nightfall," he said.

"God forbid, my father," I answered, and turned away with a heavy heart.

"*She-who-must-be-obeyed* commands thy presence, my Baboon," said the old man so soon as we passed the curtain; "but, oh, my dear son, be more careful. Yesterday I made sure in my heart that *She* would blast thee when thou didst not crawl upon thy stomach before her. She will sit in the great hall presently to do justice upon those who would have smitten thee and the Lion. Come, my son; come swiftly."

I turned, and followed him down the passage, and when we reached the central cave I saw that many Amahagger, some robed, and some clad only in the sweet simplicity of a leopard skin, were hurrying along it. We mingled with the throng, and walked up the enormous and, indeed, almost interminable cavern. All its walls were most elaborately sculptured, and every twenty paces or so passages opened out of it at right angles, leading, Billali told me, to tombs, hollowed in the rock by "the people who were before." Nobody visited those tombs now, he said; and I admit that my heart rejoiced when I thought of the opportunities of antiquarian research which lay open to me.

At last we came to the head of the cave, where there was a rock daïs almost exactly similar to the one on which we had been so furiously attacked, a fact that proved to me that these daïs must have been used as altars, probably for the celebration of religious ceremonies, and more especially of rites connected with the interment of the dead. On either side of this platform were passages leading, Billali informed me, to other caves full of dead bodies. "Indeed," he added, "the whole mountain is peopled with dead, and nearly all of them perfect."

In front of the daïs were gathered a great number of people of both sexes, who stood staring about in their peculiar gloomy fashion, which would have reduced Mark Tapley himself to misery within five minutes. On the platform was a rude chair of black wood inlaid with ivory, having a seat made of grass fibre, and a footstool formed of a wooden slab attached to the framework of the chair.

Suddenly there rose a cry of "Hiya! Hiya!" ("She! She!"), whereupon the entire crowd of spectators instantly precipitated themselves to the ground, and lay still as though they were individually and collectively stricken dead, leaving me standing like some solitary survivor of a massacre. At that moment, too, a string of guards began to defile from a passage to the left, and ranged themselves on either side of the daïs. Then came about a score of male mutes, followed by as many women mutes bearing lamps, and lastly a tall white figure, swathed from head to foot, in whom I recognised She herself. She mounted the platform, and, sitting down upon the chair, spoke to me in *Greek*, I suppose because she did not wish those present to understand what she said.

"Come hither, O Holly," she said, "and sit thou at my feet, and see me do justice on those who would have slain thee. Forgive me if my Greek doth halt like a lame man; it is so long since I have heard the sound of it that my tongue is stiff, and will not bend rightly to the words."

I bowed, and, mounting the daïs, sat down at her feet.

"How hast thou slept, my Holly?" she asked.

"I slept not well, O Ayesha!" I answered with perfect truth, and with an inward fear that perhaps she knew how I had passed the heart of the night.

"So," she said, with a little laugh; "I, too, have not slept well. Last night I had dreams, and methinks that thou didst call them to me, my Holly."

"Of what didst thou dream, Ayesha?" I asked indifferently.

"I dreamed," she answered quickly, "of one I hate and one I love," and then, as though to turn the conversation, she addressed the captain of her guard in Arabic, saying: "Let the men be brought before me."

The captain bowed low, for the guard and her attendants did not prostrate themselves, but remained standing, and departed with his underlings down a passage to the right.

Then came a silence. *She* leaned her swathed head upon her hand and appeared to be lost in thought, while the multitude before her continued to grovel upon their stomachs, only twisting their heads round a little so as to have a view of us with one eye. It seemed that their Queen so rarely appeared in public that they were willing to undergo this inconvenience, and even graver risks, to gain the opportunity of looking on her, or rather on her garments, for no living man there except myself had ever seen her face. At last we caught sight of the waving of lights, and heard the tramp of men advancing down the passage. Then in filed the guard, and with them the survivors of our would-be murderers, to the number of twenty or more, on whose countenances a natural expression of sullenness struggled with the terror that evidently filled their savage hearts. They were ranged in front of the daïs, and would have cast themselves upon the floor of the cave like the spectators, but *She* stopped them.

"Nay," she said in her softest voice, "stand; I pray you stand. Perchance the time will soon come when ye shall grow weary of being stretched out," and she laughed melodiously.

I saw a cringe of terror run along the rank of the doomed wretches, and, wicked villains as they were, I felt sorry for them. Some minutes, perhaps two or three, passed before anything fresh occurred, during which *She* appeared from the movement of her head—for, of course, we could not see her eyes—to slowly and carefully examine each delinquent. At last she spoke, addressing herself to me in a quiet and deliberate tone.

"Dost thou, O my guest, recognise these men?"

"Ay, O Queen, nearly all of them," I said, and I saw them glower at me as I said it.

"Then tell to me, and this great company, the tale whereof I have heard."

Thus adjured, in as few words as I could I related the history of the cannibal feast, and of the attempted torture of our poor servant. The narrative was received in perfect silence, both by the accused and by the audience, and also by *She* herself. When I had done, Ayesha called upon Billali by name, and, lifting his head from the ground, but without rising, the old man confirmed my story. No further evidence was taken.

"Ye have heard," said *She* at length, in a cold, clear voice, very different from her usual tones—indeed, it was one of the most remarkable things about this extraordinary creature that her voice had the power of suiting itself in a wonderful manner to the mood of the moment. "What have you to say, ye rebellious children, why vengeance should not be done upon you?"

For some time there was no answer, but at last one of the men, a fine, broad-chested fellow, well on in middle life, with deep-graven features and an eye like a hawk's, spoke. He said that the orders which they had received were not to harm the white men; none were given as to their black servant, so, egged on thereto by a woman who was now dead, they proceeded to try to "hot-pot" him after the ancient and honourable custom of their country, with the view of eating him in due course. As for their attack upon ourselves, it was made in an access of sudden fury, and they deeply regretted it. He ended by humbly praying that mercy might be extended to them; or, at least, that they might be banished into the swamps, to live or die as it might chance; but I saw it written on his face that he had very little hope of mercy.

Then came a pause, and the most intense silence reigned over the dim place, which, faintly illuminated by the flicker of the lamps striking out broad patterns of light and shadow upon the rocky walls, seemed strange as any I ever saw, even in that unholy land. Upon the ground before the daïs were stretched scores of the corpselike forms of the spectators, till at last the long lines of them were lost in the gloomy background. Before this prostrate audience were the knots of evildoers, trying to cover up their natural terrors with a brave appearance of unconcern. On the right and left stood the silent guards, robed in white and armed with great spears and daggers, and men and women mutes watching with hard, curious eyes. Then, seated in her barbaric chair above them all, with myself at her feet, was the veiled white woman, whose loveliness and awesome power seemed to shine visibly about her like a halo, or rather like the glow from some unseen light. Never have I seen her veiled shape look more terrible than it did at that time while she gathered herself up for vengeance.

At last it came.

"Dogs and serpents," *She* began in a low voice that gradually gathered power as she went on, till the place rang with it—"Eaters of human flesh, two things have ye done. First, ye have attacked these strangers, being white men, and would have slain their servant, and for that alone death is your reward. But this is not all. Ye have dared to disobey me. Did I not send my word unto you by Billali, my servant, and the father of your household? Did I not bid you to hospitably entertain these strangers, whom now ye have striven to slay, and whom, had not they been brave and strong beyond the strength of men, ye would cruelly have murdered? Hath it not been taught to you from childhood that the law of *Hiya* is an ever-fixed law, and that he who breaketh it by so much as one jot or tittle shall perish? And is not my lightest word a law? Have not your fathers taught you this, I say, whilst as yet ye were but children? Do ye not know that as well might ye bid these great caves to fall upon you, or the sun to cease its journeying, as to hope to turn me from my courses, or make my word light or heavy, according to your minds? Well do ye know it, ye Wicked Ones. But ye are all evil—evil to the core—the wickedness bubbles up in you like a fountain in the springtime. Were it not for me, generations since ye had ceased to be, for of your own evil way ye had destroyed each other. And now, because ye have done this thing, because ye have striven to put these men, my guests, to death, and yet more because ye have dared to disobey my word, this is the doom whereto I doom you: That ye be taken to the cave of torture,* and given over to the tormentors, and that on the going down of to-morrow's sun those of you who yet remain alive be slain, even as ye would have slain the servant of this my guest."

She ceased, and a faint murmur of horror ran round the cave. As for the victims, as soon as they knew the full hideousness of their doom their stoicism forsook them, and they flung themselves down upon the ground and wept, imploring for mercy in a way that was dreadful to behold. I, too, turned to Ayesha, and begged her to spare them, or at least to mete out their fate in some less awful way. But she proved hard as adamant.

"My Holly," she said, again speaking in Greek which, to tell the truth, although I have always been considered a better scholar of that language than most men, I found it rather difficult to follow, chiefly because of the change in the fall of the accent.[†] "My Holly, it cannot be.

---

*"The cave of torture."—I afterwards saw this dreadful place, also a legacy from the pre-historic people who lived in Kôr. The only objects in the cave itself were slabs of rock arranged in various positions to facilitate the operations of the torturers. Many of these slabs, which were of a porous stone, were stained quite dark with the blood of ancient victims that had soaked into them. Also in the centre of the room was a place for a furnace, with a cavity wherein to heat the historic pot. But the most dreadful thing about the cave was that over each slab was a sculptured illustration of the appropriate torment being applied. These sculptures were so awful that I will not harrow the reader by attempting a description of them.—L. H. H.

[†]Ayesha, of course, talked with the accent of her contemporaries, whereas we have only tradition and the modern tongue to guide us as to the exact pronunciation.—L. H. H.

Ayesha gives judgment.

Were I to show mercy to those wolves, your lives would not be safe among this people for a day. Thou knowest them not. They are tigers to lap blood, and even now they hunger for your lives. How thinkest thou that I rule this people? I have but a regiment of guards to do my bidding, therefore it is not by force. It is by terror. My empire is of the imagination. Once in a lifetime mayhap I do as I have done but now, and slay a score by torture. Believe not that I would be cruel, or take vengeance on anything so low. What can it profit me to be avenged on such as these? Those who live long, my Holly, have no passions, save where they have interests. Though I may seem to slay in wrath, or because my mood is crossed, it is not so. Thou hast seen how in the heavens the little clouds blow this way and that without a cause, yet behind them is the great wind sweeping on its path whither it listeth. So is it with me, O Holly. My moods and changes are the little clouds, and fitfully these seem to turn; but behind them the great wind of my purpose blows ever. Nay, the men must die; and die as I have said." Then, suddenly turning to the captain of the guard, she added:

"As my word is, so be it!"

XVI

THE TOMBS OF KÔR

After the prisoners had been removed Ayesha waved her hand, and the spectators, turning round, began to crawl away down the cave like a scattered flock of sheep. When they were at some distance from the daïs, however, they rose and walked, leaving their Queen and myself alone, with the exception of the mutes and a few guards, for the most of these had departed with the doomed men. Thinking this a good opportunity, I asked *She* to come to visit Leo, telling her of his serious condition; but she would not, saying that he certainly would not die before the evening, as people never died of that fever except at night-fall or the dawn. Also she said it would be better that the sickness should spend its course as much as possible before she cured it. Accordingly, I was rising to leave, when she bade me follow her, as she would talk with me, and show me the wonders of the caves.

I was too much involved in the web of her fascinations to say her no, even had I wished it, so I bowed in assent; whereon she rose from her chair, and, making some signs to the mutes, descended from the daïs. As she came four of the girls took lamps, and ranged themselves two in front of and two behind us, but the others went away, as also did the guards.

"Now," she said, "wouldst thou see some of the wonders of this place, O Holly? Look upon this great cave. Sawest thou ever its like? Yet was it, and many others, hollowed out by the hands of the dead race that once lived here in the city on the plain. A great and a wonderful people they must have been, those men of Kôr, but, like the Egyptians they thought more of the dead than of the living. How many men, thinkest thou, working for how many years, did it need to the hewing of this cave and all its endless galleries?"

"Tens of thousands," I answered.

"So, O Holly. This people was an old people before the Egyptians were. A little can I read of their inscriptions, having found the key to them—and, see thou here, this was one of the last of the caves that they fashioned," and, turning to the rock beside her, she motioned the mutes to hold up the lamps. Carven over the daïs was the figure of an old man seated in a chair, with an ivory rod in his hand, and it struck me that his features were exceedingly similar to those of the man whose embalmment was represented in the chamber where we took our meals. Beneath the chair, that, by the way, was shaped exactly like the one in which Ayesha had sat to give judgment, was a short inscription in the extraordinary characters whereof I have already spoken, but which I do not remember sufficiently to reproduce. It looked more like Chinese writing than any other that I am acquainted with. This inscription, with some difficulty and hesitation, Ayesha proceeded to read aloud and to translate. It ran as follows:—

"In the year four thousand two hundred and fifty-nine from the founding of the City of imperial Kôr was this cave (or burial place) completed by Tisno, King of Kôr, the people thereof and their slaves having laboured thereat for three generations, to be a tomb for their citizens of rank who shall come after. May the blessing of the heaven above the heaven rest upon their work, and make the sleep of Tisno, the mighty monarch, the likeness of whose features is graven above, a sound and happy sleep till the day of awakening,* and also the sleep of his servants, and of those of his race who, rising up after him, shall yet lay their heads as low."

*This phrase is remarkable, as seeming to indicate a belief in a future state.—EDITOR.

"Thou seest, O Holly," she said, "this people founded the city, of which the ruins yet cumber the plain yonder, four thousand years before this cave was finished. Yet, when first mine eyes beheld it two thousand years ago, it was even as it is now. Judge, therefore, how old must that city have been! And now, follow thou me, and I will show thee after what fashion this great people fell when the time was come for it to fall." Then she led the way to the centre of the cave, stopping at a spot where a round rock had been let into a kind of large manhole in the flooring, accurately filling it just as the iron plates fill the holes in the London pavements down which the coals are thrown. "Thou seest," she said. "Tell me, what is it?"

"Nay, I know not," I answered; whereon she crossed to the left-hand side of the cave (looking towards the entrance) and signed to the mutes to hold up the lamps. On the wall was something painted with a red pigment in similar characters to those hewn beneath the sculpture of Tisno, King of Kôr. This long inscription Ayesha translated to me, the pigment still being quite fresh enough to show the form of the letters. It ran as follows:—

"I, Junis, a priest of the Great Temple of Kôr, write this upon the rock of the burying-place in the year four thousand eight hundred and three from the founding of Kôr. Kôr is fallen! No more shall the mighty feast in her halls, no more shall she rule the world, and her navies go out to commerce with the world. Kôr is fallen! and her mighty works and all the cities of Kôr, and all the harbours that she built and the canals that she made, are for the wolf and the owl and the wild swan, and the barbarian who comes after. Twenty and five moons ago did a cloud settle upon Kôr, and the hundred cities of Kôr, and out of the cloud came a pestilence that slew her people, old and young, one with another, and spared not. One with another they turned black and died—the young and the old, the rich and the poor, the man and the woman, the prince and the slave. The pestilence slew and slew, and ceased not by day or by night, and those who escaped from the pestilence were slain of the famine. No longer could the bodies of the children of Kôr be preserved according to the ancient rites, because of the number of the dead, therefore were they hurled into the great pit beneath this cave, through the hole in the floor of the cave. Then, at last, a remnant of this the great people, the

*light of the whole world, went down to the coast and took ship and sailed
northwards; and now am I, the Priest Junis, who write, the last man left
alive of this great city of men, but whether there be any yet left in the other
cities I know not. This do I write in misery of heart before I die, because
Kôr the Imperial is no more, and because there are none to worship in her
temple, and all her palaces are empty, and her princes and her captains
and her traders and her fair women have passed off the face of the earth
for ever."*

I sighed in astonishment—the utter desolation depicted in that
rude scrawl was overpowering. It was terrible to think of this solitary
survivor of a mighty people recording its fate before he too went down
into darkness. What must the old man have felt as, in ghastly terrifying
solitude, by the light of one lamp feebly illumining a little space of
gloom, in a few brief lines he daubed the history of his nation's death
upon the cavern wall? What a subject for the moralist, or the painter, or
indeed for any one who can reflect!

"Dost thou not think, O Holly," said Ayesha, laying her hand upon
my shoulder, "that those men who sailed north may have been the fathers of the first Egyptians?"

"Nay, I know not," I answered; "it seems that the world is very old."

"Old? Yes, it is old indeed. Time after time have nations, ay, and rich
and strong nations, learned in the arts, been, and passed away to be forgotten, so that no memory of them remains. This is but one of several;
for Time eats up the works of man, unless, indeed, he digs in caves like
the people of Kôr, and then mayhap the sea swallows them, or the
earthquake shakes them in. Who knows what hath been on the earth,
or what shall be? There is no new thing under the sun, as the wise Hebrew wrote long ago. Yet these people were not utterly destroyed, as I
think. Some few remained in the other cities, for their cities were
many. But the barbarians from the south, or perchance my people, the
Arabs, came down upon them, and took their women to wife, and the
race of the Amahagger that is now is a bastard brood of the mighty
sons of Kôr, and behold it dwelleth in the tombs with its fathers'
bones.* But I know not: who can know? My arts cannot pierce so far

into the blackness of Time's night. They were a great people. They conquered till none were left to conquer, and then they dwelt at ease within their rocky mountain walls, with their manservants and their maidservants, their minstrels, their sculptors, and their concubines, and traded and quarrelled, and ate and hunted and slept and made merry till their time came. But come, I will show thee that great pit beneath the cavern whereof the writing speaks. Never shall thine eyes witness such another sight."

Accordingly I followed her to a side passage opening out of the main cave, then down a great number of steps, and along an underground shaft which cannot have been less than sixty feet beneath the surface of the rock, and was ventilated by curious borings that ran upward, I do not know where. Suddenly the passage ended, and Ayesha halted, bidding the mutes hold up the lamps, and, as she had prophesied, I saw a scene such as I am not likely to behold again. We were standing in an enormous pit, or rather on the brink of it, for it went down deeper—I do not know how much—than the level on which we stood, and was edged in with a low wall of rock. So far as I could judge, this pit was about the size of the space beneath the dome of St. Paul's in London, and when the lamps were held up I saw that it was nothing but one vast charnel-house, being literally full of thousands of human skeletons, which lay piled up in an enormous gleaming pyramid, formed by the slipping down of the bodies at the apex as others were dropped in from above. Anything more appalling than this jumbled mass of the remains of a departed race I cannot imagine, and what made it even more dreadful was that in this dry air a considerable number of the bodies had become desiccated with the skin still on them, and now, fixed in every conceivable position, stared at us out of the mountain of white bones, grotesquely horrible caricatures of humanity. In my astonishment I uttered an ejaculation, and the echoes of

---

*The name of the tribe, "Ama-hagger," would seem to indicate a curious mingling of races such as might easily have occurred in the neighbourhood of the Zambesi. The prefix "Ama" is common to the Zulu and kindred races, and signifies "people," while "hagger" is an Arabic word meaning a stone.—EDITOR.

my voice, ringing in that vaulted space, disturbed a skull which had been accurately balanced for many thousands of years near the apex of the pile. Down it came with a run, bounding along merrily towards us, and of course bringing an avalanche of other bones after it, till at last the whole pit rattled with their movement, even as though the skeletons were rising up to greet us.

"Come," I said, "let us go hence. These are the bodies of those who died of the great sickness—is it not so?" I added, as we turned away.

"Yea. The children of Kôr ever embalmed their dead, as did the Egyptians, but their art was greater than the art of the Egyptians, for, whereas the Egyptians disembowelled and drew the brain, the people of Kôr injected fluid into the veins, and thus reached every part. But stay, thou shalt see," and she halted at haphazard by one of the little doorways opening out of the passage along which we were walking, and motioned to the mutes to light us in. We entered a small chamber similar to that in which I had slept at our first stopping-place, only instead of one there were two stone benches or beds in it. On the benches lay figures covered with yellow linen,* on which a fine and impalpable dust had gathered in the course of ages, but to nothing like the extent that might have been anticipated, for in these deep-hewn caves there is no material to turn to dust. About the bodies on the stone shelves and floor of the tomb were many painted vases, but I saw very few ornaments or weapons in any of the vaults.

"Withdraw the cloths, O Holly," said Ayesha, but when I put out my hand to obey I drew it back again. It seemed a sacrilege, and, to speak the truth, I was awed by the dread solemnity of the place, and of the presences before us. Then, with a laugh at my fears, she removed them herself, only to discover other and yet finer wrappings lying over the forms upon the stone bench. These also she withdrew, and for the first time for thousands upon thousands of years did living eyes look upon the face of that chilly dead. It was a woman; she might have been thirty-five years of age, or perhaps a little less, and certainly had been beautiful. Even now her calm clear-cut features, marked out with deli-

---

*All the linen that the Amahagger wore was taken from the tombs, which accounted for its yellow hue. If it was well washed, however, and properly rebleached, it acquired its former snowy whiteness, and was the softest and best linen I ever saw.—L. H. H.

cate eyebrows and long eyelashes which threw upon the ivory face little lines of shadow in the lamplight, were wonderfully beautiful. There, robed in white, down which her blue-black hair was streaming, she slept her last long sleep, and on her arm, its face pressed against her breast, there lay a little babe. So sweet was the sight, although so awful, that—I confess it without shame—I could scarcely withhold my tears. It took me back across the dim gulf of the ages to some happy home in dead Imperial Kôr, where this winsome lady girt about with beauty had lived and died, and dying had taken her last-born with her to the tomb. There they slept before us, mother and child, the white memories of a forgotten human history speaking more eloquently to the heart than could any written record of their lives. Reverently I replaced the graveclothes, and, with a sigh that in the purpose of the Everlasting flowers so fair should have bloomed only to be gathered to the grave, I turned to the body on the opposite shelf, and gently unveiled it. It was that of a man in advanced life, with a long grizzled beard, also robed in white, and probably the husband of the lady, who, after surviving her many years, came at the last to sleep once more for good and all beside her.

We left the place and entered others. It would be too long to describe the many things I saw in them. Each one had its occupants—for evidently the five hundred and odd years that had elapsed between the completion of the cave and the destruction of the race had sufficed to fill these catacombs, numberless as they were—and all appeared to have been undisturbed since the day when they were placed there. I could fill a book with the description of them, but to do so would only be to repeat what I have said, with variations.

Nearly all the bodies, so masterly was the art with which they had been treated, were as perfect as on the day of death thousands of years before. Nothing came to injure them in the deep silence of the living rock: they were beyond the reach of heat and cold and damp, and the aromatic drugs with which they had been saturated were, it seems, practically everlasting in their effect. Here and there, however, we saw an exception, and in these cases, although the flesh looked sound enough externally, if touched it fell in, and revealed the fact that the figure was but a pile of dust. This arose, Ayesha told me, from these particular bodies, either owing to haste in the burial or other causes, having been soaked in the preservative,* instead of its being injected into the substance of the flesh.

About the last tomb we visited I must, however, say a word, for its contents spoke even more eloquently to the human sympathies than those of the first. It had but two occupants, and they lay together on a single shelf. I withdrew the grave-cloths, and there, clasped heart to heart, were a young man and a blooming girl. Her head rested on his arm, and his lips were pressed against her brow. I opened the man's linen robe, and found over his heart a dagger-wound, while beneath the girl's fair breast was a like cruel stab, through which her life had ebbed away. On the rock above was an inscription in three words. Ayesha translated it. It read, *"Wedded in Death."*

What was the life-history of these two, who, of a truth, were beautiful in their lives, and in their death were not divided?

I closed my eyes, and imagination, taking up the thread of thought, shot its swift shuttle back across the ages, weaving a picture on their blackness so real and vivid in its detail that I could almost for a moment think that I had triumphed over Time, and that my vision had pierced the mystery of the Past.

I seemed to see this fair girl's form—the yellow hair streaming down her, glittering against her garments snowy white, and the bosom that was whiter than her robes, even dimming with its lustre the ornaments of burnished gold. I seemed to see the great cave filled with warriors, bearded and clad in mail, and, on the lighted daïs whence Ayesha had given judgment, a man standing, robed, and surrounded by the

---

*Ayesha afterwards showed me the tree from the leaves of which this ancient preservative was manufactured. It is a low bush-like tree, that to this day grows in wonderful plenty upon the sides of the mountains, or rather upon the slopes leading up to its rocky walls. The leaves are long and narrow, a vivid green in colour, but turning a bright red in the autumn, and not unlike those of a laurel in general appearance. They have little smell when green, but if boiled the aromatic odour from them is so strong that one can hardly bear it. The best mixture, however, was made from the roots, and among the people of Kôr there was a law, alluded to on some of the inscriptions which Ayesha showed me, to the effect that on pain of heavy penalties no one under a certain rank was to be embalmed with the drugs prepared from these roots. The object and effect of this law was, of course, to preserve the trees from extermination. The sale of the leaves and roots was a Government monopoly, and from it the Kings of Kôr derived a large proportion of their private revenue.—L. H. H.

symbols of his priestly office. Now up the cave there came one clad in purple, and before and behind him marched minstrels and fair maidens, chanting a wedding song. White stood the maid against the altar, fairer than the fairest there—purer than a lily, and more cold than the dew that glistens in its heart. But as this man drew near she shuddered. Then out of the press and throng there sprang a dark-haired youth, and put his arm about this long-forgotten girl, and kissed her pale face, in which the blood shot up like lights of the red dawn across the silent sky. Next there was turmoil and uproar, and a flashing of swords, and they tore the youth from her arms, and stabbed him, but with a cry she snatched the dagger from his belt, and drove it into her snowy breast, home to the heart, and down she fell. Then, with cries and wailing, and every sound of lamentation, the pageant rolled away from the arena of my vision, and once more the Past shut to its book.

Let him who reads forgive the intrusion of a dream into a history of fact. But it came so home to me—I saw it all so clearly in a moment, as it were; moreover, who shall say what proportion of fact, past, present, or to come, may lie in the imagination? What is imagination? Perhaps it is a shadow of the intangible truth, perhaps it is the soul's thought!

In an instant the picture had passed through my brain, and *She* was addressing me.

"Behold the lot of man!" said the veiled Ayesha, as she drew the winding-sheets back over the dead lovers, speaking in a solemn, thrilling voice, which accorded well with the dream that I had dreamed: "to the tomb, and to the forgetfulness that hides the tomb, must we all come at last! Ay, even I who live so long. Even for me, O Holly, thousands upon thousands of years hence; thousands of years after thou hast gone through the gate and been lost in the mists, a day will dawn whereon I shall die, and be even as thou art and these are. And then what will it avail that I have lived a little longer, holding off death by the knowledge I have wrung from Nature, since at last I too must die? What is a span of ten thousand years, or ten times ten thousand years, in the history of time? It is as naught—it is as the mists that roll up in the sunlight; it fleeth away like an hour of sleep or the melting winter snows. Behold the lot of man! Certainly it shall overtake us, and we shall sleep. Certainly, too, we shall awake and live again, and again shall sleep, and so on and on, through periods, spaces, and times, from æon unto æon, till the world is dead, and the worlds beyond the world are dead, and naught liveth save the Spirit that is Life. But for us twain and for these dead ones shall the end of ends be Life, or shall it be Death? As yet Death is but Life's Night, but out of the Night is the Morrow born anew, and doth again beget the Night. Only, when Day and Night, and Life and Death, are ended and swallowed up in that from which they came, what shall be our fate, O Holly? Who can see so far? Not even I!"

Then she added, with a sudden change of tone and manner—

"Hast thou seen enough, my stranger guest, or shall I show thee more of the wonders of these tombs that are my palace halls? If thou wilt, I can lead thee to where Tisno, the mightiest and most valorous King of Kôr, in whose day these caves were ended, lies in a pomp that seems to mock at nothingness, and bid the empty shadows of the past do homage to his sculptured vanity!"

"I have seen enough, O Queen," I answered, "for my heart is overwhelmed by the power of this present death. Mortality is weak and easily oppressed in the company of that dust which waits upon its end. Take me hence, O Ayesha!"

XVII

The Balance Turns

Following the lamps of the deaf mutes, which, held out from their bodies as a bearer holds water in a vessel, had the appearance of floating along by themselves, we came presently to a stair which led us to *She's* anteroom, the same that Billali had travelled upon all fours on the previous day. Here I wished to bid the Queen adieu, but she would not suffer it.

"Nay," she said, "enter with me, O Holly, for of a truth thy talk pleases me. Think, Holly; for two thousand years I have found none to speak with save slaves and my own soul, and though of all this thinking hath much wisdom come, and many secrets been made plain, yet I am weary of my thoughts, and have come to loathe mine own society, for surely the food that memory gives to eat is bitter to the taste, and it is only with the teeth of hope that we can bear to chew it. Now, though thy brain is green and tender, as becometh a man so young, yet is it that of one who thinks. In truth thou dost bring back to my mind certain of those old philosophers with whom in days bygone I have disputed at Athens, and at Becca in Arabia, for thou hast the same crabbed air and dusty look, as though thou hadst passed thy days in reading ill-writ

Greek, and been stained dark with the grime of manuscripts. So draw the curtain, and sit here by my side, and we will eat fruit, and talk of pleasant things. See, I will again unveil to thee. Thou hast brought it on thyself, O Holly; I have warned thee straightly—and thou shalt call me beautiful as even those old philosophers were wont to do. Fie upon them, forgetting their philosophy!"

And without more ado she stood up and shook the white wrappings from her, and came forth shining and splendid like some glittering snake when it has cast its slough; ay, and fixed her wonderful eyes upon me—more deadly than any Basilisk's—and pierced me through and through with their beauty, and sent her light laugh ringing down the air like chimes of silver bells.

A new mood was on her, and the colour of her fathomless mind had changed beneath it. It was no longer torture-torn and hateful, as I had seen it when she was cursing her dead rival by the leaping flames, no longer icily terrible as in the judgment-hall; no longer rich, and sombre, and splendid, like to a Tyrian cloth, as in the dwellings of the dead. No, her mood now was that of Aphrodité triumphing. Life—radiant, ecstatic, wonderful—seemed to flow from her and around her. Softly she laughed and sighed, and swift her glances flew. She shook her heavy tresses, and their perfume filled the place; she struck her little sandalled foot upon the floor, and hummed a snatch of some old Greek epithalamium. All the majesty was gone, or it did but lurk and flicker faintly through her laughing eyes, like lightning seen through sunlight. She had cast off the terror of the leaping flame, the cold power of judgment that even now was being done, and the wise sadness of the tombs—cast them off and put them behind her, like the white shroud she wore, and now she stood out an incarnation of lovely tempting womanhood, made more perfect—and in a way more spiritual—than ever woman was before her.

"So, my Holly, sit there where thou canst see me. It is by thine own wish, remember—again I say, blame me not if thou dost wear away thy little span with such a sick pain at the heart that thou wouldst fain have died before ever thy curious eyes were set upon me. There, sit so, and tell me, for in truth now I desire praises—tell me, am I not beautiful? Nay, speak not so hastily; consider well the point; take me feature by feature, forgetting not my form, and my hands and feet, and my hair, and the whiteness of my skin, and then say truly, hast thou ever known a woman who in aught, ay, in one little portion of her beauty, in the curve of an eyelash even, or the modelling of a shell-like ear, is justified to hold a lamp before my loveliness? Now, my waist! Perchance thou thinkest it too large, but of a truth it is not so; it is this golden snake that is too large, and doth not bind it as it should. It is a wise snake, and knoweth that it is ill to tie in the waist. But see, give me thy hands—so—now press them round me: There, with but a little force, thy fingers almost touch, O Holly!"

I could bear it no longer. I am but a man, and she was more than a woman. Heaven knows what she was—I do not! But then and there I fell upon my knees before her, and told her in a sad mixture of languages—for such moments confuse the thoughts—that I worshipped her as never woman was worshipped, and that I would give my immortal soul to marry her, which at that time I certainly would have done, and so, indeed, would any other man, or all the race of men rolled into one. For a moment she looked a little surprised; then she began to laugh, and to clap her hands in glee.

"Oh, so soon, my Holly!" she said. "I wondered how many minutes it would need to bring thee to thy knees. I have not seen a man kneel before me for so many ages, and, believe me, to a woman's heart the sight is sweet—ay, wisdom and length of days take not from that dear pleasure which is our sex's only right.

"What wouldst thou?—what wouldst thou? Thou dost not know what thou doest. Have I not told thee that I am not for thee? I love but one, and thou art not the man. Ah Holly, for all thy wisdom—and in a way thou art wise—thou art but a fool running after folly. Thou wouldst look into mine eyes—thou wouldst kiss me! Well, if it pleaseth thee, *look!*" and she bent herself towards me, and fixed her dark and thrilling orbs upon my own; "ay, and *kiss* too, if thou wilt, for, thanks be given to the scheme of things, kisses leave no scars, except upon the heart. But if thou dost kiss, I tell thee of a surety thou wilt eat out thy breast with love of me, and die!" and she bent yet further towards me till her soft hair brushed my brow, and her fragrant breath played upon my face, and made me faint and weak. Then of a sudden, even as I stretched out my arms to clasp, she straightened herself, and a quick change passed over her. Reaching out her hand, she held it over my head, and it seemed to me that something flowed from it which chilled me back to common sense, and a knowledge of propriety and the domestic virtues.

"Enough of this wanton play," she said with a touch of sternness. "Listen, Holly. Thou art a good and honest man, and I fain would spare thee; but, oh! it is so hard for woman to be merciful. I have said I am not for thee, therefore let thy thoughts pass by me like an idle wind, and the dust of thy imaginings sink again into the depths—well, of despair, if thou wilt. Thou dost not know me, Holly. Hadst thou seen me but ten hours past, when my passion seized me, thou hadst shrunk from me in fear and trembling. I am of many moods, and, like the water in that vessel, I reflect many things; but they pass, my Holly; they pass, and are forgotten. Only the water is the water still, and I still am I, and that which maketh the water maketh it, and that which maketh me maketh me, nor can my quality be altered. Therefore, pay no heed to what I seem, seeing that thou canst not know what I am. If thou troublest me again I will veil myself, and thou shalt behold my face no more."

I rose, and sank on the cushioned couch beside her, yet quivering with emotion, though for a moment my mad passion had left me, as the leaves of a tree quiver still, although the gust be gone that stirred them. I did not dare to tell her that I *had* seen her in that deep and hellish mood, muttering incantations to the fire in the tomb.

"So," she went on, "eat of this fruit; believe me, it is the only true food for man. Now tell me of the philosophy of that Hebrew Messiah, who came after me, and who, thou sayest, to-day doth rule Rome, and Greece, and Egypt, and the barbarians beyond. It must have been a strange philosophy that He taught, for in my time the peoples would have naught of our philosophies. Revel and lust and drink, blood and cold steel, and the shock of men gathered in the battle—these were the canons of their creeds."

I had recovered myself a little by now, and, feeling bitterly ashamed of the weakness into which I had been betrayed, I did my best to expound to her the doctrines of Christianity, to which, however, with the single exception of our theory of Heaven and Hell, I found that she paid but faint attention, her interest being all directed towards the Man who taught them. Also I told her that among her own people, the Arabs, another prophet, one Mohammed, had arisen, preaching a new faith, to which many millions of mankind now adhered.

"Ah!" she said; "I understand—*two* new religions! I have known so many, and doubtless there have been others since I knew aught beyond these caves of Kôr. Mankind asks ever of the skies to vision out what lies behind them. It is terror for the end, and but a subtler form of selfishness—this it is that breeds religions. Mark, my Holly, each religion claims the future for its followers; or, at the least, the good thereof. The evil is for those benighted ones who will have none of it; seeing that light which the true believers worship, as the fishes see the stars, but dimly. The religions come and the religions pass, and civilisations come and pass, and naught endures but the world and human nature. Ah! if man would but see that hope is from within, and not from without—that he himself must work out his own salvation! He is there, and within him is the breath of life and a knowledge of good and evil, as good and evil are to him. Thereon let him build and stand erect, and not cast himself before the image of some unknown God, modelled like his poor self, but with a larger brain to think the evil thing, and a longer arm to do it."

I thought to myself—which shows how old such reasoning is, being, indeed, one of the recurring quantities of theological discussion—that her argument sounded very like some that I have heard in the nineteenth century, and in other places than the caves of Kôr—with which, by the way, I totally disagree—but I did not care to try to discuss the question with her. To begin with, my mind was too weary with all the emotions through which I had passed, and, in the second place, I knew that I should get the worst of it. It is weary work enough to argue with an ordinary materialist, who hurls statistics and whole strata of geological facts at your head, whilst you can only buffet him with deductions and instincts and the snowflakes of faith, that are, alas! so apt to melt in the hot embers of our troubles. How little chance, then, should I have against one whose brain was supernaturally sharpened, and who had two thousand years of experience, besides all manner of knowledge of the secrets of Nature at her command! Feeling that she would be more likely to convert me than I should to convert her, I thought it best to leave the matter alone, and so sat silent. Many a time since then have I regretted bitterly that I did so, for thereby I lost the only opportunity I can remember of ascertaining what Ayesha *really* believed, and what was her "philosophy."

"Well, my Holly," she continued, "and so those people of mine have also found a prophet—a false prophet thou sayest, for he is not thine own, and, indeed, I doubt it not. Yet in my day it was otherwise, for then we Arabs had many gods. Allât there was, and Saba, the Host of Heaven; Al Uzza, and Manah the stony one, for whom the blood of victims flowed; and Wadd and Sawâ, and Yaghûth the Lion of the dwellers in Yaman; and Yäûk, the Horse of Morad; and Nasr the Eagle of Hamyar; ay, and many more. Oh, the folly of it all, the shame and the pitiful folly! Yet when I rose in wisdom and spoke thereof, surely they would have slain me in the name of their outraged gods. Well, so it hath ever been;—but, my Holly, art thou weary of me already, that thou dost sit so silent? Or dost thou fear lest I should teach thee my philosophy?—for know I have a philosophy! What would a teacher be without her own philosophy? And if thou dost vex me overmuch, beware! for I will have thee learn it, and thou shalt be my disciple, and we twain will found a faith that shall swallow up all others. Inconstant man! But half an hour since thou wast upon thy knees—the posture does not become thee, Holly—swearing that thou didst love me. What shall we do?—Nay, I have it! I will come and see this youth, the Lion, as the old man Billali calls him, who came with thee, and who is so sick. The fever must have run its course by now, and if he is about to die I will recover him. Fear not, my Holly; I shall use no magic. Have I not told thee that there is no such thing as magic, though there is such a thing as mastering and commanding the forces which are in Nature? Go now, and presently, when I have made the drug ready, I will follow thee."*

*Ayesha was a great chemist; indeed, chemistry appears to have been her only amusement and occupation. One of the caves was fitted up as a laboratory, and, although her appliances were necessarily rude, the results that she attained, as will become clear in the course of this narrative, were sufficiently surprising.—L. H. H.

Accordingly I went, only to find Job and Ustane in an excess of grief, declaring that Leo was in the throes of death, and that they had been searching for me everywhere. I rushed to the couch, and glanced at him: clearly he was dying. He was senseless, and breathing heavily, but his lips were quivering, and every now and again a little shudder ran down his frame. I knew enough of doctoring to see that in another hour he would be beyond the reach of earthly help—perhaps in another five minutes. How I cursed my selfishness and the folly that had kept me lingering by Ayesha's side while my dear boy lay dying! Alas and alas! how easily the best of us are lighted down to evil by the gleam of a woman's eyes! What a wicked wretch was I! Actually, for the last half-hour I had scarcely thought of Leo—and this, be it remembered, of the man who for twenty years had been my dearest companion, and the chief interest of my existence. And now, perhaps, it was too late!

I wrung my hands, and glanced round. Ustane was sitting by the couch, and in her eyes burnt the dull light of despair. Job was blubbering—I am sorry I cannot name his distress by any more delicate word—audibly in the corner. Seeing my eye fixed upon him, he went outside to give way to his grief in the passage. Obviously the only hope lay in Ayesha. She, and she alone, could save him—unless, indeed, she was an impostor, which I did not believe. I would go and implore her to come. As I started on this errand, however, Job came flying into the room, his hair literally standing on end with terror.

"Oh, God help us, sir!" he ejaculated in a frightened whisper, "here's a corpse a-coming sliding down the passage!"

For a moment I was puzzled, but presently, of course, it struck me that he must have seen Ayesha, wrapped in her grave-like garment, and been deceived by the extraordinary undulating smoothness of her walk into a belief that she was a white ghost gliding towards him. Indeed, at that very moment the question was settled, for Ayesha herself appeared in the apartment, or rather cave. Job turned, and saw her sheeted form, then, with a convulsive howl of "Here it comes!" he sprang into a corner, and hid his head against the wall; while Ustane, guessing whose the dread presence must be, prostrated herself upon her face.

"Thou comest in a good time, Ayesha," I said, "for my boy lies at the point of death."

"So," she said softly; "if he be not dead, it is no matter, for I can bring him back to life, my Holly. Is that man there thy servant, and is that the fashion wherewith the servants greet strangers in thy country?"

"He is frightened of thy garb—it has a death-like air," I answered. She laughed.

"And the girl? Ah, I see now. It is she of whom thou didst speak to me. Well, bid them both to leave us, and we will see to this sick Lion of thine. I love not that underlings should perceive my wisdom."

Thereon I told Ustane in Arabic and Job in English both to leave the room; an order which the latter obeyed readily enough, and was glad to obey, for he could not in any way subdue his fear. But it was otherwise with Ustane.

"What does *She* want?" she whispered, divided between her dread of the terrible Queen and her anxiety to remain near Leo. "It is surely the right of a wife to be with her husband when he dies. Nay, I will not go, my lord the Baboon."

"Why doth not that woman depart, my Holly?" asked Ayesha from the other end of the cave, where she was engaged in examining some of the sculptures on the wall.

"She is not willing to leave Leo," I answered, not knowing what to say. Ayesha wheeled round, and, pointing at the girl Ustane, said one word, and one only, but it was quite enough, for the tone in which she uttered it meant volumes.

"Go!"

Then Ustane crept past her on her hands and knees, and went.

"Thou seest, my Holly," said Ayesha, with a little laugh, "it was needful that I should give these people a lesson in obedience. That girl went nigh to disobeying me, but then, she did not learn this noon how I treat the disobedient. Well, she has gone; now let me see the youth," and she glided towards the couch on which Leo lay, with his face in the shadow and turned towards the wall.

"He has a noble shape," she said, as she bent over him to look upon his face.

The next second her tall and willowy form was staggering back across the room, as though she had been shot or stabbed, staggering back till at last she struck the cavern wall, and then there burst from her lips the most awful and unearthly scream that it has ever been my lot to hear.

"What is it, Ayesha?" I cried. "Is he dead?"

She turned, and sprang towards me like a tigress.

"Thou dog!" she said, in her terrible whisper, which sounded like the hiss of a snake, "why didst thou hide this from me?" And she stretched out her arm, so that I thought she was about to slay me.

"What?" I ejaculated, in the most lively terror; "what?"

"Ah!" she said, "perchance thou didst not know. Learn, my Holly, learn: there—there lies my lost Kallikrates. Kallikrates, who has come back to me at last, as I knew he must, as I knew he must!" and she began to sob and laugh, and, indeed, to conduct herself like any other lady who is overcome, murmuring, "Kallikrates, Kallikrates!"

"Nonsense," I thought to myself, but I did not dare to say it; and, indeed, at the moment I was thinking of Leo's life, having forgotten everything else in that terrible anxiety. What I feared now was that he might die while Ayesha was unnerved by hysteria.

"Unless thou art able to help him, Ayesha," I suggested humbly, "thy Kallikrates will soon be far beyond thy calling. Surely he dies even now."

"True," she said, with a start. "Oh! why did I not come before? I am shaken—my hand trembles, even mine—and yet it is very easy. Here, thou Holly, take this phial," and she produced a tiny jar of pottery from the folds of her garment, "and pour the liquid in it down his throat. It will cure him if he be not dead. Swift, now! Swift! The man dies!"

I glanced towards him; it was true enough—Leo was in his death-struggle. I saw his poor face turning ashen, and heard the breath begin to rattle in his throat. The phial was stoppered with a little piece of wood. I drew it with my teeth, and a drop of the fluid within flew out upon my tongue. It had a sweet flavour, and for a second caused my head to swim and a mist to gather before my eyes, but happily the effect passed away as quickly as it had arisen.

When I reached Leo he was on the point of expiring—his golden head turned slowly from side to side, and his mouth was slightly open. I called to Ayesha to hold his head, and this she managed to do, although the woman was quivering from head to foot, like an aspen-leaf or a startled horse. Then, forcing the jaws a little further open, I poured the contents of the phial into his mouth. Instantly some vapour arose from it, as happens when one disturbs nitric acid, and this sight did not increase my hopes, already faint enough, of the efficacy of the treatment.

One thing, however, was certain, the death-throes ceased—at first I thought because he had gone beyond them, and crossed the awful river. His face turned to a livid pallor, and his heart-beats, which had been feeble enough before, seemed to die away altogether—only the eyelids still twitched a little. In my doubt I looked up at Ayesha, whose head-wrapping had slipped back in her excitement when she reeled across the room. She was still holding Leo's head, and, with a face as pale as his own, watched his countenance with such an expression of agonised anxiety as I had never seen before. Clearly she did not know if he would live or die. Five minutes passed slowly, and I saw that she was abandoning hope; her lovely oval face seemed to fall in and visibly grow thinner beneath the pressure of a mental agony whose pencil drew black lines about the hollows of her eyes. The coral faded even from her lips, till they were as white as Leo's face, and quivered pitifully. It was shocking to see her: even in my own grief I felt for hers.

"Is it too late?" I gasped.

She hid her face in her hands, and made no answer, and I also turned away. But as I turned I heard a deep-drawn breath, and looking down perceived a line of colour creeping up Leo's face, then another and another, and, wonder of wonders, the man whom we had thought dead rolled over on his side.

"Thou seest," I said in a whisper.

"I see," she answered hoarsely. "He is saved. I thought we were too late; another moment—one little moment more—and he had been gone!" and she burst into an awful flood of tears, sobbing as though her heart would break, and yet looking lovelier than ever as she wept. At last she ceased.

"Forgive me, my Holly—forgive me for my weakness," she said. "Thou seest after all I am a very woman. Think—now think of it! This morning thou didst speak of the place of torment appointed by this new religion of thine. Hell or Hades thou didst call it—a place where the vital essence lives and retains an individual memory, and where all the errors and faults of judgment, and unsatisfied passions, and the unsubstantial terrors of the mind wherewith it hath at any time had to do, come to mock and haunt and gibe and wring the heart for ever and for ever with the vision of its own hopelessness. Thus, even thus, have I lived for full two thousand years—for some six-and-sixty generations, as ye reckon time—in a Hell, as thou callest it—tormented by the memory of a crime, tortured day and night with an unfulfilled desire—without companionship, without comfort, without death, and led on only down my dreary road by the marsh-lights of Hope, which, though they flickered here and there, and now glowed strong, and now were not, yet, as my skill foretold, would one day lead me to my deliverer.

"And then—think of it still, O Holly, for never shalt thou hear such another tale, or see such another scene, nay, not even if I give thee ten thousand years of life—and thou shalt have them in payment if thou wilt—think: at last my deliverer came—he for whom I had watched and waited through the generations—at the appointed time he came to seek me, as I knew that he must come, for my wisdom could not err, though I knew not when or how. Yet see how ignorant I was! See how small my knowledge, and how faint my strength! For hours he lay here sick unto death, and I felt it not—I who had waited for him for two thousand years—I knew it not! And then at last I see him, and behold! my chance is gone but for a hair's breadth even before I win it, for he is in the very jaws of death, whence no power of mine can draw him. And if he die, surely must the Hell be lived through once more—once more I must face the weary centuries, and wait and wait till time in its fulness shall bring my Beloved back to me. And then thou gavest him the medicine, and that five minutes passed before I knew whether he would live or die, and I tell thee that all the sixty generations that are gone were not so long as that five minutes. But they passed at length, and still he showed no sign, and I knew that if the drug worked not then, so far as I have had knowledge, it would not work at all. Then I thought that once more he was dead, and all the tortures of all the years gathered themselves into a single venomed spear, and pierced me through and through, because again I had lost Kallikrates! And then, when all was done, behold! he sighed, behold! he lived, and I was sure that he would live, for none die on whom the drug takes hold. Think of it now, my Holly—think of the wonder of it! He will sleep for twelve hours, and then the sickness will have left him—will have left him to life and me!"

She ceased, and laid her hand upon the golden head, then she bent down and kissed his brow with a chastened abandonment of tenderness that would have been beautiful to behold had not the sight cut me to the heart—for I was jealous.

XVIII

"Go, Woman!"

Then followed a silence of a minute or so, during which, if one might judge from the almost angelic rapture of her face—for she looked angelic sometimes—*She* appeared to be plunged in a happy ecstasy. Suddenly, however, a new thought struck her, and her expression became the very reverse of angelic.

"Almost had I forgotten," she said, "that woman, Ustane. What is she to Kallikrates—his servant, or——" and she paused, and her voice trembled.

I shrugged my shoulders. "I understand that she is wed to him according to the custom of the Amahagger," I answered; "but I know not."

Her face grew dark as a thundercloud. Old as she was, Ayesha had not outlived jealousy.

"Then there is an end," she said; "she must die, even now!"

"For what crime?" I asked, horrified. "She is guilty of nothing that thou art not guilty of thyself, O Ayesha. She loves the man, and he has been pleased to accept her love; where, then, is her sin?"

"Truly, O Holly, thou art foolish," she answered, almost petulantly.

"Where is her sin? Her sin is that she stands between me and my desire. I know well that I can take him from her—for dwells there a man upon this earth, O Holly, who could resist me if I put out my strength? Men are faithful for so long only as temptations pass them by. If the temptation be but strong enough, then will the man yield, for every man, like every rope, hath his breaking strain, and passion is to men what gold and power are to women—the weight upon their weakness. Believe me, ill will it go with mortal women in that heaven of which thou speakest if only the spirits be more fair, for their lords will never turn to look upon them, and their Heaven will become their Hell. For man can be bought with woman's beauty, if it be but beautiful enough; and woman's beauty can be ever bought with gold, if only there be gold enough. So was it in my day, and so it will be to the end of time. The world is a great mart, my Holly, where all things are for sale to him who bids the highest in the currency of our desires."

These remarks, which were as cynical as might have been expected from a woman of Ayesha's age and experience, jarred upon me, and I answered, testily, that in our heaven there was no marriage or giving in marriage.

"Else would it not be heaven, dost thou mean?" she put in. "Fie upon thee, Holly, to think so ill of us poor women! Is it, then, marriage that marks the line between thy heaven and thy hell? But enough of this. Now is no time for disputing and the challenge of our wits. Why dost thou always dispute? Art thou also a philosopher of these latter days? As for this woman, she must die; for, though I can take her lover from her, yet, while she lived, he might think tenderly of her, and that I cannot suffer. No other woman shall dwell in my lord's thoughts; my empire must be all my own. She has had her day, let her be content; for better is an hour with love than a century of loneliness—now night shall swallow her."

"Nay, nay," I cried, "it would be a wicked crime; and from a crime naught comes but what is evil. For thine own sake do not this deed."

"Is it, then, a crime, O foolish man, to put away that which stands between us and our ends? Then is our life one long crime, my Holly; for day by day we destroy that we may live, since in this world none save the strongest can endure. Those who are weak must perish; the earth is to the strong, and the fruits thereof. For every tree that grows a score shall wither, that the strong one may take their share. We run to place and power over the dead bodies of those who fail and fall; ay, we win the food we eat from out the mouths of starving babes. It is the scheme of things. Thou sayest, too, that a crime breeds evil, but therein thou dost lack experience; for out of crimes come many good things, and out of good grows much evil. The cruel rage of the tyrant may prove the blessing of thousands who come after him, and the sweetheartedness of a holy man may make a nation slaves. Man doeth this and doeth that from the good or evil of his heart; but he knows not to what end his sense doth prompt him; for when he strikes he is blind to where the blow shall fall, nor can he count the airy threads that weave the web of circumstance. Good and evil, love and hate, night and day, sweet and bitter, man and woman, heaven above and the earth beneath—all these things are needful, one to the other, and who knows the end of each? I tell thee that there is a Hand of Fate who twines them up to bear the burden of his purpose, and all things are gathered in that great rope to which all things are requisite. Therefore doth it not become us to say this thing is evil and that good, or the dark is hateful and the light lovely; for to other eyes than ours the evil may be the good and the darkness more beautiful than the day, or all alike be fair. Hearest thou, my Holly?"

I felt that it was hopeless to argue against casuistry of this nature, which, if it were carried to its logical conclusion, would absolutely destroy all morality, as we understand it. But Ayesha's talk gave me a fresh thrill of fear, for what may not be possible to a being who, unconstrained by human law, is also absolutely unshackled by a moral sense of right and wrong, which, however partial and conventional it may be, is yet based, as our conscience tells us, upon the great wall of individual responsibility that marks off mankind from the beasts?

Still I was most anxious to save Ustane, whom I liked and respected, from the dire fate that overshadowed her at the hands of her mighty rival. So I made one more appeal.

"Ayesha," I said, "thou art too subtle for me; but thou thyself hast told me that each man should be a law unto himself, and follow the teaching of his heart. Has thy heart no mercy towards her whose place thou wouldst take? Bethink thee, as thou sayest—though to me the thing is incredible—he whom thou desirest has returned to thee after many ages, and but now thou hast, as thou sayest also, wrung him from the jaws of death. Wilt thou celebrate his coming by the murder of one who loved him, and whom perchance he loved—one, at the least, who saved his life for thee when the spears of thy slaves would have made an end of it? Thou sayest also that in past days thou didst grievously wrong this man, that with thine own hand thou didst slay him because of the Egyptian Amenartas whom he loved."

"How knowest thou that, O stranger? How knowest thou that name? I spoke it not to thee," she broke in with a cry, catching at my arm.

"Perchance I dreamed it," I answered; "strange dreams do hover about these caves of Kôr. It seems that the dream was, indeed, a shadow of the truth. What came to thee of thy mad crime? Two thousand years of waiting, was it not? And now wouldst thou repeat this history? Say what thou wilt, I tell thee that evil will come of it; for to him who doeth, at the least, good breeds good and evil evil, even though in after days out of the evil cometh good. Offences must needs come; but woe to him by whom the offence cometh. So said that Messiah of whom I spoke to thee, and it was truly said. If thou slayest this innocent woman, I say unto thee that thou shalt be accursed, and pluck no fruit from thine ancient tree of love. Also, what thinkest thou? How will this man take thee red-handed from the slaughter of her who loved and tended him?"

"As to that," she answered, "I have already answered thee. Had I slain thee as well as her, yet should he love me, Holly, because he could not save himself therefrom any more than thou couldst save thyself from dying, if by chance I slew thee, O Holly. And yet maybe there is truth in what thou dost say; for in some way it presses on my mind. If it may be, I will spare this woman; for have I not told thee that I am not cruel for the sake of cruelty? I love not to see suffering, or to cause it. Let her come before me—quick now, ere my mood changes," and she covered her face hastily with its gauzy wrapping.

Well pleased to have succeeded even to this extent, I passed out into the passage and called to Ustane, whose white garment I caught sight of some yards away, huddled up against one of the earthenware lamps that were placed at intervals along the tunnel. She rose, and ran towards me.

"Is my lord dead? Oh, say not he is dead!" she cried, lifting her noble-looking face up to me, all stained as it was with tears, with an air of infinite beseeching that went straight to my heart.

"Nay, he lives," I answered. "*She* hath saved him. Come."

She sighed deeply, entered, and fell upon her hands and knees, after the custom of the Amahagger people, in the presence of the dread *She*.

"Rise," said Ayesha, in her coldest voice, "and come hither."

Ustane obeyed, standing before her with bowed head.

Then came a pause, which Ayesha broke.

"Who is this man?" she said, pointing to the sleeping form of Leo.

"The man is my husband," she answered in a low voice.

"Who gave him to thee for a husband?"

"I took him, according to the custom of our country, O *She*."

"Thou hast done evil, woman, in taking this man, who is a stranger. He is not of thine own race, and the custom fails. Listen: perchance thou didst this thing through ignorance, therefore, woman, do I spare thee, otherwise hadst thou died. Listen again. Go hence back to thine own place, and never dare to speak with or to set thine eyes upon this man again. He is not for thee. Listen a third time. If thou breakest this my law, that moment thou diest. Go!"

But Ustane did not move.

"Go, woman!"

Then Ustane looked up, and I saw that her face was torn with passion.

"Nay, O *She*, I will not go," she answered in a choked voice: "the man is my husband, and I love him—I love him, and I will not leave him. What right hast thou to command me to leave my husband?"

I saw a quiver pass down Ayesha's frame, and shuddered myself, fearing the worst.

"Be pitiful," I said in Latin; "it is but Nature working."

"I am pitiful," she answered coldly in the same language; "had I not been pitiful she had been dead even now." Then, addressing Ustane: "Woman, I say to thee, go before I destroy thee where thou art!"

"I will not go! He is mine—mine!" she cried in anguish. "I took him, and I saved his life! Destroy me, then, if thou hast the power! I will not give thee my husband—never—never!"

Ayesha made a movement so swift that I could scarcely follow it, but it seemed to me that she struck the poor girl lightly upon the head with her hand. I looked at Ustane, and staggered back in horror, for there upon her hair, straight across her bronze-like tresses, appeared three finger-marks *white as snow*. As for the girl herself, she lifted her hands to her head like one who is dazed.

"Great heavens!" I said, aghast at this most dreadful manifestation of inhuman power; but *She* did but laugh a little.

"Thou thinkest, poor ignorant fool," she said to the bewildered woman, "that I have not power to slay. Look, there lies a mirror," and she pointed to Leo's round shaving-glass that had been arranged by Job with other things upon his baggage; "give it to this woman, my Holly, and let her learn that which lies across her hair, and whether or no I have power to slay."

I took the glass, and held it before Ustane's eyes. She gazed, felt at her hair, then gazed again, and presently sank upon the ground with a stifled sob.

"Now wilt thou go, or must I strike a second time?" asked Ayesha, in mockery. "See, I have set my seal upon thee, so that I may know thee till thy hair is all as white as it. If I behold thy face again, be sure, too, that thy bones shall soon be whiter than my stamp upon thy hair."

Utterly awed and broken down, the poor creature rose, and, marked with that awful mark, she crept from the room, sobbing bitterly.

"Look not so frighted, my Holly," said Ayesha, when she had gone. "I tell thee I deal not in magic—there is no magic. 'Tis only a force that thou dost not understand. I marked her to strike terror to her heart, else must I have slain her. And now I will bid my servants bear my lord Kallikrates to a chamber near my own, that I may watch over him, and be ready to greet him when he wakes; and thither, too, shalt thou come, my Holly, and the white man, thy servant. But one thing remember at thy peril. Naught shalt thou say to Kallikrates as to how this woman went, and as little as may be of me. Now, I have warned thee!" And she glided away to give her orders, leaving me more absolutely confounded than ever. Indeed, so bewildered was I, so racked and torn with such a succession of various emotions, that I began to think that I must be going mad. However, perhaps fortunately, I had but little time to reflect, for presently the mutes arrived to carry the sleeping Leo and our possessions across the central cave, so for a while all was bustle. Our new rooms were situated immediately behind what we named Ayesha's boudoir—that curtained space where I had first seen her. Where she herself slept I did not then know, but it was close at hand.

That night I passed in Leo's room, but he slumbered through it like the dead, never once stirring. I also slept well, as, indeed, I needed to do, but my sleep was full of dreams of all the horrors and wonders I had undergone. Chiefly, however, I was haunted by that frightful piece of *diablerie* by which Ayesha left her finger-marks upon her rival's hair. There was something so terrible about her swift, snake-like movement, and the instantaneous blanching of that threefold line, that, if the results to Ustane had been much more tremendous, I doubt if they would have impressed me so deeply. To this day I often dream of that awful scene, and see the weeping woman, bereaved, and marked like Cain, cast a last look at her lover, and creep from the presence of her dread Queen.

Another dream which troubled me originated in the huge pyramid of bones. I dreamed that they all arose and marched past me in thousands and tens of thousands—in squadrons, companies, and armies—with the sunlight shining through their hollow ribs. On they rushed across the plain to Kôr, their imperial home; I saw the drawbridges fall before them, and heard their skeletons clank beneath the brazen gates. On they went, up the splendid streets, on past fountains, palaces, and temples such as the eye of mortal never saw. But there was no man to greet them in the market-place, and no woman's face appeared at the windows—only a bodiless voice went before them, calling: *"Fallen is Imperial Kôr!—fallen!—fallen!—fallen!"* On, through the city, marched those gleaming phalanxes, and the rattle of their bony tread echoed in the silent air as they pressed grimly forward. They passed through the city and clomb the wall, and strode along the great roadway that was made upon the wall, till at length once more they reached the draw-bridge. Then, as the sun was sinking, they returned again towards their sepulchre, and his light shone luridly in the sockets of their empty eyes, throwing gigantic shadows of their bones, that stretched away, and crept and crept like huge spiders' legs as their armies wound across the plain. Now they came to the cave, and once more one by one they flung themselves in unending files through the hole into the pit of death, and I awoke, shuddering, to see *She*, who had been standing between my couch and Leo's, glide like a shadow from the room.

After this I slept again, soundly this time, till morning, when I awoke much refreshed, and rose. At last the hour drew near when, according to Ayesha, Leo was to awake, and with it came the veiled *She* herself.

"Thou shalt see, O Holly," she said: "presently he will awake in his right mind, the fever having left him."

Hardly were the words out of her mouth when Leo turned round and, stretching out his arms, yawned, opened his eyes, then, perceiving a female form bending over him, threw his arms about her and kissed her, in mistake, perhaps, for Ustane. At any rate, he said, in Arabic, "Hullo, Ustane! why have you tied your head up like that? Have you got the toothache?" and then in English, "I say, I'm awfully hungry. Why, Job, you old son of a gun, where the deuce have we got to now—eh?"

"I am sure I wish I knew, Mr. Leo," said Job, suspiciously edging past Ayesha, whom he still regarded with the utmost disgust and horror, being by no means sure that she was not an animated corpse; "but you mustn't talk, Mr. Leo, you've been very ill, and given us a great deal of anxiety, and if this lady," looking at Ayesha, "would be so kind as to move, I'll bring you your soup."

This turned Leo's attention to the "lady," who was standing by in perfect silence. "Why!" he said, "that is not Ustane—where is Ustane?"

Then, for the first time, Ayesha spoke to him, and her first words were a lie. "She has gone from hence upon a visit," she said; "and, behold! I am here in her place as thine handmaiden."

Ayesha's silver notes seemed to puzzle Leo's half-awakened intellect as much as did her corpse-like wrappings. However, he said nothing in answer, but, drinking off his soup greedily, turned over and slept again till the evening. When he woke for the second time he saw me, and began to question me as to what had happened, but I put him off as best I could till the morrow, when he awoke miraculously better. Then I told him something of his illness and of my doings, but as Ayesha was present I could not tell him much, except that she was the Queen of the country, and well disposed towards us, and that it was her pleasure to go veiled; for though of course I spoke in English, I was afraid that she might understand what we were saying from the expression of our faces; besides, I remembered her warning.

On the following morning Leo rose almost entirely recovered. The flesh wound in his side was healed, and his constitution, naturally a vigorous one, had shaken off the exhaustion consequent on his terrible fever with a rapidity that I can only attribute to the effects of the wonderful drug which Ayesha had given to him, and perhaps to the fact that his illness had been too short to reduce him very much. With his returning health came back full recollection of all his adventures up to the time when he had lost consciousness in the marsh, and of course of Ustane also, to whom I discovered he had grown considerably attached. Indeed, he overwhelmed me with questions about the poor girl, which I did not dare to answer, for after Leo's first awakening *She* had sent for me, and again warned me solemnly that I was to reveal nothing of the story to him, delicately hinting that if I did it would be the worse for me. Further, for the second time, she cautioned me not to tell Leo anything more than I was obliged about herself, saying that she would reveal all to him in her own hour.

Indeed, her whole manner changed. After all that I had learned I expected that she would take the earliest opportunity of claiming the man whom she believed to be her old-world lover, but this, for some reason of her own, which at the time was quite inscrutable to me, she did not do. All that she did do was to attend to his wants quietly, and with a humility which was in striking contrast to her former imperious bearing, addressing him always in a tone of something very like respect, and keeping him with her as much as possible. Of course his curiosity was as much excited about this mysterious woman as my own had been, and he was particularly anxious to see her face, which, without entering into particulars, I had told him was as lovely as were her form and voice. This in itself was enough to raise the expectations of any young man to a dangerous pitch, and, had it not been that he was still suffering from the effects of his illness, and much troubled in mind about Ustane, of whose tenderness and brave devotion he spoke in touching terms, I have no doubt but that he would have entered into Ayesha's plans, and fallen in love with her by anticipation. As it chanced, however, he was merely curious, and also, like myself, somewhat awed, for, though no hint had been given to him by *She* of her extraordinary age, not unnaturally he came to identify her with the woman spoken of on the potsherd. At last, quite driven into a corner by his continual questions, which he showered on me while he was dressing on this third morning, I referred him to Ayesha, saying, with perfect truth, that I did not know where Ustane was. Accordingly, after Leo had eaten a hearty breakfast, we adjourned into *She's* presence, for her mutes had orders to admit us at all hours.

As usual, she was seated in what, for want of a better term, we called her boudoir, and on the curtains being drawn she rose from her couch and, stretching out both hands, came forward to greet us, or rather Leo; for, as may be imagined, I was now left quite in the cold. It was a pretty sight to see her veiled form gliding towards the sturdy young Englishman, dressed in his grey flannel suit; for, though he is half a Greek by blood, with the exception of his hair, Leo is one of the most English-looking men I ever saw. He has nothing of the supple form or slippery manner of the modern Greek about him, though I presume that he inherits his personal beauty from his foreign mother, whose portrait he resembles not a little. He is very tall and broad-chested, and yet not awkward, as so many big men are, and his head is set upon him in such a fashion as to give him a proud and vigorous air, which was well described by his Amahagger name of "Lion."

"Greeting to thee, my lord and guest," Ayesha said in her softest voice. "Right glad am I to see thee standing upon thy feet. Believe me, had I not saved thee at the last, never wouldst thou have stood upon those feet again. But the danger is done, and it shall be my care"—she flung a world of meaning into these words—"that it returns no more."

Leo bowed; then, in his best Arabic, he thanked her for all her kindness and courtesy in tending an unknown stranger.

"Nay," she answered softly, "ill could the world spare such a man.

Beauty is too rare upon it. Give me no thanks, who am made happy by thy coming."

"Humph! old fellow," said Leo aside to me in English, "the lady is very civil. We seem to have tumbled into clover. I hope that you have made the most of your opportunities. By Jove! what a pair of arms!"

I signed to him to be quiet, for I had caught a suspicious gleam from Ayesha's veiled eyes, which were watching me curiously.

"I trust," she went on, "that my servants have attended thee well; if there can be comfort in this poor place, be sure it waits on thee. Is there aught else that thou desirest?"

"Yes, O *She*," answered Leo hastily. "I would learn whither the woman who was with me has vanished."

"Ah!" said Ayesha: "the girl—yes, I saw her. Nay, I know not; she said that she would go, I know not where. Perchance she will return, perchance not. It is wearisome waiting on the sick, and these savage women are fickle."

Leo looked both puzzled and distressed at this intelligence.

"It's very odd," he said to me in English; and then addressing *She*, he added: "I cannot understand; the young lady and I—well—we had a regard for each other."

Ayesha laughed a little, very musically, and changed the subject.

XIX

"Give Me a Black Goat!"

The conversation after this was of so desultory an order that I do not quite recollect it. For some reason, perhaps from a desire to keep her identity and character in reserve, Ayesha did not talk freely, as was her custom. Presently, however, she informed Leo that she had arranged a dance that night for our amusement. I was astonished to hear this, imagining that the Amahagger were much too gloomy a folk to indulge in any such frivolity; but, as will presently appear more clearly, it proved that an Amahagger dance has little in common with these fantastic festivities in other countries, savage or civilised. Then, as we were about to withdraw, she suggested that Leo might like to see some of the wonders of the caves, and accordingly thither we departed, accompanied by Job and Billali.

To describe our visit would only be to repeat a great deal of what I have already said. The tombs we entered were different indeed, for the whole rock is a honeycomb of sepulchres,* but their contents varied

---

*For a long while it puzzled me to know how the enormous quantities of rock that must have been dug out of these vast caves had been disposed of; but I discovered afterwards that

but little. Afterwards we visited the pyramid of bones that had haunted my dreams on the previous night, and thence went down a long passage to one of the great vaults occupied by the remains of the poorer citizens of Imperial Kôr. These bodies were not nearly so well preserved as were those of the wealthier classes. Many of them had no linen covering on them; also, from five hundred to one thousand of them were buried in a single large vault, the corpses in some instances being piled thickly one upon another, like a heap of slain.

Of course Leo was intensely interested in this stupendous and unequalled sight, which, indeed, was enough to awaken into the most active life all the imagination a man possessed. But to poor Job it did not prove attractive. As may be imagined, his nerves, already seriously shaken by what he had undergone since we had reached this terrible country, were yet further disturbed by the spectacle of these masses of departed humanity, whereof the forms still remained perfect before his eyes, though their voices were for ever lost in the eternal silence of the tomb. Nor was he comforted when old Billali, by way of soothing his evident agitation, informed him that he should not be frightened of these dead men, as he would soon be like them himself.

"That's a nice thing to say of a man, sir," he ejaculated, when I translated this little remark; "but there, what can one expect of an old cannibal savage? Not but what I dare say he's right," and Job sighed.

When we had finished inspecting the caves we returned and ate our meal, for it was now past four in the afternoon, and we all needed food and rest—especially Leo. At six o'clock, together with Job, we waited on Ayesha, who proceeded to terrify our poor servant still more by showing him pictures on the pool of water in the font-like vessel. She learnt from me that he was one of seventeen children, and then bid him think of all his brothers and sisters, or as many of them as he could, gathered together in his father's cottage. Next she told him to look into the water, and there, reflected on its stilly surface, appeared that dead scene of many years gone by, as it was recalled to our retainer's brain. Some of the faces were clear enough, but some were

---

it was, for the most part, built into the walls and palaces of Kôr. Also it was used to line the reservoirs and sewers.—L. H. H.

mere blurs and blotches, or had one feature grossly exaggerated; the fact being that, in these instances, Job was unable to recall the exact appearances of the individuals, or recollected them only by a peculiarity of his tribe, and the water could but reflect what he saw with his mind's eye. It must be remembered, indeed, that *She's* power in this matter was strictly limited; since, except in very rare instances, she could merely photograph upon the water what was in the mind of someone present, and then only through his will. But if she was personally acquainted with a locality, as in the case of ourselves and the whaleboat, she could throw its reflection upon the water, and also, it seems, the reflection of anything extraneous that was passing there at the time. This power, however, did not extend to the minds of others. For instance, she could show me the interior of my college chapel, as I remembered it, but not as it was at the moment of vision; since, where other people were concerned, her art was limited strictly to the facts or memories present to *their* consciousness at the moment. So much was this the case that when we tried, for her amusement, to show her pictures of noted buildings, such as St. Paul's or the Houses of Parliament, the result was most imperfect; for, of course, though we had a general idea of their appearance, we were unable to recall the architectural details, and therefore the minutiæ necessary to a perfect reflection were wanting. But Job could not be made to understand this, and, so far from accepting a natural explanation of the matter, which, though strange enough in all conscience, was nothing more than an instance of glorified and perfected telepathy, he set the phenomenon down as a manifestation of the blackest magic. I shall never forget the howl of terror which he uttered when he saw the more or less perfect portraits of his long-scattered brethren staring at him from the quiet water, or the merry peal of laughter with which Ayesha greeted his consternation. Nor did Leo altogether like the performance, but ran his fingers through his yellow curls, and remarked that it gave him "the creeps."

After about an hour of this amusement, in the latter part of which Job did not participate, the mutes indicated by signs that Billali was waiting for an audience. Accordingly he was told to "crawl up," which he did as awkwardly as usual, and announced that the dance was ready to begin if *She* and the white strangers would be pleased to attend. Shortly afterwards we all rose, and, Ayesha having thrown a dark cloak over her white wrappings (the same, by the way, that she had worn when I saw her cursing by the fire), we started. The dance was to be held in the open air, on the smooth rocky plateau in front of the great cave, and thither we made our way. About fifteen paces from the mouth of the cave we found three chairs placed, and here we sat and waited, for as yet no dancers were to be seen. The night was almost, but not quite, dark, the moon not having risen as yet, which made us wonder how we should be able to see the dancing.

"Thou wilt understand presently," said Ayesha, with a little laugh, when Leo questioned her.

Scarcely were the words out of her mouth when from every point we saw dark forms rushing along, each of them bearing what at first we took to be an enormous flaming torch. Whatever these were, they burned furiously, for the flames stood out a yard or more behind their bearers. On came the men, fifty or more of them, carrying their blazing burdens and looking like so many devils from hell. Leo was the first to discover what these burdens were.

"Great heavens!" he said, "they are corpses on fire!"

I stared and stared again. He was perfectly right—the torches that were to light our entertainment were human mummies from the caves!

On rushed the bearers of the flaming corpses, and, meeting at a spot about twenty paces in front of us, built their ghastly loads crossways into a huge bonfire. Heavens! how they roared and flared! No tar barrel could have burnt as did those mummies. Nor was this all. Suddenly I saw one great fellow seize a flaming human arm that had fallen from its parent frame, and rush off into the darkness. Presently he stopped, and a tall streak of fire shot up into the air, illuminating the gloom, and also the lamp from which it sprang. That lamp was the mummy of a woman tied to a stout stake let into the rock, and he had fired her hair. On he went a few paces and touched a second, then a third, and a fourth, till at last we were surrounded on all three sides by a great ring

of bodies flaring furiously, the material with which they were preserved having rendered them so inflammable that literally the flames
would spout out of the ears and mouth in tongues of fire a foot or more
in length.

Lanterns in Kôr.

Nero illuminated his gardens with living Christians soaked in tar,
and we were now treated to a similar spectacle, probably for the first
time since his day, only happily our lamps were not alive.

But although, fortunately, this element of horror was wanting, to describe the awful and hideous grandeur of the spectacle thus presented to us is, I feel, so absolutely beyond my poor powers that I scarcely dare attempt it. To begin with, it appealed to the moral as well as to the physical susceptibilities. There was something very terrible, and yet most fascinating, about this employment of the remote dead to illumine the orgies of the living; in itself the thing was a satire, both on the living and the dead. Cæsar's dust—or is it Alexander's?—may stop a bunghole, but the office of these dead Cæsars of the past was to light a savage fetish dance. To such base uses may we come, of so little account may we be in the minds of the eager multitudes that we shall breed, many of whom, so far from revering our memory, will live to curse us for begetting them into such a world of woe.

Then there was the physical side of the spectacle, and a wild and splendid one it was. Those old citizens of Kôr burnt as, to judge from their sculptures and inscriptions, they had lived, very fast, and with the utmost liberality. What is more, there were plenty of them. So soon as a mummy was consumed to the ankles, which happened in about twenty minutes, the feet were kicked away, and another was put in its place. The bonfire was fed on the same generous scale, and its flames shot up, with a hiss and a crackle, twenty or thirty feet into the air, throwing great flashes of light far out into the gloom, through which the dark forms of the Amahagger flitted to and fro like devils replenishing the infernal fires. We all stood and stared aghast—shocked, and yet fascinated at so strange a spectacle, and half expecting to see the spirits those flaming forms had once enclosed come creeping from the shadows to work vengeance on their desecrators.

"I promised thee a strange sight, my Holly," laughed Ayesha, whose nerves alone did not seem to be affected; "and, behold! I have not failed thee. Also, it hath its lesson. Trust not to the future, for who knows what the future may bring! Therefore, live for the day, and endeavour not to escape the dust which seems to be man's end. What thinkest thou that those long-forgotten nobles and ladies would have felt had they known that in an age to be their delicate bodies should flare to light the dance of savages? But see, here come the mummers; a merry crew—are they not? The stage is lit—now for the play."

As she spoke we perceived advancing round the human bonfire two lines of figures, one of males and the other of females, to the number of about a hundred, each arrayed only in the usual leopard and buck skins. They formed up, in perfect silence, facing each other between us and the fire, and then the dance—a sort of infernal and fiendish cancan—began. To describe it is quite impossible, but, though there was a good deal of tossing of legs and double-shuffling, it seemed to our untutored minds to be a play rather than a dance, and, as is usual among this dreadful people, whose character takes its colour from the caves wherein they live, and whose jokes and amusements are drawn from the inexhaustible stores of preserved mortality with which they share their homes, the subject was most ghastly.

In the first place it represented an attempted murder, then the burial alive of the victim and his struggling from the grave; each act of the abominable drama, which was carried on in perfect silence, being rounded off and finished with a furious and very revolting dance about the supposed victim, who writhed upon the ground in the red light of the bonfire.

Suddenly, however, this pleasing piece was interrupted. There was a slight commotion, and a large powerful woman, whom I had noted as one of the most vigorous of the dancers, made mad and drunken with unholy excitement, bounded and staggered towards us, shrieking out as she came:—

"I want a Black Goat, I must have a Black Goat, bring me a Black Goat!" and down she fell upon the rocky floor, foaming and writhing, and shrieking for a Black Goat, affording as hideous a spectacle as can be conceived.

Instantly most of the dancers assembled themselves round her, though some still continued their capers in the background.

"She has a Devil," called out one of them. "Run and get a black goat. There, Devil, keep quiet! keep quiet! You shall have the goat presently. They have gone to fetch it, Devil."

"I want a Black Goat, I must have a Black Goat!" shrieked the foaming rolling creature again.

"All right, Devil, the goat will be here presently; keep quiet, there's a good Devil!"

And so on till the goat, taken from a neighbouring kraal, arrived at last, being dragged bleating to the scene by its horns.

"Is it a Black One? is it a Black One?" shrieked the possessed.

"Yes, yes, Devil, as black as night;" then aside, "keep it behind thee, don't let the Devil see that it has got a white spot on its rump and another on its belly. In one minute, Devil. There, cut its throat quick. Where is the saucer?"

"The Goat! the Goat! the Goat! Give me the blood of my black goat! I must have it, don't you see I must have it? Oh! oh! oh! give me the blood of the goat."

At this moment a terrified *bah!* announced that the poor animal had been sacrificed, and presently a woman ran up with a saucer full of the blood. This the possessed creature, who was then raving and foaming her wildest, seized and *drank,* and was instantly recovered, and without a trace of hysteria, or fits, or possession, or whatever dreadful thing it was from which she suffered. She stretched out her arms, smiled faintly, and walked back to the dancers, who then withdrew in a double line as they had come, leaving the space between us and the bonfire deserted.

I thought that the entertainment was now over, and, feeling sickened, was about to ask *She* if we could rise, when suddenly what at first I took to be a baboon came hopping round the fire, to be met upon the other side by a lion, or rather by a human being dressed in a lion's skin. Then appeared a goat, then a man wrapped in an ox-hide, with the horns swinging ludicrously to and fro. After him followed a blesbok, then an impala, then a koodoo, then more goats, and many other animals, including a girl sewn up in the shining scaly skin of a boa-constrictor, several yards of which trailed along the ground behind her. When all the maskers had collected they began to dance about in a lumbering, unnatural fashion, and to imitate the sounds produced by the respective animals they represented, until the air was alive with roars and bleating and the hissing of snakes.

This went on for a long time, till, tiring of the pantomime, I asked Ayesha if Leo and myself could walk round to inspect the human torches, and, as she did not object, we started, turning to the left. After looking at one or two of the flaming bodies, we were about to return, thoroughly disgusted with the grotesque weirdness of the spectacle, when our attention was attracted by one of the dancers, a particularly active leopard, that had separated itself from its fellow-beasts, and was whisking about in our immediate neighbourhood, but gradually drawing towards a spot where the shadow was darkest, equidistant between two of the burning mummies. Led by curiosity, we followed it, when suddenly it darted past us into the gloom beyond, and as it went erected itself and whispered, "Come," in a voice which we both recognised as that of Ustane. Without waiting to consult me Leo turned and followed her into the outer darkness, and, filled with fear, I hurried after them. The leopard crawled on for about fifty paces—a sufficient distance to be quite beyond the light of the fire and torches—and then Leo overtook it, or rather Ustane.

"Oh, my lord," I heard her whisper, "at length I have found thee! Listen. I am in peril of my life from *'She-who-must-be-obeyed.'* Surely the Baboon has told thee how she drove me from thee? I love thee, my lord, and thou art mine according to the custom of this country. I saved thy life; then canst thou cast me off, my love, my love!"

"Of course not," ejaculated Leo; "I have been seeking thee, Ustane. Let us go and explain to the Queen."

"Nay, nay, she would slay us. Thou knowest not her power—the Baboon there, he knoweth, for he saw. Hearken! There is but one way: if thou wilt cleave to me, thou must flee with me across the marshes this very hour, and then perchance we may escape."

"For Heaven's sake, Leo," I began, but she broke in—

"Nay, listen not to him. Swift—be swift—death is in the air we breathe. Even now, mayhap, *She* hears us," and without more ado she proceeded to enforce her arguments by throwing herself into his arms. As she did so the leopard's head slipped from her hair, and I saw the three white finger-marks upon it, gleaming faintly in the starlight. Terrified by the desperate nature of the position, once more I was about to interpose, for I knew that Leo is not too strong-minded where women are concerned, when I heard a little silvery laugh behind me. I turned round, and—oh horror!—there was *She* herself, and with her Billali and two male mutes. I gasped and nearly fell, for I was certain that such a situation must result in some dreadful tragedy, of which it seemed exceedingly probable that I should be the first victim. As for Ustane, loosing her lover, she covered her eyes with her hands, while Leo, not knowing the full terror of the position, merely coloured, and looked foolish, as a man caught in such a trap would naturally do.

XX

Triumph

Then followed a moment of the most painful silence that I ever endured. It was broken by Ayesha, who addressed herself to Leo.

"Nay, now, my lord and guest," she said in her softest tones, which yet had the ring of steel about them, "look not so bashful. Surely the sight was a pretty one—the leopard and the lion!"

"Oh, bother!" said Leo in English.

"And thou, Ustane," she went on, "in truth I should have passed thee by, had not the light fallen on the stripes across thy hair," and she pointed to the bright edge of the rising moon which was now appearing above the horizon. "Well! well! the dance is done—see, the tapers have burnt down, and all things end in silence and in ashes. So thou thoughtest it a fit time for love, Ustane, my servant—and I, dreaming not that I could be disobeyed, deemed thee already far away."

"Play not with me," moaned the wretched woman; "kill me, and let there be an end."

"Nay, why? It is not well to go so swift from the hot lips of love down to the cold mouth of the grave," and Ayesha motioned to the mutes, who instantly stepped up and caught the girl by either arm.

With an oath Leo sprang upon the nearest, and hurled him to the ground, and then stood over him with his face set and his fist ready.

Again Ayesha laughed. "It was well thrown, my guest; thou hast a strong arm for one who so late was sick. But now of thy courtesy I pray thee let that man live and do my bidding. He shall not harm the girl; the night air grows chill, and I would welcome her in mine own place. Surely she whom thou dost favour shall be favoured of me also."

I took Leo by the arm, dragging him from the prostrate mute, and, half bewildered, he yielded and left the man. Then we set out for the cave across the plateau, whence the dancers had vanished, and where a pile of white human ashes was all that remained of the fire which had lit their dancing.

In due course we gained Ayesha's boudoir—all too soon it seemed to me, having a sad presage of what was to come lying heavy on my heart.

Ayesha seated herself upon her cushions, and, having dismissed Job and Billali, by signs she bade the mutes tend the lamps and retire—all save one girl, who was her favourite personal attendant. We three remained standing, the unfortunate Ustane a little to the left of the rest of us.

"Now, O Holly," Ayesha began, "how came it that thou who didst hear my words bidding this evil-doer"—and she pointed to Ustane—"to go hence—thou at whose prayer I weakly spared her life—how came it, I say, that thou hadst part in what I saw to-night? Answer, and for thine own sake, I say, speak all the truth, for I am not minded to hear lies upon this matter!"

"It was by accident, O Queen," I answered. "I knew nothing of it."

"I believe thee, Holly," she answered coldly, "and well it is for thee that I do. Then does the whole guilt rest upon her."

"I do not find any guilt herein," interrupted Leo. "She is no other man's wife, and it seems that she has married me according to the custom of this awful place, so who is harmed? Any way, madam, whatever she has done I have done, so if she is to be punished let me be punished also; and I tell thee," he went on, working himself up into a fury, "that if thou biddest one of those deaf and dumb villains to touch her again I will tear him to pieces!"

Ayesha listened in icy silence, and made no remark. When he had finished, however, she addressed Ustane.

"Hast thou aught to say, woman? Thou silly straw, thou feather, who didst think to float towards thy passion's petty ends, even against the great wind of my will! Tell me, for I fain would understand, why didst thou this thing?"

Then I think that I saw the most wonderful example of moral courage and intrepidity which it is possible to conceive. For this poor doomed girl, knowing what she had to expect at the hands of her terrible Queen, knowing, too, from bitter experience, how great was her adversary's power, yet stood unshaken, and out of the very depths of her despair drew the strength to defy her.

"I did it, O *She*," she answered, drawing herself up to the full of her stately height, and throwing back the panther skin from her head, "because my love is deeper than the grave. I did it because my life without this man whom my heart chose would be but a living death. Therefore I risked my life, and now, when I know that it is forfeit to thine anger, still am I glad that I risked it, and must pay it away in the risking, ay, because he embraced me once, and told me that he loved me yet."

Here Ayesha half rose from her couch, and then sank down again.

"I have no magic," went on Ustane, her rich voice ringing strong and full, "and I am not a Queen, nor do I live for ever: but a woman's heart is heavy to sink through waters, however deep, O Queen! and a woman's eyes are quick to see—even through thy veil, O Queen!

"Listen: I know it, thou dost love this man thyself, and therefore wouldst thou destroy me who stand across thy path. Ay, I die—I die, and go into the darkness, nor know I whither I go. But this I know. There is a light shining in my breast, and by that light, as by a lamp, I see the truth, and the future that I shall not share, unroll itself before me like a scroll. When first I knew my lord," and she pointed to Leo, "I knew also that death would be the bridal gift he gave me—it rushed upon me of a sudden, but I turned not back, being ready to pay the price, and, behold, death is here! And now, even as I knew this, so, standing on the steps of doom, do I know that thou shalt not reap the profit of thy crime. Mine he is, and, though thy beauty shine like a sun among the stars, mine he shall remain for thee. Never here in this life shall he look thee in the eyes and call thee spouse. Thou too art doomed, I see"—and her voice rose like the cry of an inspired prophetess; "ah, I see——"

Then there rang an answering cry of rage and terror. I turned my head. Ayesha had risen, and was standing with her outstretched hand pointing at Ustane, who had suddenly become silent. I gazed at the poor woman, and as I gazed there fell upon her face that same woful, fixed expression of terror which I had seen before when she broke into her wild chant. Her eyes grew large, her nostrils dilated, and her lips blanched.

Ayesha said nothing, she made no sound, she only drew herself up, stretched out her arm, and, her tall veiled frame quivering like an aspen leaf, appeared to look fixedly at her victim. Even as she looked Ustane put her hands to her head, uttered one piercing scream, turned round twice, and then fell backwards with a thud—prone upon the floor. Both Leo and myself rushed to her. She was stone dead—blasted into death by some mysterious electric agency or overwhelming will-force whereof the dread *She* had command.

For a moment Leo did not quite understand what had happened. But, when it came home to him, his face was awful to see. With a savage oath he rose from beside the corpse, and, turning, literally sprang at Ayesha. But she was watching, and, seeing him come, stretched out her hand again, and he went staggering back towards me, and would have fallen, had I not caught him. Afterwards he told me that he felt as though he had suddenly received a violent blow in the chest, and, what is more, utterly cowed, as if all the manhood had been taken out of him.

Then Ayesha spoke. "Forgive me, my guest," she said softly, addressing him, "if I have shocked thee with my justice."

"Forgive thee, thou fiend!" shouted poor Leo, wringing his hands in his rage and grief. "Forgive thee, thou murderess! By Heaven, I will kill thee if I can!"

"Nay, nay," she answered in the same soft voice, "thou dost not understand—the time has come for thee to learn. *Thou* art my love, my Kallikrates, my Beautiful, my Strong! For two thousand years, Kallikrates, I have waited for *thee,* and now at length thou hast come back to me; and as for this woman," pointing to the corpse, "she stood between me and thee, therefore have I laid her in the dust, Kallikrates."

"It is a lie!" said Leo. "My name is not Kallikrates! I am Leo Vincey; my ancestor was Kallikrates—at least, I believe he was."

"Ah, thou sayest it—thine ancestor was Kallikrates, and thou, even thou, art Kallikrates reborn, come back—and mine own dear lord!"

"I am not Kallikrates, and as for being thy lord, or having aught to do with thee, I had sooner be the lord of a fiend from hell, for she would be better than thou."

"Sayest thou so—sayest thou so, Kallikrates? Nay, but thou hast not seen me for so long a time that no memory remains. Yet am I very fair, Kallikrates!"

"I hate thee, murderess, and I have no wish to see thee. What is it to me how fair thou art? I hate thee, I say."

"Yet within a very little space shalt thou creep to my knee, and swear that thou dost love me," answered Ayesha, with a sweet, mocking laugh. "Come, there is no time like the present time. Here, before this dead girl who loved thee, let us put it to the proof.

"Look now on me, Kallikrates!" and with a sudden motion she shook her gauzy covering from her, and stood forth in her low kirtle and her snaky zone, in her glorious radiant beauty and her imperial grace, rising from her wrappings, as it were, like Venus from the wave, or Galatea from her marble, or a beatified spirit from the tomb. She stood forth, and fixed her deep and glowing eyes upon Leo's eyes, and I saw his clenched fists unclasp, and his set and quivering features relax beneath her gaze. I saw his wonder and astonishment grow into admiration, then into longing, and the more he struggled the more I saw the power of her dread beauty fasten on him and take hold of his senses, drugging them, and drawing the heart out of him. Did I not know the process? Had not I, who was twice his age, gone through it myself? Was I not going through it afresh even then, although her sweet and passionate gaze was not for me? Yes, alas! I was. Alas! that I should have to confess that at this very moment I was rent by mad and furious jealousy. I could have flown at him, shame upon me! This woman had confounded and almost destroyed my moral sense, as indeed she must confound all who looked upon her superhuman loveliness. But—I do not know how—I mastered myself, and once more turned to see the climax of the awful tragedy.

"Oh, great Heaven!" gasped Leo, "art thou a woman?"

"A woman in truth—in very truth—and thine own spouse, Kallikrates!" she answered, stretching out her rounded ivory arms towards him, and smiling, ah, so sweetly!

He looked and looked, and slowly I perceived that he was drawing nearer to her. Suddenly his eye fell upon the corpse of poor Ustane, and he shuddered and stood still.

"How can I?" he said hoarsely. "Thou art a murderess; she loved me."

Observe, he was already forgetting that he had loved her.

"It is nothing," Ayesha murmured, and her voice sounded sweet as the night-wind passing through the trees. "It is naught at all. If I have sinned, let my beauty answer for my sin. If I have sinned, it is for love of thee: let my sin, therefore, be put away and forgotten;" and once more she stretched out her arms and whispered *"Come."* Then in a few seconds it was over.

I saw him struggle—I saw him even turn to fly; but her eyes drew him more strongly than iron bonds, and the magic of her beauty and concentrated will and passion entered into him and overpowered him—ay, even there, in the presence of the body of the woman who had loved him well enough to die for him. It sounds horrible and wicked indeed, but he should not be too greatly blamed, and be sure his sin has found him out. The temptress who drew him into evil was more than human, and her beauty was greater than the loveliness of the daughters of men.

I looked up again, and now her perfect form lay in his arms, and her lips were pressed against his own; and thus, with the corpse of his dead love for an altar, did Leo Vincey plight his troth to her red-handed murderess—plight it for ever and a day. For those who sell themselves into a like dominion, paying down the price of their own honour, and throwing their soul into the balance to sink the scale to the level of their lusts, must win deliverance hardly. As they have sown, so shall they reap and reap, even when the poppy flowers of passion have with-ered in their hands, and their harvest is but bitter tares, garnered in satiety.

Suddenly, with a snake-like motion, she seemed to slip from his em-brace, and again she broke out into her low laugh of triumphant mock-ery, and said, pointing to the dead Ustane:

"Did I not tell thee that within a little space thou wouldst creep to my knee, O Kallikrates? Surely the space has been no great one!"

Leo groaned in shame and misery; for though he was overcome and stricken down, he was not so lost as to be unaware of the depth of the degradation to which he had sunk. On the contrary, his better nature rose up in arms against his fallen self, as I was to learn that night.

"Come!"

Ayesha laughed a third time, then, veiling herself quickly, she made a sign to the mute, who had been watching the strange scene with cu-rious startled eyes. The girl left, and returned presently, followed by two male mutes, to whom the Queen made another sign. Thereon they all three seized the body of poor Ustane by the arms, dragging it heavily down the cavern and away through the curtains at the end. Leo watched it for a little while, then he covered his face with his hand. To my excited fancy, the glazing eyes of dead Ustane also seemed to watch us as they went.

"There passes the dead past," said Ayesha, solemnly, as the curtains shook and fell back into their places, when the ghastly procession had vanished behind them. Then, with one of those wild changes of mood of which I have already spoken, again she threw off her veil, and, after the ancient and poetic fashion of the dwellers in Arabia,* broke into a pæan of triumph, or epithalamium, that, rich and beautiful as it was, is most difficult to render into English; that ought, indeed, to be sung to music rather than written and read. It was divided into two parts—one descriptive, the other personal; and, as nearly as I can remember, it ran as follows:—

> *Love is like a flower in the desert.*
>
> *It is like the aloe of Arabia, that blooms but once and dies; it blooms in the salt emptiness of Life, and the brightness of its beauty is set upon the waste as a star is set upon a storm.*
>
> *It hath the sun above that is the Spirit, and about it blows the air of its divinity.*
>
> *At the echoing of a step Love blooms, I say; I say Love blooms, and bends her beauty down to him who passeth by.*
>
> *He plucketh it, yea, he plucketh the red cup that is full of honey, and beareth it away; away across the desert, away till the flower be withered, away till the desert is done.*
>
> *There is only one perfect flower in the wilderness of Life.*

*Among the ancient Arabians the power of poetic declamation, either in verse or prose, was held in the highest honour and esteem, and he who excelled in it was known as "Khâteb," or Orator. Every year a general assembly was held, at which the rival poets repeated their compositions, and, so soon as the knowledge of the art of writing became general, those poems which were judged to be the best were inscribed on silk in letters of gold, and publicly exhibited, being known as "Al Modhahabât," or "golden verses." In the chant given above by Mr. Holly, Ayesha evidently followed the traditional poetic manner of her people, which was to embody their thoughts in a series of somewhat disconnected sentences, each remarkable for its beauty and the grace of its expression.—EDITOR.

> *That flower is Love!*
> *There is only one fixed light in the mists of our wandering.*
> *That light is Love!*
> *There is only one hope in our despairing night.*
> *That hope is Love!*
> *All else is false. All else is shadow moving upon water. All else is wind and vanity.*
> *Who shall say what is the weight or the measure of Love?*
> *It is born of the flesh, it dwelleth in the spirit. From each doth it draw its comfort.*
> *For beauty it is as a star.*
> *Many are its shapes, but all are beautiful, and none know whence that star rose, or the horizon where it shall set.*

Then, turning to Leo, and laying her hand upon his shoulder, Ayesha went on in a fuller and more triumphant tone, speaking in balanced sentences that gradually grew and swelled from romantic prose into pure and majestic verse:—

> *Long have I loved thee, O my love; yet has my love not lessened.*
> *Long have I waited for thee, and behold my reward is at hand—is here!*
> *Far away I saw thee once, and thou wast taken from me.*
> *Then in a grave sowed I the seed of patience, and shone upon it with the sun of hope, and watered it with tears of repentance, and breathed on it with the breath of my knowledge.*
> *And now, lo! it hath sprung up, and borne fruit. Lo! out of the grave hath it sprung. Yea, from among the dry bones and ashes of the dead.*
> *I have waited, and my reward is with me.*
> *I have overcome Death, and Death has brought back to me him that was dead.*
> *Therefore do I rejoice, for fair is the future.*
> *Green are the paths that we shall tread across the everlasting meadows.*
> *The hour is at hand. Night hath fled away into the valleys.*
> *The dawn kisseth the mountain-tops.*
> *Soft shall we live, my love, and easy shall we go.*

Crowned shall we be with the diadem of Kings.
Worshipping and wonder-struck all peoples of the world,
Blinded, shall fall before our beauty and our might.
From time unto times shall our greatness thunder on,
Rolling like a chariot through the dust of endless days.
Laughing, shall we speed in our victory and pomp,
Laughing like the Daylight as he leaps along the hills.
Onward, still triumphant, to a triumph ever new!
Onward, in our power, to a power unattained!
Onward, never weary, clad with splendour for a robe!
Till accomplished be our fate, and the night is rushing down.

She paused in her strange and most thrilling allegorical chant, of which, unfortunately, I am only able to give the burden, I fear but feebly. Then she said:

"Perchance thou dost not believe my word, Kallikrates—perchance thou thinkest that I do delude thee, that I have not lived these many years, and that thou hast not been born again to me. Nay, look not thus—put away that pale cast of doubt, for oh, be sure, herein can error find no foothold! Sooner shall the suns forget their course and the swallow miss her nest, than my soul shall swear a lie and be led astray from thee, Kallikrates. Blind me, take away mine eyes, and let the darkness utterly fence me in, and still mine ears would catch the sound of thine unforgotten voice, striking more loud against the portals of my sense than can the call of brazen-throated clarions:—Stop up mine hearing also, and let a thousand touch me on the brow, and I would name thee out of all:—Yea, rob me of every sense, and see me stand deaf, and blind, and dumb, and with nerves that cannot weigh the value of a touch, yet would my spirit leap within me like a quickening child and cry unto my heart: 'Behold Kallikrates! Behold, thou watcher, the watches of thy night are ended! Behold, thou who seekest in the night season, thy morning Star ariseth.'"

She ceased awhile, and presently continued, "Stay; if thy heart is yet hardened against the mighty truth, and thou seekest some outward pledge of that which thou dost find too strange to understand, even now it shall be given to thee, and to thee also, O my Holly. Take a lamp each one of you, and follow after me whither I shall lead you."

Without pausing to think—indeed, speaking for myself, I had almost abandoned the attempt in circumstances which seemed to render it futile, since thought fell hourly helpless against a black wall of wonder—we took the lamps and followed her. Gliding to the end of her chamber, Ayesha raised a curtain and revealed a little stair of the sort that is so common in these dim caves of Kôr. As we hurried down this stair I observed that the steps were worn in the centre to such an extent that some of them had been reduced from seven and a half inches, at which I guessed their original height, to about three and a half inches. Now, the other steps that I had seen in the caves were quite unworn, as might be expected, since the only traffic which ever passed upon them was that of those who bore a fresh burden to the tomb. Therefore this fact struck my notice with the curious force with which little things do strike us when our minds are absolutely overwhelmed by a sudden rush of powerful sensations, beaten flat, as it were, like a sea beneath the first burst of a hurricane, so that each small object on its surface starts into an unnatural prominence.

At the foot of the stairway I halted, and stared at the worn steps, and Ayesha, turning, saw me.

"Dost thou wonder whose are the feet that have worn away this rock, my Holly?" she asked. "They are mine—even my own light feet! I can remember when yonder stairs were new and level, but for two thousand years and more have I passed hither day by day, and see, my sandals have eaten out the solid stone!"

I made no answer, but I do not think that anything which I had heard or seen brought home to my limited understanding so clear a sense of this being's overwhelming antiquity as the sight of this hard granite hollowed out by her soft feet. How many hundreds of thousands of times must she have glided up and down that stair to bring about such a result?

The steps led to a tunnel, and a few paces from its mouth opened a curtain-hung doorway, a glance at which told me that it was the same whence I had witnessed that terrible scene by the leaping flame. I recognised the pattern of the curtain, and the sight of it brought that dread event vividly before my eyes, and made me tremble even at its memory. Ayesha entered the tomb, for it was a tomb, and we followed her—I, for one, rejoicing that the mystery of the place was about to be cleared up, and yet afraid to face its solution.

XXI

The Dead and Living Meet

"See now the place where I have slept for these two thousand years," said Ayesha, taking the lamp from Leo's hand and holding it above her head. Its rays fell upon a hollow in the floor, where I had seen the obedient leaping flame, but now the fire was out. They fell upon the white form stretched there beneath its wrappings upon a bed of stone, upon the fretted carving of the tomb, and upon another shelf of stone opposite to the one on which the body lay, and separated from it only by the breadth of the cave.

"Here," went on Ayesha, resting her hand upon the rock—"here have I slept night by night for all these generations, with but a cloak to cover me. It did not become me that I should lie soft when my spouse yonder," and she pointed to the rigid form, "lay stiff in death. Here night by night I have slept in his cold company—till, as thou seest, this thick slab, like the stairs down which we came, has worn thin with the tossing of my form—so faithful have I been to thee even in thy space of sleep, Kallikrates. And now, my lord, thou shalt see a wondrous thing—living, thou shalt behold thyself dead—for well have I tended thee during all these years, Kallikrates. Art thou prepared?"

We made no answer, but gazed at each other with frightened eyes, the scene was so awful and so solemn. Ayesha advanced, and laid her hand upon the corner of the shroud. Then once more she spoke.

"Be not affrighted," she said; "though the thing seem wonderful to thee—all we who live have thus lived before; nor are the very shapes that hold us strangers to the sun! Only we know it not, because memory writes no record, and earth hath gathered in the earth she lent us, for none have saved our glory from the grave. But I, by my arts and by the arts of those dead men of Kôr which I have learned, have held thee back, O Kallikrates, from the dust, that the waxen stamp of beauty on thy face should ever rest before mine eye. 'Twas a mask that memory might fill, serving to summon forth thy presence from the past, and give it strength to wander in the habitations of my thought, clad in a mummery of life that stayed my appetite with visions of dead days.

"Behold!"

"Behold now, let the Dead and Living meet! Across the gulf of Time they still are one. Time has no power against Identity, though

Sleep the merciful hath blotted out the tablets of our mind, and with oblivion sealed the sorrows that else would hound us down from life to life, stuffing the brain with gathered griefs till it burst in the madness of uttermost despair. Still are they one, for the wrappings of our rest shall roll away as thunderclouds before the wind; the frozen voices of the past shall melt in music like mountain snows beneath the sun; and the weeping and the laughter of the lost hours shall be heard once more most sweetly echoing up the cliff of the innumerable years.

"Therefore have no fear, Kallikrates, when thou—living, and but lately born—shalt look upon thine own departed self, who breathed and died so long ago. I do but turn one page in thy Book of Being, and show thee what is writ thereon.

"*Behold!*"

With a sudden motion she drew the shroud from the cold form, and let the lamplight play upon it. I looked, and shrank back terrified; since, say what she might, the sight was an uncanny one—for her explanations were beyond the grasp of our finite minds, and when stripped from the mists of vague esoteric philosophy, and brought into conflict with cold and horrifying fact, they did not do much to break its force. For, stretched upon the stone bier before us, robed in white and perfectly preserved, was what appeared to be the body of Leo Vincey. I stared from Leo, standing *there* alive, to Leo lying *there* dead, and could see no difference between them; except, perhaps, that the body on the bier looked older. Feature for feature they were the same, yes, to the crop of little golden curls, which was Leo's most uncommon beauty. It even seemed to me, as I looked, that the expression on the dead man's face resembled that which I had sometimes seen upon Leo's when he was plunged in profound sleep. I can only sum up the closeness of the resemblance by saying that I never saw twins so exactly similar in appearance as were that dead and living pair.

I turned to see what effect was produced upon Leo by the sight of his dead self, and found it to be that of partial stupefaction. He stood for two or three minutes staring in silence, and when at last he spoke it was only to ejaculate—

"Cover it up, and take me away."

"Nay, wait, Kallikrates," said Ayesha, who resembled an inspired Sibyl rather than a woman, as she stood, the lamp raised above her head flooding with its light her own rich beauty and the cold wonder of the death-clothed form upon the bier, and rolled out her majestic sentences with a grandeur and a freedom of utterance which, alas! I cannot render.

"Wait. I would show thee something, that no tittle of my crime may be hidden from thee. Do thou, O Holly, open the garment on the breast of the dead Kallikrates, for perchance my lord may fear to touch his perished self."

I obeyed with trembling fingers. It seemed a desecration and an un-hallowed thing to handle that sleeping image of the living man at my side. Presently the cold breast was bare, and there upon it, over the heart, appeared a wound, evidently inflicted with a spear or dagger.

"Thou seest, Kallikrates," she said. "Know, then, that it was *I* who slew thee: in the place of Life *I* gave thee death. I slew thee because of the Egyptian Amenartas, whom thou didst love, for by her wiles she held thy heart, and her I could not smite as but now I smote yon woman, for she was too strong for me. In my haste and bitter anger I slew thee, and now for all these ages I have lamented thee, and waited for thy coming. And thou hast come, and naught can stand between thee and me, and of a truth now for death I will give thee life—not life eternal, for that none can give, but days and youth that shall endure for thousands upon thousands of years, and with them pomp, and power, and wealth, and all things that are good and beautiful, such as have been to no man before thee, nor shall be to any man who comes after. But one thing more, and thou shalt rest and make ready for the day of thy new birth. Thou seest this body, which was thine own. For all these centuries it hath been my cold comfort and my companion; now I need it no more, for I have thy living presence, and it can but serve to stir up memories of that which I would fain forget. Therefore let it go back to the dust whence I have held it.

"Behold! I have prepared against this happy hour!" Then, from the other shelf or stone ledge, which Ayesha said served her for a couch, she took a large vitrified double-handled vase, the mouth of which was covered with a bladder. This she loosed, and, having first bent down and gently kissed the white forehead of the dead man, she undid the vase, and sprinkled its contents carefully over the corpse, taking, I observed, the greatest precautions against any drop of them touching us or herself; then poured out what remained of the liquid upon the chest and head. Instantly a dense vapour arose, and the cave was filled with choking fumes, which prevented us from seeing anything while the deadly acid did its work, for I presume it was some powerful preparation of the sort. From the spot where the body lay came a fierce fizzing and crackling sound, which ceased, however, before the fumes had cleared away. At last they were all gone, except a little cloud that still hung over the corpse. In two or three minutes more this had vanished also, and, wonderful as it may seem, it is a fact that on the stone bench which had supported the mortal remains of the ancient Kallikrates for so many centuries there was now nothing to be seen but a few handfuls of smoking white powder. The acid had utterly destroyed the body, and even in places eaten into the stone. Ayesha stooped down, and taking a handful of this powder, she threw it into the air, saying at the same time, in a voice of calm solemnity—

"Dust to dust!—the past to the past!—the lost to the lost!—Kallikrates is dead, and is born again!"

The ashes floated about us and fell to the rocky floor, while in awed silence we watched them fall, too overcome for words.

"Now leave me," she said, "and sleep if ye may. I must watch and think, for to-morrow night we go hence, and the time is long since I trod the path that we shall follow."

Accordingly we bowed, and left her.

As we passed to our own apartment I peeped into Job's sleeping-place, to see how he fared, for he had gone away, just before our interview with the murdered Ustane, quite prostrated by the terrors of the Amahagger festivity. He was sleeping soundly, good honest fellow that he was, and I rejoiced to think that his nerves, which, like those of most uneducated people, were far from strong, had been spared the closing scenes of this dreadful day. Then we entered our own chamber, and here at last poor Leo, who, ever since he had looked upon that frozen image of his living self, had been in a state not far removed from stupor, burst out into a torrent of grief. Now that he was no longer in the presence of the dread *She* his sense of the awfulness of all that had happened, and more especially of the wicked murder of Ustane, who was bound to him by ties so close, broke upon him like a storm, and lashed him into an agony of remorse and terror which was painful to witness. He cursed himself—he cursed the hour when we had first seen the writing on the sherd, which was being so mysteriously verified, and bitterly he cursed his own weakness. Ayesha he dared not curse—who would dare to speak evil of such a woman, whose spirit, for aught we knew, was watching us at the very moment?

"What am I to do, old fellow?" he groaned, resting his head against my shoulder in the extremity of his grief. "I let her be killed—not that I could help that, but within five minutes I was kissing her murderess over her body. I am a degraded brute, but I cannot resist this," and here his voice sank—"awful sorceress. I know I shall do the same to-morrow; I know that I am in her power for always; if I never saw her again I should think of no other woman during all my life; I must follow her as a needle follows a magnet; I would not go away now if I might; I could not leave her, my legs would not carry me, but my mind is still clear enough, and in my mind I hate her—at least, I think so. It is all so horrible; and that—that dead man! What can I make of it? It was *I*! I am sold into bondage, old fellow, and she will take my soul as the price of herself!"

Then, for the first time, I told him that I was in but a very little better position; and I am bound to say that, notwithstanding his own infatuation, he had the decency to sympathise with me. Perhaps he did not think it worth while to be jealous, seeing that he had no cause so far as the lady was concerned. I went on to suggest that we should try to run away; but we soon rejected the project as futile, and, to be perfectly honest, I do not believe that either of us would really have left Ayesha, even if some superior power had suddenly offered to convey us from these gloomy caves and set us down in Cambridge. We could no more have left her than a moth can leave the light that destroys it. We were like confirmed opium-eaters: in our moments of reason we well knew the deadly nature of our pursuit, but certainly we were not prepared to abandon its terrible delights.

No man who once had seen *She* unveiled, and heard the music of her voice, and drunk in the bitter wisdom of her words, would willingly give up that joy for a whole sea of placid pleasure. How much more, then, was this likely to be so when, as in Leo's case, to put myself out of the question, this extraordinary creature declared her utter and absolute devotion, and gave to him what appeared to be proofs of its endurance through some two thousand years?

No doubt she was a wicked person, and no doubt she had murdered Ustane when she stood in her path; but then, she was very faithful, and by a law of nature man is apt to think but lightly of a woman's crimes, especially if that woman be beautiful, and the crimes are committed for the love of himself.

For the rest, when had such a chance ever come to a man before as that which now lay in Leo's hand? True, in uniting himself to this dread woman he would place his life under the influence of a mysterious creature of evil tendencies,* but then, that would be likely enough

*After some months of consideration of this statement I am bound to confess that I am not quite satisfied of its truth. It is perfectly true that Ayesha committed a murder, but I suspect that, were we endowed with the same absolute power, and if we had the same tremendous interest at stake, we should be very apt to do likewise under parallel circumstances. Also, it must be remembered that she looked on it as an execution for disobedience under a system which made the slightest disobedience punishable by death. Putting aside this question of the murder, her evil-doing resolves itself into the expression of views and the acknowledgment of motives which are contrary to our preaching, if not to our practice. Now at first sight this might be fairly taken as a proof of an evil nature, but when we come to consider the great antiquity of the individual, it becomes doubtful if it was anything more than the natural cynicism which arises from age and bitter experience, and the possession of extraordinary powers of observation. It is a well-known fact that very often, putting the period of boyhood out of the argument, the older we grow the more cynical and hardened we become; indeed, many of us are only saved by timely death from moral petrifaction, if not from moral corruption. No one will deny that a young man is on the average better than an old one, for he is without that experience of the order of things which in certain thoughtful dispositions can hardly fail to produce cynicism, and that disregard of acknowledged methods and established custom which we call evil. Now the oldest man upon the earth was but a babe compared to Ayesha, and the wisest man upon the earth was not one-third as wise. And the fruit of her wisdom was this that there is but one-thing worth living for, and that is Love in its highest sense, and to gain that good thing she was not prepared to stop at trifles. This is really the sum of her evil doings, and it must be remembered, on the other hand, that, whatever may be thought of them, she had some virtues developed to a degree very uncommon in either sex—constancy, for instance.—L. H. H.

to happen to him in any ordinary marriage. On the other hand, however, no ordinary marriage could bring him such awful beauty—for awful is the only word that can describe it—such divine devotion, such wisdom, and command over the secrets of nature, and the place and power which they must win, or, lastly, the royal crown of unending youth, if indeed she could give that. No, on the whole, it is not wonderful, though Leo was plunged in bitter shame and grief, such as any gentleman would have felt under the circumstances, that he was not ready to entertain the idea of running away from his extraordinary fortune.

My own opinion is that he would have been mad if he had done so. But then, I confess, my views on the matter must be accepted with qualifications. I am in love with Ayesha myself to this day, and I would rather have been the object of her affection for one short week than that of any other woman's in the world for a whole lifetime. And let me add that if anybody who doubts this statement, and thinks me foolish for making it, could have seen Ayesha draw her veil and flash out in beauty on his gaze, his view would exactly coincide with my own. Of course, I am speaking of any *man*. We never had the advantage of a lady's opinion of Ayesha, but I think it quite possible that she would have regarded the Queen with dislike; would have expressed her disapproval in some more or less pointed manner, and ultimately have been "blasted."

For two hours or more Leo and I sat with shaken nerves and frightened eyes, and talked over the miraculous events through which we were passing. It seemed like a dream or a fairy tale, instead of solemn, sober fact. Who would have believed that the writing on the potsherd was not only true, but that we should live to verify it, and that we two seekers should find her who was sought patiently awaiting our coming in the tombs of Kôr? Who would have thought that in the person of Leo this mysterious woman should, as she believed, discover the being whom she awaited from century to century, and whose former earthly tenement she had till this very night preserved? But so it was. In the face of all we had seen it was difficult for us as ordinary reasoning men any longer to doubt its truth. Therefore at last, with humble hearts and a deep sense of the impotence of human knowledge, and the insolence of the assumption which denies the possibility of that whereof it has no experience, we laid ourselves down to sleep, leaving our fates in the hands of the watching Providence which had chosen thus to allow us to draw the veil of human ignorance, and to reveal to us for good or evil a glimpse of the potentialities of life.

XXII

Job Has a Presentiment

It was nine o'clock on the following morning when Job, who still looked scared and tremulous, came in to call me, and at the same time to breathe his gratitude at finding us alive in our beds, which, it appeared, was more than he had expected. When I told him of the awful end of poor Ustane he was even more thankful for our survival, and much shocked; though, indeed, Ustane had been no favourite of his, or he of hers. She called him "pig" in bastard Arabic, and he called her "hussy" in good English, but these amenities were forgotten in face of the catastrophe that had overwhelmed her at the hands of her Queen.

"I don't want to say anything as mayn't be agreeable, sir," said Job, when he had finished exclaiming at my tale, "but it's my opinion that that there *She* is Old Nick himself, or perhaps his wife, if he has one, which I suppose he has, for he couldn't be so wicked all alone. The Witch of Endor was a fool to her, sir: bless you, she would make no more of raising every gentleman in the Bible out of these here musty tombs than I should of growing cress on a bit of flannel! It's a country of devils, this is, sir, and she's the master one of the lot; and if ever we get clear it will be more than I expect to do. I don't see no way out of it. That witch isn't likely to let a fine young man like Mr. Leo go."

"Come," I said, "at any rate she saved his life."

"Yes, and she'll take his soul to pay for it. She'll make him a witch, like herself. I say it's wicked to have anything to do with those sort of people. Last night, sir, I lay awake and read in my little Bible that my poor mother gave me about what is going to happen to sorceresses and them sort, till my hair stood on end. Lord, how the old lady would stare if she saw where her Job had got to!"

"Yes, it's a queer country, and a queer people, too, Job," I answered, with a sigh, for, though I am not superstitious like Job, I admit to a natural shrinking, which will not bear investigation, from the things that are above Nature.

"You are right, sir," he answered, "and if you won't think me very foolish, I should like to say something to you now that Mr. Leo is out of the way"—(Leo had risen early and gone for a stroll)—"and that is, that I know it is the last country as ever I shall see in this world. I had a dream last night, and I dreamed that I saw my old father with a kind of night-shirt on him, something like these folk wear when they want to be in particular full-dress, and a bit of that feathery grass in his hand, which he may have gathered on the way, for I saw lots of it yesterday about three hundred yards from the mouth of this beastly cave.

" 'Job,' he said to me, solemn like, and yet with a kind of satisfaction shining through him, more like a Methody elder when he has sold a neighbour a marked horse for a sound one and cleared twenty pounds by the job than anything I can think on—'Job, time's up, Job; but I never did expect to have to come and hunt you out in this 'ere place, Job! Such ado as I have had to nose you up; it wasn't friendly to give your poor old father such a run, let alone that a wonderful lot of bad characters hail from this place Kôr.' "

"Regular cautions," I suggested.

"Yes, sir—of course, sir, that's just what he said they was— 'cautions, downright scorchers'—sir, and I'm sure I don't doubt it, see-ing what I know of them and their hot-potting ways," went on Job, sadly. "Anyway, he was sure that time was up, and went away saying that we should see more than we cared for of each other soon, and I suppose he was a-thinking of the fact that father and I never could hit it off together for longer nor three days, and I daresay that things will be similar when we meet again."

"Surely," I said, "you don't think that you are going to die because you dreamed you saw your old father; if one dies because one dreams of one's father, what happens to a man who dreams of his mother-in-law?"

"Ah, sir, you're laughing at me," said Job; "but, you see, you didn't know my father. If it had been anybody else—my Aunt Mary, for instance, who never made much of a job—I should not have thought so much of it; but my father was that idle, which he shouldn't have been with seventeen children, that he would never have put himself out to come here just to see the place. No, sir; I know that he meant business. Well, sir, I can't help it; I suppose every man must go some time or other, though it is a hard thing to die in a hole like this, where Christian burial isn't to be had for its weight in gold. I've tried to be a good man, sir, and do my duty honest, and if it wasn't for the supercilus kind of way in which father carried on last night—a sort of sniffing at me as it were, as though he hadn't no opinion of my references and testimonials—I should feel easy enough in my mind. Anyway, sir, I've been a good servant to you and Mr. Leo, bless him!—why, it seems but the other day that I used to lead him about the streets with a penny whip;—and if ever you get out of this place—which, as father didn't allude to you, perhaps you may—I hope you will think kindly of my whitened bones, and never have anything more to do with Greek writing on flower-pots, sir, if I may make so bold as to say so."

"Come, come, Job," I said seriously, "this is all rubbish, you know. You mustn't be so silly as to get such ideas into your head. We've lived through some queer things, and I hope that we may go on doing so."

"No, sir," answered Job, in a tone of conviction that jarred on me unpleasantly, "it isn't rubbish. I'm a doomed man, and I feel it, and a wonderful uncomfortable feeling it is, sir, for one can't help wondering how it's going to come about. If you are eating your dinner you think of poison, and it goes against your stomach, and if you are walking along these dark rabbit-burrows you think of knives, and Lord, don't you just shiver about the back! I ain't particular, sir, provided it's sharp, like that poor girl, who, now that she's gone, I am sorry to have spoke hard on, though I don't approve of her morals in getting married, which I consider too quick to be decent. Still, sir," and poor Job turned a shade paler as he said it, "I do hope it won't be that hot-pot game."

"Nonsense," I broke in angrily, "nonsense!"

"Very well, sir," said Job, "it isn't my place to differ from you, sir, but if you happen to be going anywhere, sir, I should be obliged if you could manage to take me with you, seeing that I shall be glad to have a friendly face to look at when the time comes, just to help one through, as it were. And now, sir, I'll be getting the breakfast," and he went, leaving me in a very uncomfortable state of mind.

I was deeply attached to old Job, who was one of the best and honestest men I have ever had to do with in any class of life, really more of a friend than a servant, and the mere idea of anything happening to him brought a lump into my throat. Beneath all his ludicrous talk I could see that he himself was quite convinced that something was going to happen, and though in most cases these convictions turn out to be utter moonshine—and this particular one especially was to be amply accounted for by the gloomy and unaccustomed surroundings in which its victim was placed—still it did more or less carry a chill to my heart, as any dread that is obviously a genuine object of belief is apt to do, however absurd that belief may be.

Presently the breakfast arrived, and with it Leo, who had been taking a walk outside the cave—to clear his mind, he said; and very glad I was to see both, for they gave me a respite from my gloomy thoughts. After breakfast we went for another walk, and watched some of the Amahagger sowing a plot of ground with the grain from which they make their beer. This they did in scriptural fashion—a man with a bag made of goat's hide fastened round his waist striding up and down the plot and scattering seed as he went. It was a positive relief to see one of these dreadful people do anything so homely and pleasant as sow a field, perhaps because it seemed to link them with the rest of humanity.

As we were returning Billali met us, and informed us that it was *She's* pleasure that we should wait upon her. Accordingly we entered her presence, not without trepidation, for Ayesha was certainly an exception to the accepted rule: familiarity with her might and did breed passion and wonder and horror, but it certainly did *not* breed contempt.

As usual we were shown in by the mutes, and after they had retired Ayesha unveiled, and once more bade Leo embrace her, which, his heart-searchings of the previous night notwithstanding, he did with more alacrity and fervour than in strictness courtesy required.

She laid her white hand upon his head, and looked him fondly in the eyes. "Dost thou wonder, my Kallikrates," she said, "when thou shalt call me all thine own, and when we shall of a truth be for one another and to one another? I will tell thee. First must thou be even as I am, not immortal indeed, for that I am not, but so cased and hardened against the attacks of Time that his arrows shall glance from the armour of thy vigorous life as the sunbeams glance from water. As yet I may not mate with thee, for thou and I are different, and the very brightness of my being would burn thee up, and perchance destroy thee. Thou couldst not even endure to look upon me for too long a time, lest thine eyes should ache and thy senses swim, therefore"—with a little nod—"shall I presently veil myself again." (This, by the way, she did not do.) "No: listen. Thou shalt not be tried beyond endurance, for this very evening, an hour before the sun goes down, we will start hence, and by to-morrow's dark, if all goes well, and the road is not lost to me, which I pray it may not be, we shall stand in the place of Life, and thou shalt bathe in the fire, and come forth glorified, as no man ever was before thee, and then, Kallikrates, thou mayst call me wife, and I will call thee husband."

Leo muttered something in answer to this astonishing statement, I do not know what, and she laughed a little at his confusion, and went on:

"And thou, too, O Holly; to thee also I will grant this boon, and then of a truth thou shalt be evergreen, and this I will do—well, because thou hast pleased me, Holly, for thou art not altogether a fool, like the most of the sons of men, and because, though thou hast a school of philosophy as full of nonsense as those of the old days, yet hast thou not forgotten how to turn a pretty phrase about a lady's eyes."

"Hulloa, uncle!" whispered Leo, with a return of his former cheerfulness, "have you been paying compliments? I should never have thought it of you!"

"I thank thee, Ayesha," I replied, with as much dignity as I could command; "but if there be such a place as thou dost describe, and if in this strange place there may be found a fiery virtue that can hold off Death when he comes to pluck us by the hand, yet I seek none of it. For me, O Ayesha, the world has not proved so soft a nest that I would lie in it for ever. A stony-hearted mother is our earth, and stones are the bread she gives her children for their daily food. Stones to eat and bitter water for their thirst, and stripes for tender nurture. Who would endure this for many lives? Who would so load up his back with memories of lost hours and loves, and of his neighbour's sorrows which he cannot lessen, and with wisdom that brings not consolation? It is hard to die, because our delicate flesh shrinks back from the worm it will not feel, and from that Unknown which the winding-sheet curtains from our view. But harder still, to my thought, would it be to live on, green in the leaf and fair, but dead and rotten at the core, and to feel that other secret worm of memory gnawing ever at the heart."

"Bethink thee, Holly," she said; "yet do long life and strength and beauty beyond measure give power and all things that are dear to man."

"And what, O Queen," I answered, "are those things that are dear to man? Are they not bubbles? Is not ambition but an endless ladder by which no height is ever climbed till the last unreachable rung is mounted? For height leads on to height, and there is no resting-place upon them, and rung doth grow upon rung, and there is no limit to the number. Does not wealth satiate and become nauseous, and no longer serve to satisfy or pleasure, or to buy an hour's ease of mind? And is there any end to wisdom that we may hope to win it? Rather, the more we learn, shall we not thereby be able only to better compass out our ignorance? Did we live ten thousand years could we hope to solve the secrets of the suns, and of the space beyond the suns, and of the Hand that hung them in the heavens? Would not our wisdom be but as a gnawing hunger calling our consciousness day by day to a knowledge of the empty craving of our souls? Would it not be but as a light in one of these great caverns, that, though bright it burn, and brighter yet, doth but the more serve to show the depths of the gloom around it? And what good thing is there beyond that we may gain by length of days?"

"Nay, my Holly, there is love—love, which makes all things beautiful, yes, and breathes divinity into the very dust we tread. With love shall life roll on gloriously from year to year, like the voice of some great music that has power to hold the hearer's heart poised on eagles' wings above the sordid shame and folly of the earth."

"It may be so," I answered; "but if the loved one prove a broken reed to pierce us, or if the love be loved in vain—what then? Shall a man grave his sorrows upon a stone when he has but need to write them on the water? Nay, O *She*, I will live my day and grow old with my generation, and die my appointed death, and be forgotten. For I do hope for an immortality to which the little span that perchance thou canst confer will be but as a finger's length laid against the measure of the great world; and, mark this! the immortality to which I look, and which my faith doth promise to me, shall be free from the bonds that here must tie my spirit down. For, while the flesh endures, sorrow and evil and the scorpion whips of sin must endure also; but when the flesh has fallen from us, then shall the spirit shine forth clad in the brightness of eternal good, and for its common air shall breathe so rare an ether of most noble thoughts that the highest aspiration of our manhood, or the purest incense of a maiden's prayer, would prove too gross to float therein."

"Thou lookest high," answered Ayesha, with a little laugh, "and speakest clearly as a trumpet, and with no uncertain sound. And yet methinks that but now thou didst talk of 'that Unknown' from which the winding-sheet doth curtain us. Well, perchance thou seest with the eye of Faith, gazing on this brightness, that is to be, through the painted glass of thy imagination. Strange are the pictures of the future that mankind can thus draw with this brush of faith and these many-coloured pigments of the imagination! Strange, too, that no one of them tallies with another! I could tell thee—but there, to what end—

why rob a fool of his bauble? Let it pass, and I pray, O Holly, that when thou shalt feel old age creeping slowly over thee, and the dull edge of eld working havoc in thy brain, thou mayst not bitterly regret that thou didst cast away the imperial boon I would have given to thee. But so it has always been; man can never be content with that which his hand may pluck. If a lamp shines for him to light him through the darkness, straightway he casts it down because it is no star. Happiness dances ever a pace before his feet, like the marsh-fire in the swamps, and he must catch the fire, and he must win the star! Beauty is naught to him, because there are lips more honey-sweet; and wealth is poverty, because others can weigh him down with heavier shekels; and fame is emptiness, because there have been greater men than he. Thyself thou saidst it, and I turn thy words against thee. Well, thou dreamest that thou shalt clasp the star. I believe it not, and I name thee fool, my Holly, to throw away the lamp."

I made no answer, for, especially before Leo, I could not tell her that since I had seen her face I knew it must always be before my eyes, and that I had no wish to prolong an existence which must be ever haunted and tortured by her memory, and by the last bitterness of unsatisfied love. But so it was, and so, alas, is it to this hour!

"And now," went on *She,* changing her tone and the subject together, "tell me, my Kallikrates, for as yet I know it not, how came ye to seek me here? Yesternight thou didst say that Kallikrates—him whom thou sawest dead—was thine ancestor. How was it? Tell me—thou dost not speak overmuch!"

Thus adjured, Leo told her the wonderful story of the casket and of the potsherd that, written on by his ancestress, the Egyptian Amenartas, had been the means of guiding us to her. Ayesha listened intently, and, when he had finished, spoke to me.

"Did I not tell thee once, while we talked of good and evil, O Holly—it was when my beloved lay so ill—that out of good came evil, and out of evil good—that they who sowed knew not what the crop should be, nor he who struck where the blow should fall? See, now: this Egyptian Amenartas, this royal child of the Nile, who hated me, and whom even now I hate, for in a measure she prevailed against me—see,

I say, she herself hath been the guide to lead her lover to mine arms! For her sake I slew him, and now, behold, through her he has come back to me! She would have done me evil, and sowed her seeds that I might reap tares, and behold she hath given me more than all the world can give, and there is a strange square for thee to fit into thy circle of good and evil, O Holly!

"And so," she went on after a pause—"and so she bade her son destroy me if he might, because I slew his father. And thou, my Kallikrates, art the father, and in a sense thou art likewise the son; and wouldst thou avenge thy wrong, and the wrong of that far-off mother of thine, upon me, O Kallikrates? See," and she slid to her knees, and opened the white robe upon her ivory bosom—"see, here beats my heart, and there by thy side is a knife, heavy, and long, and sharp, the very knife to slay an erring woman with. Take it now, and be avenged. Strike, and strike home!—so shalt thou be satisfied, Kallikrates, and go through life a happy man, because thou hast paid back the wrong, and obeyed the mandate of the past."

He looked at her; then he stretched out his hand and lifted her to her feet.

"Rise, Ayesha," he said sadly; "thou knowest well that I cannot harm thee, no, not even for the sake of her whom thou slewest but last night. I am in thy power, and a very slave to thee. How can I kill thee?—sooner should I slay myself."

"Almost dost thou begin to love me, Kallikrates," she answered, smiling. "And now tell me of thy country—'tis a great people, is it not? with an empire like that of Rome! Surely thou wilt return thither, and it is well, for I would not that thou shouldst dwell in these caves of Kôr. Nay, when once thou art even as I am we will go hence—fear not but that I shall find a path—and then will we journey to this England of thine, and live as it becometh us to live. Two thousand years have I waited for the day when I should see the last of these hateful caves and this gloomy-visaged folk, and now it is at hand, and my heart bounds up to meet it like a child's towards its holiday. For thou shalt rule this England——"

"But we have a queen already," interrupted Leo, hastily.

"Strike, and strike home!"

"It is naught, it is naught," said Ayesha; "she can be overthrown."

At this we both broke out into exclamations of dismay, and explained that we should as soon think of overthrowing ourselves.

"But here is a strange thing," said Ayesha, in astonishment—

"a queen whom her people love! Surely the world must have changed since I dwelt in Kôr."

Again we explained that it was the character of monarchs that had changed, and that the sovereign under whom we lived was venerated and beloved by all right-thinking men in her vast realms. Also, we told her that real power in our country rested in the hands of the people; that, in fact, we were ruled by the votes of the lower and least educated classes of the community.

"Ah," she said, "a democracy—then surely there is a tyrant, for I have long since seen that democracies, having no clear will of their own, in the end set up a tyrant, and worship him."

"Yes," I said, "we have our tyrants."

"Well," she answered resignedly, "we can at any rate destroy these tyrants, and Kallikrates shall rule the land."

I instantly informed Ayesha that in England "blasting" was not an amusement that could be indulged in with impunity, and that any such attempt would meet with the consideration of the law, and probably end upon a scaffold.

"The law!" she laughed with scorn—"the law! Canst thou not understand, O Holly, that I am above the law, and so shall Kallikrates be also? All human law will be to us as the north wind to a mountain. Does the wind bend the mountain, or the mountain the wind?

"And now leave me, I pray thee, and thou, too, my own Kallikrates, for I would make me ready against our journey, and so must ye both, and your servant also. But bring no great store of garments with thee, for I trust that we shall be but three days gone. Then must we return hither, and I will make a plan whereby we can bid farewell for ever to these sepulchres of Kôr. Yea, surely thou mayst kiss my hand!"

So we went, I, for one, meditating deeply on the awful nature of the problem that now opened out before us. Evidently the terrible *She* had determined to go to England, and it made me shudder to think what would be the result of her arrival there. What her powers were I knew, and I could not doubt but that she would exercise them to the full. It might be possible to control her for a while, but her proud, ambitious spirit would be certain to break loose and to avenge itself for the long centuries of its solitude. If necessary, and if the unaided power of her beauty did not prove sufficient for her purpose, she would blast her way to any end she set before her, and, as she could not die, and for aught I knew could not even be killed,* what was there to stay her? In the end, I had little doubt, she would assume absolute rule over the British dominions, and probably over the whole earth, and, though I was sure that she would speedily make ours the most glorious and prosperous empire that the world has ever seen, it must be at the cost of a terrible sacrifice of life.

The story sounded like a dream or some extraordinary invention of a speculative brain, and yet it was a fact—a wonderful fact—of which the universe would soon be called on to take notice. What was the meaning of it all? After much thinking I could only conclude that this marvellous creature, whose passion had kept her for so many centuries chained as it were, and comparatively harmless, was now about to be used by Providence as a means to change the order of the world, and possibly, by the building up of a power that could no more be rebelled against or questioned than the decrees of Fate, to change it materially for the better.

---

*I regret to say that I was never able to ascertain if *She* was invulnerable against the accidents of life. Presumably this was so, else some misadventure would have been sure to put an end to her in the course of so many centuries. True, she suggested to Leo that he should kill her, but very probably this was only an experiment to try his temper and mental attitude towards herself. Ayesha never gave way to impulse without some valid object.—L. H. H.

XXIII

The Temple of Truth

Our preparations did not take us very long. We packed a change of clothing apiece and some spare boots into my handbag; also we took our revolvers and an Express rifle each, together with a good supply of ammunition, a precaution to which, under Providence, we subsequently owed our lives over and over again. The rest of our gear, together with our heavy rifles, we left behind us.

A few minutes before the appointed time we were summoned to Ayesha's "boudoir," and found her also ready, the dark cloak thrown over her corpselike wrappings.

"Are ye prepared for the great venture?" she said.

"We are," I answered, "though for my part, Ayesha, I have no faith in it."

"Of a truth, my Holly," she said, "thou art like those old Jews—of whom the memory vexes me so sorely—unbelieving, and slow to accept that which thou hast not known. But thou shalt see; for unless my mirror yonder lies," and she pointed to the font of crystal water, "the path is yet open as it was of old time. And now let us away, to begin the new life which shall end—who knoweth where?"

"Ah," I echoed, "who knows where?" and we passed down into the great central cave, and out into the light of day. At the mouth of the cave we found a single litter waiting, with six bearers, all of them mutes; and with these I was relieved to see our old friend Billali, for whom I had conceived a sort of affection. It appeared that, for reasons not necessary to explain at length, Ayesha had thought it best that, with the exception of herself, we should proceed on foot. This we were nothing loth to do after our long confinement in the caves, which, however suitable they might be to serve as the last home of the dead, were depressing habitations for breathing mortals like ourselves. Either by accident or by the orders of *She*, the space in front of the cave where we had witnessed that awful dance was empty of spectators. Not a man could be seen, and consequently I do not believe that our departure was known to anyone, except, perhaps, to the mutes in attendance upon *She*, who were necessarily in the habit of keeping what they saw to themselves.

In a few minutes' time we were stepping out sharply across the great cultivated plain or lake bed, framed like a vast emerald in its setting of frowning cliff. Here we found fresh opportunity to wonder at the extraordinary nature of the site chosen by these old people of Kôr for their capital, and at the marvellous amount of labour, ingenuity, and engineering skill that must have been brought into requisition by the founders of the city to drain so huge a sheet of water, and to keep it free from subsequent accumulations. So far as my experience goes, it is, indeed, an unequalled instance of what man can do in the face of nature, for in my opinion such achievements as the Suez Canal, or even the Mont Cenis Tunnel, do not approach this ancient undertaking in magnitude and grandeur of conception.

When we had been walking for about half an hour, enjoying ourselves exceedingly in the delightful cool which at this time of the day always appeared to descend upon the great plain of Kôr, and that in some degree atoned for the want of any land or sea breeze—for all wind was kept off by the rocky mountain wall—we began to distinguish clearly the buildings which, as Billali had informed us, were the ruins of the great city.

Even from that distance we could see how wonderful those ruins were, a fact which became more evident at every step. The town was not very large if compared to Babylon or Thebes, or other cities of remote antiquity; perhaps its outer ditch contained some twelve square miles of ground or a little more. Nor had the walls, so far as we could judge when we reached them, been very high, probably not more than forty feet, which was about their present height where, through the sinking of the ground, or some such cause, they had not fallen into ruin. The reason of this, no doubt, was that the people of Kôr, being protected from outside attack by far more tremendous ramparts than any that the hand of man could rear, only required walls for show and to guard against civil discord. But, on the other hand, they were as broad as they were high, built entirely of dressed stone, hewn, probably, from the vast caves, and surrounded by a great moat some sixty feet in width, many reaches of which were still filled with water. About ten minutes before the sun sank finally we reached this moat, and passed down and through it, clambering across what evidently were the piled-up fragments of a great bridge in order to do so, and then with some little difficulty over the slope of the wall to its summit. I wish that it lay within the power of my pen to give an idea of the grandeur of the sight which met our view. There, all bathed in the red glow of the sinking sun, were miles upon miles of ruins—columns, temples, shrines, and the palaces of kings, varied with patches of green bush. Of course the roofs of these buildings had long since fallen into decay and vanished, but owing to the extreme massiveness of the masonry, and to the hardness and durability of the rock employed, most of the party walls and great columns still remained standing.*

Straight before us stretched away what evidently had been the main thoroughfare of the city, for it was very wide and regular—wider than the Thames Embankment. Being, as we afterwards discovered, paved,

*In connection with the extraordinary state of preservation of these ruins after so great a lapse of time—at least six thousand years—it must be remembered that Kôr was not burnt or destroyed by an enemy or an earthquake, but deserted, because of the ravages of a terrible plague. Consequently the houses were left unharmed; also the climate of the plain is remarkably fine and dry, with very little rain or wind. As a result these unique relics have only to contend against the unaided action of time, that works but slowly upon such massive blocks of masonry.—L. H. H.

or rather built, throughout of blocks of dressed stone, such as were employed in the walls, even now it was but little overgrown with grass and shrubs, that could find no depth of soil to live in. What had been the parks and gardens, on the contrary, had become dense jungle. Indeed, it was easy even from a distance to trace the course of the various roads by the burnt-up appearance of the scanty herbage that grew upon them. On either side of this great thoroughfare were vast blocks of ruins, each block separated from its neighbour by a space of what had once, I suppose, been garden-ground, but was now thick and tangled bush. They were all built of the same coloured stone, and most of them had pillars, which was as much as we could see in the fading light as we passed swiftly up the main road, that, I believe I am right in saying, no human foot had pressed for thousands of years.*

Presently we came to an enormous pile, covering at least eight acres of ground, that we rightly took to be a temple, which was arranged in a series of courts, each one of them enclosing another of smaller size, on the principle of a Chinese nest of boxes, these courts being separated by rows of huge columns. While I think of it, I may as well describe the remarkable shape of these columns, which resembled none that I have ever seen or heard of, being fashioned to a narrow central waist, and swelling above and below it. At first we thought that this shape was meant roughly to symbolise or suggest the female form, after the common fashion of the ancient religious architects of many creeds. On the following day, however, as we climbed the slopes of the mountain, we discovered a large quantity of stately palms, whereof the trunks grew thus, and I have now no doubt but that the first designer of those columns drew his inspiration from the graceful bends of those very palms, or rather of their ancestors, that some eight or ten

---

*Billali told me that the Amahagger believe that the site of the city is haunted, and could not be persuaded to enter it upon any consideration. Indeed, I could see that he himself did not at all like defying the custom, and was only consoled because he was under the direct protection of *She*. It struck Leo and myself as very curious that a people which has no objection to living amongst the dead, with whom their familiarity has perhaps bred contempt, and even to using their bodies as fuel, should be terrified at approaching the habitations that these very departed had occupied when alive. However, this is only a savage inconsistency. —L. H. H.

thousand years ago beautified the slopes of the mountain which formed the shores of the ancient volcanic lake.

At the *façade* of this huge temple, which, I should imagine, is almost as large as that of El-Karnac, at Thebes, some of the largest columns which I measured being between eighteen to twenty feet in diameter at the base, by about seventy feet in height, our little procession was halted, and Ayesha descended from her litter.

"There was a chamber here, Kallikrates," she said to Leo, who had gone to help her to alight, "where one might sleep. Two thousand years ago thou and I and that Egyptian asp rested therein, but since then I have not set foot here, and perchance it has fallen." Then, followed by the rest of us, she passed up a vast flight of broken steps into the outer court, and looked round into the gloom. Presently she seemed to recollect, and, walking a few paces along the wall to the left, she halted.

"It is here as of old," Ayesha said, beckoning to the two mutes, who were loaded with provisions and our few packages, to advance. One of them came forward, and, producing a lamp, lit it from his brazier, for the Amahagger when on a journey always carried with them a little lighted brazier, from which to provide fire. The tinder of this brazier was made of broken fragments of mummy carefully damped, and, if the admixture of moisture is properly managed, this unholy compound will smoulder for many hours.* So soon as the lamp was lit we entered the place before which Ayesha had halted. It proved to be a cell hollowed in the thickness of the wall, and, from the fact of its containing a massive stone table, I should imagine that it had served as a living-room, perhaps for one of the door-keepers of the great temple.

Here we camped, and after cleaning the place out and making it as comfortable as circumstances and the darkness would permit, we ate some cold meat—at least Leo, Job, and I did, for Ayesha, as I think I have said elsewhere, never touched anything except cakes of flour, fruit and water. While we were still eating, the moon, which was at her

---

*After all we are not much in advance of the Amahagger in these matters. "Mummy," *i.e.,* pounded ancient Egyptian, is, I believe, a pigment much used by artists, and especially by those of them who direct their talents to the reproduction of the works of the old masters. —EDITOR.

full, rose above the mountain-wall, and began to flood the place with silver rays.

"Know ye why I have brought you here to-night, my Holly?" said Ayesha, leaning her head upon her hand and watching the great orb as she rose, a very queen of heaven, above the solemn pillars of the temple. "I brought you—nay, it is strange, but knowest thou, Kallikrates, that thou liest at this moment upon that same spot where thy dead body lay when I bore thee back to those caves of Kôr so many years ago? The scene springs to my mind again. I can see it, and it is horrible to my sight!" and she shuddered.

Here Leo jumped up hastily and changed his seat. However the reminiscence might affect Ayesha, clearly it had few charms for him.

"I brought you," she went on presently, "that ye might look upon the most wonderful sight that ever the eye of man beheld—the full moon shining over ruined Kôr. When ye have done your eating—I would that I could teach thee to eat naught but fruit, Kallikrates, but that will come after thou hast washed in the fire; once I, too, ate flesh like a brute beast—when ye have done, I say, we will go out, and I will show you this great temple and the god whom men once worshipped there."

Of course we rose at once, and started. And here again my pen fails me. To give a string of measurements and details of the various courts of the temple would only be wearisome, supposing that I had them; and yet I know not how I am to describe what we saw, magnificent as it was even in its ruin, almost beyond the power of realisation. Court upon dim court, row upon row of mighty pillars—some of them, especially at the gateways, sculptured from base to capital—space upon space of empty chambers that spoke more eloquently to the imagination than any crowded streets. And over all a dead silence of the dead, a sense of utter loneliness, and the brooding spirit of the Past! How beautiful it was, and yet how drear! We did not dare to speak aloud. Ayesha herself was awed in the presence of an antiquity compared to which even her length of days was but a little thing; we only whispered, and our whispers seemed to run from column to column, till they were lost in the quiet air. Bright fell the moonlight on pillar and court and shattered wall, hiding all their rents and imperfections in its silver garment, and clothing their hoar majesty with the peculiar glory of the night. It was a wonderful sight to see the full moon looking down on this ruined fane of Kôr. It was a wonderful thing to think for how many thousands of years the dead orb above and the dead city below had gazed thus upon each other, and in the utter solitude of space poured forth each to each the tale of their lost life and long-departed glory. The white light fell, and minute by minute the slow shadows crept across the grass-grown courts like the spirits of old priests haunting the habitations of their worship—the white light fell, and the long shadows grew, till the beauty and grandeur of the scene and the untamed majesty of its present death seemed to sink into our very souls, and to speak more loudly than the shouts of armies concerning the pomp and splendour that the grave had swallowed, and even memory had forgotten.

"Come," said Ayesha, after we had gazed and gazed, I know not for how long, "and I will show you the stony flower of Loveliness and Wonder's very crown, if yet it stands to mock time with its beauty and fill the heart of man with longing for that which is behind the veil," and, without waiting for an answer, she led us through two more pillared courts into the inner shrine of the ancient fane.

And there, in the midst of the inmost court, that might have been some fifty yards square, or a little more, we stood face to face with what is perhaps the grandest allegorical work of Art that the genius of her children has ever given to the world. For in the exact centre of the court, placed upon a thick square slab of rock, was a huge ball of dark-hued stone, about twenty feet in diameter, and standing on the ball was a colossal winged figure of a beauty so entrancing and divine that when first I gazed upon it, illuminated and shadowed as it was by the soft light of the moon, my breath stood still, and for an instant my heart ceased its beating.

This statue was hewn from marble so pure and white that even now, after all those ages, it shone as the moonbeams danced upon it; and its height, I should say, was over twenty feet. It represented the winged figure of a woman of such marvellous loveliness and delicacy of form

The Temple of Truth

that the size seemed rather to add to than to detract from its so human
and yet more spiritual beauty. She stood bending forward and poising
herself upon her half-spread wings as though to preserve her balance
as she leant. Her arms were outstretched like those of some woman
about to embrace one she dearly loved, while her whole attitude gave
an impression of the tenderest beseeching. Her perfect and most gracious form was naked, save—and here is the extraordinary thing—the

face, which was thinly veiled, so that we could only distinguish the outline of her features. A gauzy veil was thrown round and about the head, and of its two ends one fell down across her left breast, which swelled beneath it, and one, now broken, streamed out upon the air behind her.

"Who is she?" I asked, so soon as I could take my eyes off the statue.

"Canst thou not guess, O Holly?" answered Ayesha. "Where, then, is thy imagination? It is Truth standing on the World, and calling to its children to unveil her face. See what is written upon the pedestal. Without doubt it is taken from the book of the Scriptures of these men of Kôr," and she led the way to the foot of the statue, where an inscription of the usual Chinese-looking hieroglyphics was so deeply graven as to be still quite legible, at least to Ayesha. According to her translation it ran thus:—

> *"Is there no man that will draw my veil and look upon my face, for it is very fair? Unto him who draws my veil shall I be, and I will give him peace, and sweet children of knowledge and good works."*
>
> *And a Voice cried, "Though all those who seek after thee desire thee: Behold! Virgin art thou, and Virgin thou shalt go till Time be done. There is no man born of woman who may draw thy veil and live, nor shall be. By Death only can thy veil be drawn, O Truth!"*
>
> *And Truth stretched out her arms and wept, because those who wooed her might not win her, nor look upon her face to face.*

"Thou seest," said Ayesha, when she had finished translating, "Truth was the goddess of these people of old Kôr, and to her they built their shrines, and her they sought; knowing that they should never find, still they sought."

"And so," I added sadly, "do men seek to this very hour, but they find not; and, as this Scripture saith, nor shall they; for in Death only is Truth found."

Then, with one more look at this veiled and spiritualised loveliness—which was so perfect and so pure that almost we might fancy that the light of a living spirit shone through the marble prison to lead man on to high and ethereal thoughts—this poet's dream of beauty frozen into stone, which I never shall forget while I live—we turned and retraced our steps through the vast moonlit courts. I did not see the statue again, which I regret the more, because about the great ball of stone representing the World whereon the figure stood lines were drawn that, had there been light enough, probably we should have discovered to be a map of the Universe as it was known to the people of Kôr. It is at any rate suggestive of some scientific knowledge that these long-dead worshippers of Truth had recognised the fact that the globe is round.

XXIV

WALKING THE PLANK

Next day the mutes woke us before the dawn. By the time that we had rubbed the sleep out of our eyes, and refreshed ourselves by washing at a spring which still welled up into the remains of a marble basin in the centre of the north quadrangle of the vast outer court, we found *She* standing near the litter ready to start, while old Billali and the two bearer-mutes were busy collecting the baggage. As usual, Ayesha was veiled like the marble Truth, and it struck me then that she might have taken the idea of covering up her beauty from that statue. I noticed, however, that she seemed very depressed, and had none of that proud and buoyant bearing which would have betrayed her among a thousand women of the same stature, even if they had been veiled like herself. She looked up as we came—for her head was bowed—and greeted us. Leo asked her how she had slept.

"Ill, my Kallikrates," she answered, "ill! This night strange and hideous dreams have come creeping through my brain, and I know not what they may portend. Almost do I feel as though some evil overshadowed me; and yet, how can evil touch me? I wonder," she went on with a sudden outbreak of womanly tenderness, "I wonder, should aught happen to me, so that I slept awhile and left thee waking, if thou wouldst think gently of me? I wonder, my Kallikrates, if thou wouldst tarry till *I* came again, as for so many centuries I have tarried for *thy* coming?"

Then, without waiting for an answer, she went on: "Let us be setting forth, for we have far to go, and before another day is born in yonder blue we should stand in the place of Life."

In five minutes we were once more on our way through the ruined city, which loomed on either side through the grey dawning in a fashion at once grand and oppressive. Just as the first ray of the rising sun shot like a golden arrow athwart this storied desolation we gained the further gateway of the outer wall. Here, having given one more glance at the hoar and pillared majesty through which we had journeyed, and—with the exception of Job, for whom ruins had no charms—breathed a sigh of regret that we lacked time to explore it, we passed through the encircling moat, and on to the plain beyond.

As the sun rose so did Ayesha's spirits, till at length they had regained their normal level, and she laughingly attributed her sadness to the associations of the spot where she had slept.

"These barbarians swear that Kôr is haunted," she said, "and of a truth I believe their saying, for never did I know so ill a night save once. I remember it now. It was on that very spot, when thou didst lie dead at my feet, Kallikrates. Never will I visit it again; it is a place of evil omen."

After a very brief halt for breakfast we pressed on with such good will that by two o'clock in the day we were at the foot of the vast wall of rock forming the lip of the volcano, which at this point towered up precipitously above us for fifteen hundred or two thousand feet. Here we halted, certainly not to my astonishment, for I did not see how it was possible that we should advance any farther.

"Now," said Ayesha, as she descended from her litter, "our labours but commence, for here we part with these men, and henceforward must we bear ourselves." Then she added, addressing Billali, "do thou and these slaves remain here, and abide our return. By to-morrow at the midday we shall be with thee—if not, wait."

Billali bowed humbly, and said that her august bidding should be obeyed if they stopped there till they grew old.

"And this man, O Holly," said *She,* pointing to Job; "it is best that he should tarry also, for if his heart be not high and his courage great, perchance some evil might overtake him. Also, the secrets of the place whither we go are not fit for common eyes."

I translated this to Job, who instantly and earnestly entreated me, almost with tears, not to leave him behind. He said he was sure that he could see nothing worse than he had already seen, and that he was terrified to death at the idea of being left alone with those "dumb folk," who, he thought, would probably take the opportunity to "hot-pot" him.

I translated what he said to Ayesha, who shrugged her shoulders, and answered, "Well, let him come, it is naught to me; on his own head be it. He will serve to bear the lamp and this," and she pointed to a narrow board, some sixteen feet in length, which had been bound above the long bearing-pole of her hammock, I had thought to give the curtains a wider spread, but, as it now appeared, for some unknown purpose connected with our extraordinary undertaking.

Accordingly the plank, which, though tough, was very light, was given to Job to carry, and also one of the lamps. I slung the other on to my back, together with a spare jar of oil, while Leo loaded himself with the provisions and some water in a kid's skin. When this was done *She* bade Billali and the six bearer-mutes to retreat behind a grove of flowering magnolias about a hundred yards away, and there to remain under pain of death till we had vanished. They bowed humbly, and went. As he departed, old Billali gave me a friendly shake of the hand, and whispered that he had rather that it were I than he who was going on this wonderful expedition with *"She-who-must-be-obeyed,"* a view with which I felt inclined to agree. In another minute they were gone; then, having briefly asked us if we were ready, Ayesha turned and gazed at the towering cliff.

"Great heavens, Leo," I said, "surely we are not going to climb that precipice!"

Leo, who was in a state of half-fascinated, half-expectant mystification, shrugged his shoulders, and at that moment Ayesha with a sudden spring began to scale the cliff, whither of course we must follow her. It was almost marvellous to see the ease and grace with which she sprang from rock to rock, and swung herself along the ledges. The ascent, however, was not so difficult as it seemed, although we passed one or two nasty places where it was unpleasant to look back; for here the rock still sloped, and was not absolutely precipitous, as it became above.

In this way, with no great toil—for the only troublesome thing to manage was Job's board—we mounted to the height of some fifty feet beyond our last standing-place, and in so doing drew sixty or seventy paces to the left of our starting-point, for we ascended as crabs walk, sideways. Presently we reached a ledge, narrow enough at first, but which widened as we followed it, and sloped inwards, moreover, like the petal of a flower, so that we sank gradually into a kind of rut or fold of rock that grew deeper and deeper, till at last it resembled a Devonshire lane in stone, and hid us perfectly from the gaze of persons on the slope below, had anybody been there to gaze. This lane, which appeared to be a natural formation, continued for some thirty or forty yards, then suddenly ended in a cave, also natural, running at right angles to it. That it was not hollowed by the labour of man I am sure, because of its irregular, contorted shape and course, which gave it the appearance of having been blasted in the thickness of the mountain by some frightful eruption of gas following the line of the least resistance. All the caverns hollowed by the ancients of Kôr, on the other hand, were cut out with a symmetrical and perfect regularity.

At the mouth of this cave Ayesha halted, and bade us light the two lamps, which I did, giving one to her and keeping the other myself. Then, taking the lead, she advanced down the cavern, picking her way with great care, as indeed it was necessary to do, for the floor was most irregular—strewn with boulders like the bed of a stream, and in some places pitted with deep holes, in which it would have been easy to break a limb.

This cavern we pursued for twenty minutes or more. It was about a quarter of a mile long, so far as I could form a judgment, which, owing to its numerous twists and turns, was not an easy task.

At last, however, we halted at its further end, and whilst I was still trying to accustom my eyes to the twilight without a great gust of air came tearing down the cave, and extinguished both the lamps.

Ayesha called to us, and we crept up to her, for she was a little in front, to be rewarded with a view that was positively appalling in its gloom and grandeur. Before us was a mighty chasm in the black rock, jagged, torn, and splintered through it in a far past age by some awful convulsion of Nature, as though it had been cleft by stroke upon stroke of the lightning. This chasm, which was bounded by precipices, although at the moment we could not see that on the farther side, may have measured any width across, but from its darkness I do not think it can have been very broad. It was impossible to make out much of its outline, or how far it ran, for the simple reason that the point where we were standing was so far from the upper surface of the cliff, at least fifteen hundred or two thousand feet, that only a very dim light struggled down to us from above. The mouth of the cavern that we had been following gave on to a most curious and tremendous spur of rock, which jutted out through mid air into the gulf before us for a distance of some fifty yards, coming to a sharp point at its termination, and in shape resembling nothing that I can think of so much as the spur upon the leg of a cock. This huge spur was attached only to the parent precipice at its base, which was, of course, enormous, just as the cock's spur is attached to its leg. Otherwise it was utterly unsupported.

"Here must we pass," said Ayesha. "Be careful lest giddiness overcome you, or the wind sweep you into the gulf beneath, for of a truth it has no bottom;" and, without giving us further time to grow frightened, she began to walk along the spur, leaving us to follow her as best we might. I was next to her, then came Job, painfully dragging his plank, while Leo brought up the rear. It was a wonderful sight to see this intrepid woman gliding fearlessly along that dreadful place. For my part, when I had gone but a very few yards, what between the pressure of the air and the awful sense of the consequences that a slip would entail, I found it necessary to drop on to my hands and knees and crawl, and so did the others.

But Ayesha never condescended to this humble expedient. On she went, leaning her body against the gusts of wind, and not seeming to lose either her head or her balance.

In a few minutes we had crossed some twenty paces of this awful bridge, which grew narrower at every step, when of a sudden a great gust tore along the gorge. I saw Ayesha lean herself against it, but the strong draught forced itself beneath her dark cloak, wrenching it from her, and away it went down the wind flapping like a wounded bird. It was dreadful to see it go, till it was lost in the blackness.

I clung to the saddle of rock, and looked about me, while, like a living thing, the great spur vibrated with a humming sound beneath us. The sight was truly awesome. There we were poised in the gloom between earth and heaven. Beneath us stretched hundreds upon hundreds of feet of emptiness that gradually grew darker, till at last it was absolutely black, and at what depth it ended is more than I can guess. Above were measureless spaces of giddy air, and far, far away a line of blue sky. And down this vast gulf in which we were pinnacled the great draught dashed and roared, driving clouds and misty wreaths of vapour before it, till we were nearly blinded, and utterly confused.

Indeed the position was so tremendous and so absolutely unearthly, that I believe it actually lulled our sense of terror; but to this hour I often see it in my dreams, and at its mere phantasy wake up dripping with cold sweat.

"On! on!" cried the white form before us, for now that her cloak had gone *She* was robed in white, and looked more like a spirit riding down the gale than a woman; "On, or ye will fall and be dashed to pieces. Fix your eyes upon the ground, and cling closely to the rock."

We obeyed her, and crept painfully along the quivering path, against which the wind shrieked and wailed as it shook it, causing it to murmur like some gigantic tuning-fork. On we went, I do not know for how long, only gazing round now and again when it was absolutely necessary, until at last we saw that we had reached the very tip of the spur, a slab of rock, but little larger than an ordinary table, that throbbed and jumped like any over-engined steamer. There we lay, clinging to the stone, and stared round us, while, absolutely heedless of the hideous depth that yawned beneath, Ayesha stood leaning out against the wind, down which her long hair streamed, and pointed before her. Then we saw why the narrow plank had been provided, which Job and I had borne so painfully between us. In front yawned an empty space, on the other side of which was something, as yet we could not see what, for here—either owing to the shadow of the opposite cliff, or from some other cause—the gloom was that of a cloudy night.

"We must wait awhile," called Ayesha; "soon there will be light."

At the moment I could not imagine what she meant. How could more light than there was ever come to this dreadful spot? While I was still wondering, suddenly, like a great sword of flame, a beam from the setting sun pierced the Stygian gloom, and smote upon the point of rock whereon we lay, illumining Ayesha's lovely form with an unearthly splendour. I only wish I could describe the wild and marvellous beauty of that sword of fire, laid across the darkness and rushing mist-wreaths of the gulf. How it came there I do not to this moment know, but I presume that there was some cleft or hole in the opposing cliff, through which light flowed when the setting orb was in a direct line with it. All I can say is, the effect was the most wonderful that I ever saw. Right through the heart of the darkness that flaming sword was stabbed, and where it lay the light was surpassingly vivid, so vivid that even at a distance we could see the grain of the rock, while outside of it—yes, within a few inches of its keen edge—was naught but clustering shadows.

And now, by this vast sunbeam, for which *She* had been waiting, and timed our arrival to meet, knowing that at this season for thousands of years it had always struck thus at eve, we saw what was before us. Within eleven or twelve yards of the very tip of the tongue-like rock whereon we stood there arose, presumably from the far bottom of the gulf, a sugarloaf-shaped cone, of which the summit was exactly opposite to us. But had there been a summit only it would not have helped us much, for the nearest point of its circumference was some forty feet from where we were. On the lip of this summit, however, which was circular and hollow, rested a tremendous flat boulder, something like a glacier stone—perhaps it was one, for all I know to the contrary—and the end of the boulder approached to within twelve feet of us. This huge mass was nothing more nor less than a gigantic rocking-stone, accurately balanced upon the edge of the cone or miniature crater, like a half-crown set on the rim of a wine-glass; for, in the fierce light that played upon it and us, we could see it oscillating in the gusts of wind.

"Quick!" said Ayesha; "the plank—we must cross while the light endures; presently it will be gone."

"Oh Lord, sir! surely she don't mean us to walk across this here place on that there thing," groaned Job, as in obedience to my directions he thrust the long board towards me.

"That's it, Job," I holloaed in ghastly merriment, though the idea of walking the plank was no pleasanter to me than to him.

I passed the board to Ayesha, who ran it deftly across the gulf so that one end of it rested on the rocking-stone, the other remaining upon the extremity of the trembling spur. Then, placing her foot upon it to prevent it from being blown away, she turned to me.

"Since last I was here, O Holly," she called, "the support of the moving stone hath lessened somewhat, so that I am not sure whether it will bear our weight. Therefore I must cross the first, because no hurt will overtake me," and, without further ado, she trod lightly but firmly across the frail bridge, and in another second had gained the heaving stone.

"It is safe," she called. "See, hold thou the plank! I will stand on the farther side of the rock, so that it may not overbalance with your greater weights. Now come, O Holly, for presently the light will fail us."

I struggled to my knees, and if ever I felt terrified in my life it was then; indeed, I am not ashamed to say that I hesitated and hung back.

"Surely thou art not afraid," cried this strange creature, in a lull of the gale, from where she stood poised like a bird on the highest point of the rocking-stone. "Make way, then, for Kallikrates."

This decided me; it is better to fall down a precipice and die than be laughed at by such a woman; so I clenched my teeth, and in another instant I was on that narrow, bending plank, with bottomless space beneath and around me. I have always hated a great height, but never before did I appreciate the full horrors of which such a position is capable. Oh, the sickening sensation of that yielding board resting on the two moving supports. I grew dizzy, and thought that I must fall; my spine *crept*; it seemed to me that I was falling, and my delight at finding myself stretched upon the stone, which rose and fell beneath me like a boat in a swell, cannot be expressed in words. All I know is that briefly, but earnestly enough, I thanked Providence for preserving me thus far.

Then came Leo's turn, and, though he looked rather white, he ran across like a rope-dancer. Ayesha stretched out her hand to clasp his own, and I heard her say, "Bravely done, my love—bravely done! The old Greek spirit lives in thee yet!"

And now only poor Job remained on the farther side of the gulf. He crept up to the plank, and yelled out, "I can't do it, sir. I shall fall into that beastly place."

"You must," I remember answering with inappropriate facetiousness—"you must, Job, it's as easy as catching flies." I suppose that I must have said this to satisfy my conscience, because, although the expression conveys a wonderful idea of facility, as a matter of fact I know no more difficult operation in the whole world than catching flies— that is, in warm weather, unless, indeed, it is catching mosquitoes.

"I can't, sir—I can't indeed."

"Let the man come, or let him stay and perish there. See, the light is dying! In a moment it will be gone!" said Ayesha.

I looked. She was right. The sun was passing below the level of the hole or cleft in the precipice through which the ray reached us.

"If you stop there, Job, you will die alone," I called; "the light is going."

"Come, be a man, Job," shouted Leo; "it's quite easy."

Thus adjured, with a most awful yell, the miserable Job precipitated himself face downwards on the plank—he did not dare, small blame to him, to try to walk it—and commenced to draw himself across in little jerks, his poor legs hanging down on either side into the nothingness beneath.

His violent jerks at the frail board caused the great stone, which was only balanced on a few inches of rock, to oscillate in a most dreadful manner, and, to make matters worse, when he was halfway across the flying ray of lurid light suddenly went out, just as though a lamp had been extinguished in a curtained room, leaving the whole howling wilderness of air black with darkness.

"Come on, Job, for God's sake!" I shouted in an agony of fear, while the stone, gathering motion with every swing, rocked so violently that it was difficult to cling on to it. It was a truly awful position.

"Lord have mercy on me!" cried poor Job from the darkness. "Oh, the plank's slipping!" and I heard a violent struggle, and thought that he was gone.

But at that moment his outstretched hand, clasping in agony at the air, met my own, and I tugged—ah! how I did tug, putting out all the strength that it has pleased Providence to give me in such abundance—till to my joy in another minute Job was gasping on the rock beside me. But the plank! I felt it slip, and heard it knock against a projecting knob of rock. Then it was gone.

"Great heavens!" I exclaimed. "How shall we get back?"

"I don't know," answered Leo out of the gloom. " 'Sufficient to the day is the evil thereof.' I am thankful enough to be here."

But Ayesha merely called to me to take her hand and follow her.

XXV

The Spirit of Life

I did as I was bidden, and in fear and trembling felt myself guided over the edge of the stone. I thrust my legs out, but could touch nothing.

"I am going to fall!" I gasped.

"Fall then, and trust to me," answered Ayesha.

Now, if the position is considered, it will be easily understood that this was a heavier tax upon my confidence than was justified by my knowledge of Ayesha's character. For all I knew she might be in the very act of consigning me to a horrible doom. But in life we must sometimes lay our faith upon strange altars, and so it was now.

"Let thyself fall!" she cried again, and, having no choice, I did.

I felt myself slide a pace or two down the sloping surface of the rock, and then pass into the air, and the thought flashed through my brain that I was lost. But no! In another instant my feet struck against a rocky floor, and I knew that I was standing on something solid, out of reach of the wind, which I could hear singing overhead. As I stood there thanking Heaven for these small mercies, there was a slip and a scuffle, and down came Leo alongside of me.

"Hulloa, old fellow!" he exclaimed, "are you there? This is interesting, is it not?"

Just then, with a terrific howl, Job arrived right on the top of us, knocking us both down. By the time that we had struggled to our feet again Ayesha was standing among us, bidding us light the lamps, which fortunately remained uninjured, and with them the spare jar of oil.

I found my box of wax matches, and they struck as merrily there, in that awful place, as they could have done in a London drawing-room.

In another minute both lamps were alight, and they revealed a curious scene. We were huddled together in a rocky chamber, some ten feet square, and very scared we looked; that is, with the exception of Ayesha, who stood calmly, her arms folded, waiting for the lamps to burn up. This chamber appeared to be partly natural and partly hollowed out of the top of the crater. The roof of the natural part was formed by the swinging stone, and that over the back of the chamber, which sloped downwards, was hewn from the live rock. For the rest, the place was warm and dry—a perfect haven of rest compared to the giddy pinnacle above, and the quivering spur that shot out to meet it in mid air.

"So!" said *She,* "safely have we come, though once I feared that the rocking stone would fall with you, and hurl you into the bottomless deeps beneath, for I do believe that yonder cleft goes down to the very womb of the world, and the rock whereon the boulder rests has crumbled beneath its swinging weight. But now that he," nodding towards Job, who was seated on the floor, feebly wiping his forehead with a red cotton pocket-handkerchief, "whom they rightly call the 'Pig,' for as a pig is he stupid, hath let fall the plank, it will not be easy to return across the gulf, and to that end I must make some plan. Rest you a while, and look upon this place. What think ye that it is?"

"We cannot say," I answered.

"Wouldst thou believe, O Holly, that once a man did choose this airy nest for a daily habitation, and here he dwelt for many years, leaving it but one day in every twelve to seek food and water and oil that the people brought, more than he could carry, and laid as an offering in the mouth of that tunnel through which we passed hither?"

I looked at her in question, and she continued—

"Yet so it was. There was a man—Noot, he named himself—who, though he lived in the latter days, had of the wisdom of the sons of Kôr. A hermit, and a philosopher, greatly skilled in the secrets of Nature, he it was who discovered the Fire that I shall show you, which is Nature's blood and life, and that the man who bathes therein and breathes thereof shall live while Nature lives. But like unto thee, O Holly, this Noot would not turn his knowledge to account. 'Ill,' he said, 'was it for man to live, for man is born to die.' Therefore he told his secret to none, and therefore did he abide here, where the seeker after Life must pass, and was revered of the Amahagger of that day as holy, and a hermit.

"Now, when first I came to this country—knowest thou how I came, Kallikrates? Another time I will tell thee; it is a strange tale—I heard of this philosopher, and waited for him when he sought his food yonder, and returned with him here, though I greatly feared to tread the gulf. Then did I beguile him with my beauty and my wit, and flatter him with my tongue, so that he led me down to the home of the Fire, and told me the secrets of the Fire; but he would not suffer me to step therein, and, fearing lest he should slay me, I refrained, knowing that the man was very old, and soon would die. So I returned, having learned from him all that he knew of the wonderful Spirit of the World, and that was much, for this man was wise and very ancient, and by purity and abstinence, and the contemplations of his innocent mind, had worn thin the veil between that which we see and those great invisible truths, the whisper of whose wings we hear at times as they sweep through the gross air of the world. Then—it was but a very few days after, I met thee, my Kallikrates, who hadst wandered hither with the beautiful Egyptian Amenartas, and I learned to love for the first and last time, once and for ever, so that it entered into my mind to come hither with thee, and receive the gift of Life for thee and me. Therefore came we, with that Egyptian who would not be left behind, and, behold! we found the old man Noot lying but newly dead. *There* he lay, and his white beard covered him like a garment," and she pointed to a spot near to which I was sitting; "but surely he has long since crumbled away, and the wind hath borne his ashes hence."

Here I put out my hand and felt in the dust, till presently my fingers touched something. It was a human tooth, very yellow, but sound. I held it up and showed it to Ayesha, who laughed.

"Yes," she said, "it is his without a doubt. Behold what remains of Noot and the wisdom of Noot—one little tooth! Yet that man had all life at his command, but for his conscience' sake he would have none of it. Well, he lay there newly dead, and we descended whither I shall lead you, and then, gathering up all my courage, and courting death that I might perchance win so glorious a crown of life, I stepped into the flames, and behold! Life such as ye can never know until ye feel it also flowed into me, and I came forth undying, and lovely beyond imagining. And I stretched out mine arms to thee, Kallikrates, bidding thee take thine own immortal bride, and behold! blinded by my naked beauty, thou didst turn from me, to hide thine eyes upon the breast of Amenartas. Then a great fury filled me, making me mad, and I seized the javelin that thou didst bear, and stabbed thee, so that, at my feet, in the very place of Life, thou didst groan and go down into death. I knew not then that I had strength to slay with mine eyes and by the power of my will, therefore in my madness I slew with the javelin.*

"And when thou wast dead, ah! I wept, because I was undying and thou wast dead. I wept there in the place of Life so that had I been mortal any more my heart had surely broken. And she, the swart Egyptian—she cursed me by her gods. By Osiris did she curse me and by Isis, by Nephthys and by Anubis, by Sekhet, the cat-headed, and by Set, calling down evil on me, evil and everlasting desolation. Ah! I can see her dark face now lowering o'er me like a storm, but she could not harm me, and I—I know not if I could harm her. I did not try; it was naught to me then; so together we bore thee hence. Afterwards I sent

---

*It will be observed that Ayesha's account of the death of Kallikrates differs materially from that written on the potsherd by Amenartas. The writing on the sherd says, "Then in her rage did she smite him *by her magic,* and he died." We never ascertained which was the correct version, but it will be remembered that the body of Kallikrates showed a spear-wound in the breast, which seems conclusive, unless, indeed, it was inflicted after death. Another thing that we never ascertained was *how* the two women—*She* and the Egyptian Amenartas—were able to bear the corpse of the man they both loved across the dread gulf and down the shaking spur. What a spectacle the two distracted creatures must have presented in their grief and loveliness as they toiled along that awful place with the dead man between them! Probably, however, its passage was easier then.—L. H. H.

her—the Egyptian—away through the swamps, and it seems that she lived to bear a son and to write the tale that should lead thee, her husband, back to me, her rival and thy murderess.

"Such is the tale, my love, and now the hour is at hand that shall set a crown upon it. Like all things on the earth, it is compounded of evil and of good—more of evil than of good, perchance; and writ in a scroll of blood. It is the truth; I have hidden nothing from thee, Kallikrates. And now, one thing before the moment of thy trial. We go down into the presence of Death, for Life and Death are very near together, and—who knoweth—that might happen which shall separate us for another space of waiting? I am but a woman, and no prophetess, and I cannot read the future. But this I know—for I learned it from the lips of the wise man Noot—that my life is but prolonged and made more bright. It cannot endure for aye. Therefore, ere we go, tell me, O Kallikrates, that of a truth thou dost forgive me, and dost love me from thy heart. See, Kallikrates: much evil have I done—perchance it was evil but two nights since to strike that girl who loved thee cold in death, but she disobeyed me and angered me, prophesying misfortune to me, and I smote. Be careful when power comes to thee also, lest thou too shouldst smite in thine anger or thy jealousy, for unconquerable strength is a sore weapon in the hands of erring man. Yea, I have sinned—out of the bitterness born of a great love have I sinned—yet do I know the good from the evil, nor is my heart altogether hardened. Thy love, Kallikrates, shall be the gate of my redemption, even as aforetime my passion was the path down which I ran to ill. For deep love unsatisfied is the hell of noble hearts and a portion for the accursed, but love that is mirrored back more perfect from the soul of our desired doth fashion wings to lift us above ourselves, and make us what we might be. Therefore, Kallikrates, take me by the hand, and lift my veil with no more fear than though I were some peasant girl, and not the wisest and most beauteous woman in this wide world, and look me in the eyes, and tell me that thou dost forgive me with all thine heart, and that with all thine heart thou dost worship me."

She paused, and the infinite tenderness in her voice seemed to hover round us like some memory of the dead. I know that it moved me more even than her words, it was so very human—so very womanly. Leo, too, was strangely touched. Hitherto he had been fascinated against his better judgment, somewhat as a bird is fascinated by a snake, but now I think that all this passed away, and he knew that he

She paused, and the infinite tenderness in her voice seemed to hover round us like some memory of the dead.

really loved this strange and glorious creature, as, alas! I loved her also. At any rate, I saw his eyes fill with tears as, stepping swiftly to her, he undid the gauzy veil, and taking her by the hand, gazed into her sweet face, saying—

"Ayesha, I love thee with all my heart, and so far as forgiveness is possible I forgive thee the death of Ustane. For the rest, it is between thee and thy Maker; I know nothing of it. I know only that I love thee as I never loved before, and that, be it near or far, I will cleave to thee to the end."

"Now," answered Ayesha, with proud humility—"now, when my lord doth speak thus royally pardoning with so rich a hand, it becomes me not to lag behind in gifts, and thus be beggared of my generosity. Behold!" and she took his hand and, placing it upon her shapely head, she bent herself slowly down till one knee for an instant touched the ground—"Behold! in token of submission do I bow me to my lord! Behold!" and she kissed him on the lips, "in token of my wifely love do I kiss my lord. Behold!" and she laid her hand upon his heart, "by the sin I sinned, by my lonely centuries of waiting wherewith it was wiped out, by the great love with which I love, and by the Spirit—the Eternal Thing that doth beget all life, from Whom it ebbs, to Whom it must return again—I swear:—

"I swear, even in this first most holy hour of completed Womanhood, that I will cherish Good and abandon Evil. I swear that I will be ever guided by thy voice in the straightest path of duty. I swear that I will eschew Ambition, and through all my length of endless days set Wisdom over me as a ruling star to lead me unto Truth and a knowledge of the Right. I swear also that I will honour and will cherish thee, Kallikrates, who hast been swept by the wave of time back into my arms, ay, till my day of doom, come it soon or late. I swear—nay, I will swear no more, for what are words? Yet shalt thou learn that Ayesha hath no false tongue.

"So I have sworn, and thou, my Holly, art witness to the oath. Here, too, are we wed, my husband, with the gloom for bridal canopy—wed till the end of all things; here do we write our marriage vows upon the rushing winds, which shall bear them up to heaven, and round and continually round this rolling world.

"And for a bridal gift I crown thee with my beauty's starry crown, and enduring life, and wisdom without measure, and wealth that none can count. Behold! the great ones of the earth shall creep about thy feet, and its fair women shall cover up their eyes because of the shining glory of thy countenance, and its wise ones shall be abased before thee. Thou shalt read the hearts of men as an open writing, and hither and thither shalt thou lead them as thy pleasure listeth. Like that old Sphinx of Egypt thou shalt sit aloft from age to age, and ever shall they cry to thee to solve the riddle of thy greatness, that doth not pass away, and ever shalt thou mock them with thy silence!

"Behold! once more I kiss thee, and with that kiss I give to thee dominion over sea and earth, over the peasant in his hovel, over the monarch in his palace halls, and cities crowned with towers, and all who breathe therein. Where'er the sun shakes out his spears, and the lonesome waters mirror up the moon, where'er storms roll, and Heaven's painted bows arch in the sky—from the pure North clad in snows, across the middle spaces of the world, to where the amorous South, lying like a bride upon her blue couch of seas, breathes in sighs made sweet with the odour of myrtles—there shall thy power pass and thy dominion find a home. Nor sickness, nor icy-fingered fear, nor sorrow, and pale waste of flesh and mind hovering ever o'er humanity, shall so much as shadow thee with the shadow of their wings. As a God shalt thou be, holding good and evil in the hollow of thy hand, and I, even I, humble myself before thee. Such is the power of Love, and such is the bridal gift I give unto thee, Kallikrates, my Lord and Lord of All.

"And now it is done; now for thee I loose my virgin zone; and come storm, come shine, come good, come ill, come life, come death, it never, never can be undone. For, of a truth, that which is, is, and, being done, is done for aye, and cannot be changed. I have said—Let us hence, that all things may be accomplished in their order;" and, taking one of the lamps, she advanced towards the end of the chamber that was roofed in by the swaying stone, where she halted.

We followed her, and perceived that in the wall of the cone there was a stair, or, to be more accurate, that some projecting knobs of rock had been so shaped as to form a good imitation of a stair. Down these Ayesha began to climb, springing from step to step like a chamois, and after her we followed with less grace. When we had descended some fifteen or sixteen steps we found that they ended in a long rocky slope, shaped like an inverted cone or funnel.

This slope was very steep and often precipitous, but it was nowhere impassable, and by the light of the lamps we climbed down it with no great difficulty, though it was gloomy work enough travelling on thus, none of us knew whither, into the dead heart of a volcano. As we went, however, I took the precaution of noting our route as well as I could; and this was not so very difficult, owing to the extraordinary and most fantastic shapes of the rocks that were strewn about, many of which in that dim light looked more like the grim faces carven upon mediæval gargoyles than ordinary boulders.

For a considerable time we travelled on thus, half an hour I should say, till, after we had descended many hundreds of feet, I perceived that we had reached the point of the inverted cone, where, at the very apex of the funnel, we found a passage, so low and narrow that we were forced to stoop as we crept along it. After some fifty yards of this creeping the passage suddenly widened into a cave, so huge that we could see neither the roof nor the sides. Indeed, we only knew that it was a cave by the echo of our tread and the perfect quiet of the heavy air. On we went for many minutes in absolute awed silence, like lost souls in the depths of Hades, Ayesha's white and ghost-like form flitting in front of us, till once more the place ended in a passage which opened into a second cavern much smaller than the first. We could clearly distinguish the arch and stony banks of this second cave, and, from their rent and jagged appearance, we judged that it had been torn in the bowels of the rock by the terrific force of some explosive gas, like that first long passage through the cliff down which we had passed before we reached the quivering spur. At length this cave ended in a third tunnel, where gleamed a faint glow of light.

I heard Ayesha utter a sigh of relief as this light dawned upon us, which flowed we knew not whence.

"It is well," she said; "prepare to enter the very womb of the Earth, wherein she doth conceive the Life that ye see brought forth in man and beast—ay, in every tree and flower. Prepare, O Men, for here ye shall be born anew!"

Swiftly she sped along, and after her we stumbled as best we might, our hearts filled like a cup with mingled dread and curiosity. What were we about to see? We passed down the tunnel; stronger and stronger grew the glow, reaching us now in great flashes like rays from a lighthouse, as one by one they are thrown wide upon the darkness of the waters. Nor was this all, for with the flashes came a soul-shaking sound like that of thunder and of crashing trees. Now we were through the passage, and—oh heavens!

We stood in a third cavern, some fifty feet in length by perhaps as great a height, and thirty wide. It was carpeted with fine white sand, and its walls had been worn smooth by the action of fire or water. This cavern was not dark like the others—it was filled with a soft glow of rose-coloured light, more beautiful to look on than anything that can be conceived. But at first we saw no flashes, and heard no more of the thunderous sound. Presently, however, as we stood in amaze, gazing at the marvellous sight, and wondering whence the rosy radiance flowed, a dread and beautiful thing happened. Across the far end of the cavern, with a grinding and crashing noise—a noise so dreadful and awe-inspiring that we all trembled, and Job actually sank to his knees—there flamed out an awful cloud or pillar of fire, like a rainbow many-coloured, and like the lightning bright. For a space, perhaps forty seconds, it flamed and roared thus, turning slowly round and round; then by degrees the terrible noise ceased, and with the fire it passed away—I know not where—leaving behind it the same rosy glow that we had first seen.

"Draw near, draw near!" cried Ayesha, with a voice of thrilling exultation. "Behold the Fountain and the Heart of Life as it beats in the bosom of this great world. Behold the Substance from which all things draw their energy, the bright Spirit of this Globe, without which it cannot live, but must grow cold and dead as the dead moon. Draw near, and wash you in those living flames, and take their virtue into your poor bodies in all its virgin strength—not as now it feebly glows within your bosoms, filtered thereto through the fine strainers of a thousand intermediate lives, but as it is here in the very fount and source of earthly Being."

We followed her through the rosy glow up to the head of the cave, till we stood before the spot where the great pulse beat and the great flame passed. And as we went we became sensible of a wild and splendid exhilaration, of the glorious sense of such a fierce intensity of Life that beside it the most buoyant moments of our strength seemed flat and tame and feeble. It was the mere effluvium of the fire, the subtle ether that it cast off as it rolled, entering into us, and making us strong as giants and swift as eagles.

We reached the head of the cave, and gazed at each other in the glorious glow, laughing aloud in the lightness of our hearts and the divine intoxication of our brains—even Job laughed, who had not smiled for a week. I know that I felt as though the mantle of all the genius whereof the human intellect is capable had descended upon me. I could have spoken in blank verse of Shakesperian beauty; inspired visions flashed through my mind; it was as though the bonds of my flesh had been loosened, and had left the spirit free to soar to the empyrean of its unguessed powers. The sensations that poured in upon me are indescribable. I seemed to live more keenly, to reach to a higher joy, to sip the goblet of a subtler thought than ever it had been my lot to taste before. I was another and most glorified self, and all the avenues of the Possible were for a while laid open to my mortal footsteps.

Then, suddenly, whilst I rejoiced in this splendid vigour of a new-found self, from far away there came the dreadful muttering noise, that grew and grew to a crash and a roar, which combined in itself all that is terrible and yet splendid in the possibilities of sound. Nearer it came, and nearer yet, till it was close upon us, rolling down like all the thunder-wheels of heaven behind the horses of the lightning. On it travelled, and with it the glorious blinding cloud of many-coloured light, and stood before us for a space, slowly revolving, as it seemed to us; then, accompanied by its attendant pomp of sound, it passed away I know not whither.

So astonishing was the wondrous sight that one and all of us, save *She*, who stood up and stretched her hands towards the fire, sank down before it, and hid our faces in the sand.

When it was gone Ayesha spoke.

"At length, Kallikrates," she said, "the moment is at hand. When the great flame comes again thou must bathe in it; but throw aside thy garments, for it will burn them, though thee it will not hurt. Thou must stand in the fire while thy senses will endure, and when it embraces thee suck the essence down into thy very heart, and let it leap and play around thy every limb, so that thou lose no moiety of its virtue. Hearest thou me, Kallikrates?"

"I hear thee, Ayesha," answered Leo, "but, of a truth—I am no coward—but I doubt me of that raging flame. How know I that it will not utterly destroy me, so that I lose myself and lose thee also? Nevertheless I will do it," he added.

Ayesha thought for a minute, and then said—

"It is not wonderful that thou shouldst doubt. Tell me, Kallikrates: if thou seest me stand in the flame and come forth unharmed, wilt thou enter also?"

"Yes," he answered, "I will enter even if it slay me. I have said that I will enter now."

"And that will I also," I cried.

"What, my Holly!" she laughed aloud; "methought that thou wouldst naught of length of days. Why, how is this?"

"Nay, I know not," I answered, "but there is that in my heart which calleth to me to taste of the flame, and live."

"It is well," she said. "Thou art not altogether lost in folly. See now, I will for the second time bathe me in this living bath. Fain would I add to my beauty and to my length of days, if that be possible. If it be not possible, at the least it cannot harm me.

"Also," she continued, after a momentary pause, "there is another and a deeper cause why I would once again dip me in the fire. When first I tasted of its virtue my heart was full of passion and of hatred of that Egyptian Amenartas, and therefore, despite my strivings to be rid of them, passion and hatred have been stamped upon my soul from that sad hour to this. But now it is otherwise. Now is my mood a happy mood, and I am filled with the purest part of thought, and thus I would ever be. Therefore, Kallikrates, will I once more wash and make me pure and clean, and yet more meet for thee. Therefore also, when in turn thou dost stand in the fire, empty all thy heart of evil, and let contentment hold the balance of thy mind. Shake loose thy spirit's wings, muse upon thy mother's kiss, and turn thee toward the vision of the highest good that hath ever swept on silver wings across the silence of thy dreams. For from the seed of what thou art in that dread moment shall grow the fruit of what thou shalt be for all unreckoned time.

"Now prepare thee, prepare! even as though thy last hour were at hand, and thou wast about to cross through Death to the Land of Shadow, and not by the Gates of Glory into the realm of Life made beautiful. Prepare, I say, Kallikrates!"

XXVI

WHAT WE SAW

Then followed a few moments' pause, during which Ayesha seemed to be gathering up her strength for the fiery trial, while we clung to each other, and waited in utter silence.

At last, from far, far away, came the first murmur of sound, that grew and gathered till it began to crash and bellow in the distance. As she heard it Ayesha swiftly threw off her gauzy wrapping and loosened the golden snake from her kirtle. Then, shaking her lovely hair about her like a garment, beneath its cover she slipped off the white robe and replaced the snaky belt around her outside the masses of her falling locks. There she stood before us as Eve might have stood before Adam, clad in nothing but her abundant hair, held round her by the golden band; and no words of mine can tell how sweet she looked—and how divine. Nearer and nearer drew the thunder wheels of fire, and as they came she pushed one ivory arm through the dark masses of her hair and wound it about Leo's neck.

"Oh, my love, my love!" she murmured, "wilt thou ever know how I have loved thee?" and she kissed him on the forehead, hesitated a little as though in doubt, then advanced and stood in the pathway of the flame of Life.

There was, I remember, something very touching to my mind about her words and that embrace upon Leo's forehead. It was like a mother's kiss, and seemed to carry a benediction with it.

On came the crashing, rolling noise, and the sound of it was as the sound of a forest being swept flat by a mighty wind, to be tossed up again like so much grass, and hurled in thunder down a mountain-side. Nearer and nearer it approached; now flashes of light, forerunners of the revolving pillar of flame, were passing like arrows through the rosy air; and now the edge of the pillar itself appeared. Ayesha turned towards it, and stretched out her arms to greet it. On it rolled very slowly and lapped her round with fire. I saw the essence run up her form. I saw her lift it with both hands as though it were water, and pour it over her head. I even saw her open her mouth and draw it down into her lungs, and it was a dread and wonderful sight.

Then she paused, and, stretching out her arms, she stood quite still, a heavenly smile upon her face, as though she were the very Spirit of the Flame.

The mysterious fire played up and down her dark and rolling locks, twining and twisting itself through and around them like threads of golden lace; it gleamed upon her ivory breast and shoulder, from which the hair had slipped aside; it slid along her pillared throat and delicate features, and seemed to find a home in the glorious eyes that shone and shone, more brightly even than the burning spiritual ether.

Oh, how beautiful she looked there in the flame! No angel out of heaven could have worn a greater loveliness. Even now my heart faints before the recollection of it, as naked in the naked fire she stood and smiled at our awed faces, and I would give half my remaining time upon this earth thus to see her once again.

But suddenly—more suddenly than I can tell—an indescribable change came over her countenance, a change which I could not define or explain, but none the less a change. The smile vanished, and in its stead there crept a dry, hard look; the rounded face seemed to grow pinched, as though some great anxiety was leaving its impress there.

"I saw the essence run up her form."

The glorious eyes, too, lost their light, and, as I thought, the form its perfect shape and erectness.

I rubbed my eyes, thinking that I was the victim of some hallucination, or that the radiance of the intense light produced an optical delusion; and, as I marvelled, the flaming pillar slowly twisted and thundered on to whithersoever it passes in the bowels of the great earth, leaving Ayesha standing where it had been.

So soon as it was gone she stepped forward to Leo's side—it seemed to me that there was no spring in her step—and stretched out her hand to lay it upon his shoulder. I gazed at her arm. Where was its wonderful roundness and beauty? It looked thin and angular. And her face—by Heaven!—*her face was growing old before my eyes!* I suppose that Leo saw it also; certainly he recoiled a little.

"What is it, my Kallikrates?" she said, and her voice—what was wrong with those deep and thrilling notes? They sounded high and cracked.

"Why, what is it—what is it?" she said confusedly. "I am dazed. Surely the quality of the fire hath not altered. Can the principle of Life alter? Tell me, Kallikrates, is there aught wrong with my eyes? I see not clear," and she put her hand to her head and touched her hair—and oh, *horror of horrors!*—it all fell upon the floor.

"*Look!—look!—look!*" shrieked Job, in a shrill falsetto of terror, his eyes starting from his head, and foam upon his lips. "*Look!—look!—look! she's shrivelling up! she's turning into a monkey!*" and down he fell upon the ground, foaming and gnashing in a fit.

True enough—I faint even as I write it in the living presence of that terrible recollection—Ayesha *was* shrivelling up; the golden snake that had encircled her gracious form slipped over her hips and to the ground. Smaller and smaller she grew; her skin changed colour, and in place of the perfect whiteness of its lustre it turned dirty brown and yellow, like to an old piece of withered parchment. She felt at her head: the delicate hand was nothing but a claw now, a human talon resembling that of a badly preserved Egyptian mummy. Then she seemed to understand what kind of change was passing over her, and she shrieked—ah, she shrieked!—Ayesha rolled upon the floor and shrieked.

Smaller she grew, and smaller yet, till she was no larger than a monkey. Now the skin had puckered into a million wrinkles, and on her shapeless face was the stamp of unutterable age. I never saw anything like it; nobody ever saw anything to equal the infinite age which was graven on that fearful countenance, no bigger now than that of a two-months' child, though the skull retained its same size; and let all men pray they never shall, if they wish to keep their reason.

At last she lay still, or only moving feebly. She, who but two minutes gone had gazed upon us—the loveliest, noblest, most splendid woman the world has ever seen—she lay still before us, near the masses of her own dark hair, no larger than a big ape, and hideous—ah, too hideous for words! And yet, think of this—at that very moment I thought of it—it was the *same* woman!

She was dying: we saw it, and thanked God—for while she lived she could feel, and what must she have felt? She raised herself upon her bony hands, and blindly gazed around her, swaying her head slowly from side to side as does a tortoise. She could not see, for her whitish eyes were covered with a horny film. Oh, the horrible pathos of the sight! But she could still speak.

"Kallikrates," she said in husky, trembling tones. "Forget me not, Kallikrates. Have pity on my shame; I die not. I shall come again, and shall once more be beautiful, I swear it—it is true! *Oh—h—h—*" and she fell upon her face, and was still.

Yes, thus, on the very spot where more than twenty centuries before she had slain Kallikrates the priest, Ayesha herself fell down and died.

Overcome with the extremity of horror, we too sank to the sandy floor of that dread place, and swooned away.

———

I know not how long we remained thus. Many hours, I suppose. When at last I opened my eyes the other two were still outstretched upon the floor. The rosy light yet beamed like a celestial dawn, and the thunder-wheels of the Spirit of Life yet rolled upon their accustomed track, for as I awoke the great pillar was passing away. There, too, lay the hideous little monkey frame, covered with crinkled yellow parchment, that once had been the glorious *She*. Alas! it was no hideous dream—it was an awful and unparalleled fact!

What had chanced to bring about this shocking change? Had the nature of the life-giving fire varied? Did it, perhaps, from time to time send forth an essence of Death instead of an essence of Life? Or was it that the frame once charged with its marvellous virtue could bear no more, so that were the process repeated—it mattered not at what lapse of time—the two impregnations neutralised each other, and left the body on which they acted as it was before ever it came into contact with the very spring of Being? This, and this alone, would account for the sudden and terrible ageing of Ayesha, as the whole length of her two thousand years took effect upon her. I had not the slightest doubt myself but that the shape now lying before me was just what the frame of a woman would be if by any extraordinary means life could be preserved in her till at length she died at the age of some two-and-twenty centuries.

But who can tell *what* happened? There was the fact. Often since this awful hour I have reflected that it requires no great stretch of imagination to see the finger of Providence in the matter. Ayesha locked up in her living tomb, waiting from age to age for the coming of her lover, worked but a small change in the order of the World. But Ayesha strong and happy in her love, clothed with immortal youth, godlike beauty and power, and the wisdom of the centuries, would have revolutionised society, and even perchance have changed the destinies of Mankind. Thus she opposed herself to the eternal law, and, strong though she was, by it was swept back into nothingness—swept back with shame and hideous mockery!

For some minutes I lay, faintly turning these terrors over in my mind, while my physical strength came back to me, which it did quickly in that buoyant atmosphere. Then I bethought me of the others, and staggered to my feet, to see if I could arouse them. But first I took up Ayesha's kirtle and the gauzy scarf with which she had been wont to hide her dazzling loveliness from the eyes of men, and, averting my head so that I might not look upon it, I covered up that dreadful relic of the glorious dead, that shocking epitome of human beauty and human life. This I did hurriedly, fearing lest Leo should recover, and see it again.

Then, stepping over the perfumed masses of dark hair that were scattered upon the sand, I went to Job, who was lying upon his breast, and turned him over. As I lifted him his arm fell back in a way that I did not like—which sent a chill through me, indeed—and I glanced sharply at his face. One look was enough. Our old and faithful servant was dead. Already shattered by all he had seen and undergone, his nerves had utterly broken down beneath this last dire sight, and he had died of terror, or in a fit brought on by terror. I had only to look at his features to be assured of it.

This was another blow; but it may help people to understand how overwhelmingly awful was the experience through which we had passed when I say that we did not feel it much at the time. It seemed quite natural that the poor old fellow should be dead. When Leo came to himself, which he did with a groan and trembling of the limbs about ten minutes afterwards, and I told him that Job was dead, he merely said, *"Oh!"* And, mind you, this was from no heartlessness, for he and Job were much attached to each other; and he often talks of him now with the deepest regret and affection. It was only that his mind would bear no more. A harp can give out but a certain quantity of sound, however heavily it is smitten.

Well, I set myself to recovering Leo, who, to my infinite relief, I found was not dead, but only fainting, and in the end I succeeded, as I have said, and he sat up. Then I saw another dreadful thing. When we entered that awful place his curling hair had been of the ruddiest gold; now it was turning grey, and by the time we gained the outer air it was snow white. Besides, he looked twenty years older.

"What is to be done, old fellow?" he said in a hollow, dead sort of voice, when his brain cleared a little, and a recollection of what had happened forced itself upon him.

"Try and get out, I suppose," I answered; "that is, unless you would like to go in there," and I pointed to the column of fire, which was once more rolling by.

"I would if I were sure that it would kill me," he said with a little laugh. "It was my cursed hesitation that did this. If I had not been doubtful *She* might never have tried to show me the road. But I am *not* sure. The fire might have the opposite effect upon me. It might make me immortal; and, old fellow, I have not the patience to wait a couple of thousand years for her to come back again as she did for me. I had rather die when my hour comes—and I should fancy that it isn't far off either—and go my ways to look for her. Do you try it, if you like."

But I merely shook my head; my excitement was as dead as ditch-water, and my distaste for the prolongation of our mortal span had come back upon me more strongly than ever. Besides, we neither of us knew what the effects of the essence might be. The result upon *She* had not been of an encouraging nature, and of the exact causes which produced that result we were, of course, ignorant.

"Well, my boy," I said, "we cannot stop here till we follow those two," and I pointed to the little heap under the white garment and to the stiffening corpse of poor Job. "If we are going we had better go. But, by the way, I expect that the lamps have burnt out," and I took one up to look at it, and sure enough it had.

"There is some more oil in the vase," said Leo indifferently—"if it is not broken, at least."

I examined the vessel in question—it was intact. With a trembling hand I filled the lamps—luckily there was still some of the linen wick unburnt. Then I lit them with one of our wax matches. While I did so we heard the pillar of fire approaching again as it went on its never-ending journey, if, indeed, it was the same pillar that passed and repassed in a circle.

"Let us see it come once more," said Leo; "we shall never look upon its like again in this world."

It seemed but idle curiosity, yet somehow I shared it, and so we waited till, turning slowly upon its own axis, the burning cloud had flamed and thundered by; and I remember wondering for how many tens of thousands of years this phenomenon had recurred in the bowels of the earth, and for how many more thousands it would continue to recur. I wondered also if any mortal eyes would ever again mark its passage, or any mortal ears be thrilled and fascinated by the swelling volume of its majestic sound. I do not think so; I believe that we are the last human beings who will ever see that unearthly sight. Presently it had gone, and we too turned to go.

But before we went each of us took Job's cold hand and shook it. It seemed a ghastly ceremony, but it was the only means in our power of showing our respect to the faithful dead and of celebrating his obsequies. The heap beneath the white garment we did not uncover. We had no wish to look upon that terrible sight again. But we went to the pile of rippling hair that had fallen from her in the agony of the hideous change which was worse than a thousand natural deaths, and each of us drew from it a shining lock. These locks we still have, the sole memento that is left to us of Ayesha as we knew her in the fulness of her grace and glory. Leo pressed the perfumed hair to his lips.

"She called to me not to forget her," he said hoarsely; "and swore that we should meet again. By Heaven! I never *will* forget her. Here I swear that, if we live to escape from this, I will not for all my days have aught to do with any other living woman, and that wherever I go I will wait for her as faithfully as she waited for me."

"Yes," I thought to myself, "if she comes back as beautiful as we knew her. But supposing she came back *like that!*"*

And then we went. We went, and left those two in the presence of the secret well and fount of Life, but gathered to the cold company of Death. How lonely they looked as they lay there, and how ill assorted! That little heap had been for two thousand years the wisest, loveliest, proudest creature—I can hardly call her woman—in the whole universe. She was wicked, too, in her way; but, alas! such is the frailty of the human heart, her wickedness had not detracted from her charm. Indeed, I am by no means certain that it did not add to it. After all it was of a grand order; there was nothing mean or small about Ayesha.

And poor Job! His presentiment had come true, and there was an end of him. Well, he has a strange burial-place—no Norfolk hind ever

---

*What a terrifying reflection it is, by the way, that nearly all our deep love for women who are not our kindred depends—at any rate, in the first instance—upon their personal appearance. If we lost them, and found them again dreadful to look on, though otherwise they were the very same, should we still love them?—L. H. H.

had a stranger, or ever will; and it is something to lie in the same sepulchre with the poor remains of the imperial *She*.

We looked our last upon them and the indescribable rosy glow in which they lay; then with hearts far too heavy for words we left them, and crept thence broken-down men—so broken down that we renounced the chance of practically immortal life, because all that made life valuable had gone from us, and we knew even then, that to prolong our days indefinitely would only be to prolong our sufferings. For we felt—yes, both of us—that having once looked Ayesha in the eyes, we could not forget her for ever and ever while memory and identity remained. We both loved her now and for all time; she was stamped and carven on our hearts, and no other woman or interest could ever raze that splendid die.

And I—there lies the sting—I had and have no right to think thus of her. As she told me, I was nothing to her, and never shall be through the unfathomed depth of Time, unless, indeed, conditions alter, and a day comes at last when two men may love one woman, and all three be happy in the fact. It is the only hope of my broken-heartedness, and a somewhat faint one. Beyond it I have nothing. I have paid down this heavy price, all that I am worth here and hereafter, and that is my sole reward. With Leo it is different, and often and often I bitterly envy him his happy lot, for if *She* was right, and her wisdom and knowledge did not fail her at the last, which, arguing from the precedent of her own case, I think most unlikely, he has some future to look forward to. But I have none, and yet—mark the folly and the feebleness of the human heart, and let him who is weak learn wisdom from it—yet I would not have it otherwise. I mean that I am content to give what I have given and must always give, and to take in payment those crumbs that fall from my mistress's table: the memory of a few kind words, the hope one day in the far undreamed future of a sweet smile or two of recognition, a little gentle friendship, and a little show of thanks for my devotion to her—and Leo.

If this does not constitute true love, I do not know what does, and all I have to say is, that it is a very bad state of mind for a man on the wrong side of middle age to fall into.

XXVII

We Leap

We passed through the caves without trouble, but when we came
to the slope of the inverted cone two obstacles stared us in the face.
The first of these was the laborious nature of the ascent, and the next
the extreme difficulty of finding our way. Indeed, had it not been
for the mental notes that I had fortunately taken of the forms of various rocks, I am sure that we never should have managed it at all, but
have wandered about in the dreadful womb of the volcano—for I suppose it must once have been something of the sort—until we died of
exhaustion and despair. As it was we went wrong several times, and
once nearly fell into a huge crack or crevasse. It was terrible work
creeping about in the dense gloom and awful stillness from boulder to
boulder, and examining them by the feeble light of the lamps to see if
I could recognise their shapes. We rarely spoke; our hearts were too
heavy for speech. We simply stumbled along in a dogged fashion,
falling sometimes and cutting ourselves. The fact was that our spirits
were utterly crushed, and we did not greatly care what happened to us.
Only we felt bound to try to save our lives whilst we could, and indeed
a natural instinct prompted us to it. So we blundered on for some three

or four hours, I should think—I cannot tell exactly how long, for we had no watch left that would go. During the last two hours we were completely lost, and I began to fear we had wandered into the funnel of some subsidiary cone, when at length I suddenly recognised a very large rock which we had seen shortly after we began our descent. It is a marvel that I should have known it; indeed, we had already passed it going at right angles to the proper path, when something about it struck me, and I turned back and examined it in an idle sort of way, and, as it happened, this accident proved our salvation.

After this we gained the rocky natural stair without much difficulty, and in due course found ourselves again in the little chamber where the benighted Noot had lived and died.

But now a fresh terror confronted us. It will be remembered that owing to Job's fear and awkwardness the board upon which we walked from the huge spur to the rocking-stone had been whirled off into the tremendous gulf below.

How were we to cross without the plank?

There was only one answer—we must try and *jump* it, or else perish where we were. The distance in itself was not so very great, between eleven and twelve feet I should think, and I have seen Leo jump over twenty when he was a young fellow at college; but then, think of the conditions! Two weary, worn-out men, one of them on the wrong side of forty, a rocking-stone to take off from, a trembling point of rock some few feet across to land upon, and a bottomless gulf to be cleared in a raging gale! It was bad enough, God knows; but when I pointed out these things to Leo, he put the whole matter in a nutshell by replying that, merciless as the choice was, we must choose between the certainty of a lingering death in the chamber and the risk of a swift one in the air.

There was no gainsaying this argument, but it was clear that we could not attempt to leap in the dark; the only thing to do was to wait for the ray of light which pierced through the gulf at sunset. How near to or how far from sunset we might be neither of us had the faintest notion; all we did know was, that when at last the light came it would not endure for more than two minutes at the outside, so that we must be prepared to meet it. Accordingly, we made up our minds to creep on to the top of the rocking-stone and lie there in readiness. We were the more easily reconciled to this course by the fact that our lamps were once more nearly exhausted—indeed, one had gone out bodily, and the other was jumping up and down as the flame of a lamp does when the oil is done. So, by the aid of its dying light, we hastened to crawl out of the little chamber and clamber up the side of the great stone.

At this moment the lamp expired.

The change in our situation was sufficiently remarkable. Below, in the little chamber, we had only heard the roaring of the gale overhead—here, lying face downwards on the swinging stone, we were exposed to its full force and fury, as the great draught drew first from this direction and then from that, howling against the mighty precipice and through the rocky cliffs like ten thousand despairing souls. We lay there hour after hour in terror and misery of mind so deep that I will not attempt to describe them, and listened to the wild storm-voices of that Tartarus, while, set to the deep undertone of the spur opposite, whereon the wind hummed as through some awful harp, they called to each other from precipice to precipice. No nightmare dreamed by man, no dark invention of the romancer, can ever equal the living horror of that place, and the weird crying of those voices of the night, as we clung like shipwrecked mariners to a raft, and tossed on the black, unfathomed wilderness of air. Fortunately the temperature was not a low one; indeed, the wind was warm, or we should have perished. So we clung and listened, and while we were stretched out upon the rock a thing chanced which was so curious and suggestive in itself, though doubtless a mere coincidence, that it added to, rather than lightened, the burden on our nerves.

It will be remembered that when Ayesha was standing on the spur, before we crossed to the stone, the wind tore her cloak from her, and whirled it away into the darkness of the gulf, we could not see whither. Well—I hardly like to tell the story; it is so strange—as we lay there upon the rocking-stone, this very cloak came floating out of black space, like a memory from the dead, and fell on Leo—so that it covered him almost from head to foot. At first we could not imagine what it was, but soon discovered by its texture, and then, for the first time, poor Leo gave way, and I heard him sobbing there upon the stone. No doubt the cloak had been caught upon some pinnacle of the cliff, and thence was blown hither by a chance gust; at the least, it was a most curious and touching incident.

Shortly after this, suddenly, without the slightest previous warning, the red knife of light appeared stabbing the darkness through and through—struck the swaying stone on which we were, and rested its lurid point upon the spur opposite.

"Now for it," said Leo; "now or never."

We rose and stretched ourselves, looking first at the cloud-wreaths stained the colour of blood by that scarlet ray as they tore through the sickening depths beneath, then at the empty space between the swaying stone and the quivering rock, and, in our hearts, despaired, preparing for death. Surely we could not clear it—desperate though we were.

"Who is to go first?" said I.

"Do you, old fellow," answered Leo. "I will sit upon the other side of the stone to steady it. You must take as much run as you can, and jump high; and may God have mercy on us!"

I acquiesced with a nod, and then I did a thing I had never done since Leo was a little boy. I turned and put my arm round him, and kissed him on the forehead. It sounds rather French, but I was taking my last farewell of a man whom I could not have loved more if he had been my own son twice over.

"Good-bye, my boy," I said; "I hope we shall meet again, wherever it is that we go to."

The fact was I did not expect to live another two minutes.

Next I retreated to the far side of the rock, and waited till one of the chopping gusts of wind got behind me; then I ran the length of the huge stone, some three or four and thirty feet, and sprang wildly into the dizzy air. Oh! the sickening terrors which I felt as I launched myself at that little point of rock, and the horrible sense of despair which shot through my brain as I realised that I had *jumped short*! But so it was; my feet never touched the point, they went down into space, only my hands and body came in contact with it. I gripped at it with a yell, but one hand slipped, and I swung right round, holding by the other, so that now I faced the stone from which I had sprung. In agony I clutched with my left hand, and this time managed to grasp a knob of rock, and there I hung in the fierce red light, with thousands of feet of empty air beneath me. My hands were holding to either side of the under part of the spur, so that its point was touching my head. Therefore, even had I found the strength, I could not have pulled myself up. The most that I could do would be to hang for about a minute, and then drop down, down into the bottomless pit. If any man can imagine a more hideous position, let him speak! All I know is that the torture of that half-minute nearly turned my brain.

I heard Leo give a cry, and then suddenly I saw him in mid air springing up and out like a chamois. It was a splendid leap that he took under the influence of his terror and despair. Clearing the horrible gulf as though it were nothing, and landing well on to the rocky point, he threw himself upon his face, to avoid pitching off into the depths. I felt the spur above me shake beneath the shock of his impact, and as it shook I saw the huge rocking-stone, that had been violently depressed by him as he sprang, fly back when relieved of his weight till, for the first time during all these centuries, it swung beyond its balance, falling with a most awful crash right into the rocky chamber which had once served the philosopher Noot for a hermitage, and, I have no doubt, for ever sealing the passage that leads to the Place of Life with some hundreds of tons of rock.

All this happened in a second, and, curiously enough, notwithstanding my terrible plight, I noted it, involuntarily as it were. I even remember thinking that no human being would go down that dread path again.

Next instant I felt Leo seize me by the right wrist with both hands. By lying flat on the point of rock he could just reach me.

"You must let go and swing yourself free," he said in a calm and collected voice, "and then I will try and pull you up, or we will both fall together. Are you ready?"

By way of answer I loosed the rock, first with my left hand, and then with the right, and, as a consequence, swayed out clear of the overshadowing point, my weight hanging upon Leo's arms. It was a dreadful moment. He was a very powerful man, I knew, but would his strength be equal to lifting me up till I could get a hold on the top of the spur, when owing to his position he had so little purchase?

"I swung to and fro."

For a few seconds I swung to and fro, while he gathered himself for the effort, and then I heard his sinews cracking above me, and felt myself lifted up as though I were a little child, till I hooked my left arm round the rock, and my body was supported by it. The rest was easy; in two or three more seconds I was up, and we lay panting side by side, trembling like leaves, with the cold perspiration of terror pouring from our skins.

Then, as before, the light went out like a lamp.

For some half-hour we rested thus without speaking a word, but at length we began to creep along the great spur as best we might in the dense gloom. As we drew towards the face of the cliff, from which the spur sprang out like a spike from a wall, the light increased, however, though only very little, for it was night overhead. After this the gusts of wind lessened, and we made better progress, and at last reached the mouth of the first cave or tunnel. But now a fresh trouble awaited us: our oil was gone, and the lamps, no doubt, were crushed to powder beneath the fallen rocking-stone. We were even without a drop of water to stay our thirst, for we had drunk the last in the chamber of Noot. How were we to see to make our way through this boulder-strewn cavern?

Clearly all that we could do was to trust to our sense of touch, and attempt the passage in the dark; so in we crept, fearing that if we delayed to do so our exhaustion would overcome us, and we should probably lie down and die where we were.

Oh, the horrors of that last tunnel! The place was strewn with rocks, and we fell over them and knocked ourselves up against them till we were bleeding from a score of wounds. Our only guide was the side of the cave, which we kept touching, and so bewildered did we grow in the darkness that thrice we were seized with the terrifying thought that we had turned, and were travelling the wrong way. On we went, feebly, and still more feebly, for hour after hour, stopping every few minutes to rest, for our strength was spent. Once we fell asleep, and, I think, must have slept for some hours, for, when we woke, our limbs were quite stiff, and the blood from our blows and scratches had caked, and was hard and dry upon the skin. Then we dragged ourselves on again, till at last, when despair was entering into our hearts, we saw the light of day once more, and found ourselves outside the tunnel in the rocky fold or lane that, it will be remembered, led into it from the outer surface of the cliff.

It was early morning—that we could tell by the feel of the sweet air and the look of the blessed sky, which we had never hoped to see again. We entered the tunnel, so near as we knew, an hour after sunset, so it followed that it had taken us the entire night to crawl through this dreadful place.

"One more effort, Leo," I gasped, "and we shall reach the slope where Billali is, if he has not gone. Come, don't give way," for he had cast himself upon his face. He rose, and, leaning on each other, we scrambled down that fifty feet or so of cliff—I have not the least notion how. I only remember that we found ourselves lying in a heap at the bottom, and then once more began to crawl along upon our hands and knees towards the grove where *She* had told Billali to wait her return, for we could not walk another foot. We had not gone forty yards in this fashion when suddenly one of the mutes emerged from some trees on our left, through which, I presume, he had been taking a morning stroll, and ran to us to see what strange animals we were. He stared, and stared, then held up his hands in horror, and nearly fell to the ground. Next, he started as fast as he could go for the grove, which was some two hundred yards away. Small wonder that he was horrified at our appearance, for we must have been a shocking sight. To begin with, Leo, his golden curls turned to a snowy white, his clothes nearly rent from his body, his worn face, and his hands a mass of bruises, cuts, and blood-encrusted filth, was a sufficiently alarming spectacle, as he painfully dragged himself along the ground, and I have no doubt that I was little better to look on. I know that two days afterwards, when I inspected my face in some water, I scarcely recognised myself. I have never been famous for beauty, but there was something besides ugliness stamped upon my features that I have not lost to this day, something resembling that wild look with which a startled person awakes from deep sleep. And really it is not to be wondered at. What I do wonder at is that we escaped at all with our reason.

Presently, to my intense relief, I saw old Billali hurrying towards us, and even then I could scarcely help smiling at the expression of consternation on his dignified countenance.

"Oh, my Baboon! my Baboon!" he cried, "my dear son, is it indeed thou and the Lion? Why, his mane that was as ripe corn is white like the snow. Whence come ye? and where is the Pig, and where, too, is *She-who-must-be-obeyed*?"

"Dead, both dead!" I answered; "but ask no questions; help us, and give us food and water, or we too shall die before thine eyes. Seest thou not that our tongues are black for want of water? How, then, can we talk?"

"Dead!" he gasped. "Impossible! *She* who never dies—dead, how can it be?" Then, perceiving, I think, that his face was being watched by the mutes who had hastened to us, he checked himself, and motioned to them to carry us to the camp, which they did.

Fortunately when we arrived some broth was boiling on the fire, and with this Billali fed us—for we were too weak to feed ourselves—thereby, I firmly believe, saving us from death by exhaustion. Then he bade the mutes wash the blood and grime from us with wet cloths, and after that we were laid down upon piles of aromatic grass, and instantly fell into the dead sleep which follows absolute prostration of mind and body.

XXVIII

Over the Mountain

The next thing I recollect is a feeling of the most dreadful stiffness, and a curious, vague idea passing through my half-awakened brain that I was a carpet that had just been beaten. I opened my eyes, and the first object they fell on was the venerable countenance of our old friend Billali, who was seated by the side of the improvised bed upon which I was sleeping, and stroking his long beard thoughtfully. His presence at once brought back to my mind a memory of all that we had recently endured, which was accentuated by the vision of poor Leo lying opposite to me, his face black with bruises and his beautiful curling hair turned from yellow to white.* At that sight I shut my eyes again and groaned.

"Thou hast slept long, my Baboon," said old Billali.

"How long, my father?" I asked.

"A round of the sun and a round of the moon, a day and a night hast thou slept, and the Lion also. See, he sleepeth yet."

---

*Curiously enough, lately Leo's hair has to some extent regained its colour—that is to say, it is now a yellowish grey, and I am not without hopes that in time it will quite recover itself.—L. H. H.

"Blessed is sleep," I answered, "for it swallows up recollection."

"Tell me," he said, "what has befallen you, and what is this strange story of the death of Her who dieth not. Bethink thee, my son: if this be true, then is thy danger and the danger of the Lion very great—nay, almost is the pot red wherewith ye shall be potted, and the stomachs of those who shall eat you are already hungry for the feast. Knowest thou not that these Amahagger, my children, these dwellers in the caves, hate you? They hate you as strangers, and they hate you more because of their brethren whom *She* put to the torment for your sake. Assuredly, if once they learn that there is naught to fear from Hiya, from the terrible One-who-must-be-obeyed, they will slay you by the pot. But let me hear thy tale, my poor Baboon."

Thus adjured I began, and told him—not everything, indeed, as I did not think it desirable to do so, but sufficient for my purpose, which was to make him understand that *She* was in fact no more, having fallen into a volcanic fire, and—as I put it—been consumed therein; for the truth would have been incomprehensible to him. I also told him some of the horrors we had undergone in effecting our escape, which impressed him deeply. But I saw clearly that he did not believe in the report of Ayesha's death. He believed, indeed, that we thought that she was dead, but his explanation was that it had suited her to disappear for a while. Once, he said, in his father's time, she had vanished for twelve years, and there was a tradition in the country that many centuries back no one had seen her during a whole generation, when she reappeared suddenly, and destroyed a woman who had assumed the position of Queen. I said nothing to this, but only shook my head sadly. Alas! I knew too well that Ayesha would return no more, or at any rate that Billali would never see her again. Elsewhere we may find her, and, as I believe, shall find her, but not here.

"And now," concluded Billali, "what wouldst thou do, my Baboon?"

"Nay," I said, "I know not, my father. Can we not escape from this country?"

He shook his head.

"It is very difficult. By Kôr you cannot pass, for you would be seen, and so soon as those fierce ones found that you were alone—well," and he smiled significantly, lifting his hand as though he were placing a hat upon his head. "But there is that way over the cliff whereof once I spoke to thee, by which they drive the cattle out to pasture. Beyond these pastures are marshes, in width three days' journey, and after that I know not, but I have heard that seven days' march thence runs a mighty river, which flows down to the black water. If you could reach its banks, perchance you might escape, but how can you come thither?"

"Billali," I said, "once, thou knowest, I saved thy life. Now pay back the debt, my father, and save me mine and that of my son, the Lion. It shall be a pleasant thing for thee to think of when thine hour comes, and something to set in the scale against the evil doing of thy days, if perchance thou hast done any evil. Also, if thou art right, and if *She* does but hide herself, surely when she comes again she will reward thee."

"My son the Baboon," answered the old man, "think not that I have an ungrateful heart. Well do I remember how thou didst rescue me when those dogs stood by to see me drown. Measure for measure I will repay, and if thou canst be saved, surely I will save thee. Listen: by dawn to-morrow be prepared, for litters shall be here to bear you away across the mountains, and through the marshes beyond. This I will do, saying it is the word of *She* that it be done; and he who obeyeth not the word of *She*, food is he for the hyænas. Then, when you have crossed the marshes, must you strike with your own hands, so that perchance, if good fortune go with you, you may live to come to that black water whereof you told me. And now, see, the Lion wakes, and you must eat the food I have made ready for you."

Leo's condition when once he was thoroughly aroused proved not to be so bad as might have been expected from his appearance, and we both us made a good meal, which, indeed, we needed sadly. After this we limped down to the spring and bathed, and then came back and slept again till evening, when once more we ate heartily. Billali was absent all that day, no doubt making arrangements about litters and bearers, for we were awakened in the middle of the night by the arrival of a considerable number of men in the little camp.

At dawn the old man himself appeared, and told us that by using *She's* dreaded name, though with some difficulty, he had succeeded in impressing the necessary men, and with them two guides to conduct us across the swamps. Also he urged us to start at once, at the same time announcing his intention of accompanying us, to protect us against treachery. I was much touched by this act of kindness on the part of that wily old barbarian towards two utterly defenceless strangers. A journey through those deadly swamps which, allowing for his return, would occupy six days was no light undertaking for a man of his age, but he consented to it cheerfully in order to promote our safety. This proves that even among those dreadful Amahagger—who with their gloom and their devilish and ferocious rites are certainly by far the most terrible savages that I ever heard of—there are people with kindly hearts. Of course self-interest may have had something to do with it. Billali may have thought that *She* would reappear suddenly and demand an account of us at his hands. Still, with all deductions, it was a great deal more than we could expect under the circumstances, and I can only say that for so long as I live I shall cherish a most affectionate remembrance of my nominal parent, Billali.

Accordingly, having breakfasted, we started in the litters, feeling, physically, almost recovered after our long rest and sleep. The condition of our minds I must leave to the imagination.

Then followed a terrible pull up the cliff. Sometimes the ascent was natural, more often it was a zigzag roadway, cut in the first instance, no doubt, by the old inhabitants of Kôr. The Amahagger say they drive their spare cattle over it once a year to pasture beyond; but if this is so, those cattle must be unusually active on their feet. Of course the litters were useless here, so we were obliged to walk.

By midday, however, we reached the great flat top of that mighty wall of rock, and grand indeed was the view from it, with the plain of Kôr, in the centre of which we could clearly discern the pillared ruins of the Temple of Truth, to the one side, and on the other the boundless and melancholy marsh. This wall of rock, which no doubt had once formed the lip of the crater, proved to be about a mile and a half thick, and was still covered with clinker. Nothing grew upon it; but here and there, wherever there was a little hollow, the eye was relieved by the sight of occasional pools of water, for rain had lately fallen. We clambered over the flat crest of this mighty rampart, and then came our downward march, which, if not so difficult a matter as the ascent, was still sufficiently break-neck, and took us till sunset to accomplish. That night, however, we camped in safety upon the wide slopes that rolled away to the marsh beneath.

On the following morning, about eleven o'clock, began our dreary journey across those awful seas of swamp which I have already described.

For three whole days, through stench and mire, and the all-prevailing flavour of fever, did our bearers struggle along, till at length, beyond that most desolate, and without guides utterly impracticable, district we came to open rolling ground, covered with game of all sorts, but quite uncultivated, and mostly treeless. And here on the following morning, not without some regret, we bade farewell to old Billali, who stroked his white beard and blessed us solemnly.

"Farewell, my son the Baboon," he said, "and farewell to thee too, O Lion. I can do no more to help you. But if ever you come to your country, be advised, and venture not again into lands that you know not, lest you never should return, but leave your white bones to mark the limit of your journeyings. Farewell once more; often shall I think of you; nor wilt thou forget me, my Baboon, for though thy face is ugly thy heart is true." Then he turned and went, and with him went the tall and sullen-looking bearers, and this was the last that we saw of the Amahagger. We watched them winding away with their empty litters like a procession bearing dead men from a battle, till the mists of the marsh gathered round them and hid them, and then, left utterly desolate in the vast wilderness, we turned and gazed around us and at each other.

Three weeks ago four men had entered the swamps of Kôr, and now two of us were dead, and we who lived had suffered adventures and experiences so strange and terrible that Death himself hath not a more fearful countenance. Three weeks—and only three weeks! Truly time should be measured by events, and not by the lapse of hours. It seemed like thirty years since we were captured in our whale-boat.

"We must strike out for the Zambesi, Leo," I said, "but God knows if we shall ever get there."

Leo nodded; he had become very silent of late. So we started with nothing but the clothes we stood in, a compass, our revolvers and Express rifles, and about two hundred rounds of ammunition, and thus ended the history of our visit to the ancient ruins of mighty and imperial Kôr.

———

As for the accidents and dangers that subsequently befell us, strange and varied though they were, after deliberation I have determined not to record them here. In these pages I give only a short and clear account of an occurrence which I believe to be unprecedented, and this I do, not with a view to immediate publication, but merely to put on paper, while they are yet fresh in my memory, the details of our journey and its result, which will, I believe, prove interesting to the world if ever we decide to make them public. It is not, however, our present intention that this should be done during our joint lives.

For the rest, it is of no public interest, resembling as it does the experience of more than one Central African traveller. Suffice it to say that, after incredible hardships and privations, we did reach the Zambesi, which proved to be about a hundred and seventy miles south of the spot where Billali left us. There for six months we were imprisoned by a savage tribe, who believed us to be supernatural beings, chiefly on account of Leo's youthful face and snow-white hair. From these people we escaped, and, crossing the Zambesi, wandered southwards, where, when on the point of starvation, we were sufficiently fortunate to fall in with a half-caste Portuguese hunter who had followed a troop of elephants farther inland than he had ever been before. This man treated us most hospitably, and, after innumerable sufferings and adventures, ultimately, through his assistance, we reached Delagoa Bay, more than eighteen months from the time when we emerged from the marshes of Kôr, and on the next day were so fortunate as to catch one of the steamboats that trade round the Cape to England. Our journey home was prosperous, and we set foot on the quay at Southampton exactly two years from the date of our departure upon our wild and seemingly ridiculous quest. Now I write these last words with Leo leaning over my shoulder in the old room in my college, the same into which some two-and-twenty years ago my poor friend Vincey stumbled on the memorable night of his death, bearing with him the iron chest.

Here ends this history so far as it concerns science and the outside world. What its end will be as regards Leo and myself is more than I can guess. But we feel that is not reached yet. A story that began more than two thousand years ago may stretch a long way into the dim and distant future.

———

Is Leo really a reincarnation of that ancient Kallikrates of whom the inscription tells? Or was Ayesha deceived by some strange hereditary resemblance? And, another question: In this play of reincarnations, had Ustane aught to do with the Amenartas of long ago? The reader must form his own opinion on these as on many other matters. I have mine, which is that, as regards Leo, *She* made no mistake.

Often I sit alone at night, staring with the eyes of my mind into the blackness of unborn time, and wondering in what shape and form the great drama will be finally developed, and where the scene of its next act will be laid. And when, ultimately, that *final* development occurs, as I have no doubt it must and will occur, in obedience to a fate that never swerves and a purpose which cannot be altered, what will be the part played therein by that beautiful Egyptian Amenartas, the Princess of the royal race of the Pharaohs, for the love of whom the Priest Kallikrates broke his vows to Isis, and, pursued by the inexorable vengeance of the outraged Goddess, fled down the coast of Libya to meet his doom at Kôr?

SHE

To H. R. H.

Not in the waste beyond the swamps and sand,
   The fever-haunted forest and lagoon,
Mysterious Kôr thy walls forsaken stand,
   Thy lonely towers beneath the lonely moon—
   Not there doth Ayesha linger, rune by rune
Spelling strange scriptures of a people banned.
   The world is disenchanted; over soon
Shall Europe send her spies through all the land.

Nay, not in Kôr, but in whatever spot,
   In town or field, or by the insatiate sea,
Men brood on buried loves, and unforgot,
   Or break themselves on some Divine decree,
Or would o'erleap the limits of their lot—
   There, in the tombs and deathless, dwelleth SHE!

NOTES

DEDICATION

Andrew Lang: Andrew Lang (1844–1912) was a classics scholar and critic who was among Haggard's earliest admirers and promoters. Lang and Haggard became close friends; they sought each other's advice and assistance, collaborated on various projects, and each dedicated works to the other. In 1887, Lang published *He*, a parody of Haggard's novel. He is also, incidentally, the author of the postscripted poem "She: to H. R. H." (see p. 314).

INTRODUCTION

p. 3, lines 7–8 "vir doctissimus et amicus meus": Latin for "a most educated man and my friend."

p. 4, line 2 *a statue of Apollo:* Apollo was the Greek god of prophecy, poetry, and the sun. The physical image of Apollo handed down from antiquity is that of a tall, blond young man of great beauty and utter implacability.

line 7 *They call him "Charon":* In Greek mythology, Charon is the boatman who ferries the shades of the dead across the river Styx and into Hades. He was depicted as a grim and ugly old man who was not so much malevolent as distant and uncaring.

lines 22–23 *the Zulu people, I think, for I had just returned from the Cape at the time:*

Starting at the age of nineteen, Haggard worked in southern Africa for six years, first as the unpaid secretary to the lieutenant governor of the English colony in Natal. During his years in Africa, Haggard absorbed much of the information, including an intimate knowledge of the Zulu people, that was to figure in his African-set novels. The cape at the southern tip of Africa is the Cape of Good Hope.

p. 5, lines 20–21 *recently read with much interest a book of yours describing a Central African adventure:* This is clearly a reference to Haggard's earlier book *King Solomon's Mines,* published in 1885.

line 35 *Central Asia:* the location of *Ayesha: The Return of She,* Haggard's 1905 sequel, in which Leo and Holly travel to a lost city in Tibet.

p. 6, lines 12–13 *the maintenance of the* bona fides: *bona fides* is Latin for "good faith."

p. 7, line 8 *when I came to look at the MS.:* "MS." is the abbreviation for the word "manuscript."

footnote *THE EDITOR:* In order to support the idea that this story is true, Haggard does not take direct responsibility for the content of the narrative that follows. As he says in the first paragraph of the Introduction, "I am not the narrator but only the editor of this extraordinary history." Throughout the story, Holly speaks in the first person while Haggard makes appearances only in the footnotes that he as "EDITOR" inserts to explain elements of Holly's story.

I. MY VISITOR

p. 9, lines 8–9 *go up for my fellowship:* Fellowships were lifetime memberships in a college (see note on "college," below) that ensured the fellow's right to study and live at the college and that provided room and board at the college's expense.

line 9 *expected by my tutor:* The Oxford and Cambridge university systems assign a tutor to each student seeking a degree; the tutor oversees the students' studies and reading as they prepare to sit for final exams at the end of their course of study.

lines 9–10 *and my college:* Oxford and Cambridge are composed of many individual colleges that operate as essentially independent schools. The university as a whole administers shared facilities, such as libraries, but the academic and social lives of the students and faculty are entirely centered on their own particular college.

p. 10, line 13 *Like Cain, I was branded:* Cain, the son of Adam and Eve, was physically marked for murdering his brother Abel. "And the Lord said unto him, therefore whosoever slayeth Cain, vengeance shall be taken on him sevenfold. And the Lord set a mark upon Cain, lest any finding him should kill him" (Genesis 4:15).

lines 23–24 *the monkey theory:* a mocking name for the theory of evolution as proposed by Charles Darwin in *The Origin of Species,* published in 1859. Darwin's publication was one of the most controversial scientific theories in history, and as his theory was published only twenty-seven years before the appearance of *She,* it was still very much in the minds of Haggard's readers.

line 31 *"if I am Beauty, who are you?":* This is a clear allusion to the "Beauty and the Beast" fairy story; perhaps more notably, this entire episode, climaxing in this line, bears a striking resemblance to a romantic disappointment suffered by Haggard in his twenties.

p. 12, line 10 *my sixty-fifth or sixty-sixth lineal ancestor:* Since the date given for the death of Kallikrates is roughly 339 B.C., about 2,200 years pass until the day Vincey (Leo's father, that is) visits Holly and gives him his charge. This equates to roughly thirty-three years per generation, which makes Haggard's calculus generally believable.

lines 10–11 *an Egyptian priest of Isis:* The most important of the ancient Egyptian goddesses, Isis was the sister and wife of the god Osiris and was revered by the Egyptians as the divinity of fertility and the source of humankind's agricultural knowledge.

line 13 *Hak-Hor, a Mendesian Pharaoh:* Otherwise known as Achoris, Hakor (as it's more commonly spelled nowadays) was a pharaoh of the Twenty-ninth Dynasty (399–380 B.C.), also known as the Mendesian Dynasty because its pharaohs came from the powerful Egyptian city of Mendes. Hakor ruled for thirteen years, from 393 to 380, dates that fit nicely with the supposed service of Kallikrates' father in Hakor's army.

line 15 *mentioned by Herodotus:* Herodotus, who lived in the fifth century B.C., was the first historian of the ancient world; his great subject, in nine books, was the Greco-Persian wars.

line 20 *Delagoa Bay:* Now known as Maputo Bay, it is an inlet off the Indian Ocean in southern Mozambique and the harbor of Maputo, the chief port and capital of Mozambique.

footnote 1 *The Strong and Beautiful, or, more accurately, the Beautiful in strength:* The name Kallikrates does, in fact, mean "Beautiful in strength." The name καλλικρατεσ derives from the Greek words καλλοσ, meaning "beautiful," and κρατοσ, meaning "strength." Such apotropaic (meant to ward off evil) names were not uncommon in classical Greece; the name was to impart its qualities to the name-holder, like the name of Nicias (victory), an Athenian general in the Peloponnesian War.

footnote 2, line 36 *buried among the* ἱρένες (*young commanders*): This subject is in fact treated by Herodotus (ix.85:1–2).

p. 13, line 11 *assumed the cognomen:* The cognomen was the third of a Roman man's three names. The first, the praenomen, was a given name, like Gaius or Quintus. The second, the nomen, was the name of his *gens,* his clan, like Julius or Horatius. The last, the cognomen, was the name of the branch of the family to which he belonged, like Caesar or Flaccus. Cognomen were sometimes taken from the name of the town from which a man's family came, but they were often derived like nicknames, making special reference to an attribute of the family—such as Caesar, which means "having fine hair," or Felix, which means "lucky."

line 13 *Charlemagne invaded Lombardy:* Charlemagne (A.D. 742–841), Frankish king and eventually "the Emperor of the West," invaded Lombardy in 771, marching on the capital, Pavia, in order to defend Pope Adrian I, who was being pressured to anoint Charlemagne's repudiated nephews as Frankish kings.

line 17 *Edward the Confessor:* Edward III reigned from 1042 to 1066.

line 18 *William the Conqueror:* ruler of England from 1066 to 1087.

line 25 *the time of Charles II:* ruler of Great Britain from 1660 to 1685.

p. 14, line 26 *two thousand two hundred a year:* Since Vincey's money is, as we later find out, all in the form of consols, treasury bonds with no maturity that paid out roughly 3 percent a year, we can assume that his principle is roughly seventy or eighty thousand pounds, a considerable amount of money in the 1880s.

line 34 *a ward of Chancery:* The Courts of Chancery, under the aegis of the Lord High Chancellor, had the authority to assume the guardianship of orphans.

p. 16, lines 31–32 *my despatch-box:* A despatch (in American English, dispatch) box would be used for carrying papers and documents when traveling.

line 32 *a large portmanteau:* A portmanteau is a suitcase of stiff leather, opening into two separate compartments, for carrying large articles of clothing.

p. 17, lines 1–2 *the gyp who waited on Vincey and myself:* "Gyp" is a slang term, particular to Cambridge, for a college servant.

II. THE YEARS ROLL BY

p. 19, lines 20–21 *the 9th instant:* "Instant" is a term meaning the current month.

line 21 *in —— College Cambridge:* It was a common convention in eighteenth- and nineteenth-century novels to exclude specific information in a narrative, especially names of people, names of places, and dates. (The concealment of specific or private information is meant to further the illusion that the events portrayed actually occurred.) This convention is also reflected in the Introduction, when Haggard is reluctant to commit to the location of his first meeting with Holly and simply says, "a certain University, which for the purposes of this history we will call Cambridge."

lines 24–25 *invested in Consols:* See the note for p. 14, l. 26 on Vincey's income.

p. 21, line 5 *to find a nurse:* not a medical nurse, but a nursemaid or nanny.

lines 16–17 *Job—that was the young man's name:* The servant's name is obviously an allusion to the long-suffering and selfless servant of God in the Bible.

p. 22, line 17 *brandy-balls:* a brandy-flavored candy popular in England, scarcely intoxicating but perhaps inappropriate for a youngster.

lines 35–36 *It was the chaff:* "Chaff" is a slang term for good-natured teasing.

p. 23, lines 24–25 *read for the Bar:* To "read" is to study. Leo is going to study to become a barrister, a lawyer.

lines 25–26 *going to London to eat his dinners:* Since law was not taught at universities in Haggard's day, the only way to become a lawyer was to apprentice at one of the legal firms at London's Inns of Court.

III. THE SHERD OF AMENARTAS

p. 25, line 1 *my Sèvres china:* Porcelain of outstanding quality was produced in the factories in Sèvres, France.

line 2 *Marat had used just before he was stabbed in his bath:* Jean-Paul Marat (1743–93) was a French politician, journalist, and radical revolutionary. He suffered from a discomfiting skin disease and spent a considerable amount of time soaking in a medicinal bath; it was in his bath that he was assassinated by Charlotte Corday, a moderate Republican.

line 25 *into the wards:* Wards are the ridges in a lock mechanism that serve to exclude any but the correct key from operating it; they're also, by association, the notches cut into a key that fit these ridges.

p. 27, line 6 *formed of Sphinxes:* A sphinx is a mythological creature with the head of a man (sometimes a woman) and the body of a lion. Sphinxes are almost invariably portrayed as the hostile guardians of secrets and, as perhaps most famously in the story of Oedipus, the asker of mysterious riddles.

line 24 *Uncial Greek Writing:* "Uncial" refers to a style of writing both the Roman and Greek alphabets characterized by rounded capital letters.

line 28 *black-letter Latin:* a style of writing, later referred to by Haggard as Old English, similar to the typeface known as Gothic, in which the letters have thick black bodies and are elaborately decorated.

p. 28, lines 1–2 *an ordinary amphora:* An amphora is a long ceramic container with two handles used by the Greeks and Romans to store and carry liquids like wine.

line 19 *scarabæus:* The scarabaeus was a beetle held sacred by the Egyptians; the word is also used for any depiction of the beetle when it serves, as in this case, as a talisman or charm.

line 21 *Rā or the Sun:* Ra was the greatest of the Egyptian gods. He was associated with the sun and depicted as a man with the head of a hawk.

p. 29, line 29 *the time of Elizabeth:* Elizabeth I was the ruler of England from 1558 to 1603.

line 32 *the Zambesi:* more commonly now "Zambezi": a major river of southern Africa flowing from Zambia southwest to Mozambique.

p. 30, line 13 *brought me to Aden:* Aden is the capital of Yemen, on the southwest tip of the Arabian peninsula, across a very narrow body of water from Ethiopia and Somalia on the African continent.

line 16 Omnia vincit amor: Latin for "Love conquers all."

page 31, line 15 *"thus far shalt thou go, and thus much shalt thou learn":* This is not a direct quotation from any particular source so much as a description of what God meant in his admonition to Adam and Eve to stay away from the Tree of Knowledge. Vincey is saying that God may perhaps wish to have certain subjects remain unknown and unexplored by people.

p. 34, footnote *Nekht-nebf, or Nectanebo II:* Haggard is conflating Nectanebo I (Nekhtnebf), the founder of the 30th Dynasty, who died in 363 B.C., with Nectanebo II (Nekhthareb), the last pharaoh of that dynasty, whose fate after his departure for Nubia (Ethiopia) is unknown.

p. 37–38, lines 40–1 *the cartouche already mentioned:* A cartouche is a figure in Egyptian hieroglyphics that encircles the name of a member of royalty or a divinity.

p. 38, lines 18–19 HOC FECIT DOROTHEA VINCEY: Latin for "Dorothea Vincey made this."

p. 39, line 16 *Ætate sua 17:* Latin for "His age is seventeen."

line 23 A.U.C.: An abbreviation of the Latin phrase *ab urbe conditia,* "from the founding of the city."

line 24 (cvi): simply, the Roman numeral for 106.

p. 43, line 10 *Armoryke which ys to seien Britaine ye Lesse:* mock Middle English meaning "Armoric, which is to say Britain the Lesser." The British Isles were, at the time of Roman occupation, ethnically Celtic. Following the collapse of the Roman Empire, though, repeated influxes of German peoples from the north and east began to drive the Celts to the fringes of the

British Isles, to places like Cornwall and Wales. A group of Celts known as the Bretons, however, crossed the English Channel around the sixth century and established themselves in what is now known as Brittany, in northwestern France—"Armorica" is the ancient name for this area.

The story of the sherd as it's presented in this section is one of Haggard's attempts to make believable the progress from Kallikrates to the Vinceys, from ancient Greece to modern England. This affinity between Brittany and England allows for a seemingly natural progression for the potsherd and the family in moving from the continent to England.

"Armorica" is a largely literary name that appears, among other places, in Chaucer's *Canterbury Tales*. One of several uses of "Armorica" is in the Franklin's Tale: "In Armorik, that called is Britayne, / Ther was a knyght that loved and dide his payne / To serve a lady in his beste wise" (Franklin's Tale, l. 21–23).

Finally, Haggard's description of the writing as being "Old English Black-Letter" again refers to the style of writing (see the note for p. 27, l. 28 on this subject) rather than to the language, which is clearly Middle English, not Old English (also known as Anglo-Saxon).

line 13 *Sathanas hym selfe:* Satan himself.

line 22 *Lorenzo Marquez:* the original name given to Maputo, the capital of Mozambique, when it was founded. The city was named after the Portuguese explorer who visited the area in 1544. Since the entry on the sherd is dated 1564 and as the city that came to be named Lorenzo Marquez was only widely settled in the eighteenth century, this points to a probable anachronism on Haggard's part—it is unlikely that the name would have been used as early as the sixteenth century.

p. 44, line 20 *duxerunt autem nos ad reginam* advenaslasaniscoronantium: They took us, moreover, to the queen of the people who crown strangers with pots.

p. 50, line 10 *bound for Zanzibar:* Zanzibar is an island off the coast of what is now Tanzania; historically, it was ruled variously by Arabs, by the Portuguese, by the German East Africa Company, and by the British.

IV. THE SQUALL

p. 51, line 6 *the huge sail of our dhow:* A dhow is a single-masted ship used for trade and transportation throughout the Indian Ocean and along the African coast.

line 12 *monsoon:* A monsoon is a pattern of winds that prevail in one direction during one season, and prevail in the opposite direction in another. At this point in the story, the winds are in the right direction to allow Holly and Leo's expedition to proceed easily, "running," southward along the African coast.

p. 53, line 10 *centre-board:* A center-board is a retractable board that is inserted through a boat's hull and vertically into the water; it is necessary to sailing because it allows the horizontally applied force of the wind to be transferred into forward motion.

line 26 *beat back against it:* To beat back is to sail into the wind.

line 32 *the sight of these blackamoors:* A blackamoor is any person with dark skin, regardless of race, from North Africa. It is not, as Job's use of the term makes brutally clear, a complimentary term.

p. 54, line 14 *let go the halyards:* A halyard is a line used to raise or lower a sail.

lines 15–16 *the parrel jammed and the yard would not come down:* A parrel is a loop of rope used to raise and lower a yard or spar (a piece of wood or metal that supports rigging) attached to a mast.

line 26 *We were pooped:* That is to say, the poop deck (the stern) of the ship was momentarily submerged.

p. 56, line 25 *pulled a tub upon the homely Cam:* that is, rowed a boat on the Cam River, which flows through Cambridge.

p. 57, line 5 *to back water:* to row in the direction that is the opposite of the boat's motion in order to slow it down or stop it.

V. THE HEAD OF THE ETHIOPIAN

p. 62, line 24 *the Old Gentleman:* a polite slang phrase for the Devil.

p. 63, lines 13–14 *"You are an unbelieving Jew, Uncle Horace," he said. "Those who live will see.":* a reference to Acts 14:2 ("But the unbelieving Jews stirred up the Gentiles, and made their minds evil affected against the brethren"), in which the Jews turn the Gentiles against the apostles.

p. 64, line 5 *an excellent potted tongue:* Potting is a method of preserving meat by cooking it, seasoning it, and sealing it in a pot.

footnote *Sikkim:* formerly a kingdom, now an Indian state, in the Himalayas, near Nepal.

p. 65, footnote, line 8 *Sir John Kirk:* Sir John Kirk (1832–1922) was a companion of David Livingstone, the missionary explorer of Africa, and a colonial administrator of Zanzibar from 1863 to 1887.

p. 67, line 12 *a "sport":* a joke; that is, a freak of nature.

line 16 *doses of quinine:* Quinine was a well-established anti-malarial at the time of Haggard's writing, when little was known about malaria's transmission by mosquitoes. Haggard reflects the common understanding of the day that it was the fetid air of the swamp, not the mosquito-borne parasite, that can cause fever.

line 24 *a beautiful waterbuck:* Waterbuck are a breed of antelope from central Africa.

line 31 *Express rifle:* Express rifles were primarily sporting rifles—as opposed to military rifles—and characteristically fired small, light bullets with very high velocities, which allowed hunting at long distances.

p. 70, lines 3–4 "h*eat us," he added nervously, picking up an "h" in his agitation:* Haggard depicts Job as having the vestiges of a lower-class accent that shows itself in a moment of panic. One of the characteristics of his accent, which is similar to Cockney, is that the initial *h* is dropped on most words (e.g., "orse" for "horse"), and that, as here, words starting with a vowel sometimes gain an *h.*

VI. An Early Christian Ceremony

p. 73, line 3 *the alligator:* Haggard means "crocodile" (the term he properly used in the previous chapter). Alligators are native only to the Americas.

lines 11–12 *"biltong," as, I believe, the South African Dutch call flesh thus prepared:* This is one of many pieces of trivia Haggard gained while working in Natal that he incorporates into his novel.

p. 75, line 13 *purgatives that we swallowed:* In Haggard's day, one of the common—and quite unhealthy—treatments to prevent malaria was to combine the use of emetics and purgatives along with regular doses of quinine.

p. 76, line 23 She-who-must-be-obeyed: the Amahagger name for Ayesha. "She-who-must-be-obeyed" has an interesting history with Henry Rider Haggard. As a small child, it's been reported, Haggard's nursemaid would often terrorize him by leaving him in the charge of a grotesque rag doll who went by this name (see Biographical Note).

p. 78, lines 19–20 *the East African Somali:* Somalis are lighter-skinned Africans. Haggard is subscribing to the consensus of his day, which decreed that the lighter-skinned the race, the more likely civilized. This use of skin color thus allowed the Europeans to create a hierarchy of more and less civilized races in Africa.

p. 79, lines 11–12 *Mammon of Unrighteousness:* In the New Testament, Mammon is the personification of avarice of all kinds.

p. 80, line 1 *Amahagger, the People of the Rocks:* The derivation of the name of the Amahagger and its supposed meaning, "the People of the Rocks," is not certain and is likely a wholly original coinage by Haggard, despite his editorial note to the contrary in Chapter XVI (see p. 183).

line 12 *a rocky defile:* A defile is a narrow pass, especially through mountains.

p. 81, line 17 *crisped like a negro's:* that is to say, naturally curled.

p. 82, line 22 *who was called Ustane:* Ustane's name is also, very likely, Haggard's coinage. Norman Etherington, in his excellent *The Annotated She* (Indiana University Press, 1991), suggests that the proper pronunciation of the name is "Oo-sta-nay," not "Oo-*stayn.*"

VII. USTANE SINGS

p. 84, line 1 coram populo: Latin for "in public."

p. 89, lines 17–18 *I wished Job's scruples had been at Jericho:* The slang meaning of "Jericho" is a place of concealment, exile, or—as Holly is using the term—great and desirable distance.

lines 34–35 *Norfolk red-poll stock:* a breed of reddish, hornless cattle from England.

p. 91, line 28 *the great balls of fire that move about there:* Holly is referring to ignis fatuus (literally, "foolish fire"), or will-o'-the-wisps, eerie lights seen over marshland at night. These may result from the ignition of methane escaping from dead plants or animals, or from some sort of phosphorescence. They are generally held to presage death, or at least the bedevilment of travelers foolish enough to follow them.

VIII. THE FEAST, AND AFTER!

p. 97, lines 8–9 *to avoid whom Job had played the* rôle *of another Scriptural character:* specifically Joseph, who, in Genesis 39, is imprisoned for alleged sexual misconduct.

p. 98, line 9 *Kafir corn:* sorghum.

lines 15–16 *the viscera of the dead, after the fashion of the Egyptians:* The ancient Egyptians would remove all bodily organs and separate them before the process of embalming a mummy began.

line 18 *the case of Etruscan amphoræ:* The Etruscans, as other ancient cultures did, placed in large earthenware jars commodities that would be of use to the dead, and left them in their burial chambers.

lines 33–34 *an eland or a koodoo:* These are both breeds of large African antelope.

p. 99, lines 19–20 *an entertainment of the Barmecide stamp:* In *The Arabian Nights,* the Barmecides were a family in Baghdad who, at one point, entertain a beggar by feeding him imaginary food.

p. 101, lines 22–23 *anthropophagous customs:* cannibalism.

p. 103, line 17 *"playing 'possum":* playing dead. When opposums are attacked, they're said to feign death (or, alternately, to slip into comas).

line 33 *beneath my gripe:* "Gripe" is simply a variant of "grip."

p. 104, line 2 *Peace Society:* The New York Peace Society, possibly the first pacifist organization, was founded in 1815. In 1828 it joined with other such groups to form the American Peace Society. Presumably, the group had expanded into England by Haggard's time.

IX. A LITTLE FOOT

p. 108, line 23 *these hyæna-men:* Billali applies this epithet to the cannibals because hyenas are scavengers.

p. 112, line 18 *an unctuous and sooty mark:* "Unctuous" means oily, or fatty.

X. SPECULATIONS

p. 117, line 7 *quoting the saying of a politician:* Despite the fact that Haggard probably did have some specific politician's remark in mind, this quotation has not proven traceable.

p. 118, lines 15–16 *teal, coot, snipe, and plover:* Teal are freshwater ducks with brightly colored feathers. Coot are aquatic birds that, strictly speaking, are not inhabitants of Africa. Snipe are small shore birds with long bills, like sandpipers. Plover are a family of wading birds with large, round bodies.

p. 123, line 20 *Bacchus with ivy leaves:* Bacchus, the Roman god of wine (a variant on the Greek Dionysus), is usually depicted wearing a crown of leaves.

XI. THE PLAIN OF KÔR

p. 125, line 13 *wandering globes of fen fire:* another reference to ignis fatuus.

p. 128, lines 19–20 *clouds of jewelled honeysuckers:* Honeysuckers, also called honeyeaters, are small birds native, actually, to Australia and the South Pacific.

line 23 *quagga:* Quagga, now extinct, were wild horses closely related to zebras, and indigenous to southern Africa. Attempts are being made, as of this writing, to revive the species by breeding them out of zebras.

line 27 *single-barrel sporting Martini:* A Martini rifle was a breech-loading hunting rifle.

p. 132, lines 34–35 *sculptures in bas-relief:* low-relief carvings in which the sculpted figures do not protrude much from their background. Bas-relief carvings are technically rather difficult and connote a great deal of craftsmanship on the part of the sculptors.

p. 133, line 29 *not unlike a Zanzibar mat:* possibly referring to a prayer mat; the population of Zanzibar is predominantly Muslim.

XII. "SHE"

p. 135, line 9 *Norfolk jacket:* a belted jacket with box pleats in the front and back.

p. 138, lines 10–11 *instruments resembling a lyre:* Lyres are small harps, extant in ancient Greece, with U-shaped frames and crossbars to which the strings are attached. Lyres were employed almost exclusively to accompany recitations or singing.

p. 139, lines 17–18 *generally used for signets:* A signet is a seal, often mounted upon a ring.

p. 140, line 34 *"kootooing":* Kowtowing (as it's more commonly rendered; Haggard's spelling here seems to be unique), a Chinese practice, involves paying respect to a superior by kneeling and knocking one's head against the floor.

p. 141, line 18 *Mary, Queen of Scots, going to execution in a play:* Mary Stuart (1542–87), the daughter of James V of Scotland, was next in line to the British throne after the children of Henry VIII. Her life was rife with intrigue, adventures, plots, etc., and ended when her cousin Elizabeth I had her beheaded. She had the last, albeit posthumous, laugh when her son James succeeded the childless Elizabeth to the English throne. Her life has been repeatedly dramatized, most famously by Swinburne (in a trilogy), Friedrich Schiller, and (after Haggard's death) Maxwell Anderson.

p. 143, line 4 *instinct with beauty:* that is, imbued with it.

line 30 *an ancient tongue, that sweet child of the old Syriac:* Ayesha is referring to Arabic, which she mistakenly says is descended from Syriac, a now dead Aramaic language of the Near East that survives in several religious contexts. Although both Syriac and Arabic are Semitic languages and have, ultimately, the same roots, Syriac is scarcely the ancestor of Arabic—the two developed side by side for centuries.

XIII. AYESHA UNVEILS

p. 147, lines 19–20 Yárab, the son of Kâhtan: Arabic names are traditionally given in the form of the bearer's own name plus the name of his father. Women identified themselves through their father's and grandfather's names.

line 21 *Yaman the Happy:* Yemen.

lines 29–30 *the Persian Ochus, or are the Achæmenians gone:* Ochus (also known as Artaxerxes III) was the king of Persia and, upon mercilessly defeating the Egyptians, became the first pharaoh of the Thirty-first Dynasty; he ruled Egypt from 343 to 338 B.C., when he was murdered by one of his ministers, the eunuch Bagoas. Ayesha refers to Ochus and his descendants as the

Achaemenians because the Persians she knew were of the Achaemenian dynasty.

p. 148, line 2 *since then the Ptolemies:* The Ptolemy dynasty was founded by the Macedonian Ptolemy I (c. 367–283 B.C.), a general under Alexander the Great who was given Egypt and Libya on Alexander's death and the partition of his empire. There were fifteen kings of Egypt named Ptolemy; the name Cleopatra was favored by the family's queens and princesses: The Cleopatra of Julius Caesar and Marc Antony was Cleopatra VII.

lines 12–13 *does the Temple stand that the Wise King built:* Ayesha refers to the Temple of Solomon, built as a resting place for the Jews' Ark of the Covenant and completed in 957 B.C.

line 19 *"Herod!" she said. "I know not Herod.":* Of course she doesn't. Ayesha would not know Herod, known as Herod the Great (37 B.C.–A.D. 4), because she had gone into seclusion hundreds of years before his birth. She is speaking of Solomon's Temple, destroyed by Nebuchadnezzar, while Holly is referring to the Temple built during Herod's reign to replace the edifice constructed in the sixth century B.C., after the Jews' exile in Babylonia, and seriously damaged by the Romans Pompey and Crassus. Herod's Temple, completed decades after his death, was promptly destroyed by the Romans in A.D. 70.

line 25 *Solitudinem faciunt, pacem appellant:* "They make a desert, they call it peace." This phrase (in fuller version: "To robbery, slaughter, and plunder they give the false name of empire; and where they make a desert, they call it peace") was recorded by the Roman historian Tacitus in the *Agricola* and attributed to Calgacus, a Caledonian chieftain conquered by the Romans.

p. 149, line 4 *Their Messiah came:* The entire following paragraph is a (false) portrayal of the Jews as the crucifiers of Christ and as being too avaricious to accept any god that does not bring them "wealth and power." Though Haggard was an early Zionist and wrote sympathetically of the Jews in some of his novels, he was not immune from the general anti-Semitism of his time, and in his old age his Zionism faded and his distaste for Jews grew more pronounced.

lines 15–16 *a vessel of Him they call Jehovah, ay, and a vessel of Baal, and a vessel of Astoreth:* Ayesha is comparing the Jewish God to the two principal gods of the Phoenicians: Baal, the principal male deity of power and fertility, and Astoreth, his female counterpart. One of the reasons this is such a galling comparison is that Baal, in the Jewish tradition, is taken as the ultimate false idol.

lines 19–20 *Why, if I remember, so said one of their prophets:* perhaps a reference to

Zechariah 13:7: "Awake, O sword, against my shepherd, and against the man that is my fellow, saith the Lord of hosts: smite the shepherd, and the sheep shall be scattered: and I will turn mine hand upon the little ones."

p. 150, lines 20–21 *that Grecian Helen:* Helen, the daughter of Leda and Zeus, was the wife of Menelaus, king of Sparta, and the most beautiful woman in the world. Her abduction by Paris, a prince of Troy, brought on the Trojan War.

p. 151, line 20 *a span in thickness:* A span is a unit of length equal to the distance between the tip of the thumb and the tip of the little finger in an outstretched hand—about nine inches.

line 30 *I ween:* I think.

p. 154, lines 21–22 *Actæon who perished miserably:* In Greek mythology, Actaeon was a hunter who, because he saw the goddess Artemis naked, was turned into a stag and killed by his own hunting dogs.

p. 156, line 9 *her white kirtle:* "Kirtle" is an archaic term for a woman's shift or tunic.

line 12 *argent of her breast:* "Argent" is silver, or silvery white.

p. 157, line 10 *Venus Victrix:* literally, Venus the conqueror. Venus might be depicted in Roman art and on Roman coins not only as the goddess of love but as the goddess of victory.

XIV. A Soul in Hell

p. 160, line 8 diablerie: fiendishness, witchcraft.

line 27 *the original Circe:* In the Odyssey, Circe is the temptress witch who turns Odysseus' men into pigs.

p. 161, lines 6–7 vive la guerre!: French for "Long live war!"

XV. Ayesha Gives Judgment

p. 172, line 24 *Mark Tapley himself:* Mark Tapley is a character in Charles Dickens's 1844 novel, *Martin Chuzzlewit,* who is constantly cheerful and good-humored.

p. 175, line 35 *one jot or tittle:* slang for "a tiny, little bit." The word "jot" derives from "iota"; a tittle is a tiny diacritical mark. Perhaps Ayesha's usage is Haggard's conscious echo of Jesus' "For verily I say unto you, Till heaven and earth pass, one jot or one tittle shall in no wise pass from the law, till all be fulfilled" (Matthew 5:18).

XVI. THE TOMBS OF KÔR

p. 182, lines 27–28 *There is no new thing under the sun, as the wise Hebrew wrote:* See Ecclesiastes 1:9.

p. 183, lines 19–20 *the space beneath the dome of St. Paul's in London:* This is a large area of more than 8,000 square feet (given that the diameter of St. Paul's inner dome is 101 feet). More interesting than the area is Haggard's means of conveying it, alluding to a landmark that any of his readers could easily visualize.

XVII. THE BALANCE TURNS

p. 189, line 17 *Becca in Arabia:* "Becca" is a variant name for the holy city of Mecca.

p. 190, line 10 *more deadly than any Basilisk's:* The basilisk is a mythological dragon with deadly breath and, most infamously, deadly eyes.

line 17 *Tyrian cloth:* cloth dyed with the most expensive dye of the ancient world, Tyrian purple, which was produced in Tyre, a Phoenician city on the eastern coast of the Mediterranean.

lines 22–23 *old Greek epithalamium:* An epithalamium is a lyric poem written in honor of a wedding.

p. 194, line 10 *we Arabs had many gods:* The names that follow are all names of idols worshiped throughout Arabia by the pre-Islamic Arabs.

XVIII. "GO, WOMAN!"

p. 202, lines 18–19 *no marriage or giving in marriage:* "For when they shall rise from the dead, they neither marry, nor are given in marriage; but are as the angels which are in heaven" (Mark 12:25).

p. 203, line 23 *casuistry of this nature:* Casuistry is specious or sophistic reasoning intended to mislead or confuse.

XIX. "GIVE ME A BLACK GOAT!"

p. 216, line 5 *Nero illuminated his gardens with living Christians:* According to Tacitus, Nero held a party in which the illumination was Christians tied to burning crosses.

p. 217, line 8 *Cæsar's dust—or is it Alexander's?—may stop a bunghole:* It's Alexander's, actually, at least according to Shakespeare: "Why may not imagination trace the noble dust of Alexander, till he find it stopping a bunghole?" (*Hamlet*, V.1).

p. 219, line 1 *a neighbouring kraal:* In Afrikaans, a kraal is a corral.

lines 25–26 *blesbok, then an impala, then a koodoo:* Blesboks, impalas, and koodoos (kudus) are African antelopes.

XX. TRIUMPH

p. 227, lines 22–23 *Venus from the wave, or Galatea from her marble:* Both are images of perfect female forms being unveiled for the first time. The first is the image of Venus's birth, as she stepped forth fully formed from the sea and onto the shore of Crete. The second is that of Galatea, the statue carved out of marble that was so beautiful that its sculptor, Pygmalion, fell in love with it, and the statue was transformed into a real woman.

XXI. THE DEAD AND LIVING MEET

p. 237, lines 1–2 *inspired Sibyl:* In ancient Greece and Rome, sibyls were female prophets.

p. 239, line 34 *confirmed opium-eaters:* In the nineteenth century, eating opium was the most common method of self-administration. Opium, in various forms, was legal and widely available.

XXII. JOB HAS A PRESENTIMENT

p. 243, line 12 *Old Nick himself:* the Devil.

lines 13–14 *The Witch of Endor:* the mystical woman whom the despairing King Saul sought for a prophecy before he fought the Philistines (I Samuel 28). She raised from the dead the spirit of the prophet Samuel.

page 244, line 7 *what is going to happen to sorceresses:* Job is talking about the admonition in Exodus 22:18: "Thou shalt not suffer a witch to live."

p. 244, line 25 *more like a Methody elder:* A "Methody elder" would be a Methodist lay preacher. It's perhaps worth noting, given this attack on the honesty of Methodists, or at least of their lay preachers, that Haggard himself was a Methodist.

p. 248, line 16 *winding-sheet:* the sheet in which corpses are wrapped, a shroud.

p. 250, lines 2–3 *dull edge of eld:* senility; "eld" meaning age.

line 11 *heavier shekels:* Shekels are ancient units of measurement and currency; here the meaning is coins, or money in general.

p. 251, line 35 *But we have a queen already:* The queen is, of course, the beloved Victoria (1819–1901).

XXIII. THE TEMPLE OF TRUTH

p. 256, lines 26–27 *the Suez Canal, or even the Mont Cenis Tunnel:* These were both great feats of Victorian-era civil engineering. The Suez Canal, which was completed in 1869, connected the Mediterranean Sea with the Red Sea. The Mont Cenis Tunnel, completed in 1871, runs eight and a half miles under the Alps, connecting Modane, France, to Bardonecchia, Italy.

p. 257, line 29 *the Thames Embankment:* a pathway built along the north shore of the Thames River in London in the mid-nineteenth century; its construction significantly diminished the width of the river. Again we see Haggard's deft use of an allusion his readers could readily grasp.

p. 259, line 4 *El-Karnac, at Thebes:* Karnak, in Egypt, is one of the world's largest temple complexes. Built over a period of hundreds of years, it features immense walls and massive columns.

p. 261, line 2 *their hoar majesty:* "hoar," or "hoary," means white with age.

line 4 *this ruined fane:* A fane is a temple.

XXIV. WALKING THE PLANK

p. 268, lines 16–17 *Devonshire lane in stone:* Throughout Devonshire, a mostly rural county in the southwest of England, are very narrow, winding roads that have hedges or stone walls on either side.

p. 271, line 10 *Stygian gloom:* relating to the River Styx and, by association, Hades, the underworld, the realm of the dead.

line 36 *like a half-crown:* A half-crown is a coin, now out of circulation in Britain, worth two shillings sixpence.

p. 273, line 5 *like a rope-dancer:* like a tightrope walker.

p. 274, lines 13–14 *"Sufficient to the day is the evil thereof":* from the Sermon on the Mount, Matthew 6:34.

XXV. THE SPIRIT OF LIFE

p. 276, line 7 *wax matches:* Wax matches, more like little candles than matches, are essentially combustible match heads set atop rolled wax paper; they're fairly long, do not blow out easily, and burn for a relatively long time before going out.

p. 278, lines 21–22 *the swart Egyptian:* "Swart" means swarthy, or dark-skinned.

lines 22–24 *By Osiris did she curse me and by Isis, by Nephthys and by Anubis, by Sekhet, the cat-headed, and by Set:* The curse names virtually all of the most important ancient Egyptian gods. Osiris and Isis we have already met;

Nephthys was the goddess associated with the ritual of the dead and the wife of Set, the evil god with the head of a long-snouted beast; Anubis was the jackal-headed god who brought the souls of the dead to their final judgment; Sekhet was a goddess of the sun with the head of a lion.

p. 283, line 2 *like a chamois:* Chamois are agile antelopes from the mountains of Europe.

p. 285, line 18 *to soar to the empyrean:* The empyrean is the highest sphere of the heavens, in which the ancients believed there was nothing but fire and light.

XXVI. WHAT WE SAW

p. 296, line 31 *no Norfolk hind:* A hind is a farm-laborer or, more generally, a rustic, or country person; presumably this is a reference to Job's ancestry.

XXVII. WE LEAP

p. 300, lines 16–17 *storm-voices of that Tartarus:* Tartarus was an underworld below and far worse than Hades; it was there that Zeus imprisoned the Titans, who ruled the earth before the Olympians.

XXVIII. OVER THE MOUNTAIN

p. 310, line 33 *covered with clinker:* Clinker is the vitrified rock and sludge expelled from a volcano.

p. 312, line 28 *round the Cape:* again referring to the Cape of Good Hope, at the southern tip of Africa, to be passed on the return voyage up the west side of Africa.

READING GROUP GUIDE

1. Consider the great effort that the author makes to pass off the events of the novel as real (presenting himself merely as the editor of the manuscript rather than its author, the detailed presentation of the shard, the extensive footnotes, etc.). Does this actually make the novel seem true to life? Do you think that the author's contemporaries were taken in, or did they readily recognize the game the author was playing?

2. Discuss the novel's presentation of women, blacks, Muslims, and Jews. Do you think that Job's and Holly's misogyny is actually the author's? Do you find the discussions of nonwhites and non-Christians objectionable? How do you imagine Haggard's readers reacted?

3. It's been suggested that many of the book's themes—particularly its fascination with the implacable, all-powerful, aggressive female at its center— were not entirely understood by the author, that he was writing from his unconscious feelings and fears. Do you agree?

4. Haggard was one of the bestselling authors of his day. Do you think that the quality of his writing justifies his huge success?

5. Consider the author's allusions to things and ideas that would be familiar to his readers: the Thames Embankment, St. Paul's Cathedral, Mary, Queen of Scots. Do you find such imagery helpful, or are these now obscure references a block between the twenty-first-century reader and his or her enjoyment of the novel?

6. Haggard spent some years living in Africa. Do his depictions of the African landscape and its people feel authentic to you?

7. *She* is often considered the progenitor of the modern fantasy/quest novel. How do you think it compares in quality, style, or content to the Ring trilogy by Tolkien, the Narnia books of C. S. Lewis, or, for that matter, to the Indiana Jones movies and J. K. Rowling's Harry Potter books? Do you think that its influence can be felt in works you're familiar with?

8. Fictional characters in possession of immortality are often presented as miserable, monstrous, or decadent, and the two-thousand-year-old Ayesha is depicted as coldhearted, morbid, almost inhuman. Wouldn't extended life be a benefit? Or would a longer-than-normal life span invariably lead to a distance from normal feelings?

A Note on the Text

This Modern Library Paperback Classics edition of *She* is based on a 1912 printing of the revised Longmans, Green, and Co. edition of 1896.

She was first serialized in *The Graphic* between October 1886 and January 1887. The first U.S. edition of the complete novel was published by Harper's Franklin Square Library on December 24, 1886. Longmans, Green published the first U.K. edition of the complete novel on January 1, 1887. The Greiffenhagen and Kerr illustrations, many of which appear in this edition, were added in a November 1, 1888, Longmans, Green edition that also included hundreds of minor textual corrections (further alterations appeared in the 1891 "New Edition"), and the Andrew Lang sonnet at the conclusion of the text was added in an 1896 edition.

The editors wish to express their gratitude to Jessica Amanda Salmonson of Violet Books (www.violetbooks.com) for her invaluable assistance in the preparation of this edition, and to acknowledge Norman Etherington's exhaustive *The Annotated She* (Indiana University Press, 1991).

A NOTE ON THE TYPE

The principal text of this Modern Library edition
was set in a digitized version of Janson, a typeface that
dates from about 1690 and was cut by Nicholas Kis,
a Hungarian working in Amsterdam. The original matrices have
survived and are held by the Stempel foundry in Germany.
Hermann Zapf redesigned some of the weights and sizes for
Stempel, basing his revisions on the original design.

MODERN LIBRARY IS ONLINE AT
WWW.MODERNLIBRARY.COM

MODERN LIBRARY ONLINE IS YOUR GUIDE
TO CLASSIC LITERATURE ON THE WEB

THE MODERN LIBRARY E-NEWSLETTER

Our free e-mail newsletter is sent to subscribers, and features sample chapters, interviews with and essays by our authors, upcoming books, special promotions, announcements, and news.

To subscribe to the Modern Library e-newsletter, send a blank e-mail to: sub_modernlibrary@info.randomhouse.com or visit www.modernlibrary.com

THE MODERN LIBRARY WEBSITE

Check out the Modern Library website at
www.modernlibrary.com for:

- The Modern Library e-newsletter
- A list of our current and upcoming titles and series
- Reading Group Guides and exclusive author spotlights
- Special features with information on the classics and other paperback series
- Excerpts from new releases and other titles
- A list of our e-books and information on where to buy them
- The Modern Library Editorial Board's 100 Best Novels and 100 Best Nonfiction Books of the Twentieth Century written in the English language
- News and announcements

Questions? E-mail us at **modernlibrary@randomhouse.com**.
For questions about examination or desk copies, please visit
the Random House Academic Resources site at
www.randomhouse.com/academic